The Golden Grasshopper
A Story Of The Days Of
Sir Thomas Gresham

by

William Henry Giles Kingston

Double 9
BOOKS

The Golden Grasshopper
A Story Of The Days Of Sir Thomas Gresham
by William Henry Giles Kingston

ISBN: 978-93-61420-24-5

Published by

DOUBLE 9 BOOKS

2/13-B, Ansari Road
Daryaganj, New Delhi – 110002
info@double9books.com
www.double9books.com
Tel. 011-40042856

ABOUT THE AUTHOR

William Henry Giles Kingston (February 28, 1814 – August 5, 1880), sometimes known as W. H. G. Kingston, was an English author of boys' adventure stories. On February 28, 1814, William Henry Giles Kingston was born in Harley Street, London. He was the oldest child of Lucy Henry Kingston and Frances Sophia Rooke, a granddaughter of Sir Giles Rooke, a Court for Common Pleas Judge. Kingston's paternal grandfather, John Kingston (1736-1820), was a Member of Parliament who, although owning a plantation in Demerara, was a staunch supporter of the Abolition of the Slave Trade. Kingston's father, Lucy, started a wine business in Oporto, and he lived there for many years, making frequent trips to England and establishing a lifelong love of the sea.

CONTENTS

Chapter One
Persecution

In the year of Grace 1551, Antwerp was not only the chief city of the Netherlands, but the commercial capital of the world. Its public buildings were also celebrated for the elaborate carving of their exteriors, for their richly-furnished interiors, and for their general architectural beauty.

In one of the principal streets of that city there stood a handsome house, the property of that wealthy and highly-esteemed merchant—Jasper Schetz. In a private room, the walls richly adorned with carving and tapestry, sat at a dark oak writing table a gentleman in a black velvet suit, having a black cap of the same material on his head. On a high-backed chair near him hung his cloak and rapier, while at his side he had a short dagger, with a jewelled hilt, ready for use. He was still young, but his features were grave, and his brow full of thought. His figure was tall and slight, though perhaps somewhat too stiff to be graceful. He was evidently a person of note, one more accustomed to guide men by his counsels, perhaps, than to command them in the field— rather a financier or diplomatist than a military commander. Another person was in the room, standing at a high desk at a little distance. He was a somewhat older man than the former, shorter in figure, and more strongly built. His countenance also exhibited a considerable amount of intelligence, as well as firmness and decision of character.

"Write to their lordships, Master Clough, that I have secured a loan from Lazarus Tucker of 10,000 pounds for six months, with interest at the rate of 14 per cent, per annum. Acknowledge that the rate is somewhat high, but the loan could not be procured for less. Say I have paid over to our good friends Schetz Brothers the sum of 1,000 pounds, according to the command of the King, as an acknowledgment to them for the last loan which they obtained for his Majesty."

The gentleman first described continued dictating to the latter, his secretary, for some time, much in the same style. He then branched off into other subjects, and gave a sketch of the political events which had lately occurred in the Netherlands, then ruled by the Emperor Charles the Fifth of Germany and King of Spain, his sister Queen Mary of Hungary acting as Regent for him. He continued: "Protestant principles have made great progress, even though the fatal Inquisition flourishes in the country more actively than heretofore. The Emperor has just drawn up a new set of instructions for the guidance of the Inquisitors. These men are empowered to inquire, proceed against, and chastise all they call heretics, or persons suspected even of heresy, and their protectors. It is dreadful to think of the power placed in their hands. Already thousands of the inhabitants of the Netherlands have been burned, or drowned, or hung, or killed on the rack; those who can taking to flight, till many parts are well-nigh depopulated. Nothing can be more dreadful than the system of torture employed. The accused person is carried off to prison, often without knowing the crime he is accused of, or his accusers. He is tortured to make him confess. The torture takes place at midnight in some gloomy dungeon, dimly-lighted by torches. The victim, whether man, woman, or tender virgin, is stripped naked, and stretched upon a wooden bench. Water, weights, fires, pulleys, screws, all the apparatus by which the sinews can be strained without cracking, the bones bruised without breaking, and the body racked without giving up the ghost, is now put into operation. If the victim, to escape further torture, confesses, he is at once carried off to execution; if not, he is restored to prison to recover somewhat from the effects of the torture, when he is again brought back to suffer, in the hopes of extorting a confession. However, I have already spun out my letter to too great a length, and I must bring it to a conclusion. Your lordships will see how differently situated the Netherlands are at the present time to our happy England, under the rule of our gentle sovereign, King Edward."

Master Clough having added some further remarks, closed the letter, and sealed it carefully with the signet ring of his employer, the Worshipful Master Thomas Gresham (the device on which was a grasshopper).

Thomas Gresham at that time held the honourable post of Royal agent at Antwerp. The letter being carefully done up with other papers in a silk covering, Richard Clough took it out of the room, and delivered it into the hands of a special messenger who was to convey it to England. He soon returned, saying that a lady earnestly craved an audience.

"I know her not," he added, "but she will in no wise receive a refusal. She is a matron of comely appearance, though her cheeks are pale, and her eyes betoken grief and anxiety. She is accompanied, too, by a young boy, who appears to be her son, and stands holding her hand, trembling as if lately put in great bodily fear."

"Let her come up by all means, Master Clough," answered the merchant; "if we can assist her in her distress, we are bound to do so. The Lady Anne will, I doubt not, if she finds her worthy, be interested in her case."

"I will obey you, sir," said Richard Clough, hurrying out. In a short time he returned with a lady, who although not young, yet retained many traces of beauty. She led by the hand a boy apparently about nine years of age, who, as Master Clough had remarked, looked completely terrorstricken. The merchant rose, and with becoming courtesy placed a chair for the lady opposite to where he sat.

"Pray, madam, tell me how I can assist you," he said, "for I see at once that you are in distress."

"Indeed, indeed, I am, sir," she answered. "I come to pray a great boon of you. I am your countrywoman, though married to a Netherlander. My husband, Karl Van Verner, may not be unknown to you, as he is a wealthy and highly honoured burgher of Antwerp. My maiden name was Bertram, and my family, as well as that of my husband, have long been attached to the Protestant faith. We had till lately worshipped God in private, according to the way we considered most acceptable to Him, not intruding, however, our opinions on our neighbours, but, alas! my husband's wealth was coveted by those in power. Some secret enemy informed against us, and only this morning the officers of the Inquisition suddenly entered our house. We had just assembled for morning prayer. As my young boy beheld them seize his father, he cried out with terror, at the same time attempting to drag him out of their hands. I could not help at first giving way to my grief and terror. In vain my husband expostulated with them, and promised to accompany them quietly if they would set him at liberty. He contrived, however, to whisper to me, to place our boy in safety, and to endeavour to escape myself. In spite of my tears and entreaties, my beloved husband was then dragged off by the officers of the Inquisition, and I hastened away to obey his directions. My husband's fate is, I fear, too certainly sealed. The Bible was found in his hands. He had long been known to be a consistent Protestant. What may be my fate, I know not, but my desire and hope are to share his. Again, I ask you, sir, will you, in the abundance of your compassion and charity, take charge of this boy—soon, I verily believe, to be an orphan? Ernst is his Christian name. He will, in return, I feel sure, serve you well, and prove true and faithful."

The merchant cast an eye of compassion on the boy. The mother saw the look, and trusted that she had gained an advantage.

"Oh! take him, sir, take him! I implore you!" she exclaimed, clasping her hands. "Should he be deprived of his father and me, as I feel sure he soon will be, though his life may be spared, he may be brought up by the priests in the fearful errors of the Romish faith. I appeal to you as a Protestant. Oh! save him from such a fate! I know no one else who is able to protect him, but you can do so fully and completely. I ask you not to bestow wealth on him. I will make over all we possess to you, if I have the power. Let him only labour for you, and be brought up in the Reformed faith."

While the lady was speaking, the merchant had been considering how far granting her request might imperil his own position, where his business led him into constant intercourse with numerous Roman Catholics, and sometimes even with the very ministers of the Emperor. Still his heart leaned towards the side of compassion. His features gradually relaxed as his feelings softened towards the distressed lady and her child.

"Whatever the risk, I will befriend your boy, madam," he said. "Come here, Ernst; your mother wishes you to trust to me. Lady, I would gladly afford you also any assistance in my power," he continued, interrupted, however, by Madame Verner, who poured out before him her feelings of gratitude.

"I am resolved to share the lot of my husband," she answered. "While he lives I will not desert him."

"You are a noble lady, and I would not interfere with your purpose," said the merchant; "but consider that you will not be, able to aid your husband, and you may only sacrifice your own life."

"That I am prepared to do," said the lady, rising. "May God reward you, as you protect my child!"

She pressed the boy to her bosom, again uttered an expression of gratitude to the merchant, and, not daring to trust herself with another look at her child, hastened from the room. I was that little boy, Ernst Verner. It was the last time I heard the voice of my beloved mother. I saw her, yes, once, but oh! my heart sickens even now as I bring the fearful vision to my sight.

Chapter Two
Faithful Unto Death

Master Gresham, leaving Richard Clough at his desk, took Ernst Verner by the hand, and led him out of the room. They passed along a gallery with a richly carved balustrade on one side, and portraits of burgomasters, warriors, and stately dames, hanging from the wall on the other. Opening a door, several female voices saluted them.

At one end of the room sat a tall and graceful lady, young and handsome, with an embroidery frame before her. Her head-dress was a small sort of hood, richly ornamented, with a veil falling behind. She had a long waist with an embroidered stomacher, and a handsome girdle which hung down in front. Her gown was open, showing a richly-decorated petticoat beneath, so long as completely to hide her feet when she stood up on the entrance of her husband, Master Gresham. On either side of the room were several damsels with spinning-wheels and distaffs by their sides, or else actively plying their needles. A little boy, fair and delicate—a year or two younger than Ernst, he appeared—was playing on the ground near the couch on which the lady sat, with some of those wonderful toys for which Holland was already celebrated. The lady looked up as Master Gresham approached.

"What child have you there, my dear lord?" she asked.

"One in whom perchance you will take an interest, Lady Anne, when you hear his history," answered Master Gresham; and he detailed in a few words the visit of the boy's mother, and her petition that the child might be taken care of.

"We cannot refuse the charge which Heaven has sent us," answered the lady. "He may be a companion and playmate to our little Richard, and I doubt not a blessing to us, if we are faithful to our trust."

From that day forward Ernst became one of the family of Master Thomas Gresham. In the house he had many amusements; but his life was a somewhat dull one notwithstanding, for he was never allowed to go abroad, unless in the company of his patron. The reason of this did not occur to him. Master Gresham, however, acted wisely. He knew that those who had seized the child's parents might seize the boy also, and though from his youth he might escape death, he would certainly be brought up as a Romanist—a proceeding which the honest Protestant Englishman greatly dreaded. There was no lack of company, however, in the house. Often entertainments were given to various guests. Seldom indeed was the merchant's hospitable board spread without several visitors being present.

Soon after Ernst had become an inmate of Master Gresham's house, a personage arrived who was treated with great consideration. He had come from the South, after having visited the Holy Land, and appeared to have seen much of the world besides. Indeed, there were few countries about which he had not something to say. There was nothing very remarkable about his appearance. He was slightly built, and of middle size; but he had that hardy, wiry look, which showed that he was capable of undergoing great fatigue and enduring an excess of heat without inconvenience, if not of cold. His ordinary dress was that of a simple gentleman, with a flat cap, having a coif tying beneath the chin and completely concealing his hair. His cloak, or gown, was of fine cloth, trimmed with rich fur, and having long sleeves. Beneath it was a closely-buttoned waistcoat, while he wore long hose, and puffed breeches, reaching but a short way down the upper part of the leg. The upper part of his shoes were pointed, a jewelled dagger hung to his waist by a belt, in which were stuck his gloves when not in use, and leathern purse also hanging to it. He was addressed by Master Gresham as Sir John De Leigh, and was treated by him as a person of consideration. A banquet was given in honour of his arrival, to which a number of the principal merchants, magistrates, and other civil officers of Antwerp were invited. It made a never-forgotten impression on Ernst, young as he was. It took place in the grand hall on the ground floor of the house. With interest he watched the placing of the tables and the spreading of the cloths, while at one end the butler arranged on the buffet the rich pieces of plate and other vessels, giving a magnificent appearance to that part of the hall, and standing out well against the dark tapestry hung up behind them. In the centre of the table was first placed a silver vessel of large size, containing salt; and small round cakes of bread were arranged where each guest was to sit. Drinking-cups also, of glass, were placed along the table, with a plate and napkin for each guest.

About thirty persons had been summoned, among whom were a few dames to bear the Lady Anne company. At the further end of the hall was a gallery where the musicians were stationed; while cushioned chairs were arranged on each side of the table and covered with handsome tapestry work.

When the guests began to arrive, the servitors came forward with basin, ewers, and towels, that each might wash his hands before sitting down to the meal.

Master Gresham and Lady Anne received them with due courtesy, when each guest was conducted to the place assigned to him at the table; Sir John De Leigh and other personages of distinction being seated at the upper part, while Master Clough and several other secretaries and attendants took their seats at the further end below the salt-cellar.

And now the musicians struck up a lively tune. The servitors entered with the good cheer, which was, in due course, served round.

It would be impossible to describe all the luxuries. Among them a boar's head was seen, highly ornamented, while on either side were two peacocks, the feathers of their tails spread out, while on their necks hung two golden grasshoppers, the armorial bearings of the host. The peacocks, which had been roasted, and covered with the yolk of eggs, after having cooled, had been sewed into their skins, and thus looked almost as if they were alive. There were two pair of cocks which had been roasted, and then covered, one with gold, and the other with silver foil. There was also venison, a swan boiled, roasted pheasant and roasted bittern, with fish of various sorts—pike and perch. A variety of ornaments, too, made their appearance, subtilties, they were called, and ornamental devices in pastry. One was a lofty castle, covered with silver, flags of gold waving on its summit. However, it would take up too much space to describe the numberless dishes which appeared at this banquet.

The musicians at intervals played for the amusement of the guests, and toward the end, lest they might have become weary of too many sweet sounds, the doors of the hall opened, and a band of maskers entered habited in various grotesque costumes. With a deep obeisance to the master of the feast, as well as to the lady and their visitors, the leader of the party commenced an oration the subject of which Ernst Verner was too young at the time to note down, and has long since forgotten. It was followed by the representation of a Morality, the subject of which also, for the same reason, is not noted in this diary. Ernst, with his young companion, little Richard Gresham, were running about the hall hand in hand, watching the maskers, and amusing themselves by observing the guests. One of the former, wearing a huge cloak which completely concealed his form, during the performance separated himself from his companions. His eye was fixed on the two boys. It might have been that he supposed no one observed him; but, even though attending to her guests, the mother's glance was following her young Richard. With cautious steps the masker slowly moved up towards where the little boys were standing, their attention occupied with one of the most exciting portions of the mystery. At length the masker stood close to the boys. And now the eyes of every one in the hall were riveted on the performers. On a sudden, the cloak was thrown round the boys. No cry was heard, and the masker glided rapidly towards the door of the hall, still left open. So quick were his movements, that he would have escaped unobserved had not Lady Anne's voice been heard, exclaiming, "Stop him! Stop him! He has carried off the children!" Richard Clough started from his seat, and drawing his dagger, rushed after the abductor. The man, turning his head at the cry, saw that he was pursued, and letting go one of the children—it was the little Richard—fled more rapidly. Honest Master Clough, however, with the excited feelings of a warm-hearted Welshman, pursued him. The man had just reached the door, when Master Clough caught him by the cloak, and would have struck his dagger into his neck, had he not loosened the garment and let go the little Ernst, whose head had been so muffled in a cloth that he had been unable to cry out. The man sprang from the door before Master Clough could again seize him, exhibiting, now deprived of his cloak, the dark dress of an ecclesiastic, though his head, still concealed by his large mask, prevented his features being visible. A number of persons were at the time passing, and the stranger was thus able to make his escape. Indeed, honest Master Clough, having gained his object of rescuing the children, probably considered that it might be wise not to continue the pursuit in the open street, where perchance he might have found more enemies than friends.

As may be supposed, after this Master Gresham was chary of letting his young charge go without his doors, unless with a strong escort. But one day, having to pay a visit of ceremony to an important person at the farther end of the city, he set forth on horseback, attended by Master Clough, two of his other secretaries, and several attendants, all well-armed. Ernst, as the Lady Anne thought, having suffered from being deprived of the free air, was carried along with the party, being placed on the saddle in front of one of the serving-men. Ernst gazed about him, enjoying the free air and the warm sun, which shone down from the blue sky. The scene in the streets, however, was at no time lively; the dresses both of men and women being of a sombre hue, the latter wearing the large dark cloaks with hoods which had been introduced from Spain, while a gloomy expression sat generally on the countenances of the men. The visit was paid, Ernst remaining in the hall with the attendants, while Master Gresham with his secretaries proceeded into the audience chamber of the great man. They were on their way back, when, approaching the wide thoroughfare of the Mere, a crowd of persons was seen proceeding in that direction. It was necessary for Master Gresham's party to proceed through the Mere, or he would have turned aside to avoid the throng. As they entered the place, a procession was seen advancing down one of the streets which led into it. First came a band of acolytes, swinging censers and chanting hymns to the honour of the

Virgin. Next to them marched on either side of the street a guard of soldiers, having in their midst a large party of priests, between whom were seen four persons with their hands fastened behind them, their heads bare, and clothed in long coarse robes; blood-red banners were borne aloft by some of the priests. Then came a brotherhood, also in dark garments, with cowls on their heads and their faces masked. A party of officials on horseback, magistrates, and others, with another body of troops, brought up the rear. Slowly the procession wound its way into the Square, on one side of which was now seen a scaffold with a pulpit raised above it, and a booth or stand, covered with cloth, with seats arranged within. At one end were two lofty gibbets; while below, in the open space, two stout posts appeared fixed in the ground, with iron chains hanging to them, and near at hand large piles of faggots.

So completely closed round by the throng were the English party, that they could neither move forward nor recede. The procession reached the stage, when the prisoners were led up upon it, the magistrates and other officials taking their places on either side, the brotherhoods forming a dark line below the platform. The priests seemed to be exhorting the prisoners, but the distance was too great to allow what was being said to be heard. The preacher, lifting a crucifix in the air, waved it round, and addressed the multitude below. He was met rather by glances of hatred and fear than by looks of sympathy. Still he continued, now in a loud voice thundering anathemas on the heads of heretics, and threatening the vengeance of Heaven on those who sheltered them, or refused to give them up into the hands of the Inquisitors. Sometimes the crowd appeared to be violently agitated, and here and there persons were seen moving among them, as if to urge them forward in an attempt to rescue those about to suffer; but the stern looks of the well-trained Spanish troops kept them in awe. The sermon—if a fierce harangue composed of invectives against simple Christianity could so be called—was brought to a conclusion; and now, in a loud voice, the presiding Inquisitor asked the accused for the last time whether they would recant and make confession of their sins, promising them absolution and a sure entrance into heaven, with a more easy death than the terrible one to which they were condemned. The gag was removed from the mouth of the chief prisoner that he might give his answer.

"No, no!" he exclaimed, "I accept not such mercy as you offer. I hold fast to a simple faith in Christ's meritorious death, and that alone is sufficient to secure my salvation. I look upon the sacrifice of the Mass as an act dishonouring Him. I believe that no human person has power to absolve me from sin; that all must enter the kingdom of heaven here who are to belong to it hereafter, and thus that masses for the dead are a deceit and fraud;

that Christ hears our prayers more willingly than any human mediator or being who has once dwelt on earth; that His mother was honoured among women, but not above women; that her heart was less tender than His; and that she can no more hear prayers or intercede with Him than can any other person of the seed of Adam requiring, like all others, to be cleansed by His blood."

"Off with him to the stake! to the stake!" shouted the priests as these words were uttered.

A female—a graceful lady—was next asked whether she would recant.

"I hold to the opinion my dear husband has uttered," she answered.

Master Gresham turned pale when he heard her speak, for he recognised the features of one he had seen but a short time before. At that moment the little boy, who had been eagerly watching the scene, uttered a loud shriek.

"Oh! my father! my dear mother!" he cried out; "let me go to them—let me go to save them!"

With difficulty the groom held him on his horse, for he struggled desperately to be free. "There's kind Bertha, my nurse; and honest, good Gunter too! Let me go, I say, that I may help them!"

The English party were too far off to allow those on the stage to observe them. Even the servants refused to recant, though promised their lives and liberty if they would do so.

Karl Van Verner and his wife were led down from the platform by the steps towards the two stakes, which stood close to each other. And now the members of the brotherhood on whom had been imposed the sad office of executing the victims, rushed forward with faggots, which they piled up round them. Two professional executioners, who had been summoned for the purpose, secured the victims by the chains to the stakes. While fire was set to the piles, the members of the brotherhood burst forth into a melancholy *miserere*, which rose up even above the groans and sighs of the people.

Master Gresham ordered his attendants to try and force their way out of the crowd. At length, many persons, unwilling to witness the suffering of the victims, retired along the various streets leading into the Mere, thus giving an opportunity to the English party to retreat. Once more the young boy cast a terrified glance towards the horrible spectacle, when the groom, in mercy, throwing a cloak round his head, pushed on through the crowd, the whole party making their way as rapidly as they could towards the royal merchant's residence.

For days, for months, for years even, did that dreadful spectacle occur again and again to the mind of the child. Thus perished his parents, with their two faithful attendants, their only crime that of reading God's Word, singing His praises, and holding together family prayer.

Theirs was no solitary fate. Every week, every day almost, victims were offered up to the papal Moloch by those who thus hoped to stamp out the very existence of Protestantism from the land. Vain efforts! The seed of religious truth, scattered far and wide, was springing up and bearing fruit—sometimes bitter enough, it must be owned—but such as was not to be destroyed by Roman Pontiff or Spanish King.

Chapter Three
News from England

For several days the young Ernst did not recover from the effects of the dreadful scene he had witnessed. No smile ever beamed on his countenance, his cheeks were pale, his eyes dim. His kind protectors began to fear that he had received a blow which might cast a gloom over his life, if it did not quickly shorten it. Even Sir John De Leigh, the philosopher, the man of the world, who declared that no circumstances of life, no human suffering, should produce any effect on the mind of a man of sense, compassionated the orphan boy. He even condescended to call the child to him, to tell him of the scenes he had witnessed in foreign lands—how he had seen the Grand Bashaw and the Great Mogul,—the splendour of their palaces, and the obedience of their subjects; how he himself had ridden under a silken canopy on the back of a huge elephant, and traversed the burning desert, placed between the humps of a swift dromedary. By degrees he won back the boy to take an interest in what was going on around him, though often little Ernst would start, and burst forth again into bitter tears.

The boy and his young companion were, for a large portion of each day, with the Lady Anne, who took a pleasure in instructing him. Already he could read without difficulty, and she now placed paper and pen in his hand, and instructed him in the art of writing, an art very soon to stand him in good stead, and to enable him to serve his generous patron, Master Gresham.

Of that kind patron some account ought now to be given.

Master Thomas Gresham came, so Ernst believed, of a line of honourable merchants. Sir Richard Gresham, his father, of whom he was the youngest son, died some three years before this, having been some time Lord Mayor of London. Sir Richard had a brother, Sir John Gresham, who was employed as Royal agent to King Henry the Eighth in Flanders, a post to which the patron of Ernst Verner afterwards succeeded. Sir Richard's eldest son was named after his uncle, and became Sir John Gresham. Sir Richard had two daughters, the eldest of whom married the wealthy Sir John Thynne, of Longleat, in Wiltshire.

Although it was not customary for merchants to send their sons to college, so much talent was exhibited by Thomas Gresham, that his father determined to give him the advantage of a University education. When only three years old he was deprived of his mother's care, a loss he ever bewailed. According to his father's purpose, he was sent to Cambridge, and admitted a pensioner at Gonville and Caius College. He there undoubtedly imbibed that attachment to the Protestant faith for which he was ever afterwards conspicuous, and for which his Hall was at that time distinguished. He there also gained a taste for literature, and a respect for learned men, for which he was noted throughout life, and which none of the subsequent cares of business were ever able to extinguish in him.

Expediency probably, rather than inclination, made him a merchant; at the same time the advantages to be derived from foreign commerce were then so considerable, that, with the splendid examples of his father and of his uncle before him, it can be no matter of surprise, that he forsook the quiet walk of life which his college might have afforded, for one of honour and emolument. Before going to college he had been bound apprentice to his uncle, Sir John Gresham, in consequence of which he was, in 1543, admitted a member of the Mercers' Company, being then in the twenty-fifth year of his age.

He had at the time the event here described occurred, for some time been holding the post of Royal agent at Antwerp, greatly to the satisfaction of the King and their lordships.

In consequence of the maritime position of Antwerp, it far surpassed, in size and wealth, Brussels, and every other Flemish town. Its population was estimated at 100,000 souls. Its internal splendour was unequalled, the wealth of its merchants unsurpassed. They attracted hither traders of all nations—English, French, Germans, Danes, Osterlings, Italians, Spaniards and Portuguese. Of these the Spaniards were by far the most numerous. For many years, the city exhibited the uncommon spectacle of a multitude of nations, living together like one large family, where each used its own customs, and spoke its own language. The inhabitants were talented, and noted for their hospitality. The ladies were highly educated: many of them could converse in several different languages; while during most days of the week there was a constant succession of gay assemblies, banquets, dances and nuptial parties, while music, singing, and cheerful sounds might be heard by the passer-by in every street. What a fearful change was in a few short years to be wrought in this state of things! Shrieks of agony, cries of despair, hideous, brutal slaughter, blood flowing down the doorsteps of every house, flames bursting forth from amid those once festive halls!

Ernst was sorry when Sir John De Leigh took his departure. The boy had gained a powerful friend, though he was not aware of it. Little more need be said for the present of Ernst Verner's life at that time. He was treated with the greatest kindness and consideration by Master Gresham and his lady. Indeed, there was no difference in the care they bestowed on him and on their little Richard. More than one journey was made by Master Gresham to England and back, while his family remained at the house of Caspar Schetz. The Baron Grobbendonck, for that was his title, who was at that time one of the greatest merchants of Antwerp, and the chief supporter of the Bourse, was one of the four brothers who formed an influential mercantile establishment.

Once more Master Gresham returned to Antwerp. At length news came from England. It was observed that he looked more serious than was his wont.

The young Protestant King Edward the Sixth was very sick. There would probably be disturbances in England, for he had set aside the devise of Henry the Eighth to his daughters Mary and Elizabeth, and had given the Crown to the heirs of the Lady Frances, the Duchess of Suffolk, she herself being passed over. The Lady Jane Grey was the eldest of her three daughters; she had no male heir. Fifteen Lords of the Council, nine judges, and other officers had signed a paper, agreeing to maintain the succession contained in the King's notes delivered to the judges. Master Gresham observed that he feared greatly that this arrangement would cause disturbances in England. Shortly after this, another dispatch arrived. It contained the news that King Edward had died on the 6th of July, twenty-two days after he had thus solemnly excluded his sisters from the throne.

He acted undoubtedly from right motives, believing this arrangement to be the best, in order to secure a Protestant ruler and a Protestant faith to England.

Already had the Reformed faith made great progress. The last prayer of the young King showed his earnest and abiding love of that faith: "O Lord God! save Thy chosen people of England. O my Lord God! defend this realm from papistry, and maintain Thy true religion!" were almost his dying words.

Master Gresham's anticipations of evil were too soon fulfilled. While the Duke of Northumberland and his party supported Lady Jane and her husband (the Earl of Dudley), the larger portion of the nation rallied round Queen Mary, not because she was a Romanist, but because she was considered to be the legitimate heiress to the Crown, while the unfortunate Lady Jane was shut up in the Tower. Mary arrived in London, and was triumphantly proclaimed as Queen on the 3rd of August, A.D. 1553.

In a short time the estimation in which Master Gresham was held by the new Romish sovereign of England was made manifest, as he was deprived of his office and ordered to return home. The journey was performed on horseback, the Lady Anne riding a horse alone, but each of her maidens being placed behind a groom. Ernst and the little Richard were carried in the same manner. They took the road to Bruges, from thence intending to proceed on to Dunkirk and Calais, that Lady Anne might not be exposed to a long sea-voyage. The journey was of necessity performed at a very slow rate, many sumpter mules being required to carry the baggage and bedding, and some of the inns at which they had to stop being without any but the roughest accommodation. At Bruges they rested a day, that the Lady Anne might see some of the churches and public buildings of that fine city. The eyes of all the party were, however, grieved with a spectacle which they would willingly have avoided, since they could not prevent it. Ernst Verner was the first to apprehend what was about to take place, and his cry of horror drew the attention of the rest of the party to the scene. Just such a procession as he had beheld two years before was passing through the streets. There were Spanish soldiers, and priests in various coloured vestments, with boys waving censers and banners borne above their heads. A vast crucifix, with the figure of the Lord of light and life—that Holy One, full of love and mercy—nailed to it. How His heart must grieve, as looking down from heaven He beholds the deeds of cruelty and injustice performed in His name. The procession had just arrived at the place of execution, and soon, with but little ceremony or form, five victims were chained to the stakes there erected, and the flames burst up, consuming their bodies. The people looked on, if not with indifference, at all events without exhibiting their feelings, kept in awe by the Spanish troops, and their dread of the power of the Emperor. Lady Anne entreated that they might hasten from the city.

"Alas! my wife, I fear, that though we proceed onwards, we may meet with similar scenes till we are beyond the boundaries of the country. And now we have a Popish sovereign on the throne of England, I know not what events may there take place."

"Surely the Princess Mary has herself not escaped suffering, and has been so exemplary in her conduct, that she would not permit such deeds to be done as we hear of in this country."

"Her training has been that of the Emperor Charles. She has been brought up, as he was, by the priests of Rome; and the same training will in most instances produce the same results," answered the merchant. "But let us be wise, my wife, and not speak of these things where any eavesdropper may overhear them. Now that I have lost my firm friend and patron, the

Duke of Northumberland, I feel much uncertainty as to my own position. There are those who hate me, both because I am a Protestant, and because they are jealous of my success. The old Marquis of Winchester has ever turned a green eye towards me, and is even now plotting to do me ill. He, I doubt not, has been the chief cause of my recall."

Ernst heard these remarks, though he did not give much heed to them at the time, but still it left the impression on his mind that his kind patron was in danger.

Calais was at length reached, and the party once more found themselves under the protection of the British flag. While waiting for the rise of the tide to float the vessel out of the river, Master Gresham took a walk round the fortifications; and he saw enough to convince him that they had been allowed to go to decay, and were not in a condition to enable them to resist any sudden attack of the enemy. Although England was at that time at peace with France, yet at any moment war might be declared between the rival powers; and any simple man might know, as well as the most experienced general, that Calais would be the first place attacked. Master Gresham determined to make this important fact known to the Queen's Council on his arrival in England.

Ernst now for the first time saw the open sea rolling up through that narrow passage, across which England and France can gaze on each other. Ernst heard Master Gresham remark that, long time as they had taken to accomplish the journey, it was his wont when riding post, with relays of fleet horses along the road, to perform it in three days.

The wind was fair, and the white cliffs of Dover, seen when leaving the land, gradually rose up more distinctly before the eyes of the voyagers, till the sloop coming to an anchor, they were conveyed on shore in a small boat. Master Gresham's party, with his servants, who were all well-armed, was a strong one. On the road they passed several suspicious characters, who looked greatly inclined to examine the inside of the leathern purses of the merchant and his attendants. But gold may be bought too dearly, and the gentlemen, with glances of regret, allowed the travellers to pass on.

They had just crossed London Bridge on their way to Master Gresham's house in Lombard Street, when a concourse of people was seen coming up along the road from the west. There were troops with their halberds glittering in the sun, banners waving, with trumpets sounding, horsemen in rich armour, and horse soldiers with lances and streamers. Master Gresham's party had to draw up on one side to allow the procession to pass, and it was soon known that the Queen was coming on her way from Westminster to the Tower. Soon she appeared in an open chariot, ornamented with tissue of gold and silver, and drawn by six steeds. She was dressed in a gown of blue velvet, furred with powdered ermine, while on her head hung a cloth of tinsel, beset with pearls and precious stones, and outside round her head was a circlet of gold, so richly ornamented with jewels, that their weight compelled her to support her head with her hands. Her small size was not perceived as she thus sat in her chariot, though it was seen that her countenance was thin and pale, betokening ill-health.

"Will she visit the Lady Jane in the Tower, I wonder—she who might have been Queen instead, had those who supported her proved faithful?" whispered Lady Anne into her husband's ear.

"Hush! hush, wife!" answered Master Gresham; "such words are dangerous. We have seen many sad things done in the Netherlands. If we would be safe, now we have come to England, we must hold our peace."

The procession having moved onward towards the east, the travellers proceeded on their way, and in a short time were comfortably lodged in Master Gresham's own mansion in Lombard Street. Although English was the native tongue of his mother, as yet young Ernst spoke it but imperfectly. It was therefore deemed advisable by his kind patron that he should be sent to school, where he might acquire a greater acquaintance with the language, and other knowledge besides.

Chapter Four
Saint Paul's School

Ernst Verner felt somewhat sad and lonely in London. Antwerp was a large city, but London was far larger, and he was afraid to venture out by himself, lest he should not find his way back again to Lombard Street. Lady Anne too was very kind, but she was somewhat stately and cold, and could not replace one whom he still remembered with tender love. With Richard he was more at home, but Richard was delicate, and did not seem inclined to enter into the sports for which Ernst sighed. Master Gresham was as kind as Lady Anne, but he was at all hours engaged in business, and often appeared not to take notice of the young boy depending on him. He told Ernst that he was to go to school, but the time passed by, and Ernst still remained at home, picking up such knowledge as a worthy man, Master Dickson, who came every day to instruct Richard, was willing to impart.

At length, one evening when Master Gresham was seated before the fireplace, in which blazed several logs, Ernst, who had been sitting silently in one corner for some time, with his face over a book, ventured to address him. Ernst was in no way afraid of his patron, whose genial, easy manners had from the first put him at his ease.

"Master Gresham," he said, "I now speak English well enough to go to an English school. You said I was to go: when may that time be?"

"Few boys are in a hurry to put themselves under the power of a pedagogue's birch," answered Ernst's patron, looking down upon him. "Have you thought on that subject, Ernst? The road to learning is not always one of roses. You must be prepared for many things to which you have not been accustomed, boy."

"I do not expect to find many roses in this big city," answered Ernst; "but yet I would lief get more learning than I at present possess."

"Well, lad, you shall have your will. As soon as Saint Paul's School opens again after the holidays, you shall go to it," answered Master Gresham. "You have heard of it, may be. It was founded by a ripe scholar—Dean Colet— and it is well able to turn out ripe scholars, I am told. Dr Freeman, the head master, is a learned man, and a thorough disciplinarian, and it is the fault of his pupils if they do not imitate his example. The Honourable Company of Mercers, to which I belong, are the trustees of the school, and although you are not native born, I shall be able to obtain a nomination for you. In Dean Colet's trust he especially declares, in the statutes of the school, that it shall be open to the children of all nations and countries indifferently. Indeed there is no doubt that while he limited the number of scholars to 153—so many fishes as were caught in the net by the apostles (John twenty-one, verse 11), he wished the offspring of our foreign brethren in the reformed doctrines to have a share in his benefits. No boys are, however, to be admitted, but such as can say their Catechism, as well as read and write competently; but as you can do that, Ernst, already, I may promise you an admission."

Ernst thanked his patron, for he had a desire to gain knowledge, though he did not clearly understand what sort of place a school was. As he was anxious to make a good appearance on entering, he attended with more assiduity than ever to his studies at home, and thus he had made very fair progress before the day of admission arrived. At that time there was less difficulty than there had been previously in obtaining admission to the school. Romanists would not send their children to it, and Protestant parents were often afraid of doing so, lest they should bring suspicion on themselves, or lest some day Bishop Gardiner should insist on the pupils being brought up in the Romish doctrines.

The day at length arrived for Ernst's admission. Master Gresham himself was too much occupied to go with him. He therefore deputed Master Elliot, his factor in Lombard Street, to perform the duty of introducing the boy. It was a bitter cold morning, but Ernst was up betimes, and having eaten his breakfast, he slung his new satchel, which Lady Anne had procured for him, over his back. He had, too, thick shoes, with bright red cloth hose, and a long blue coat, which kept his knees warm, though it somewhat impeded his running.

Master Elliot and his charge soon reached Saint Paul's, and turning to the left, stood before the entrance of the school. Ernst looked up, and thought the building a very fine one. There were none around to be compared to it.

On either side were two dwelling-houses, which Master Elliot told him were the habitations of the masters. Passing under a fine porch, they found themselves in the entrance-hall, where the younger pupils were assembled, who were under the especial charge of the chaplain. In a second large hall were boys of more advanced age, who were instructed by the under master, while in a third division were the boys of the upper forms, who were under the especial superintendence of the high master himself. The last two divisions were separated only by a large curtain, which could be drawn at will. Master Elliot passing on, stood before the head master's chair at the further end of the hall. Dr Freeman received his salute, and descending from his chair, inquired the name of the boy he had brought.

"Ah! yes," he said, on hearing Ernst's name, "a ward of the worshipful Master Gresham—that *ditissimus mercator*, as my honoured friend Dr Caius calls him. I am glad to have the youthful Verner under my charge. I will presently see that he possesses the necessary qualifications for entering, of which, however, I entertain no doubt, being fully persuaded, from what Master Gresham wrote, that he is far more proficient than many who come here."

Ernst did not exactly understand all that the Doctor was saying; at the same time he heard enough to give him courage, and with less anxiety and alarm than might have been expected, he bade his friend the factor farewell.

"Keep thy wits about thee, my lad," whispered Master Elliot, "and do credit to your name and country. There is nothing very difficult for you to go through, depend on that, or those dull-headed boys we passed as we entered would never have taken their places in the school."

Ernst found his friend's remarks correct.

His reading, in spite of his foreign accent, was considered fluent, and his writing very good. To the questions put to him he answered in a way to obtain the approbation of the Doctor, and he was forthwith sent to take his place in the lower school. Ernst found that each class contained sixteen boys. The one who was at the head of his class had a little seat to mark his honourable position, arranged above the benches on which the other boys were placed.

As at that early hour lights were required, each boy had brought a wax candle, it being against the rules laid down by Dean Colet that any tallow candles should be used. As soon as the day became sufficiently bright, the candles were immediately extinguished, to be ready again in the evening. Ernst, by attending diligently to his studies, gained the approbation of his masters, and, greatly to his surprise, was in a short time promoted to the seat of honour at the head of the class. He observed that when Master Elliot entered he laid down fourpence, which he found was the fee for his admission into the school. This sum was given to a certain poor scholar, who was engaged to attend to the schoolrooms, swept them out, and also kept the seats and desks clean—John Tobin was his name. Ernst took a liking to the lad because he seemed so humble and quiet, and ready to oblige. His cheeks were somewhat hollow and his garments threadbare, for in truth the fourpence he received, though not a sum to be despised, was not sufficient to maintain him in much luxury. John Tobin had also a widowed mother, already advancing in life, whom he did his utmost to support, and he looked forward to the time when he should, by the result of his labours, enable her to live in more comfort than she then could. Ernst, in course of time, made friends with several of his schoolfellows, who will be mentioned hereafter. He had to be up early every morning to take his breakfast and be away to school, as the hours of study were from 7 to 11 a.m., and from 1 to 5 p.m.

On one side of the hall was a chapel, where the pupils assembled for prayers on first collecting in the morning, as also at noon, and again in the evening. Ernst, having been brought up a strict Calvinist, was not altogether pleased at seeing, over the chair of the head master, an image of the boy Jesus, albeit it was a beautiful work of art.

It was in the gesture of teaching. All the scholars on going into the hall, as also on departing, were taught to salute it with a hymn. Above the figure there was a painting, intended to represent God the Father, under which was written the words, "Hear ye Him!" These words were placed there, Ernst heard, at the suggestion of the great Dutch scholar Erasmus, who was a friend of Dean Colet, and who, some years before, had visited London. Under the figure also were some lines in Latin, written by the same learned person. Behind the school was a playground surrounded by cloisters, where the pupils played in rainy weather.

As is well-known, it was the custom for the elder boys in some schools, and other youths, to assemble on stages at Barthelmy Fair, where they held disputations on various subjects, much in the way as is done in the Netherlands. The scholars at Dean Colet's school were, however, interdicted from this amusement, he considering it as tending only to idle jabbering.

His great wish was that they all should learn pure and chaste Latin, and he prohibited them from studying the later writers, after Sallust and Cicero. Ernst found that there were very few holidays at the school, Dean Colet holding that keeping the Saints' days, as had been the custom, was a great cause of idleness and dissipation. He remarked that those countries where the Saints were thus honoured were the poorest, and most immoral in Christendom. The students were, however, allowed to act plays, interludes, and moralities, and were trained by the head master and others to speak their parts with correctness and grace; indeed, so perfect did they become, that they at times exhibited their talents before their Sovereign.

Ernst's days were not altogether pleasant ones. He was jeered at by the other boys on account of his foreign tongue. The discipline too of the school was very strict. The ferule and the birch were constantly employed. If he was perchance late at school, either in the morning or afternoon, he had additional tasks and impositions, not that he often suffered on that account.

He attended with great assiduity to his studies, anxious to improve himself, and to show that he was worthy of the kind patronage of Master Gresham. He soon made himself acquainted with Paul's *Accidents*, written by Dean Colet for the use of his scholars, and consisting of the rudiments of grammar, with an abridgment of the principles of religion.

Ernst had mixed so little with other boys, that he was unaccustomed to defend himself against the attacks of his companions. Thus at first even very small boys dared to assail him, he looking upon them with pity, or it may have been with contempt, just as a large mastiff, when little dogs are barking at his heels, refrains from retaliating. This gave them courage to continue their persecutions. One day, however, several of the bigger boys thought fit to unite with them, mimicking Ernst, and inquiring what had become of his parents, that they allowed him thus to be sent to a foreign land.

"They were burnt for their religion," answered Ernst at last; "because they would not bow down to idols, or attend the Popish mass."

"Oh! oh! young master, heretics were they!" exclaimed some of the boys; for at this time, although the principles of the school existed as before, Romanism was apparently in the ascendant. "Then you are a heretic, I doubt not, and will some day come to the stake."

A big boy was standing by whom Ernst had often seen, though never spoken to. He listened eagerly to what Ernst was saying, as also to the exclamations of the other boys.

"I am ready to burn for the true faith," said Ernst. "It were well for some of you to try and learn what that true faith is, instead of abusing a foreigner sent among you."

"Are you, young jackanapes, to teach us?" exclaimed several of the big boys together; and the younger ones, set on by them, once more began to attack Ernst, to pull his coat tails, and to give him cuffs on the head. He stood it for some time in his usual way, till one of the big ones began to treat him in the same manner. Instantly turning round, he struck his new assailant a blow between the eyes, which sent him reeling backwards. The boy, enraged, flew upon Ernst, and would have punished him severely, had not at that moment the lad who, has been spoken of sprung forward.

"Fair play!" he exclaimed, "fair play! English boys, if you forget what that is, I intend to see it carried out. Now as Ernst Verner is a slight boy, and I am a stout one, whoever wants to attack him must attack me first—who is ready? Come on! you all know me, Andrew A'Dale, that I never flinch from a fight; and with a good cause to fight for, I am not going to do so now."

The boy who had been attacking Ernst, blinded with anger, flew at A'Dale, who sent him back reeling among his companions.

"Does anybody else want to attack Verner?" he exclaimed; "let him come on now, or ever afterwards keep quiet."

No one answered the challenge. The bigger boys walked off one by one with looks of anger turned towards A'Dale, while the younger ones slunk away, and Ernst was left standing near A'Dale. Ernst thanked A'Dale warmly for the protection he had afforded him.

"I never stood up for another more willingly," answered A'Dale. "You are a foreigner, and without friends, and more than that you are a Protestant, and your parents have suffered for a good cause. Both those things would make me wish you well, but I like you for yourself, and for the spirit you have shown, so say no more about it."

From that day forward Ernst and Andrew A'Dale became firm friends.

Soon after this the whole school went in procession, according to custom, to attend the service of the Boy Bishop. He was one of the choristers of the cathedral, one of whom every year was selected for this office. He was habited in a bishop's full dress, though it cannot be said that he looked altogether as dignified as might have been desired. Still he managed to ape with tolerable accuracy the movements and mode of proceeding of a full-grown bishop. One thing might truly be said, that had he played many strange antics, he would scarcely have out-done Bishop Bonner, albeit such a remark would have been dangerous to make at that time. The boys of the school were arranged, as has been said, in their seats, when the bishop, ascending the pulpit, and with crozier in hand, delivered his address. His companions now and then made signs to him which betokened no great amount of respect. As the boys of Saint Paul's School, however, had the eyes of their masters fixed on them, they behaved with sufficient decorum. A'Dale, however, who disliked such mummeries as much as did Ernst, did not altogether keep his countenance. He was in sight of the altar, where the priest was about to perform the high mass. That ceremony was gone through in the usual way, both A'Dale and Ernst, and some others may be, chafing not a little at being obliged to be present at it. Ernst's quick sight had detected the eyes of the priest fixed on him and A'Dale. He whispered to his companion.

"Yes, possibly we are marked," answered A'Dale; "but the priest can do us little harm, I should think; and at all events we must brave it out." The two boys, it must be owned, took little pains to conceal their feelings. Before leaving the church each boy of the school had to take up one penny, and present it to the Boy Bishop for his maintenance, and thus every year he collected a goodly number of pennies. It may be remarked that the Boy Bishop was chosen by the other choristers to officiate from Saint Nicholas Day to the evening of Innocents' Day. Should he die during that period, he was always buried in the habit of a bishop. The following day Ernst and A'Dale saw, not without some anxiety, the priest who had been officiating at the altar enter the school. After speaking with the head master, he cast his eyes round the classes and pointed to A'Dale and Ernst.

"Some harm will come out of this," they thought; but they wisely said nothing. Again the priest consulted with the head master, who seemed to be expostulating with him, and finally took his departure, casting a frowning glance on the two boys. Having reached the door he turned round, as if to watch what the head master would do. Dr Freeman on this called up A'Dale and Ernst, and spoke in a loud voice with great severity to them, threatening them with condign punishment for their irreverent behaviour. As, however, he did not proceed further than words, they had reason to hope that he did not consider them guilty of any very atrocious crime. As soon as the priest had taken his departure, they were allowed to return to their seats, with an admonition, that in future, whatever they might think of such matters, not to express their thoughts by their gestures.

It may be supposed, though, that the masters were not personally favourable to the re-introduction of the Popish forms and ceremonies which was then taking place throughout the country. There was more to come out of this than the boys thought.

Chapter Five
An Insurrection

Queen Mary had been for some months seated on the throne. The nation was becoming uneasy. The Protestant Bishop Latimer was committed to the Tower on the 13th of November, and Archbishop Cranmer was sent there on the 14th, while, at the same time, deprived Bishops, among whom were Bonner, Bishop of London, and Gardiner, Bishop of Winchester, were restored to their sees, both well-known for their virulent hatred of the Reformation. And now the intended match of the Queen with Philip of Spain, the son of Charles the Fifth, was openly talked of. It was known in a short time that the Queen had herself selected him. This was further confirmed by a statement, that on the 30th of October, having sent for the Spanish Ambassador into her chamber, the Queen repeated the *Veni Creator*, and kneeling before the host, gave him her sacred promise that she would marry no other man than Philip.

The Queen thus hoped, with a Popish husband, and with the aid of Spain, that she might restore within the realm the faith of Rome to which she clung. A secret agent had arrived from Rome—Francis Commendone by name. At first he was unable to gain access to the Queen, but, being well-known to Sir John De Leigh, the knight arranged his introduction. To him the Queen expressed her desire to re-establish the Romish Church in the country. She sent letters also by him to the Pope, which it is said were so acceptable to Julius the Third, that he wept for joy, in the belief that his pontificate would be honoured by the restoration of England to its ancient obedience. These facts becoming known, and many more statements being made which were untrue, the hatred of the people to the proposed marriage increased.

Ernst with many of his schoolfellows were in the street, when the report was spread that a large body of Spaniards, being chiefly the retinue of the Count and his harbingers, were riding through London. The dislike which Ernst naturally entertained for the people of that nation, who were so cruelly tyrannising over his native country, now blazed up, "Let's treat these people as they deserve!" he cried out to his companions. "Let us show them that though Englishmen love freedom and free men, they hate tyranny and tyrants!"

A loud hurrah was the response to this appeal. It was in the depth of winter, and the snow was lying somewhat thickly in the streets. The boys soon gathered snow-balls, with which each one loaded himself. As they moved along their numbers increased, till Ernst and his companions were almost lost sight of. They hurried on to a spot they knew the Spaniards must pass. The Count's attendants were congratulating themselves on their safe arrival in the country, and at the thoughts of being soon comfortably housed after their long ride.

"Now, boys, now!" shouted Ernst. "Give them a taste of our quality. Let us show them we will have no Spaniards in this country to reign over us. Give it them! give it them!"

As he spoke, every hand was raised on high, and a shower of snow-balls came flying about the ears of the astonished Spaniards. At first they stopped, in the vain hope of catching their assailants. The boys flew off, mocking them with their laughter. Again they moved on, when the hardy crowd collected again, and sent rapidly flying round them a complete storm of snow-balls. They were no soft or harmless missiles—some were hard as stone—masses of ice. Several of the cavaliers were cut and bruised, two or three were nearly hurled from their horses. The gay doublets of all were thoroughly bespattered with snow, and sometimes with other materials mixed with it. Ernst was more eager even than the rest, urging on his companions to continue the assault. The more angry the Spaniards became, the more the boys laughed, especially when one or two ecclesiastics among them got hit. The people who came out from their houses, although taking no part in the sport, stood by, applauding the boys, and laughing heartily. As Ernst was running here and there, encouraging his companions, re-collecting them when they were dispersed, and bringing them up again to the assault, he suddenly felt his arm grasped by a man's hand. Looking up he saw a stranger. "What is it you want of me?" he asked; "let me go, I wish to have another cast."

"Stay, boy, stay, you are acting foolishly," answered the stranger. "I know you, though you do not remember me. I was in search of you. Come with me; I have something of importance to communicate."

"I cannot! I cannot!" cried Ernst. "I must not desert my companions! I must have another throw at the Spaniards. See! it was I who hit that grim old gentleman in the eye. I think I could just catch the tip of his long nose if I was to try again. Let me go, I say! Hurrah! boys, shoot away! We will show the Dons what Englishmen think of them and their Romish faith. We want no idolatry and masses and confessions, and priests to play the tricks they used to do!"

"Foolish lad! come with me!" again exclaimed the stranger. "Such exclamations as these may cause you your life, and injure, not only yourself, but those who have protected you."

This last remark had more effect on Ernst Verner than any of the others.

"Well," he said, "I will go with you, sir, and hear what you have got to say. We have given the Spaniards a taste of our quality, and have made them understand that they are no welcome visitors to the shores of Old England."

The last remark was made as the stranger led off Ernst down a narrow street, or lane rather, such as branched off in every direction from the thoroughfares of the City. They stopped under an archway where they were free from observation.

"What is it you would have with me?" asked Ernst, looking up at the stranger, nothing daunted, though of course he was in the man's power, and the stroke of a dagger might have left him lifeless on the pavement, no one being witness to the deed, while his murderer would, to a certainty, have escaped.

"Listen to me, foolish boy," said the stranger. "I am in the service of a certain worthy gentleman—a friend of your patron, Master Gresham. He sent me to look for you, for it appears he holds you in more esteem than were he acquainted with your proceedings to-day he would be inclined to bestow on you. Now listen. He would not himself communicate directly with Master Gresham, but he desires you, as you would wish to show your gratitude to your patron, as well as to him, to hasten forth to Master Gresham's house: tell him to boot and saddle, and to hie him with all speed to his country house at Intwood. Danger threatens him. The fate his old friend and patron has lately suffered may be his. After he reaches it, let him make such arrangement of his affairs as he deems necessary, and go into hiding. When the danger has blown over, he who sends me will give him advice thereof; but if his enemies continue to seek his life, he must remain concealed, or fly for safety to some foreign land."

"Pardon me for my vehemence and rudeness, sir," said Ernst, when the stranger ceased speaking. "I will thankfully convey your message; I understand it clearly. My only fear is, lest I may have been observed, as one of those engaged in the attack on the Spaniards, and may be impeded on my way."

"I will take care of that," said the stranger. "I will watch you at a distance, and, should you be stopped, will endeavour to obtain your release. I may have more influence with the people in authority than you may suppose.

Now hasten away, you will not go so fast that I cannot keep up with you; but remember that you must yourself deliver the message to Master Gresham in person. Let it not pass through any other hands. He will excuse you for your absence from school, and will probably send a message to your master that may enable you to escape punishment. Now hie thee away, lad. I will follow, and will go to thy rescue, should any attempt to stop thee."

Ernst, thus understanding that his patron was in danger, tucked up the skirts of his long gown closely round his waist, and hurried away at the top of his speed. The stranger must have had to keep up a rapid pace to hold him in sight. Ernst sped on. His chief fear was that he might meet some of his companions, who would inquire the cause of his haste. On he went. He saw several of them at a distance; but, by turning down one lane and running up another, he avoided them. He forgot that in so doing he should probably get out of sight of the stranger, but he little heeded that: he rather trusted to his own adroitness than to any assistance which might be given him. Breathless he reached the door of his patron's house.

Hurriedly knocking, he was admitted. Master Gresham was out. He hastened to the Lady Anne's apartments. With anxious looks she inquired the cause of his coming.

"It is better that you should endure some alarm than that my dear master should suffer evil," said Ernst, as he delivered the message which he had received. "It will be well to make preparations for his journey, that the instant he returns he may be able to set forth."

"Wisely spoken, lad," answered Lady Anne; "you have well repaid the care we have taken of you. While I am seeing that such garments as my lord may require are put up, do you go and tell the factor, John Elliot, to have the horses in readiness; and let James Brocktrop know that he is to ride with his lord. Tell him not where, but that he must be prepared for a long journey."

All these arrangements were made before the return of Master Gresham: he had been presiding at a meeting of the Mercers' Company. Seldom had he appeared so much out of spirits, even before he heard the account Ernst had to give him. The merchants of London, he said, were universally against this Spanish marriage. They were too well acquainted with the affairs of Europe, and with the character of the Emperor and his son, not to dread the worst consequences to England. The cruelties exercised over the inhabitants of the Low Countries had driven numerous skilled artisans to England; but if Philip was ruler here, they would be afraid to come, dreading lest the same cruelties might be exercised upon them in the land of their adoption.

Lady Anne interrupted these remarks by bringing forward Ernst. The merchant listened calmly to the account given him by the lad.

"The warning is from a friend," he remarked; "it should not be disregarded. Yet I have no fancy to fly away like a traitor or criminal: I would rather remain and stand the brunt of any attack made on me."

"Oh, my dear lord, be not so rash!" exclaimed Lady Anne. "If the Queen desires again to establish the Romish faith in England, surely she will endeavour to remove all those who, from their rank or wealth and sound Protestant principles, are likely to interfere with her project."

Ernst added his entreaties to those of the Lady Anne, assuring his patron that the man who had spoken to him had urged instant flight as the only sure means of escaping the threatened danger. Master Gresham at length yielded to the entreaties of his wife; and having put on his riding-dress, and secured his arms round him, accompanied by his faithful attendant James Brocktrop, he took his departure from his house. He was soon clear of the City, riding along the pleasant lanes and open fields towards the north of London. Ernst ran behind the horses, keeping a little way off, for a considerable distance, till he saw them safe out of the City, and then returned to make his report to the Lady Anne, who failed not to pray that her lord might be protected on his journey. Again she thanked Ernst for the benefit he had done her lord.

And now the boy returned, with his heart beating more proudly than it had ever beaten before, back to school: a line from Lady Anne, explaining that he had been employed by his patron, saved him from the penalty which he might have had to suffer for his absence.

Ernst got back to school: the master asked no questions. He might have been aware that some of his boys had been out pelting the Spaniards with snow-balls; but the crime, perchance, was not a great one in his eyes.

The following day, the Earl of Devonshire and a large assemblage of other lords and gentlemen went down to the Tower Wharf to receive the Spanish Ambassador, who came to arrange the terms of the Queen's marriage. He travelled in great state, attended by a number of nobles and others. He was Flemish—the Count of Egmont; hereafter to be seen by Ernst under very different circumstances. As he landed thus in great state, the Earl of Devonshire gave him his right hand, and assisted him to mount a richly-caparisoned steed standing ready to carry him. Thus the cavalcade of nobles, in their furred cloaks, proceeded on through Cheapside, and so forth to Westminster. As the Count looked round him, he might have suspected that his master Philip was in no respect welcome to the English. There were many people, notwithstanding the cold, in the streets; but none of them shouted or waved their hats, but on the contrary held down their heads and turned aside, well knowing that his visit boded no good to their country. Still more hateful were the thoughts of the marriage to the people when the terms of the treaty became known. The boys at Saint Paul's School were the first to invent a new game, one half calling themselves Spaniards, the other English. Ernst would never consent to join the Spaniards.

"No," he said; "they burned my father and my mother, and while I live I will never unite with them. I tell you, boys, they will burn you and your fathers and your mothers, and all you love, who dare to call themselves Protestants, if they ever get power in this country of England."

Often the battle raged furiously in the playground between the two parties. On no occasion would the English allow themselves to be beaten: indeed, those who represented the Spaniards seemed to feel that they had a bad cause; and whether they charged each other, or one party pursued the other, the Spaniards invariably gave way.

And now troublous times began in England. News was received that various gentlemen and others were up in arms to resist the coming of the King of Spain—Sir Thomas Carew in Devonshire and Sir Thomas Wyatt in Kent. The Duke of Suffolk also caused proclamation to be made against the Queen's marriage. News reached London that an army of insurgents under Sir Thomas Wyatt was marching on the City. The boys from the schools were sent to their friends, no one knowing what might occur. Willingly the Lady Anne would have followed her lord into the country; but she feared that by going thither she might betray the place of his retreat. She therefore waited in London, hoping that she might receive tidings of his safety. Day after day, however, passed by, and no news reached her. Ernst endeavoured to console her, entreating that he might be allowed to set off to visit Master Gresham.

"That would cause almost as much risk as my going," she answered. "Your foreign tongue, my boy, would betray you, and you might easily be traced. No; we must put our trust in God that He will protect my lord amid the dangers which surround him."

Not many days after this the insurgents came to the south side of the Thames. Those of the inhabitants of London who held to Queen Mary armed themselves for her defence; and as the army of Sir Thomas Wyatt passed on the Surrey side in sight of the Tower, the ordnance which was placed thereon was discharged at them. Though the guns roared loudly, however, no injury was inflicted. When they came to London Bridge they found the gates shut and the drawbridge cut down. Onward they marched therefore to Kingston, there being no other means of passing the Thames till they could reach that place. Here also the bridge was broken down; but the Queen's men being dispersed, the insurgents crossed in boats, and, marching on, halted not till they had reached Knightsbridge. Ernst, hearing of what was taking place, was eager to go out and join them, and he failed not to find a number of companions who were willing to unite with him in the expedition. They had no arms, but they arranged a plan to obtain daggers and bows and arrows, and they hoped with these to perform some mighty exploit, so as to prevent the hateful Spanish match.

Ernst was captain of this youthful band, and Andrew A'Dale and the young Richard Gresham lieutenants. They had full fifty others with them. That they were not sent off to prison at once, with no small risk of afterwards being hung up, as were many older men, was owing to the prudence of Ernst Verner. He advised that, should any demand their intentions, their replies should be that they were arming for the protection of their country, and that as yet they had not decided on their plan of operation. Thus, while the citizens were assembling in the public places or marching here and there, they also were able to go forth, no one doubting that they were prepared to defend the City against the insurgents. It may have been, however, that some of those of more advanced age had the same intentions, and that, had Sir Thomas Wyatt been successful, they would gladly have joined him. And now there was a great commotion, it being known that the insurgents were approaching close to the west end of London. On this Queen Mary came into the City, and arriving at Guildhall, where a large concourse of people was assembled, made a vehement oration against Wyatt and his followers, Bishop Gardiner exclaiming as she concluded, "How happy are we, to whom God has given so wise and learned a Queen!"

Not long after, however, when Wyatt drew still closer to the City, many of the followers of the Queen went to her, crying out that all was lost, and urged her to take boat, so that she might go down the river and escape. Her women, too, were shrieking through terror, and endeavouring to hide themselves away, thinking that the insurgents would speedily come in and slay them. It might have been a happy thing for this kingdom and people, if the advice of these timorous soldiers had been followed. Some probably were only too glad at having an excuse for persuading the Queen to leave the kingdom. She, however, refused to move, declaring "that now she was Queen—Queen she would remain." One thing certainly must be said of Queen Mary: she was a bold, brave woman, determined in purpose, though all gentle feelings were completely overcome by the influence of her bigotry and superstition; thus, having once tasted of blood, her disposition seemed that of a veritable tiger.

The sound of guns was now heard in the City. Ernst and his companions were very eager to march forth, but obtaining no certain information, they knew not in which direction to proceed. He, therefore, with one faithful companion—Andrew A'Dale—agreed to set forth to gain information.

Poor Lady Anne was by this time in great agitation about her young charges, they having strayed out unknown to her, and she being unable to tell what had become of them.

Ernst and Andrew, hiding their weapons, hurried along, passing through Cheapside, and going on till they arrived at Ludgate. Joining an armed band who were going forth, they slipped out through the gate. And now they took their way along Fleet Street to Temple Bar. They had not gone far before they saw a large body of armed men approaching. They guessed rightly. They formed part of the army of Sir Thomas Wyatt.

"We will join them," said Ernst; but A'Dale was cautious. "Let us draw aside," he observed, "and see what they are about."

On marched the insurgents. Some had fire-arms, but many had only long pikes and scythes, and other hastily-formed weapons. Still as they advanced, the people shouted, "A Wyatt! a Wyatt!"

The boys now joined the band, which with loud shouts marched onward till they arrived at Ludgate. The gate was, however, shut. Wyatt having thus far been successful, hoped that he should have no difficulty in entering the City; but when he knocked at the gate, Lord William Howard, who was there commanding, shouted out:

"Avaunt, traitor! Thou shalt not enter in here."

In vain the insurgents thundered at the gate. They could by no means force it. Some were slain in making the attempt. Two or three were struck down by arrows close to where Ernst and his companion were standing.

"We shall do well to retreat," observed A'Dale, in a low voice; "we shall gain no honour here. I fear that these men will not force the gate."

He spoke too truly. The order was given to retreat. The boys were now hurried back by the crowd, from which it was impossible to extricate themselves.

Chapter Six
In Fleet Prison

Ernst Verner and Andrew A'Dale began bitterly to repent their folly in having come out of the City. Still more so did they when the insurgents met a body of the Queen's troops near Temple Bar. Sir Thomas Wyatt's men, though they for some time fought bravely, many losing their lives, were at length put to flight, and a herald advancing, urged their leader to yield himself a prisoner, and to submit to the Queen's clemency. The friends around him, however, entreated him rather to fly than to trust to one under such evil influences as was her Majesty, but in despair he at length yielded himself up to Sir Maurice Berkley. It was a sad sight to see poor Sir Thomas mounted on a horse behind Sir Maurice, and carried off to Westminster. As this is not a record of public events, it may briefly be said that the clemency afforded to Sir Thomas Wyatt was that of death, he being some time afterwards executed.

There can be no doubt that this insurrection hastened the execution of the young and talented Lady Jane Grey, and of her husband, Lord Guilford Dudley. The event just described took place on the 7th of February, 1554, and on the 12th Lord Guilford Dudley was led out of his prison to die on Tower Hill. Ernst and A'Dale heard, as boys are apt to hear, that some event of importance was about to take place, and together they found their way to the spot, little knowing, however, what they were to witness. The bell tolled slowly when the young nobleman was led forth from the Tower to the scaffold. He gazed round him on that cold winter's morning; yet colder seemed the hearts of those who were thus putting him out of life. After a short time allowed him for prayer, he laid his head on the block. The executioner held it up, and declared it to be the head of a traitor. It was then wrapped in a cloth, and his body was taken back in a cart to the Tower. The boys, with many other persons, now made their way within the walls, supposing that they were to witness the interment of the young lord, but shortly they found themselves beneath the walls of the White Tower. There, on the green open space, a scaffold appeared. While they were wondering why it was there placed, a door at the foot of the Tower opened, and forthwith came several guards and other persons. In their midst walked a lady, young and lovely, moving with grace, and her countenance, though grave and sad, yet beaming with a radiance which seemed to the boys angelic.

Young indeed she was, for she had as yet numbered only seventeen summers. She walked on with a firm step, not a tear appearing in her eyes. In her hand she held a book, from which she read, praying as she walked. Thus she came to the scaffold. There she knelt down and again lifted up her heart in prayer to God. She was the Lady Jane Grey, thus about cruelly to be put to death for no crime—no fault of hers. When she rose, she handed her book from which she had been reading, to an officer who stood by her side. He was Master Brydges, brother of the Lieutenant of the Tower. In vain the priests who stood round endeavoured to persuade her to die in the faith of Rome. She who had a short time before uttered these memorable words, "I ground my faith upon God's Word, and not upon the Church, for if the Church be a good Church, the faith of the Church must be tried by God's Word, and not God's Word by the Church," could not, while God's grace supported her, abandon the pure Protestant truth she held. And now she was well prepared to die, for she trusted in the risen Saviour, all-powerful to keep her to the end. Tying the kerchief about her eyes, she felt for the block, and said, in a sweet, low voice, "What shall I do? Where is it?"

One of those standing by guided her to the block, on which she then laid down her head as if on a pillow, and stretched forth her body, seemingly about to rest, saying: "Lord, into Thy hands I commend my spirit." No other word she spoke. The gleaming axe descended, and the life of that young and virtuous and highly talented lady was thus cut short. Had Ernst been alone he would have fallen to the ground, so faint and sick at heart did he become at the spectacle he had witnessed. But A'Dale was of somewhat firmer stuff, and taking his companion by the arm, led him again out of the precincts of the Tower. The gates were once more closed.

Such was the commencement of horrors which the City of London was to witness.

On the following day, when morning broke, in all parts of London gallows were found erected, from Billingsgate in the east to Hyde Park Corner in the west, and in nineteen different places were these instruments of death set up; and ere the close of that black day, forty-eight men had been suspended on them, all accused of joining in the rebellion of Sir Thomas Wyatt. Still the prisons were full of captives; and a few days afterwards several leaders and twenty-two common rebels were marched out of London under a strong escort to suffer death in Kent, there to strike terror into the hearts of the inhabitants.

It was melancholy at that time to walk about London, for in every direction the sight of men hanging in gibbets met the eye. Ernst declared that he would not again leave the house, and yet a feverish curiosity compelled him, with A'Dale, often to traverse the streets.

Still no news came of Master Gresham, and Lady Anne became very anxious to hear of his safety.

At length, one night, the wind blowing, and the rain pattering down on the roof, a loud knocking was heard at the door, and after some time the porter, being aroused, went to the watch-hole to see who was without. As there was but a single horseman, the porter asked his business.

"Don't you know me, knave?" asked the voice of James Brocktrop; "open quickly! I have a message for our lady!"

Saying this, as soon as the door was opened, he brought his horse into the paved hall, and led it through to the back of the house, where the stables were situated.

"Now hie thee to bed, knave," he said to the porter. "I will get for thee a cup of sack, that thou mayest sleep sounder after being thus aroused."

In a short time Ernst was summoned by Lady Anne, and directed to bring James Brocktrop into her presence, to hear the news he had brought from her lord. They spoke for a short time together, when both went down to the hall, Lady Anne calling Ernst to her. The door was opened, and James Brocktrop sallied forth, leaving Lady Anne and Ernst to watch at the door.

In a short time Brocktrop returned, accompanied by another person, with a cloak wrapped closely round him which shaded his features. No sooner was he inside than the door was again closed, and, without speaking a word, Lady Anne led him along to the stairs, and together they ascended to the upper part of the house.

"Who is that?" asked Ernst of Brocktrop; "surely I know the figure of the stranger."

"It will be wise in you to know nothing about the matter, young master," answered Brocktrop: "some knowledge is dangerous, especially in these times."

Ernst formed his own opinion on the subject. He had little doubt who the stranger was.

"Now hie thee to bed, lad, hie thee to bed," said Master Brocktrop, "and forget, if thou canst, that thou hast been awakened out of thy sleep; and if thou art cross-questioned at any time, thou wilt remember that which has passed to-night is but an idle dream not to be spoken of."

Ernst went back to his room, which he shared with the young Richard Gresham, and was soon again fast asleep.

After this, Lady Anne no longer spoke of her anxiety regarding the fate of her husband; but she saw no guests, and those who called on business were told that as soon as Master Gresham returned, and was able to see them, he would willingly hear what they had to communicate.

Master Gresham was not the only Protestant gentleman of repute who was at this time anxious about himself. Many who had come prominently forward during the reign of King Edward were now placed in great fear in consequence of the proceedings of the Queen's ministers. A sermon, a short time before preached by Gardiner, Bishop of Winchester, before the Queen, greatly alarmed the minds of those who held Protestant principles, in which he had entreated that, as before open rebellion and conspiracy had sprung out of her leniency, she would now be merciful to the body of the commonwealth and conservation thereof, which could not be unless the rotten and hurtful members thereof were cut off and consumed. In truth, it was well-known that she and her counsellors had determined to carry through the matter of restoring the Popish faith by fire and blood. Ernst especially trembled when he heard that Philip, the son of the cruel persecutor of the Netherlands, had arrived in England, and that he had been married to Queen Mary on the 25th of June, the festival of Saint James, the Patron Saint of Spain, and that henceforth he was to be called King of England. Gardiner, who performed the ceremony, was treated with great respect, and at the banquet which followed was the only person permitted to sit upon the daïs with the King and Queen.

And now all the gibbets in London were taken down, so that the dead bodies hanging thereon might not offend the sight of the King, who, however, had been too much accustomed to see the subjects of his father burned because they trusted in God's Word to have felt any great repugnance to the spectacle.

Everywhere the streets of London were filled with Spaniards, who walked haughtily about with their cloaks over their shoulders and swords by their sides, greatly to the displeasure of the citizens, who often seemed disposed to place them all, with their Prince, on board the vessels in the Thames, and send them forthwith again out of the country. And now preparations were complete for the state visit of the King and Queen to the City.

Banners were hung out along the streets; all sorts of designs were prepared, while all public spots which would allow of paintings were ornamented with various devices; among others, the conduit in Gracechurch

Street was decorated with pictures of Henry the Eighth and Edward the Sixth, and of the nine worthies. Henry was represented with a Bible in his hand, on which was written, "Verbum Dei."

Now the Queen and a vast number of nobles—English, Flemish, and Spanish—rode through the City in great state; but few of the mob cheered, or cried, "God save the King and Queen!" Many, indeed, uttered very different exclamations, at which Mary, and Bishop Gardiner, were very wroth, scarcely attempting to conceal their anger. Still more angry was the Bishop when he arrived in Gracechurch Street, and saw the representation of King Henry with a Bible in his hand. Immediately he sent some one to call the painter before him, who, on his appearing, had numerous foul words showered down on his head.

"Thou art an accursed traitor!" he added. "Who bade thee thus paint the good King with a book in his hand? Thou shalt be sent to the Fleet because thou art a fool, if not a traitor."

The poor painter humbly apologised, saying that he thought, as King Henry had allowed the Bible to be read in all churches, it was right to paint him in that manner.

"No, no, knave!" answered the bishop. "Such a painting is against the Queen's Catholic proceedings. She does not esteem the Bible as the vile heretics do. Now go and paint out the book, or thy head will grace one of the first fresh gibbets which will soon be erected in the City."

The painter hastened off, and painting out the Bible, put in the King's hands a pair of gloves in its stead.

Ernst, as has been said, was watching the procession, but with a bitter heart. He did not intend to make any sign of disrespect: he simply avoided shouting, or showing that he was pleased at the arrival of the Prince, when suddenly he found his arm seized by a person with a firm grasp.

"What want you with me?" he asked, looking up, and almost expecting to see the person who had before warned him that Master Gresham was in danger.

"Thou art a young traitor, and must prepare to go with me to prison," said the officer of justice. "I saw thee just now make signs of hatred towards the Queen. For this alone thou deservest to die; we can have no traitors in England."

In vain Ernst pleaded that he had not done any wrong, and that though he had not shouted, neither had the great mass of people standing round. This seemed somewhat to stagger the officer. The man was about, indeed, to let Ernst go, when a priest, who had been standing near, stepped forward, and looking the boy earnestly in the face, exclaimed: "Oh! young traitor, I saw thee when I was performing mass at Saint Mary Overy, and the rebels under Wyatt attacked the church. Thou wert among those who stripped the altar, and endeavoured to carry off the silver candlesticks. Young heretic and traitor that thou art! Off to the Fleet with him! I wot that his father and friends are as bad as he is; and when they come to look for him they shall be secured likewise. I can swear to his countenance. See! he trembles and turns pale. He is guilty, there is no doubt of it."

"Indeed I am not, master!" exclaimed Ernst. "At the time you speak of, I was on the north side of the river. Only once, when I entered London, did I ever cross London Bridge."

"Thou wouldest swear to any falsehood, young traitor," answered the priest. "Thy word is of no value."

"But I can swear that he did not cross London Bridge on that day!" exclaimed Andrew A'Dale, who had been at some little distance from Ernst at the time, but, seeing him seized hold of by the guard, had hurried up, and heard the last remarks of the priest.

"Ah, ah!" exclaimed the priest, looking at Andrew, "why, of course thou wilt swear anything for thy companion, for thou wert there thyself. Thy nature is shown clearly enough, because thou didst not shout for the good Queen Mary and her loving spouse. Seize him also: carry them both away to the Fleet. They are a brace of traitors and heretics. Away with them! Away with them!"

On this both the lads were seized, and, in spite of all their expostulations and assertions of their innocence, were being dragged off by the officers of the so-called justice. At that instant, a richly-dressed gentleman on horseback, who had for some reason remained somewhat behind the royal party, was passing by in order to rejoin them. Observing the youth struggling in the hands of the guards, he turned his head aside. He gave a second glance at Ernst's countenance, and after doing so stopped his horse, and made a sign to the guard to allow the boys to approach. "What, my lad," he exclaimed, "have you been breaking the peace? Of what crime are you accused?"

Ernst looked up at the speaker, and recognised Sir John De Leigh.

"I am wrongfully accused of having been, with other boys, at the church of Saint Mary Overy when it was sacked; but to my knowledge I have never been near the place, and during the whole of that day was on the north side of the river."

"I believe your words, my boy, and will see what can be done for you," answered Sir John.

He spoke to the guards, but they shook their heads. The boys had been given into their charge by Father Overton, and they dared not let them go free. In vain Sir John offered to be answerable for them. "The father is in the service of Bishop Gardiner, and he is not one likely to pardon us, should we allow the prisoners to escape."

"Well, my lads, I am afraid you must submit to it," said Sir John, in a kind voice. "But trust to me; I will see after you, and hope, if you can prove yourselves innocent, to get you set free."

"Thank you, sir," said Ernst; "but, in the meantime, I fear me much that Lady Anne will be anxious at not hearing of me, and so will A'Dale's friends; will you, therefore, send to her, and beg her also to let them know what has become of him?"

"You are a thoughtful boy," answered Sir John; "I will see to it;" and slipping a purse into Ernst's hands, he rode on, whispering as he did so, "You will require that to obtain some few necessaries in prison."

Seeing there was no help for it, the boys walked on rapidly, endeavouring to look as little like prisoners as possible. Their guards, indeed, with their heavy arms, had some difficulty in keeping up with them. Proceeding down Cheapside, they reached Ludgate, and then turning to the north by the banks of the river Fleet, they arrived at the entrance of the prison, surrounded by strong walls. On either side of the entrance, which had a room overhead, were two low, tower-like buildings facing a flight of steps leading down to the river. The porter quickly opened the gate, and eagerly received his prisoners, well pleased at the thoughts of the fees they might bring him.

"Glad to see you, my young masters; we shall find you pleasant apartments, I doubt not; and maybe you will occupy them to the end of your days—or perchance until you go forth to grace one of the gibbets with which our ancient city has of late been adorned."

The guards, having received a proper acknowledgment from the warden of the delivery of the prisoners, demanded a fee, that they might have the honour of drinking their healths, and were evidently disappointed when A'Dale stoutly refused to yield to their demands. The boys were now carried before the governor of the prison, or sub-warden, as he was called, who farmed the management from the warden, his chief business being to wring, as much out of the prisoners as he possibly could, either by threats, or barbarous treatment, or offers of favour to be shown them.

A'Dale, who was a well-practised London lad, and knew its ways thoroughly, whispered to Ernst to produce only one of his coins at a time, being very sure that the sub-warden would otherwise not grant them any favour until he had possessed himself of the greater number. Ernst accordingly at once placed a couple of marks in the warden's hands.

"There, Master Warden," he said; "we are unjustly brought in here; but we would desire, while we remain, to enjoy such conveniences as the place can afford."

"Of course, young masters, all who come hither consider themselves brought here unjustly. You shall have an upper chamber, or at least a portion of one, as perchance you may have companions, whence you can enjoy a view of the Fleet river, and the barges passing up and down it. Such bedding as many a dignitary of the Church has had to rest on, and food from my own buttery. More, surely, you cannot desire; and, hark you! these two marks are very well as a beginning, but I must see more of them, or you will find your quarters and your fare changed pretty speedily." The sub-warden having thus, as he said, examined his prisoners, summoned the jailer to conduct them to the apartments he indicated.

Chapter Seven
Deliverance

Ernst and A'Dale were led through many passages, in which the air was close and heavy, and their nostrils were assailed with many foul odours. At length the jailer unlocked a door at the end of a long passage, and, pointing to the inside of the room, told them they might walk in. With sinking hearts they entered, and the man, without more ado, turned the lock upon them.

The room was almost destitute of furniture, and dirty in the extreme, evidently not having been cleaned out since its last occupant was dismissed. In one corner was a truckle bed, covered with a cloth and a pile of loose straw. There was a rickety table of rough boards, with three legs, and a couple of stools of the same character. The window was long and narrow, with bars across it; though a moderately stout man could not have squeezed through, even had the bars been wanting. It was only by standing on one of the stools they could look out of the window, whence, as the warden had told them, they could see the muddy waters of the Fleet flowing by, with Fleet Street beyond, winding its way to Temple Bar.

"This is a scurvy place to put us in," observed A'Dale, "we who are innocent of any crime."

"Better men have been placed in a worse situation," answered Ernst. "In my country hundreds, nay thousands, of persons, for no crime but that of worshipping God according to their consciences, have been not only committed to prison and tortured, but burned, and otherwise put to death."

"Surely the people of England would never submit to such tyranny as that!" exclaimed A'Dale.

"I know not," observed Ernst; "may be they will have no choice. Had there been more men of true heart among them, they would have rescued that sweet Lady Jane Grey and her young and handsome husband. When I found that the Queen had the heart to allow them to be put to death, I felt sure that she would not hesitate to destroy all who might oppose her will."

"I hope we may escape from her power," observed A'Dale. "Who was the gallant gentleman who spoke to you? Do you think he can help us?"

Ernst told his friend. "I know little of him," he added; "but he seems to be a man of influence, and kindly disposed towards me."

The warden fulfilled his promise to the lads, though not exactly as they desired. A mattress was brought them, and a coarse and not over-clean covering; food also on a trencher, and a mug of ale was sent in, but the food was badly cooked, and the ale was none of the best. There was, however, a sufficiency to satisfy hunger and thirst; and they hoped for little more than that. They had been on foot all day. They were glad, when it grew dark, to throw themselves on their rough bed, and there in a short time they forgot their anxiety in sleep. The next day they waited anxiously for news from Sir John De Leigh, but none came. Ernst hoped also that some messenger might arrive from Lady Anne, trusting that Sir John had fulfilled his promise by informing her what had happened to them. They were doomed, however, to be disappointed. Towards evening, Master Babbington, the sub-warden, failed not to make his appearance.

"You remember my remark of yesterday evening, my young masters," he observed. "I have to demand a further payment, or I must place another person in this chamber instead of you, and remove you to one below, which may not be so pleasant."

"We are willing to pay yet further, Master Warden," answered Ernst; "but I would beg you also to give us more liberty. We neither desire nor have the power of quitting the prison, having reason to believe that our friends will intercede in our behalf; but to be shut up all day in this room is far from pleasant; and we will pass our words not to escape for the next week, should we be confined as long."

The warden laughed grimly. "That were a pretty way of looking after prisoners," he observed. "However, on payment of another mark each, you may perchance obtain the liberty of taking the air, on passing your word that you will make no attempt to leave the prison."

The money and the promise were at once given, and the boys were told that at certain hours of the day they would have liberty to take the air in the courtyard below.

The very thought of this gave the boys considerable satisfaction. They did not sleep soundly that night, and both were awoke, it might have been about midnight, by hearing groans, as of a person in pain, proceeding apparently from the chamber below them. They listened attentively, and now they heard a human voice; it seemed lifted up in prayer. Getting out of bed, and putting their ears to the floor, they could distinguish the very words. Fervent and earnest was the prayer. It was addressed neither to the Virgin nor to saints, but to One always ready to hear prayer—to One who "so loved the world that He gave His only begotten Son, that whosoever believeth in Him should not perish, but have everlasting life." The voice was deep-toned and earnest. Sometimes it trembled like that of a man advanced in life, or suffering from great bodily sickness. The boys felt almost that they had no right to listen to words which were spoken to God alone. Still they felt their own spirits revive, and their courage strengthened. The speaker seemed to think that the hour of his death was fast approaching, that he might have to stand before a tribunal of his fellow-men, and he prayed that strength might be given him to make a good confession, to hold fast to the faith. At length the prayer ceased, and once more the boys lay down in their beds, and were soon again asleep.

The following day, at the hour of noon, the door of their ward opened, and the red nose of Master Babbington appeared at it.

"You may go forth, young masters," he observed; "but remember you are watched, and if you are seen spying about, instead of the leniency you have hitherto experienced, you will be treated with no small amount of rigour." Saying this, the warden went on his way to visit other prisoners.

The boys, glad to find themselves in the enjoyment of even such limited liberty as was given them, hastened from the room and found their way into the courtyard. There were several other persons brought into the prison, for slight offences probably. Most of them were engaged in various games, some of ball or tennis, while others were content to walk up and down, to stretch their legs and to inhale such air, close and impure as it was, as they were allowed to breathe.

HE INQUIRED WHY THEY WERE IN PRISON.

As Ernst and A'Dale were on their way back to their chamber, the hour of their liberty having expired, they met a venerable personage, accompanied by a guard, proceeding along the passage. He stopped and gazed at them with an air of commiseration, and inquired for what cause, they, so young and innocent-looking, had been committed to prison.

"On a false accusation, sir," answered Ernst; and in a few words he explained what had happened to them.

"There are many who are brought here on false accusations," observed the venerable-looking stranger. "However, you are young, and may, I hope, bear your imprisonment with less suffering than I do. Better far that you should be brought here innocent than guilty; and yet, my young friends, let me ask you—How do you stand before God, innocent or guilty?"

"Very guilty, I am afraid, sir," answered Ernst, looking up.

"If you are judged by your own merits, yes," answered the stranger; "but if by faith you have put on Christ's righteousness, you stand free and guiltless in the sight of the Judge of all things."

"Oh yes, sir! yes!" answered Ernst; "I know that the just shall live by faith."

"Well answered, my boy," replied the stranger. "Trust not to works, not to ordinances, not to forms, not to creeds, but simply to the all-sufficient merit of Christ. You must take Him as your own Saviour, as He offers salvation, and rely on Him, and Him alone through faith. It is an important truth; and happy are you that you have been brought into this prison if you accept it."

"Come, move on, move on!" exclaimed a rough voice. "We cannot let you teach your heresy to these boys, albeit the fire will probably purge you and them of it ere long."

Ernst, looking round, saw the burly form of Master Babbington, the warden of the prison, approaching.

He and A'Dale, respectfully wishing the old man farewell, hurried on, that they might avoid an encounter with the jailer. The stranger was no other than the venerable John Hooper, late Bishop of Worcester and Gloucester. Ernst afterwards learned much about him from one who wrote the lives of many martyrs of the true faith. It was his prayer which they had heard on the second night of their coming to the prison. The room in which he was lodged was foul and damp; and there he was kept for many months suffering from disease, till he was finally led forth and carried to Gloucester, where he was cruelly put to death by fire, holding to the true faith to the last moment of his life.

Ernst and A'Dale, in consequence of their speaking to the good bishop, were deprived of their liberty; but it mattered little, for in two days officers arrived at the prison to carry up numerous persons to be examined before the Bishop of Winchester. Among others, Ernst and A'Dale were summoned. They went willingly, thinking that they could surely with ease free themselves.

Many of the prisoners as they were led forth looked sick and pale, as if they had been kept in unwholesome wards, with scanty food. Some were weeping, not knowing what might be the result of their trial. It was rumoured, not without reason, that the Queen proposed to crush out the Reformed religion with fire and sword; and they remembered that in King Henry's time, that sweet young lady—Anne Askew—had been burned at

Smithfield; and it was evident that Queen Mary had much of the nature of her father. The prisoners were led over London Bridge to the Church of Saint Mary Overy—the very place in which the priest declared that Ernst had been seen with other rioters attacking the altar.

The Bishop of Winchester and other bishops, among whom was Bonner, Bishop of London, were seated in great state, when the prisoners were brought up before them. A few were faint-hearted, and when asked their opinions on the supremacy of the Pope, on transubstantiation and other points, declared themselves believers in the doctrine of Rome. Others, however, boldly denied that the Pope had any authority in this realm of England, while they as bravely asserted the Protestant doctrine for which they had been cast into prison. Many of them, of all ranks, some poor and illiterate, did in no wise shrink from the abuse heaped on them by Gardiner and Bonner especially.

And now the priest who had accused Ernst and A'Dale appeared in court. He fixed his eyes sternly on them, as if he would frighten them into submission, and pointing at them a finger of scorn, declared that they were among the worst of those present, having committed sacrilege and robbery, as he could clearly show. In vain the boys looked round for any one to plead their cause.

"Off with them to prison!" shouted Gardiner; "they are fit food for the flames, which ere long they must be given to feed."

The rest of the accused were sent back to their prison, King Philip being still in the country, and the Queen not being, as yet, willing to commence the burning of her loving subjects. It was not till she was left alone, deserted by her husband, that she gave full way to the spirit of bigotry which dwelt in her heart.

"As for these lads," exclaimed the bishop, "let them be put in the foulest dungeon in the Fleet, and that, I wot, is bad enough! In a few days they will have the means of drying their clothes and limbs too, if I mistake not."

The hearts of the two boys, which had hitherto held up bravely, now sunk very low; but just at that moment, as Ernst cast one more imploring glance round the court, a gentleman in a rich suit entered, and at once going up to the lads, led them before Gardiner, the Chancellor. He exchanged a few words with him, and seemed, by his gestures and the expression of his countenance, to be pleading hard in their favour.

"Well, well, Sir John, you must have your way," answered the Bishop. "If I mistake not, they will very soon be again within the power of the court;

and another time, remember, they will not escape so easily." The priest, seeing that his victims were about to escape him, addressed the Chancellor, but was quickly silenced; and Sir John De Leigh, in triumph, led the boys out of the building. The priest scowled fiercely at them as they passed.

"I know that Father Overton—he will try to work you mischief," observed Sir John; "but you must keep out of his way. These vultures, when once they fix their talons on their prey, like not to have it torn away from them, and will follow it eagerly, in the hopes of regaining it."

Ernst and A'Dale found a horse in readiness, held by a groom, on which Sir John told them to mount; and together they rode back over London Bridge, between the row of houses which rose up above them on either side.

On their arrival at the house in Lombard Street, the Lady Anne hurried downstairs, cordially welcoming Ernst, while little Richard followed, and threw his arms round his neck in his joy at his recovery.

"I cannot thank you enough, Sir John, for all you have done for us," she said, as the knight saluted her. "My husband desires to see you, and to thank you also. Our young friend here must also come up, though, as he is older than Ernst, we cannot help being angry with him, believing that he may have led his companion into mischief."

"No, no, I led him!" exclaimed Ernst, quickly and boldly. "I am ready to suffer punishment, but blame not him, for I deserve it more than he does."

"We will not talk of punishment," said Sir John, smiling. "Most people would think that you had had enough, with a week's sojourn in the Fleet Prison. I hope that you may never again in the course of your lives see the inside of it. It is difficult in the present time for even honest men to keep outside, if there are any who have a desire to put them in."

These words were spoken as they were proceeding upstairs. Lady Anne opened the door of the usual sitting-room, and there, reclining in a chair, suffering apparently somewhat from sickness, they beheld Master Gresham himself. He rose to welcome Sir John, and to thank him for the favour which he had done him. It was no less, indeed, than having procured his acquittal from the charges which Lord Winchester and others had brought against him. Not only this, but the Queen's Council, finding their affairs in the Netherlands greatly disordered, and it being necessary to raise further loans, had looked about for a fit person to fill the post of Royal agent, and none was found in whom all could confide so completely as in Master Gresham. Instead, therefore, of being committed to the Fleet, and perchance left to die there of disease, he had received this honourable appointment, the notice of which had only just before been sent him by Sir John De Leigh.

Master Gresham received Ernst very kindly, but admonished him to be careful in future, and on no account to allow himself to be led away by his feelings, or to mingle in any popular disturbance. "Patience and forbearance will, in the end, gain more than haste and violence," he observed. "It is seldom that a short road can be found to any great object—at least, if that object is to be secured permanently. I do not say that there are not times and seasons when men must fight for objects they hold dear, but in most cases those objects are most likely to be secured with the sword sheathed—by perseverance and firm language."

Ernst expected to be sent back to Saint Paul's School, to which A'Dale had to return; but, by the advice of Sir John De Leigh, Master Gresham agreed to take him back to Antwerp.

"He will be no longer recognised there," observed the knight; "but that priest, whom I know well, and who has accused him, will not rest till he has again got him into trouble. Why he has thus marked him down I know not, but that he has done so I am certain. Till you commence your journey, I would advise that he remains in the house, or only goes forth under your charge, and no one will now dare molest you. Had they not required your services, I fear that my influence would have availed little; but, being fully aware of your value, they are too wise to cut down the tree from which they hope to pluck golden fruit. Now, farewell, my friend; I must hie me back to court, there to attend on my loving sovereign." The knight spoke in a somewhat satirical tone.

"Remember, my good friend, that there are some persons from whom faithful service obtains but a scant recompense," observed Master Gresham. "As a tree, too, is known by its fruit, surely, judging by its produce, the Church of Rome must be of a very bitter nature, and not such as a man like you would desire to support."

"I was brought up a faithful son of the Church of Rome; and as that appears to have the upper hand at present, I see no reason why I should quit it," answered the knight; "and if I did so, I should have little chance of helping myself, much less my friends; so you, at all events, should not advise me to take any such step."

Master Gresham sighed.

"Such principles as these will soon bring ruin on our country," he said to himself; for he could not utter such thoughts aloud. The knight seemed to divine them, however.

"It is well that all people do not think as Bishops Gardiner and Bonner, or, forsooth, as the Queen's majesty herself, or perchance there might be as many burnings and hangings in fair England as there have been in the Netherlands. We cannot stop the tide altogether, but we can help to quell its fury. However, farewell, honest friend; I am glad to have done thee a service."

Saying this, the knight took a cordial farewell of Master Gresham and of Lady Anne, giving Ernst a kind shake of the hand.

Chapter Eight
A Storm at Sea

The shades of evening had settled down over the great City, the only lights being those of the lanterns of the costermongers' stalls scattered up and down in various directions, and the occasional glare of a link, as the citizens went to and fro from each other's houses. Another knock was heard at Master Gresham's door.

"A stranger desires to see you, sir," said the porter. "He declines giving his name, but he says you know him, and will, he is sure, greet him kindly."

"What is he like?" asked Master Gresham. "I cannot admit strangers. Beg him to write his name on this tablet; but do not tell him that I am within till I hear who he is."

This caution, as may be supposed, was not unnecessary in those dangerous times; for though Master Gresham had had the assurance of Sir John Leigh that he need no longer apprehend danger, he yet knew the treachery of which Bishop Gardiner was capable, and that, did he wish to get rid of him, he would not hesitate to do so, in spite of the support he might be receiving from other friends. The tablet was soon brought back.

"Admit him—admit him instantly," said Master Gresham, as soon as he saw the name; and, rising from his seat as the stranger entered, he stretched forth both his hands.

"My dear friend, Master John Foxe, I greet you heartily," he said, leading him to a chair. "My wife, here is one whom I have known from my youth upwards—a true and bold champion of the faith. And what is your pleasure, Master Foxe? it would be mine to aid you if I had the power."

"In troth, Master Gresham, it is to advise me how I can best leave this fair kingdom of England, and to help me in so doing," answered the visitor. "I had hoped that a humble man like me might have escaped persecution, but I have received notice that if I remain my life will have to pay the penalty; so I am about to put the seas between myself and our sovereign Lady and her fire-loving Bishop; for although I am ready to burn, if called on to witness to the faith, yet I see no reason why I should not fly from danger, if by so doing I may live to bear a faithful testimony in after years."

"You speak wisely, Master Foxe," said Master Gresham. "Even now I am about to start for the Netherlands; and we will bear each other company. The wind holds from the north, and I propose therefore taking ship from Ipswich. We may thus speedily reach a port in Flanders, whence we can travel on to Antwerp. You may there for a time as a foreigner be safe from persecution under my protection, unless you take to public teaching and preaching. In that case I should be unable to protect you."

"Thank thee, my friend," answered Master Foxe. "I look to One for protection from man's malice more powerful than man himself; but while I am in your company I will follow your wishes, albeit it is hard when occasion offers not to speak to our fellow-men of God's love and mercy to man as shown in His Gospel. I would ask you to afford your protection, not only to me, but to my wife and children; for I would not leave them behind, lest they also become exposed to the malice of those who hate the truth."

Master Foxe had wisely sent his family on a day's stage beyond London, having been greatly assisted by his friend the Duke of Norfolk. He had rendered him all the aid in his power, and supplied all the articles for his voyage.

Master Gresham and his company set forth the next morning at an early hour. They journeyed as usual on horseback, without making more show than needful, each man, however, being well-armed with sword and arquebuse, so that, should they be attacked by robbers, they might defend themselves. No robbers appeared, but soon after they left London two persons, on sleek, well-fed steeds, were seen riding at a distance behind them. They wore long cloaks; their features concealed greatly by their wide-topped hats and the coifs they wore beneath. When the travellers stopped these men stopped also, and when they reached a hostel the strangers took up their abode in the same, keeping at the farther end of the table, where they, however, might hear what was spoken by the guests. At other times no notice might have been taken of them, but after the warning Master Foxe had received, he naturally began to suspect that they had some object in view which might interfere with his liberty. He therefore, like a wise man, kept his tongue mostly silent when they were within hearing. The matter might have remained in doubt, but Ernst, on one occasion slipping round where they sat talking, so it seemed, earnestly to one another, had the means of observing the countenance of one of them. Coming back, he whispered into the ear of the Lady Anne, "I thought so from the first: it is Father Overton, the very priest who brought the accusation against me and A'Dale. He is one of Bishop Bonner's runners, that is clear. His presence bodes us no good. It is well to know our enemies, to escape their malice, though we should wish to do them no harm."

"You have acted wisely, Ernst; keep silence, and do not stray from us, though I suspect that the object of the priest in following us is to try and lay hold of Master Foxe. He would prove more valuable game than you are, my boy."

Ernst said he would warn Master Foxe, and did so. The preacher thanked him.

"I thought as much," he said; "but One mighty to save watches over us. We will go on fearlessly, trusting to Him."

Ernst trembled at the thought of again getting into the power of the priest, and kept carefully with his friends, lest by any chance he might be carried off.

The next day the priest and his companion were seen following as before, not knowing, perchance, that their character had been discovered. Master Gresham showed no little discomfort at seeing them; still, to avoid them was impossible. He and his companions therefore travelled on steadily, trying to heed them as little as possible, and saying nothing which might give them an excuse for arresting any of the party.

Master Gresham had already sent on to secure a vessel, which was in readiness for their reception on their arrival. They were not alone, however, for several other persons who had become conspicuous for their Protestant principles during the reign of King Edward had either received warning that their lives were in danger, or, knowing themselves to have acted often in opposition to the principles of the new Queen, had thought it wise to escape from her anger. Thus, a very large number were collected on board the galley. Ere the sails were hoisted, Master Foxe summoned them together, and entreated them to join him in prayer to God that they might escape from the malice of their enemies, and find a home whither they were going, where they could worship Him in spirit and in truth. They failed not also to speak of their gratitude at having escaped from the danger which threatened them.

Then the seamen came on board, the heavy anchor was hove up, and the vessel stood away from the shore. The weather, however, was threatening; dark clouds flew rapidly across the sky. The wind, blowing strong, was increasing. The danger to be found at sea was great; yet the passengers entreated the captain to continue the voyage—they dreaded having again to land. Already some of their friends had been seized and cast into prison; they knew that such might be their fate should they remain on shore.

The arrival of the priest at Ipswich, even though he was disguised, had become known, and it was suspected that his object was no good one. The shores of England were rapidly fading from view, but the wind continued to increase. The waves rose high on either side of the vessel, tipped with foam, and threatening every moment to break down over her deck; still she struggled on. The seamen made all secure, and prayed the passengers to go below. Ernst, however, continued on deck, holding firmly to the shrouds. There was another person near him who stood up, securing himself in the same way: it was Master Foxe. Although the wind howled in the rigging, the waves roared round on either side, and the spray came dashing in thick showers over them; although the sky was dark, and the waters around were troubled, the countenance of the preacher was calm and undismayed. He gazed on the shores of England; it was his native land, and he loved it well. Now he looked up at the threatening sky, and along over the dark, foam-topped seas. He was going forth an exile, perchance never to return, and yet he felt that rather would he trust the threatening ocean than the tender mercies of those who now had sway in England.

The captain came to him at length.

"You seem, good sir, a leading man among my passengers," he observed. "I fear me much, that if we attempt to continue the voyage, my stout ship may be overwhelmed, and we may together go with her to the bottom of the ocean. I fear me, therefore, that we must return, and wait till the gale has subsided."

"I would pray you to continue on the voyage," answered Master Foxe. "Let us trust to Him who rules the waves and winds. He will not allow us to perish."

"But we must trust to our own right judgment, sir," answered the captain. "Now, as a seaman, I know that the peril of proceeding is very fearful indeed, and therefore I opine that we should not tempt God by exposing ourselves to it."

"You speak justly, captain," answered Master Foxe. "As a good seaman, knowing the danger, you are right not to expose those under your charge to it. Still, I for one would rather trust myself into the hands of God, during such a gale as this, than run back and put ourselves into the power of such persons as now rule our fair land of England."

"You speak too truly," answered the captain. "We will hold on yet a little longer; but should the gale continue, we must, to save the vessel and our lives, put back to shore; as an honest man I cannot act otherwise."

Not many minutes had passed, when a furious blast struck the vessel. Over she heeled, the waters rushing in on one side, and seeming about to overwhelm her.

"Hold on for your lives!" shouted the captain. "Put up the helm! ease away the after sheets!"

Slowly the vessel came round, and ran before the blast. Before she had been struggling with the seas, but now she fled before them, though even then they hissed and bubbled up on either side, as if eager to hold her in their grasp. On, on she flew, faster and faster. Once more the shores of England appeared in sight. Anxiously the captain and his mate looked out to try and distinguish the landmarks, that they might steer the vessel so as to arrive at the entrance of the port of Harwich. The shades of evening were, however, coming on, a mist hung over the land, so as to render objects scarcely discernible. The passengers had begun to gather on deck; for, feeling the movement of the vessel more easy, they believed that the storm had abated, and that they were again in safety. Various were their exclamations when they found the sea raging as furiously as ever, and the dark clouds hanging over their heads.

Among those who had come on deck was Master Gresham. He held little Richard by the hand. Too often had he crossed the Channel to be surprised at what he saw, and yet perhaps he, more than any one else besides the captain, knew the dangerous position of the vessel.

Calmly he consulted with him as to the best course to pursue. Another person also stood calm and collected as Master Gresham: it was the minister, Master Foxe. Ernst watched him with admiration, as even amidst the roughest tossings of the ship a smile of confidence played over his features. And yet as the vessel rose on the summit of a sea, and then rushed down again into the hollow, the waters hissing and foaming high above her bulwarks, it seemed indeed as if she would never rise again, but must sink down, down, till she reached the depths of the ocean. At this time many gave way, unable to refrain from showing their fear by loud cries. Yet then the voice and look of Master Foxe would reassure them. "Fear not, my friends," he exclaimed; "if ye are Christ's, if ye have not only turned away from the idolatries of Rome, but have given your hearts to Him, you are safe in His keeping. Dread nothing therefore: He will, if He thinks fit, take you safely to land, or if not, will call you to Himself, to be with Him where He is. Now is the time to show your trust in the loving Saviour, all-powerful to save you from temporal death as from death eternal."

Thus the faithful minister continued speaking, till all who heard him felt their faith and courage revive, and no longer did any give way to expressions of fear. Still the danger continued to increase. In vain the captain endeavoured to pierce the thick gloom. No land could he discern; no beacon-fire burst forth to show of a friendly harbour. Lady Anne remained below, and thither Master Gresham conveyed little Richard.

"Should there be danger of the vessel striking, I will come for you," he said: "wife, I will save you or perish with you. Ernst, to your charge we commend our boy; you are a brave swimmer, and may be able to rescue him."

"Oh! my dear lord, do rather try and save our boy; leave me to my fate, if the fearful danger you speak of arrives!" exclaimed Lady Anne.

To this Master Gresham would not consent.

"No," he said, "I cannot let you, my wife, perish; and our boy is as safe in the keeping of Ernst as he would be in mine. I know that he will save the boy, or lose his own life in the attempt."

Ernst felt very proud on hearing these remarks, and gladly promised to watch over his friend Richard.

Onward rushed the vessel. At length it seemed to those who stood on deck that the wind did not blow so furiously as before. A short time passed, and it became evident that the gale was abating. Still, those who were acquainted with the dangers of the sea knew full well that, should the vessel be cast on the beach, how great would be the peril of their lives. The hardy seamen were at their posts. The captain ordered all to keep silence. One of the mates went forward, looking out for the land. The captain stood near the helmsman. In a clear voice he issued his orders. The sea as well as the wind had decreased. Now the sails were taken in one by one.

"Stand by with the anchor," cried the captain. "Let go!"

A plunge was heard, and the hempen cable flew quickly out. The vessel rode head to wind with her stern to the shore, not perceived by any but the seamen, so hardly could a landsman's eye pierce the thick gloom around. Still she plunged heavily into the seas which rolled towards it. Now and then the captain shouted to his mates—"Does she hold?"

The answer was satisfactory. Yet it seemed scarcely possible that iron anchor and hempen cable could prevent a ship forced by those furious billows from driving onward to the shore. Thus the night passed away. No stars were seen; no moon to cheer the voyagers. Anxiously they waited for the dawn. It came at last. Then, for the first time, they saw the shore stretching out for some distance in the west—a long line, on which the raging breakers burst furiously without a break. Once more the anchor was lifted, the sails were set, and the vessel stood closer in.

A small creek appeared, into which the captain thought the boat could run. Only a few, however, could be carried at a time. The boat was lowered into the water, but not without difficulty could the passengers be placed within it. The women and children were first lowered, and all entreated that

Master Foxe would accompany them. He was unwilling, however, to quit the vessel; and not till warmly pressed by all round him would he consent, believing that it might be for the common good.

Ernst remained with his patron. Anxiously they watched the boat which contained the Lady Anne and little Richard. Away it went, urged on by the sturdy arms of the bold seamen. One of the mates, an experienced mariner, steered the boat. Now she sank into the hollow of the sea, now she was seen rising to the summit of the wave, the foam dancing round her. Once more she was hid from sight. Now she rose again. Thus she proceeded onward. As may be supposed, Master Foxe employed all his powers to cheer and comfort those with him, for often it seemed to them, as they saw the dark seas rushing after them, that their frail boat would be overwhelmed; or when they looked towards the shore, and beheld the white curling waves, they thought it impossible she could ever pass through them in safety. Thus the boat rushed on. Now she rose on the summit of a sea. The sturdy mate stood up to gaze around him. Firmly he grasped the tiller. Sinking down again, the boat glided into the very mouth of the little river, and arriving at a steep bank the mate urged his passengers to land speedily, that he might return to bring their companions to the shore. He had to make two other trips. Master Gresham and Ernst were the last to leave the ship, the captain promising, should he be able to weather out the gale, to return for them. They also safely reached the shore. Not far from where they landed a bridle road passed by, leading from the south. Master Gresham instantly set forth with Ernst and others to seek for some farmhouse where the party might be accommodated. They had not gone far when two horsemen were perceived coming along the road. As they drew near, they and the voyagers exchanged looks, and knew each other, even before they had time to utter greetings, had they so desired. In an instant Master Gresham recognised Father Overton, the priest, and his companion, who had followed them to Ipswich.

Chapter Nine
The Abdication of Charles the Fifth

Bishop Gardiner was not a person to allow his prey to escape him if he could help it. Notice was brought to him that John Foxe was proceeding to Ipswich, to embark thence for the Continent; he therefore had despatched Father Overton and another priest on his track, hoping by some means to entrap him.

Great was the disappointment, therefore, of Father Overton, when he found that Foxe was in the company of Master Gresham, whom he knew well to be a prudent man; and still greater when, after all the trouble he had taken, the whole party got safely on board and proceeded to sea.

His satisfaction may be supposed when he found that they had again landed. He now felt confident that by some means or other he should be able to get them into his power.

The only farmhouse in the neighbourhood where the voyagers could obtain shelter was inhabited by Romanists. Indeed, a large number of the country people were of that faith. Father Overton, guessing that they would go there, rode off as fast at his steed could carry him, and arrived first at the farmhouse.

Farmer Hadden and his wife were at home.

He speedily explained the object of his visit.

"They are fearful heretics," he remarked, "endeavouring to escape the vengeance of our just laws against such people, and it would be a holy and pious work in you, my friends, if you will follow my directions and endeavour to deliver them into my hands. Feed them well, and treat them well, and afterwards profess that you are followers of the Church of Rome; but express your desire to be informed of the Protestant tenets, and show an inclination to leave your present Church. Inform me of all that is said; or, better still, is there not some place in the house where you can conceal me, so that I may overhear their words? Thus, without doubt, we shall get these people into our power, and you will have performed a meritorious act."

Farmer Hadden and his dame listened to what was said. Now, although they had not left the ancient faith, this was owing possibly to their never having heard the Gospel preached. The proposal of the priest was not, at all events, to their taste, and their hearts revolted at the thought of the treachery they were required to undertake.

Still, they were timid people, and dreaded to offend the priest. A third person, however, was present. It was their daughter Margery. She had on several occasions heard the preachers, in King Edward's time, telling in simple language the truths of the Gospel. She had also, with her savings, purchased a Bible, which she carefully treasured up, and kept in her own room, bringing it down at times to read to her father and mother. Thus they, too, also had a knowledge of God's Word. Father Overton, finding that they did not willingly enter into his views, began to threaten them, telling them how many people had already been cast into prison, to be given ere long to the flames, and that unless they showed their love to the mother Church they too might suffer the same fate. Margery said nothing, but, with her eyes cast on the ground, kept spinning away as if scarcely heeding the words which were spoken.

At length the dame, fearing that the Father would put his threats into execution, agreed to follow his wishes. Father Overton, therefore, telling his companion to lead away their horses to a farm at some distance, desired Farmer Hadden to place him in a cupboard whence he could overhear all that was said by their guests. Margery well knew that though he might hear he could not see. As soon, therefore, as he was shut in, she, placing her spinning-wheel aside, threw her kerchief over her head and hurried out to meet the voyagers.

She speedily encountered Master Gresham with John Foxe and Ernst. Her voice trembled with agitation as she told them what had occurred; "But do not blame my parents," she exclaimed; "they are forced to act as they are about to do, and they themselves hate the very notion of betraying you, their guests. Only be cautious, therefore, and remember that whatever is said will be heard by hostile ears."

"Thank you, maiden; we will be cautious; but nevertheless we will speak freely from God's Word. The fear of what man can do unto us should not make us hold our tongues," replied Foxe.

Margery having given her warning, hurried back to the farm.

In a short time Master Gresham, with the preacher and Ernst, arrived, and made arrangements with the farmer and his wife for the accommodation of the whole party. Dame Hadden might have suspected that Margery had warned her guests, but she said nothing, busily employing herself in preparing provisions for them, aided by her daughter and serving-maid. The fire was made up, pots put on to boil, and meat placed to roast, while the farmer drew some flagons of his best beer. He resolved not to show any lack of hospitality to those persecuted men, albeit they differed from the Church to which he belonged. A blessing had been asked by Master Foxe ere the feast began, and at its conclusion he rose also to return thanks. He then from his pocket produced a copy of God's Word, and spoke to all present of the love of God to perishing sinners. "Could we but remember that 'not a sparrow falls to the ground' but God knoweth it, while 'all the hairs of our heads are numbered,' surely we should trust Him in all things, and understand how He is our loving Father and Friend, and thus go to Him, trusting in the complete salvation which Christ has wrought for us. We should go to Him on all occasions direct for what we need, without any other mediator. Oh! remember these words: 'God so loved the world that He gave His only begotten Son, that whosoever believeth in Him should not perish, but have everlasting life.' Remember also these words, which Christ Himself spoke: 'Verily, verily, I say unto you, he that heareth My word, and believeth on Him that sent Me, hath everlasting life, and shall not come into condemnation, but is passed from death unto life. Verily, verily, I say unto you, the hour is coming, and now is, when the dead shall hear the voice of the Son of God, and they that hear shall live.' Yes, my dear friends, many who are now dead in trespasses and sin, who have never yet been born again, shall listen to the simple truth of the Gospel, and gladly accept its life-giving offers."

Thus in the same strain he continued for some time, showing forth God's love to man, man's need of a Saviour, the perfect and complete salvation wrought by that Saviour for all who accept it, even though, like the thief on the cross, they are deeply sunk in sin, and have not, till the last hour of their lives, heard the sound of the Gospel. Even Margery was surprised to hear Master Foxe speak thus, knowing that he was aware who was listening to his words.

The day closed, and the visitors were shown to such sleeping chambers as the house afforded. When all was quiet the farmer went to the cupboard and released the priest. He came forth.

"I pray you, sir, that you will not betray these good people. Surely nothing that was said deserves death or punishment of any sort. But hie thee away from hence, and let me entreat you to forget what thou hast heard," whispered Farmer Hadden, in an imploring tone.

"No, no," answered the priest; "I would not for much forget those words spoken by Master Foxe. I knew not that such words were to be found in the Scriptures. That they are there I am sure, or so learned a man as he is would not have spoken them. Christ tells us that if we believe in Him we have eternal life, and that is, I opine, glory and happiness unspeakable. Not that we shall have, but that we have it; that we have passed from death unto life. Christ Himself spoke those words. He does not say that we have any works to do, any penances to perform, but simply that we are to put faith in Him. The Church, I know, says differently; but there is a sweet and gracious meaning in those words which struck deep into my heart. I will stay and have more conversation with Master Foxe."

"I will summon him then," said the farmer; "I too would fain hear more of these things from his lips."

Most willingly the preacher rose from his couch, and sat himself down with the farmer and Father Overton. The lamps were lighted, so that God's Word might be read; and thus they sat till the grey light of morning broke into the room: the minister explaining the simple plan of salvation, drawing all his words from the fountain source. The sun rose in a clear sky, and scarcely was the morning meal concluded, before one of the shipmen came up to announce that the wind was fair, the sea calm, and that they might all return quickly on board. Another passenger was added to them. Father Overton desired to accompany the party abroad. "My house, and all I possess, I will leave behind me," he observed; "and no small amount of wealth, to gather which I was imperilling my soul. If I went back, the fate I was designing for others would assuredly be mine; and I would rather learn more of God's Word, and have my faith increased, than go back yet ignorant, and perchance relapse again into the fearful errors of Rome."

In God's good providence the vessel arrived in two days at Newport in Flanders, whence the party travelled to Antwerp. There, among the Protestants of that city, most of the voyagers found refuge; Master Foxe and his family being entertained by Master Gresham. After some time, the preacher, finding that he had many enemies in Antwerp who might deliver him up to the secular power as a heretic, proceeded with his family to Frankfort. Thence he continued on up the Rhine till he reached Basle in Switzerland, where were found great numbers of Englishmen who had been driven from their homes by persecution. That city was already famous for printing, and here Foxe began his inestimable work, giving an account of the martyrs who had suffered for the faith from the earliest times; but these matters Ernst Verner did not hear for some time afterwards.

With much sorrow Ernst Verner saw that true and faithful servant of Christ take his departure from Master Gresham's house. He won the hearts of all who knew him, and no one esteemed him more than did Master Gresham and Lady Anne. Yet the lessons of wisdom he had given were greatly interrupted by the life which the young lad was now called on to live. A great and important ceremony was about to be performed at Brussels; and Master Gresham, desiring to go there in proper state, took Ernst with him to attend on him as his page. The sober citizen's gown which the merchant generally wore was now exchanged for one of richer materials, and cut according to the Spanish fashion of the times. Ernst too was habited in a richer dress than he had ever before worn.

All arrangements being made, Ernst and several servants set off in attendance on Master Gresham for the capital city of the Netherlands. It had been for some time known that the Emperor—Charles the Fifth—purposed to abdicate the throne in favour of his son Philip the Second, now titular King of England, as well as of several small kingdoms and provinces. The day fixed was the 25th of October of the year 1555. In the magnificent hall of the residence of the Dukes of Brabant, the great ceremony was to take place. At one end a spacious platform had been erected, below which was a range of benches for the deputies of the seventeen provinces, while upon the stage were rows of seats covered with tapestry for the knights and guests of high distinction. In the centre of the stage was a splendid canopy, decorated with the arms of Burgundy, beneath which were placed three gilded armchairs.

At an early hour the larger portion of the hall was filled with persons whose magnificent dresses and general bearing showed that they belonged to the upper orders. Vast as was the hall, only such as they could find room.

As the clock struck three, the Emperor entered—a decrepit man who, although numbering only thirty-five years, looked much older. With one arm he leaned on the shoulder of a tall and graceful youth, while his other rested on a crutch. His hair was white, close-cropped, and bristly, his beard grey and shaggy, his eye dark blue, his forehead spacious, and his nose aquiline, but crooked; while his under lip was heavy and hanging, the lower jaw projecting so far beyond the upper, that he could with difficulty bring his shattered teeth together, so as to speak with clearness. Behind him came his son Philip, and Queen Mary of Hungary, the Archduke Maximilian, and other great personages following, accompanied by a glittering throng of warriors, councillors, lords and Knights of the Fleece. There was no lack of priests. The Bishop of Arras was among them, serene and smiling, whatever might have been passing in his heart. There, too, Ernst recognised one whom he had seen in London—the Count of Egmont. His tall figure, delicate features, and dark flowing hair, were not easily forgotten. His costume was magnificent, unsurpassed by any. Near him stood the Count of Horn, a brave admiral, but bold and quarrelsome—an unpopular man. Little did they think that ere long they were to be betrayed by pretended friends, and doomed to death by the sovereign whom they had faithfully served. On the same platform were two other gallant men, the Marquis Berghen and the Lord of Montigny—also doomed to suffer a cruel fate by their treacherous master. Near Philip stood his favourite companion—a man with a pallid face, coal-black hair, a slender and handsome figure—the famous Ruy Gomez. Such were some of the many noted characters who had assembled at the call of the Emperor.

As that man of hideous countenance and tottering steps entered the hall, all present rose to their feet. At a sign from him they again took their seats. He then seated himself in the centre of three chairs—one occupied by Queen Mary of Hungary, the other by his son. A long oration was now delivered by Philibert de Bruxelles, setting forth the Emperor's reasons for abdicating the throne, his boundless love for his subjects, and the imperative necessity he felt of maintaining the Catholic religion in its purity. The deed of cession was then read, by which Philip received all the Emperor's Burgundian property, including the seventeen Netherlands.

Cries of admiration burst from the assembly as the address was concluded. The Emperor then rose, and beckoning the Prince of Orange, he leant as before on his shoulder, resting his other hand on his crutch. The Prince had but recently returned from the camp on the frontier, where, notwithstanding his youth, he had been appointed by the Emperor to command his army against Admiral Coligny and the Duc de Nevers. The Emperor spoke of his numerous expeditions and campaigns, as also of eleven voyages by sea, his plans for the security of the Roman Catholic religion, and his desire that his magnificent empire should be governed by his son in a worthy manner, entreating the nation to render obedience to their new sovereign, and above all things to preserve the Catholic faith. Humbly he begged them also to pardon him for all errors and offences he might have committed during his reign. The great Emperor, sinking into his chair, wept like a child, while sobs were heard throughout every portion of the hall.

Even Philip appeared touched. Dropping on his knee, he kissed his father's hand. Charles, placing his hands on his son's head, then blessed him, and raising him, embraced him affectionately, while Philip uttered a few words expressive of his duty to his father, and his affection for his people. He expressed his regret that he could not address them in either French or Flemish, deputing the Bishop of Arras to act as his interpreter. This duty was performed by the prelate in smooth, fluent, and well-turned common-places, being replied to by Jacob Mass, member of the Council of Brabant, much in the same style. Queen Mary of Hungary, who had long been acting as Regent of the Netherlands, imitating her brother in language, also rose and resigned her office.

After a few more orations the ceremony terminated, and the Emperor slowly left the hall as he had entered. A stranger might have supposed from what he had heard that the country had ever been happily and well governed, and that there was every prospect of peace and prosperity for the subjects of the new monarch. Alas! how different was the truth. Ernst Verner, in spite of all that was said, could not forget the number of innocent persons who had already been sacrificed on the altar of bigotry and tyranny. Young as he then was, he knew full well the meaning of those exhortations of the Emperor as to the necessity of maintaining the Catholic religion in all its purity. It meant burn, slay, destroy, or drive out of the realm, all who oppose the religion of the priests of Rome—crush out with an iron heel every spark of liberty of conscience, of freedom of thought, of Protestant principles. Ernst found afterwards that Master Gresham's thoughts had agreed with his, and that he anticipated fearful evils for the people of the Netherlands.

Chapter Ten
Ernst Verner begins his Journal

I, Ernst Verner, had by this time sufficiently mastered the art of penmanship to enter the events of the day in my journal with facility, which I seldom failed to do. My notes are, however, far too numerous to be copied. I therefore write out only such as I deem most likely to be interesting to my friends.

On our return to Antwerp; Master Gresham busied himself greatly in the business which had brought him to that city. We were all busily employed from morning till night writing and making up accounts. Not only were monetary transactions to a vast amount carried on, but large purchases were made of arms and ammunitions of war. Bullion to a considerable amount also was required in England; of this Master Gresham possessed himself for the advantage of the Queen.

We were also employed in purchasing gunpowder, military stores, and other necessary tackle for the Queen's ships of war, which at that time were greatly deficient in these articles. I consider that it was greatly owing to this forethought of my kind patron that England was afterwards in a condition to defeat the efforts of Spain to bring her under subjection; but I am now referring to events which did not take place for some time after the period of which I am speaking.

It was with considerable regret that I heard that my kind patron was directed once more to return to England, and that he purposed taking Lady Anne and his family with him.

On our arrival in London I was sent back to Saint Paul's School to finish my education. I was received kindly by the masters, who had not been changed, although they were compelled to be circumspect in their conduct, lest they should be accused of heresy, of which they knew themselves to be guilty, according to the ideas entertained by those of the Romish Church. The times were very sad. On my first holiday I went out in search of my old friend A'Dale, for he had left school. I found that he had been apprenticed to a mercer in Cheapside. He had grown into a big lad. As he had been somewhat daring and fond of excitement as a boy, he was, as may be supposed, not unwilling to find himself in a turmoil, where a pair of stout fists or a thick cudgel would serve him in good stead. I had somewhat lost my taste for such things during the courtly life I had lately led. He laughed at my effeminacy, and urged me to arouse myself, and to practise the old English sports, which would fit me for the rough life I might be destined to go through. He promised to call for me whenever he could, and, as he had a good deal of liberty, his visits were not unfrequent.

A'Dale entertained as strong a dislike to the mass as I did, and we had agreed that, in spite of the risk we ran of being accused of heresy, nothing should compel us to attend it. One evening we were proceeding through the streets, when we found ourselves pressed in by a crowd, which was hurrying up to see a procession of priests pass along. There walked Bishop Bonner under a golden canopy supported on poles by four priests, all richly arrayed. A vast crucifix was carried before him, and other priests bore banners with various devices. There came also a priest, under another canopy, bearing the host, before which numbers fell down, and worshipped as if it were some idol. Those who did not so were frowned at by the priests. Some were buffeted and told that they were heretics, and fit only for the fires of Smithfield. There were also bands of men in various disguises, and there were figures of saints and other devices, before which the people were made to bow, albeit the saints, being badly carved, some of them looking most unsaintly and unbeautiful, were jeered at, and laughed at by those at a distance, those near being compelled to bow down as they did to the host. And then followed bands of waits playing all sorts of instruments. On either side marched men with burning torches, lighting up the streets as if it were day.

"Alas! there is no true worship here. The souls of these people, even if they desire to be fed, are sent away empty," I said to myself. A'Dale and I, who had been forced in with the crowd, now attempted to make our escape. As we were doing so, I found a hand placed on my shoulder.

"What, my young friend, have you become a follower of the true faith? I thought you had been a heretic," said a person, whose voice was that of a stranger.

I looked up. A friar, so it seemed by his dress, was standing near me. For some moments I was at a loss to recollect who he was, till I recognised him as the companion of Father Overton. I had the presence of mind, however, to be silent till I could frame a wise answer.

"Perchance you mistake me for some one else," I answered. "I am a young man still under instruction; but, young as I am, I desire to follow the true faith."

"You are cautious in your speech," said the friar; "but go on—I find I am not mistaken. I wish to have a word with you in private. I mean you no harm. You can tell me of one in whom I am interested."

Keeping hold of A'Dale's arm, I at length found myself again in the street. We went down the hill towards Ludgate, and then turning along the bank of the Fleet, soon found ourselves in a quiet spot, free from observation. The friar had kept us in sight, and soon again joined us.

"I thank you for this confidence, young sir," he said. "These are dangerous times, and those who trust others may fare ill; but of you I have no fear. I want to learn from you news of one whom you knew as Father Overton. I have received several epistles from him, and by their means I have been brought to hold very different doctrines to those I had before believed were true; yet hitherto I have not dared to express them, but I feel that I can keep silence no longer. My great desire is to go forth and preach the great doctrine of justification by faith, held by Luther and those true and pious bishops who have lately been committed to the flames. Their deaths, testifying as they did to the truth, were, with the exhortations of my friend Overton, the means of turning me from the Church of Rome. I trust that you have not fallen back into the errors of that Church."

"No, indeed, I have not," I answered. "I rejoice to find that you, as well as Father Overton, have deserted them. With regard to him, I saw him several times at Antwerp, where he was supported by my patron, Master Gresham, but suddenly he disappeared, and no one could tell what had become of him. The fears were that he had been carried off by the Inquisition."

"We shall ere long meet again," said the friar, after we had exchanged a few more words. "However tempted, my young friends, hold fast to the faith. I never knew happiness till I embraced it. I am very sure that bitter regret and misery will be the lot of those who have once known and then deserted it."

Thus saying, he pressed our hands, and hurried away along the banks of the river. We slowly returned homewards, afraid of exchanging our thoughts, lest we should be overheard.

The next day was a holiday, for it was the festival of some saint in the Romish Calendar. A'Dale and I were on foot early. Finding a large concourse of people going in the direction of the northern part of the City outside the gates, known as Smithfield, we followed them. On one side were some high and ancient houses, but on the other the ground was entirely open, with meadows and woods beyond.

"It is to be the grandest burning we have had yet," I heard a person remark. "There is a priest to be burnt, and two women, besides a knight and two other laymen."

My heart sickened when I heard this, for I had no wish to see the burning, but A'Dale urged me on. "He liked to be in a crowd," he said, "and we might come away before the fire was set to the piles." We found that none of the prisoners had as yet passed. At length we saw them coming along from Newgate, the Fleet, and other prisons. They walked on with their hands bound, and a few guards only, and priests on either side. I wondered that none of the crowd attempted to rescue them. It might have been done with great ease, though, perchance, to escape afterwards might have been more difficult.

Occasionally the friends of the prisoners came up and spoke to them, and received their farewells. Some, indeed, kept by their side the whole way, the guards not interfering. Among them, nearly the last, walked a lady. Her figure was tall and graceful, though she stooped somewhat, bowed down by sickness or sorrow. Her features were deadly pale, their whiteness increased by the black dress she wore, her raven hair flowing over her shoulders, for her head was bare. People looked on her with a pitying eye, but no one came up to her. She alone of all the victims appeared to have no friends in that vast crowd. Yet every now and then she lifted up her eyes, and glanced round as if in search of some one. As she passed near where A'Dale and I were standing, it struck me she looked earnestly at me. Fearless of consequences, I darted forward, and took my place by her side.

"Can I be of any service to you?" I said.

She looked at me with an inquiring glance. Her lips opened. "Who are you?" she asked.

"My parents died for the truth at Antwerp, as you are about to die, lady," I replied. "I would thankfully render you the aid which it was denied me to offer them."

"I will trust you," she said. "You will not deceive a dying woman."

As she spoke, she hastily took a parchment from her bosom, and handed it to me.

"There! conceal it," she said, "ere it is perceived by others. It contains the certificate of my marriage to my husband, now in foreign lands, and the title-deed of an estate which should be my child's. I have but one—a young girl. I know not to a certainty where she is; for when I was seized I urged her to fly and to put herself under the protection of some Protestant family, who, for the love of the faith, would support her till the return of her father from abroad. I dared not trust this paper into the hands of my cruel jailers; but I feel sure I may confide it to you, and that you will, to the best of your power, do as I desire."

I promised the lady that I would faithfully obey her wishes; and so interested did I feel in her fate, that I offered to continue by her side to the last.

"No, no! you will be watched, perchance, if you do, and bring the same doom I suffer on your own head."

"I WILL TRUST YOU," SHE SAID.

Still I entreated her to allow me to remain; but she insisted upon my quitting her, not only for my own sake, but lest I might run the risk of losing the important document she had given me.

While I was thus speaking to her as we moved slowly on through the crowded streets, another person came up, whom I at once recognised as the friar I had met on the previous day. He took no notice of me, however, but at once addressed himself to the lady. At first, with somewhat of a look of scorn, she desired him to depart; but after he had whispered a few words in her ear her manner changed, and as they walked along he continued addressing her. I guessed the purport of his conversation. Her countenance even brightened as he spoke. Now and then the priests with the other prisoners cast suspicious glances towards him; but he continued to walk on, speaking so low that no one else but the unhappy lady could hear him; and thus the band of prisoners arrived at Smithfield. Here they were saluted by the ribald shouts of the populace, who seemed to delight in hurling all sorts of abusive epithets on their heads. A'Dale wanted to remain, but I kept to my purpose. My chief interest was with the unhappy lady. I rejoiced, however, to see that her countenance was calm and unmoved; indeed, a serene joy seemed occasionally to play over it. I suspect, indeed, that some of those who stood by thought that the friar had brought her an offer of freedom, but it was not so; the only freedom she desired was to be liberated from this state of care and pain, and to mount upwards to be with her risen Lord. Onward marched the sad procession; but of all those I saw, none appeared to tremble or to desire to escape the dreadful fate awaiting them.

A'Dale, taking me by the arm, endeavoured to drag me into the front rank. "I want to judge how these people behave themselves at the stake," he said. "You and I perhaps, Ernst, may one day have to go through the same, and it may be well to take a lesson, so as to know how to comport ourselves."

I did not like his tone; it appeared more mocking than serious. It was not so, however. His heart was really as grieved as mine, but more indignant: such was his temper. Yet he really wished to see the burning.

"No, no," I answered. "Spare me, A'Dale, I cannot. I would be ready, if called on, to burn, myself, but to see others suffer, willingly I cannot. That poor lady, too, with a young child and a husband loving her, thus to be separated from them. How glorious and firm must be her faith to support her under such a trial; or rather, I should say, how gracious is the Holy Spirit who gives her strength for her need! It is that which supports her."

Still A'Dale would have me accompany him; and, though I was unwilling, he dragged me forward. I felt faint and sick and confused. The recollections of the past crowded on me with such force that they almost shut out, as it were, the scene before my eyes. I remember being in the midst of a vast crowd, and seeing on a high platform the sheriffs and a number of great officers in rich dresses, and below huge posts with chains secured to them, and a number of guards and priests below the platform, while other persons with their hands bound were in their midst, and rude rough men carrying faggots to and fro and piling them up near the posts; and then other persons were brought forward and secured to the posts, and more words were spoken, and priests seemed to be exhorting their prisoners, but none were released. And then the faggots were thrown round them, and the flames ascended, but no exclamation of fear burst from their breasts. I could gaze no more. Sick unto death, I uttered a cry and fled from the spot, scarcely knowing where I went.

Chapter Eleven
A Meeting with Master Overton

I left Smithfield far behind me, and found myself again amidst the streets of the City, when, overcome by my feelings, I sank on one side of the road, just within an archway. How long I remained there I know not, when I heard a voice addressing me by name:

"Rise, my boy; rise, Ernst Verner; I will conduct you to your home."

I looked up and saw the friar whom I had met in the morning.

"I am thankful I found you," he said, "or in your fainting state you might have suffered injury from some of the thieves and cut-purses who infest this City. What has happened to you?"

I told him that I had fled from the burnings at Smithfield.

"I do not wonder at that," he answered; "it was a fearful sight."

"And the poor lady with whom I saw you on her way thither, has she escaped?" I asked.

"No; she was among those who suffered death. She witnessed a good confession, and died, I believe, rejoicing, without feeling one pang of pain."

While the friar was speaking I gradually recovered.

"We will now set forward," he said, "for I must leave this City, and continue my search for my friend, who has, I believe, returned to England. I did not say this to you before, but I do so now I know that I may trust you. Should you by chance meet him, let him know that he who was once Friar Roger is so no longer, and earnestly desires to see him."

I assured him that I should be ready to help him, as well as Master Overton, and that I believed nothing would induce me to betray them.

"Yes, I know that I can trust you," he said. "And now I have to ask you, did not the lady give you a packet, desiring you to carry out the wishes which are therein expressed?"

"Yes," I answered, feeling in the bosom of my frock, in which I placed it. "I have it here safe, and hope to do as she desired."

"It might, however, be better if you were to give it to me," he observed. "You are but a youth, and might lose it, or may be unable to fulfil her request."

I could not help looking at the speaker suspiciously as he said this. Was his object to deprive me of the packet, that he might make use of it for his own purposes? If such was the case, he might have done so while I lay in a swoon.

"You will pardon me, my friend," I answered, after a minute's consideration; "that poor lady confided the packet to me, almost with her dying breath, and I purpose, if I have the power, to carry out her wishes."

Friar Roger looked at me and smiled.

"You act wisely," he answered. "You have not yet proved my fidelity, and are right not to trust me; and, besides, I think you have a greater prospect of remaining in this life than I have, for assuredly if my heresy were discovered I should speedily be brought into the same state as the poor people you saw this morning."

We had not gone far when A'Dale came hurrying after me. He had not at first missed me when I fled from Smithfield, but hearing some one remark with a laugh that a lad had been frightened by the fires, and had taken to flight, he concluded that I was the person spoken of. Friar Roger expressed his satisfaction at the appearance of A'Dale, and, confiding me to his charge, wished us farewell.

At length I reached Master Gresham's house in Lombard Street. The Lady Anne remarked upon my pale face and haggard features, and inquired what had occurred. Knowing her kind disposition, I told her the occurrences of the morning.

"Alas! alas!" she answered. "We must commiserate their fate, though I believe firmly that all of them are tasting the joys of heaven. But for that poor lady you speak of I feel more particularly. Can you tell me her name?"

I bethought me of the packet, for to the Lady Anne I knew that I could confide it properly.

"That will tell us," I observed.

We carefully opened the packet, which I drew from my bosom. Lady Anne read it.

"Alas! alas!" she said; "even while you were describing the poor lady I had an idea that she might be one I knew well in my early days, and for whom I had a warm affection. Even at that time I thought her opinions dangerous. And, my sweet Barbara, has such been indeed your fate? I would that I had the means of discovering her daughter; this document gives but a slight clue, saying little more than she told you. She believes that her child will be found among certain Flemish artisans settled at Norwich. There are many in that city, and thus among them it will be difficult to discover her. Still it must be done, and I will consult my husband on his return."

"Could I not go down to Norwich and search among the artisans there?" I asked. "I have indeed a fellow-feeling for the poor young lady, and I would thankfully be employed on such a service."

"I will think about it," answered Lady Anne; "but Norwich is a long way off, and you are young to undertake such a journey alone. If James Brocktrop can be spared I will send him, though he might not undertake the task with the zeal I should desire."

"But could not I accompany him?" I asked. "The holidays will soon begin, and if Master Gresham does not return, I shall be at liberty."

"Have patience, my boy; I will consider it," repeated Lady Anne.

When I told A'Dale, he was eager to accompany me. I knew I could trust him. It wanted but two weeks to the holidays; and we agreed that if Lady Anne could not then send Brocktrop, we ourselves, with her permission and that of my patron, would set forth together.

At length term time was over, and I was at liberty.

"I have consulted my lord's factor, Master John Elliot, and he will send James Brocktrop, for the purpose of inquiring into the trade and produce of Norwich, where he is given to understand a considerable amount of manufactures has been produced by the Flemish refugees settled in that city," said Lady Anne. "You can accompany him, and you will thus have a favourable opportunity of inquiring for the young girl."

I was greatly pleased at this arrangement; it was so exactly what I wished. A'Dale likewise obtained leave to make holiday and to accompany us. Horses were provided for our journey, and with a change of clothes and other necessaries packed in our valises and strapped before us, with thick cloaks to guard us from the inclemency of the weather, our equipment was complete.

To enable us to defend ourselves, we each of us also had a brace of pistolets, and an arquebus, which hung at the saddlebow. Thus well provided, we set forth to the North. I found the roads very different to those I had been accustomed to in the Low Countries. Instead of affording a broad level way, they were full of ruts and inequalities. Sometimes we had to pass through a wide extent of mud, and at other times to pick our way amidst the boulders, rocks, and stones which lay before us. This prevented us from proceeding as rapidly as we should have desired. We could talk, however, as we rode along, and had many subjects of conversation.

At length we reached the ancient town of Norwich, standing on its ten hills. In the late reign numerous Flemish families, driven out of the Netherlands by dread of the Edicts and the Inquisition, had settled here.

Brocktrop had been supplied with a sufficient excuse for his visit, being sent thither by the well-known mercer, Master Gresham, to examine into the state of trade and make purchases accordingly, assisted by me; while A'Dale had a similar commission from his employer. We were thus able to go about through the town and to visit the houses of the settlers for the purpose of examining the produce of their looms. Some we found employed in the manufacture of lutestrings, brocades, paduasoys, tabinets, and velvets, while a considerable number were engaged in making cutlery, knives, daggers, swords, lancets and other articles for the use of surgeons, as also clocks and watches. Lace-making we also found carried on extensively.

Still during our search we had not discovered the child of the martyred lady. At last one day we entered a humble cottage where a man was seated at a loom. His back was turned towards us. Even to my eye he did not appear to be as expert as others we had visited. Still he worked on diligently; the material he was producing being of a somewhat rough character, Brocktrop turned away, seeing that the stuff would not suit his purpose, when I apologised to the workman for intruding: on him. He turned round as I did so, and I saw a countenance with the features of which I was acquainted. Brocktrop and A'Dale had just gone out of the door. The workman rose.

"I would speak with you," he said. "Are those to be trusted?"

"Yes, sir, I am sure they are," I answered; and I at once saw that the person speaking to me was he whom I had first known as Father Overton.

He greeted me cordially, and so I ran out and begged Brocktrop and A'Dale to wait for me for a few minutes.

"I have been anxious to hear of you since we parted at Antwerp," I said. "John Foxe, too, in his letters has inquired of you, and we feared that you had fallen into evil plight."

"I left Antwerp secretly," he answered, "for I was in danger. Besides, I had a longing to return to England, first to minister to these poor refugees who had been driven by persecution from their native land, and also to spread the truth among my own countrymen. Having learned the art of weaving, I have remained here for some time in disguise; though I believe I am already suspected, and perhaps may again have to seek for safety in flight—though ready, if needs be, to suffer as a martyr for the truth."

I replied that I hoped he would yet escape till better times, which might come, seeing that there was no prospect of the Queen's Majesty having a son to succeed her. I then told him of the happy conversion of Friar Roger, by means of the letters he had written from Antwerp, and that he desired once more to meet with him.

A gleam of satisfaction passed over the countenance of Overton.

"I trust it is so," he answered; "and yet it may be prudent in me not to place myself in his power until I am sure of his fidelity." He then inquired what had brought me to Norwich. I at once told him the secret object of our visit, mentioning the name of the unhappy lady who had been put to death.

"Barbara Radford, did you say? Alas! alas! has she been murdered by these bloodthirsty bigots? Tell me how she looked; what she said. My sister, my dear sister, you were ever true and faithful! It would have rejoiced your heart to know that the brother you ever treated so affectionately had been brought to a knowledge of the truth. But oh! Ernst Verner, think what are my feelings when I tell you that it was I, in my blindness and bigotry, who first brought the family of the Radfords before the notice of the cruel Bonner as firm and uncompromising Protestants. Yet I loved my sister as much as any priest of Rome, imbued with its principles, can entertain love; but I thought it right to crush all such feelings, for the sake of advancing the cause I advocated. In what a different light do I now view such conduct!"

"The great Apostle Paul was a fearful persecutor, and yet he became one of the most mighty instruments in God's hands for spreading the truth," I replied.

"Yes, yes; but it becomes not me to liken myself to such a man," he answered. "You say that you believe that my sister's child is even now in this town? Then my heart did not deceive me. Not many days ago I met a lovely little girl in the family of some poor Flemish weavers. They told me that she was not their own child, but that they felt themselves bound to support her as if she were, and would sacrifice all that they possess rather than allow her to want. I made no further inquiries then, for a stranger coming in they were silent. Yet I well remember that while I spoke to her, a look came over her countenance which reminded me of my once-loved sister. I thought it was fancy, and banished it from my mind. I now feel sure that my feelings did not mislead me. But I cannot leave my work. I owe my safety, I believe, to never going forth during the day; for so well-known are my features, that I might be recognised. When evening sets in, return hither, and I will accompany you to the cottage where the family of Crugeot reside."

I bade my friend farewell, and hurried after my companions.

"Ask no questions," I said; "it will be the safest; but I have a clue at length to the object of which we are in search, and I trust that we may be able to carry out the Lady Anne's beneficent designs."

Having concluded our rambles about the city, and James Brocktrop having gained all the information he required, we returned to our hostelry. I begged that I might go forth alone when it was dark. I had full confidence in the faithfulness of Brocktrop, as well as in the discretion of A'Dale; but yet I was sure that the fewer who knew Overton's secret the better. One who like him had left the Church of Rome, if discovered, would be sure to meet with no mercy.

I accordingly set out by myself through the streets of Norwich. I had noted the house where I had seen him, and fully believed that I should find it again. There are, however, so many ups and downs in the city, and the streets wind about so much, that it is no easy matter to find the way, especially dark as it then was. Here and there only a light gleamed forth from some artisan's workshop, making the obscurity in other places still more dense. At last I recognised a building I had seen in the morning, and knew that Master Overton's house was not far on one side of it. I hastened on and knocked. A voice told me to come in, and I saw him, as before, with a small lamp by his side, working away at his loom.

"I thank you very much, my young friend, for coming," he said; "I am anxious, as you are, to try and discover my niece. I have no doubt, however, that she will be found. We will soon go forth in search of the worthy Flemings in whose company I saw her."

Saying this, he threw a cloak round him such as was worn by the Flemings, and taking me by the arm we together left the house, which he locked carefully behind him. My eyes had now become accustomed to the darkness of the streets, and I could without difficulty walk on by the side of my companion. We had not gone far, when he stopped at the door of a low cottage. We listened, for a sweet, low hymn was being sung by some one within. It was one of Marot's, such as my own dear parents had delighted in. The sound melted me almost to tears. Now another voice joined in: it was that of a woman. And now a man's tones were heard, full and rich. I would not for much have interrupted that hymn. Perhaps the singers scarcely knew the risk they ran, for had any Romish priests heard them they might have recognised the hymns as those of the Protestant poet of France; he whose verses had afforded consolation to many a persecuted Christian, to many an exile from his native land. At length the hymn ceased. Overton knocked gently at the door. It was opened by a woman, the light from within falling on her person, showing by her costume that she was a Fleming.

"I am a friend," said Overton; "you know me. I have come to see you, and ask a few questions."

"You are welcome, Master Holt," she said in broken English. "Come in, for I know you to be a friend to the people of our faith."

We entered. The woman looked at me. "He is trustworthy," said Overton. "I saw a young girl in your company the other day," he continued; "I am anxious to talk with her, for a strange communication has been made me, and I think I know more about her than you may suppose." The woman listened attentively.

"She is in the back room," she said; "I will call her. I told you that she is not my child, but I love her as if she were. I would not part with her, unless it was greatly to her benefit."

"If she is the child I believe her to be, she is my niece," answered Overton, "and a lady of wealth and distinction is ready to take charge of her. A sound Protestant, moreover. Would you not then yield her up?"

"I would not selfishly prevent the dear girl from doing anything which would advance her interests. But you may be wrong; perhaps she is not the child you seek. However, I will call her, and you can speak to her yourself."

The Flemish woman, opening a door, called, and in an instant a girl eleven or twelve years old came bounding into the room. She was very fair, with blue eyes, her countenance full of animation, her light-brown hair long and silky.

"Aveline," she said, "here is a worthy gentleman who wishes to speak with you. He thinks he knew your dear mother. Will you describe her to him, that he may judge whether he is right?"

Aveline ran up to Overton, and taking his hand, exclaimed:

"Oh yes! she was an angel, so sweet and loving and kind, and her figure so tall and graceful."

"Yes, yes," said Overton, looking eagerly in the child's face; "but her name, what was her name?"

"My dear father, before he went away, always called her Barbara."

"Ah! yes," said Overton, "that was the name; but the surname; by what name was your father known?"

"My father's name was Radford—Captain Radford. He went away a long time ago, in a big ship, belonging to some merchant adventurers, and he has never since come back, and poor dear mamma was accused of reading the Bible, and of loving God's people more than the ways of the world, and some cruel men came and dragged her off to prison. They very nearly took me, but she told me to fly away, and to get clear of them, and that I must throw myself on the mercy of the first Protestant family I could meet. I ran and ran on, wishing to obey my mother, and fearing that the Queen's guards would be in pursuit of me, till I came upon an encampment of travellers by the roadside. I stopped and listened; they were singing a hymn. I knew that it was a Protestant hymn, and thus I knew that I might trust them. They did not understand much I said, for they had not been long in the country. Yet I made myself understood, and when they heard my tale they undertook to afford me protection. In vain I have since frequently begged that I might go forth and search for my mother, but they always shook their heads, and said it was of no use. Still I am sure that I shall meet her again. Do you not think so, sir?"

"Yes, dear child; there is a place where all who are clothed in the robes of the Lamb will assuredly meet, and there I trust that you will meet with your mother."

Aveline looked up in Overton's face with an inquiring glance. "What do you mean?" she asked eagerly; and then in a deep low whisper, painfully drawing her breath, she said, "Is she dead?"

"The body in which you knew her has returned to dust, but she herself is now rejoicing with a joy unspeakable. Do not mourn for her, my child. Only accept the same gracious offer she accepted, and follow the course she has followed, and assuredly you will be reunited to her."

"Yes, yes, I will indeed!" exclaimed Aveline, clasping her hands and looking upwards.

Never had I seen a countenance more beautiful and radiant. Already an angelic expression rested on it, such as I am sure it will wear when glorified in heaven.

The husband, Crugeot, now came forward, for before his wife had opened the door he had concealed himself in the further room; even a humble family, such as I have described, in those days lived in dread of persecution. Yet even they would not altogether hold their tongues, but desired to witness for the truth.

We had interrupted, I found, their usual evening service, and on our knocking they had scattered, not knowing who might be about to enter.

Overton now explained to Aveline that he was her uncle, and asked her whether she would go and reside with a rich lady who would be her patroness. She looked at Dame Crugeot.

"I cannot leave her," she said, "unless she wishes to part with me."

"I do not wish to part with you, my child; but yet I would advise you to accept the generous offer which has been made."

"But will they talk to me as you have done, of the Saviour and of my dear mother? I cannot go to people who will not do that," said the little girl firmly.

Her uncle explained that she could enjoy all the advantages of wealth; but promised amusements and luxuries did not tempt her. Almost unwillingly, however, at last, by the urgent advice of her uncle, she consented to leave her Flemish friends. Hitherto I had said very little. I merely again repeated Lady Anne's offer, and told her how kind and generous a friend she had been to me, and that I was sure she would prove the same to her.

"But you will not take me to-morrow," she said; "let me have another day with my kind nurse, or more than nurse—my second mother."

I was sure that James Brocktrop would consent to remain another day; indeed, our horses required a longer rest before they were fit for the return journey.

Chapter Twelve
Disappearance of Aveline

A'Dale and I felt very proud as we escorted Mistress Aveline Radford towards London. Brocktrop had supplied her friends with money to purchase proper attire suitable to her position, for she was in truth a young lady in all respects, having been nurtured delicately, and well instructed. I foresaw that she would quickly become a favourite with the Lady Anne, for she was a damsel much suited to her taste. I esteemed her greatly, and so did A'Dale: I soon saw that. She rode on a pillion behind Master Brocktrop, whose horse was more suited to carry her than were our steeds, which were much smaller; besides, he was well accustomed to carry ladies, Lady Anne herself often thus going out. A'Dale and I rode on either side, talking to her, and endeavouring to keep up her spirits, for she was much cast down, at leaving her kind friends, and more so at the thought of the sad fate her dear mother had suffered.

Master Overton would not quit Norwich for the present. He had there work to do, and were he to venture into London, he would quickly be recognised and put to death. We journeyed more slowly than we had done when going north, as we were afraid of tiring the little lady.

We reached Lombard Street without any adventure. Lady Anne stretched out her arms towards Aveline when she saw her, almost as if she had been her own child, and pressed her to her bosom.

"I will be a mother to you," she said, gazing at her affectionately. Truly Lady Anne had a tender heart. In a short time the little girl recovered her spirits, though even in the midst of her play with young Richard she would sometimes stop, and the tears would come into her eyes. I knew then that she was thinking of her mother.

Richard was a delicate boy. He had gone to school at first with me, but was unable to bear the rough treatment there, and he accordingly remained at home, his mother being well competent to teach him various branches of learning, while certain masters came at times to impart other knowledge. He and Aveline soon became great friends. He watched over her as if she was his sister, and she regarded him in the light of a brother. He was never weary of playing with her, albeit she now and then gave herself not a few airs when he was inclined to humour her. Yet she was in no degree wayward, but always obedient and affectionate to the Lady Anne.

Master Gresham returned from Spain, and proceeded again in the course of a few days to Antwerp.

I may say here, that I did not note down his comings and goings. Sometimes he remained in England only four or five days, scarcely sufficient to recruit his strength, and then once more returned about the Queen's business to Antwerp. He came over while King Philip was in England, and I heard him tell Lady Anne that he was greatly disconcerted with the course events were taking; that a war with France would neither be profitable nor honourable; but the King had set his mind on it; and the Queen, from her foolish fondness, would carry out his wishes, even though it might prove the destruction of her kingdom.

A'Dale came to me one day about this time, and told me that he was growing tired of the life of a mercer's apprentice, and that he was minded to join the English forces who were going out to aid the Spanish army on the Flemish frontier. It was to consist of seven thousand men: four of infantry, one of cavalry, and two of pioneers. I had two strong reasons to urge against this; one was that he would be united with Romanists and supporting the cause of Rome and tyranny; and the other, that being in an honourable position which must some day become profitable to him, when he might marry and settle down as a citizen, he would be wrong to abandon it for one where he might lose his life or limbs, and, moreover, be employed in slaughtering his fellow-creatures. He laughed at what he called my new ideas. I said that I was sure they were right ideas, and that God never intended men to fight and destroy one another.

"But if our country were attacked by foes, would you not fight?" he asked.

"That is a different case," I said. "If I found myself a soldier, a soldier I would remain, or if the country were attacked, I would become one for the sake of defending it; but you have an honourable, peaceable calling, and you propose quitting it without necessity for the sake of going and fighting on the side of a people for whom you have no love, against a nation many of whom are true Protestants and friendly disposed to England."

He replied that he would think over what I had said; but I was afraid I had made but little impression on him.

The army set forth without him, however. Some time after this I had still greater difficulty in persuading him to remain at home, when news came of the great battle fought on the banks of the Somme, near the town of Saint Quentin. On one side were the Spanish, English, Flemish, and German host, under the Duke of Savoy. The French were under Constable Montmorency. They were beaten, with a dreadful loss. Never since the fatal day of Agincourt had the French suffered a more disastrous defeat. Six thousand were slain, and there were as many prisoners taken. The Admiral Coligny bravely defended Saint Quentin to the last, but the place was at length taken by storm, amidst horrors unspeakable.

When we heard of them, I asked A'Dale whether he still could wish he had been there.

"No," he said; "honestly, I am thankful that I had not to take part in such scenes."

And now I must briefly run over the events I find noted in my diary.

I bade farewell to school, and though Master Gresham talked of letting me go to college, as he had gone, he afterwards altered his intentions, since the Universities were under the complete control of Cardinal Pole and his commissioners. "The object of going to college is to enlarge the mind and gain knowledge; but while people such as these rule there, I opine that neither one object nor the other is likely to be attained," observed Master Gresham. "I will therefore keep you with me, Ernst; you can serve in my shop, and there gain a knowledge of such business as may be greatly useful to you."

Master Gresham's house, I should have said, was one of the best in Lombard Street, which was beyond doubt the handsomest street in London.

Over the door was a crest—a large metal grasshopper, so that no stranger had any difficulty in finding the house. As is well-known, this street gained its name from the Italian merchants who came from Genoa, Lucca, Florence, and Venice, and were known as Lombards. They were very useful to the Italian clergy who had benefices in England, and who were thus able to receive their incomes drawn from England without difficulty. Thus the English supported a number of foreign priests, from whom they received no benefit whatever. By degrees Englishmen entered into the same business.

As may be supposed, it would be difficult to describe the variety of affairs in which my patron was engaged. Among others we bought and sold plate, and foreign gold and silver coins. These we melted and culled. Some were recoined at the Mint, and with the rest we supplied the refiners, plate-workers, and merchants who required the precious metals. Whenever we received money at usury, we gave a bond, and my patron was always able to lend it out again, either to the Government or to others at a still higher rate of usury. At times, the stranger from the country might have supposed that all the gold and silver in England had been collected in Lombard Street, for here were magnificent silver vessels exposed for sale, and vast quantities of ancient and modern coins. Gold chains, too, were seen hung up, and jewels of all sorts. In truth, all articles of value might there be purchased or disposed of. Master John Elliot was at this time factor and manager of the establishment, my patron being seldom in England, or remaining, when he did come, but a few days at a time. I was expecting every day to be summoned to Antwerp. This would have been much to my sorrow, for I felt unwilling to leave the Lady Anne, and still more so, I may confess, to part from the little Aveline. My affection for her was that of a brother for a sister—at least I thought so, and so it might have been.

At length Master Gresham returned. I knew not why, but suspected it was owing to some difference with the Council. For some time, therefore, he attended to his own private affairs. It had been arranged that he, with Lady Anne, was to go down to Osterley, whither he delighted to retire from the the cares of business.

I was one afternoon seated at my desk writing away rapidly, and intent on my work, when the porter told me that a stranger wished to speak with me. On going to the entrance, I found, standing in a recess where no light fell, a person who, as I came up, uttered my name.

"Ernst Verner," he said, and I at once recognised the voice of Master Overton, "you have already conferred on me a great favour; will you increase it? I wish to see my young niece. I am about again to leave England, and even this night hope to embark. The search after me is, I find, very hot, and had I not managed to mislead my pursuers, who believe that I am gone to the North, I could not have ventured into London, even though I am so disguised that few would discover me. Did I think that there would be any risk to the girl, I would not ask the favour; but she is the only being on earth now remaining to whom I am allied by ties of blood. Her mother was my dearest sister, and she was the last of several who had before her death left this world."

The request seemed very simple, and I undertook to convey it to Lady Anne, who would, I hoped, without difficulty grant it. A short way off was an archway, beneath which I thought Overton could speak to his niece unobserved, and I promised, should I obtain permission, to conduct her there. Master Gresham was from home, and Lady Anne, when I told her of Overton's request, had some hesitation as to allowing Aveline to go out to meet him. The little girl, however, as soon as she heard the invitation, entreated that she might bid farewell to her uncle. It had become almost dark, but I assured Lady Anne this would make no difference. At length, reluctantly, she gave Aveline permission to visit the place appointed. I agreed to wait for her at a little distance. This arrangement was safer, certainly, than allowing a condemned priest to enter the house.

Overton was at the spot appointed. "I have a few farewell words to speak to my young niece," he said, "and in ten minutes I beg you to return to escort her back."

Scarcely had I retired, when I heard a cry, and through the gloom I saw several persons crowding into the gateway. I ran towards it, wondering what had occurred, but arrived in time only to catch a glimpse of Overton and Aveline in the midst of a party who were hurrying them along. I ran after them, but they heeded me not. One, however, suddenly turned round and dealt me a blow which brought me to the ground, almost senseless. When I recovered, they had disappeared, and I knew not what road they had taken. I could not bring myself to go back with the sad news to Lady Anne. I knew not in what direction to follow. But I ran blindly on, hoping by some means I might overtake them. The dreadful fear came over me that he was a traitor, and that all he had said was but a cloak to cover his designs.

At length, broken-hearted, I returned to Lombard Street. Lady Anne received me with a look of grief, not unmixed with indignation, such as I had never seen.

"I have known you all your life, Ernst," she said at length, "or otherwise I could not believe you innocent in this matter, so suspicious an air does it wear. You must, though having no bad intentions, have been most cruelly deceived by this man Overton; and yet what object could he have had in carrying off the girl?"

When Master Gresham returned, he also was very indignant against Overton, declaring his belief that he was a hypocrite; though what could have been his object in taking away his niece it was impossible to say. My patron bethought him of going immediately to the Privy Council, and getting a warrant for the apprehension of the stranger; but he himself was so much out of favour at that time, that he believed no object would thus be gained. He had been so interested with Aveline's history, though he had seen little of her, that he was sincerely grieved at what had occurred, and at my suggestion ordered out several servants with torches, directing them to proceed to various parts of the City, in the hopes of meeting with Overton and his niece, or with those who had carried them off, should this have occurred without his connivance. I eagerly set out, calling on A'Dale to join in the search.

Such occurrences as I have described were too common to cause much observation. People at that time were nightly dragged out of their beds by the emissaries of Bishop Bonner, and hauled off to prison. At length, as we were proceeding towards the river, we met a serving-man with a torch, who was on his way to conduct his master back to his house in that neighbourhood. He told us, in reply to our inquiries, that a short time before he had met an armed band with a man, who seemed to be a prisoner, and a young girl; that they had taken boat, and proceeded up the Thames. I inquired whether he was sure that they had gone up, and had not rather proceeded down the stream. He was certain, he said, that they had gone upwards; that he had heard some one speak the word "Lambeth," if that would prove any guidance to us.

This convinced me that Overton had truly fallen into the power of the cruel Bonner, and that Aveline, found in his company, had been carried off with him.

Once more I returned with the information we had gained to Lady Anne and my patron. Never had I felt so great a sorrow. A'Dale and I devised all sorts of plans for liberating Aveline; but, alas! one after the other was thrown aside as hopeless. Master Gresham promised to exert all his influence rather than allow her to suffer.

"Surely her Majesty would not wish that an innocent young girl like Aveline should suffer hurt," cried Lady Anne.

"My dear wife, she who thinks she is doing God's service in burning pious bishops and youths and maidens, such as some who have been brought to the stake, would not hesitate to inflict the same doom on your Aveline."

Lady Anne burst into tears. She was not a lady given to weeping, and I had never seen her so moved before. Indeed, I could have joined her, so grieved was I for the loss of Aveline, if lost she was.

Master Gresham began to chide, and told her not to weep. "I will see what can be done for the damsel," he said. "I have seen so little of her, that I knew not she had thus won upon your affections."

As my patron said this, my hopes began to revive; for I thought him all-powerful, and that anything he undertook he would most assuredly accomplish.

Some time passed by, and no tidings could be gained of Overton or his niece. Meantime disastrous news came from the army in France, which did not soften the disposition of Queen Mary nor of Bishop Bonner. Every misfortune which occurred made her believe still more firmly than ever that it was sent because she did not sufficiently support the Catholic religion, and because so many of her subjects remained opposed to that faith. To show her zeal and love for it, therefore, she resolved to take further steps for the extirpation of what she called heresy.

Chapter Thirteen
Accession of Queen Elizabeth

Once again the fires at Smithfield, as well as in other parts of the country, never long together extinguished, burned up brightly and frequently.

The people submitted, though with an ill grace.

One day A'Dale came and told me there was to be another great burning. We had heard that several persons—priests, laymen, and women—were about to be committed to the flames.

"The people have been murmuring more than ever, and would, I believe, if led on by bold men, attempt to rescue the prisoners. What say you, Verner? I am ready to risk my life if there is a prospect of success."

"And I likewise," I answered, after a moment's thought. "Well then, there is no time to be lost. Get your cloak and sword, and if there is an opportunity we will not let it pass by."

We hurried on. Large crowds were collecting from all quarters. It is strange that human beings should desire to see the sufferings of their fellow-creatures. Many, however, were going, we hoped, like ourselves, to sympathise with the sufferers, or to afford them assistance. As we went along, we judged from the words we heard uttered that we should not lack support.

I have had so often before to describe the scenes at Smithfield, that I will not do so again.

As we arrived at the place, we found the wide space entirely surrounded by a dense crowd, while every window and other elevated spot in the neighbourhood was thronged with people, who might gaze upon what was going forward. There was the platform with the great officers who had been directed to superintend the executions, and the pulpit for the friars who were to preach, and the stakes with chains and piles of faggots.

We heard it again asserted by other bystanders that two priests were to be burned, and some said there was a little girl. On hearing this, A'Dale and I started, and inquired earnestly of the speaker if he knew that what he said was true.

"Too true, I fear me, young masters," he answered. "These people would burn infants if they could get no others to burn."

"Are men with hearts in their bosoms, and swords in their hands, to see such things take place, and not attempt to prevent it?" exclaimed A'Dale, in a determined voice.

I seconded him; for at once the fearful suspicion came across me that our little Aveline might be the child spoken of. We were rejoiced to find that several bystanders echoed our sentiments. The feeling that something should be done to rescue the prisoners spread through the crowd. I wondered that such had not been done before: it might have saved the lives of many innocent men; for those tyrant priests would never have dared to inflict punishment on their victims if the nation had boldly risen up against them.

We were at too great a distance from the platform clearly to distinguish the features of the prisoners; but when the guards opened out a little, so as to expose them to view, we saw two persons in the dress of priests, and in a group of women a young girl, whose figure was exactly that of Aveline. My heart sank as I saw her, and then it seemed to rise again and throb and boil with indignation. I felt capable of daring and doing everything to save the dear little girl. Even should it not be Aveline, I would do much; but I would risk liberty and life, and run every prospect of suffering the same fate, for the sake of rescuing her.

And now the priests were led up to the platform, where stood a Bishop — whom we supposed to be Bonner himself — with several other ecclesiastics round him. These seized the unhappy priests, and tore their robes from their backs, and then scraped on the crown of their heads and the tips of their fingers: this being to signify that the oil of anointing was scraped off. This operation occupied some time. It seemed as if the Bishop and his vile myrmidons took pleasure in prolonging the torment of their victims. Fierce words were spoken to the priests in loud tones. Though we could not hear the words, we knew this by the gestures and by the occasional sounds which reached our ears.

At length, one by one, the martyrs were led down again from the platform towards the stakes to which they were to be secured for burning.

Again they were asked if they would recant.

Their reply was a stern refusal to give up what they knew to be the truth. Having stirred up the people round us, A'Dale and I, knowing full well the risk we ran, worked our way up still nearer to the platform, waiting here and there to ascertain the temper of the multitude. As far as we could judge, they were all in the same mood; all equally hating Rome and its fearful proceedings. As we got nearer, we had no longer any doubts as to who were the intended victims. In one of the priests I recognised my friend Overton; in the other, Friar Roger, whom I had wrongfully suspected; and there too stood with the females our little Aveline. She seemed perfectly undismayed. Her eyes were cast upward, and, so it seemed to me, an angelic smile played over her countenance. Could those demons in human shape have the heart to burn so young and innocent a creature? A'Dale and I, seeing this, began to speak more boldly to the people round us. We asked them if they were men to submit to such tyranny. Would they wish to see their own daughters, and wives, and sisters, burn before their eyes?

"You see those innocent people about to be put to a cruel death!" exclaimed A'Dale; "after burning them, the same men will proceed on to burn those you love. Strike a brave blow now, and you will make them quail before you."

The people applauded us, but few seemed disposed to move. They had no weapons except thick sticks, and the guards were well-armed. Whether notice of the temper of the crowd reached the ears of the authorities, I know not, but they seemed eager to hasten on with the executions. A band of vile ruffians, who for wretched pay would commit any atrocity, were engaged in surrounding each stake with faggots. In a few minutes more, fire would be set to the piles.

"There is no time to be lost!" I exclaimed to A'Dale; "we must make the venture now, or it will avail nothing."

"Men, Englishmen, countrymen, will you allow those innocent ones to perish before your eyes, and not endeavour to save them?" exclaimed A'Dale. "On, men, on!" but the crowd stood back.

A few bold spirits joined us in urging on the rest; but unless a general rush were made, nothing could be done. I felt as if my heart would burst with indignation and dread—indignation that strong men should see innocent ones suffer, dread lest our efforts might be unavailing. A'Dale and I rushed among the crowd, calling on them to come on. Our actions were perceived, though our words may not have been heard, by those in authority. Guards were advancing towards us. The magistrates ordered the executioners to proceed with their work.

Already the victims were chained to the stakes, and the ruffian assistants hurried forward with faggots. We shouted—we implored the people to face the guards, and to rescue the prisoners. All our efforts, we feared, would be in vain. The magistrates shouted to the executioners to bring forward the torches. Happily they had been forgotten, and no one was ready with a light.

The Bishop and the priests stormed and raged. At length some ruffians were seen in the distance, waving torches and hurrying on towards the stakes, where the victims were thus cruelly kept. But their hearts were lifted up in prayer, their eyes turned towards heaven. They heeded not what was taking place around them. The young Aveline knew that there her sainted mother had yielded up her life, and she was sure that the pathway she was about to tread would carry her in the same direction.

And now there was a loud cry, and a man on horseback was seen galloping towards the spot. We could not hear the words spoken, but there seemed to be great agitation among the magistrates and priests. The crowd swayed to and fro to let the horseman pass.

"Stay the execution! Stay the execution!" he shouted, seeing that the men with torches were about to cast them on the piles of faggots. "I command you in the Queen's name. She will have no more burning in Smithfield!"

"This is an impostor!" exclaimed the Bishop. "Our good Queen would not hinder so holy a work."

"What Queen sends you?" asked the magistrate.

"Queen Elizabeth!" cried the herald. "Queen Mary is dead! And by the command of our new Queen, Sir William Cecil despatched me instantly to put a stop to these murderous proceedings. Long live Queen Elizabeth!"

The cry was taken up by the crowd, who, rushing forward, dragged away the faggots from round the prisoners. The magistrates and the priests fled, the guards dispersed. Those who had charge of the garments of the prisoners brought them. A'Dale and I rushed forward to assist Aveline, who threw herself, weeping, upon my shoulder. When the friars' garments were brought to Overton and Roger Upton—such was his name—they put them aside.

"No, no; we will never again use those habits of the worst of slaveries," they answered; and, on hearing this, some kind people in the crowd brought them cloaks and hats, which they thankfully put on. Of the other persons who were about to suffer death, I need not make mention. They all had friends, who joyfully came forward to receive them. The cruel cords which had bound Aveline's ankles and wrists to the stake had so hurt her that she could with difficulty walk. A'Dale and I were about to lead her off, though she was in a sad plight to pass through the streets, when a female in the crowd stepped forward, and, in a gentle voice, begged that her servants might be allowed to carry her.

"I have a hand-litter close by; she is not fit to be taken to her home in any other way."

We were thankful to accept this offer. The lady was, from her appearance, evidently of rank. Two men who attended her lifted Aveline up, and carried her off amidst the crowd. Just as they were going, the body of the guards returned, and seeing Overton and Upton still there, took them again into custody.

"We have no order for your release," they said; "and it will not do to let all our prisoners escape us."

"As you will, my masters," said Overton; "we would rather have had our liberty, but we will not resist your authority."

I heard that they were to be carried to the Fleet, and had just time to bid them farewell, and hurry after Aveline.

"You are right to be watchful over the young girl," said the lady, when I overtook them, "as you cannot tell what treachery might be played her. I came, however, to this terrible place in the hopes of being able to assist some poor person who might perchance escape the flames. Many of those I loved on earth have been cut off during the late unhappy reign, and I have devoted myself to soothe and comfort those who are about to suffer, or those who might escape death."

The lady now asked me in what direction Aveline desired to go. I told her to Master Gresham's house in Lombard Street. She seemed well pleased at hearing this, and hastened onwards. I was in fear, however, all the way lest those who had taken Overton and his companion into custody might come in search also of Aveline. On what account they did not seek her, I could not tell; but thankfully we reached Master Gresham's house in safety. Lady Anne's joy on seeing Aveline was very great, for news had been brought her of the fearful fate to which she had been destined. On seeing the lady, she greeted her with much respect, appearing to know her, although she did not address her by name. The lady, after exchanging a few words with Lady Anne, took her departure.

"She desires not to be known," observed Lady Anne, when I inquired who she was.

Richard's delight on the recovery of Aveline was very great; he scarcely liked to let her out of his sight. The young girl had suffered greatly, and it was necessary to have a physician to attend on her. He ordered that she should be kept perfectly quiet, and sent some cooling draughts, by which her nerves might be quieted. Lady Anne wisely forbore questioning her as to how she had been carried off, or what had afterwards happened to her.

Next morning, I went to the Fleet, where I was able without difficulty to gain access to Overton. He told me that he had been seen by some of

Bonner's spies when he entered London, that he had been followed from place to place, and that the most convenient opportunity of seizing him had occurred when he was speaking to Aveline. His friend, Roger Upton, had been seized at the same time, and very speedily condemned to death, a fate to which Bishop Bonner had also doomed his young niece.

The next day Master Gresham summoned me to attend him to Hatfield, where he was about to pay his respects to her Majesty. We arrived there early in the day, when my patron was at once admitted to an audience. He was very cordially received by Queen Elizabeth, who promised to attend to his interests. He did not fail also to give her Majesty wise counsel. Among other things, she promised him that, when he was abroad on her business, she would not only keep one ear shut to hear him on his return, but also that should he do her even as much service as he had done to King Edward and to Queen Mary, she would give him as much land as they both had done. These two promises greatly inspirited my patron. Before he took his departure, the Queen desired him to proceed forthwith to Antwerp, where there was business of importance for him to perform. As the journey was a hurried one, and he would not be long absent, he did not on this occasion take me with him.

In the meantime Aveline had recovered from the effects of her cruel imprisonment, and the great terror of her life into which she had been put. Through the intervention of Master Gresham, Overton and his friends were liberated, he liberally offering them an asylum in his house until they could obtain employment.

Great was the happy change which the nation experienced. It was soon known that Queen Elizabeth was no friend to the Romish customs. Directly she came to the throne, she refused to attend mass. This was on Christmas Day. The Queen had gone to the chapel as usual, and there she sat while the Gospel was read; but as soon as it was concluded, having seen a Bishop preparing himself by putting on his robes in the old form, she and her nobles left the chapel and retired to her privy chamber. Two days after this, a proclamation was issued, forbidding the elevation of the host. It was also ordered that the Gospels and Epistles, the Creed, and Lord's Prayer, the Ten Commandments, and the Litany should be used in English. Her respect for the Bible, and her desire to have it spread throughout her realms, was still more clearly shown on the occasion of her progress from the Tower to Westminster, the day before her coronation, on the 15th of January, 1559.

I cannot describe the magnificent way in which the City was decorated, nor the numerous pageants which were prepared to do her honour. From one, a child—who was intended to represent Truth—let down, by a silk lace, an English Bible, richly bound, before the Queen. She kissed both her hands, with both her hands she received it, afterwards applying it to her breast, and lastly, standing up and thanking the City for its gifts, promised to be a diligent reader thereof. When any good wishes were cast forth for her virtuous and religious government, she would lift up her hands towards heaven, and desired the people to answer "Amen."

My patron was not long absent. I had been labouring in the shop that day, and at supper had joined the family, my master, who had been absent at court, having just returned, when Sir John Leigh came in. The conversation turned on various matters abroad. News had just been received that King Philip had actually quitted Flanders and gone to reside for the future in Spain. The Queen's ministers had therefore resolved to send an ambassador resident to his court. For this office Sir Thomas Chaloner, who had hitherto been in Flanders, was appointed.

"And I understand my friend Sir Thomas Gresham is to fill his place at Brussels in the capacity of an ambassador," observed Sir John Leigh, bowing to my patron.

"What!" exclaimed Lady Anne. "You are not joking with my husband?"

"No, assuredly," answered Sir John; "this very day he has received the honour of knighthood, and as I came here I heard of the appointment I have mentioned."

"Sir John speaks the truth, my dear wife," said my patron, turning to Lady Anne. "I have received that honour from the Queen's Majesty, but I wished that another might tell you of it rather than myself. I am ready to devote my powers to the service of our good Queen, and therefore gladly accept the office she has put upon me, albeit it may be rather to my loss than profit."

I will not repeat the congratulations of Lady Anne, or of the guests who were present. No time was to be lost, as the matter was pressing; and I was well pleased to find that I was to accompany my patron in the character rather of a secretary than a page. Truly he had been kind and generous to me.

Chapter Fourteen
Events in Antwerp

Once more we were in Antwerp. We stayed there, however, but a short time, to confer with Master Clough on various financial and commercial matters. I should mention that an attempt was made by the Papists to stir up enmity against the new Queen of England among the people of Antwerp, in order, if possible, to prevent Sir Thomas Gresham from obtaining the point he required. For this purpose a friar was engaged to preach a sermon. He furiously attacked the Queen, abused her as a heretic and a heathen, who cared not for God nor religion, and whose great object was to make all her people heathens, telling his hearers that any Catholic would be justified in putting her to death; not only that, but he would thereby perform a meritorious work, highly pleasing to the Church and to God. The indignation, however, of the people of Antwerp on hearing this sermon was very great, for at that time there were fully fifty thousand professed Protestants in that city, besides many more who secretly approved of their principles. Had the friar ventured abroad, there would have been little doubt that he would have been well bastinadoed by the populace. He must have suspected that such would be his fate if he showed himself.

The following day Sir Thomas received a visit from Master Lazarus Tucker. He came, he said, on the part of the friar to request that Sir Thomas would throw his protection over him, to save him from the treatment he was likely to receive. I had seldom seen my patron so amused.

"By my troth," he answered, "this is impudence! Here is a villainous fellow who preaches black treason in the name of religion, and then sends to me, the envoy of the Queen's Majesty, to protect him! No, no! let him go forth if he lists, and if he is well bastinadoed by the people, he will only obtain his desert."

The friar, however, remained shut up in his house, but shortly afterwards, through the aid of Cardinal Granvelle, secretly left the city, and took refuge in Brussels. No man in authority was more hated at that time in the Netherlands than was Cardinal Granvelle. When Philip went to Spain, he had been left behind in Flanders. His ambition had procured for him a cardinal's hat, and, by his insolent and imperious bearing, he soon incurred such deep hatred, that the first noblemen of the country conspired against him, and vowed to effect his ruin.

I was present on one occasion when the spirit which was abroad, even among people of the highest rank, exhibited itself. When at Brussels, our old friend Jasper Schetz, now Lord of Grobbendonck, invited Sir Thomas to a banquet. A large party of Flemish nobles were collected, among whom I felt myself a very humble person. The conversation turned upon the thoroughly hated Cardinal Granvelle, his luxurious style of living, and the air of haughty superciliousness with which he treated all who approached him. As the wine circulated, the abuse of the Cardinal became more vehement. His magnificent equipages, liveries, and the arrangements of his household, excited their derision; the way he lived, and the tinsel and glitter in which the prelate pranked himself, were contrasted with the simple habits and garments of the nobles of Germany.

At length it was proposed that the plainest possible livery should be adopted for the servants of all present, as unlike as possible to that worn by the menials of the Cardinal. Some one also proposed that a symbol should be added to the livery, to show the universal contempt for Granvelle. By whom should it be designed? was the question. It was agreed that the matter should be decided by lot. Dice were called for. Count Egmont won. A few days afterwards his retainers appeared in doublet and hose of the coarsest grey, long hanging sleeves, such as were worn by the humblest classes, the only ornament being a monk's cowl, or a fool's cap and bells, embroidered on the sleeves. The other nobles, who had been present at the dinner, ordered all their servants to appear in the same costume, which now became so popular, that all the tailors in Brussels could scarcely furnish those in demand. Many of them, indeed, wore in front of their dress a fool's head with a cardinal's hat upon it.

The Regent, Margaret of Parma, at first laughed with the rest at this proceeding, as she had no love for Granvelle. She induced the nobles to omit the fool's cap from the livery, and to substitute a bundle of arrows, or a wheatsheaf. The Cardinal, who was soon after this recalled, took care to avenge himself on those who had thus mocked him. He represented to Philip, that though he could easily forgive the fools' caps and cowls, yet the wheatsheaf and the bundle of arrows betokened the existence of a conspiracy against the authority of the Prince himself; and probably on that very occasion the death of Count Egmont was determined on by Philip and the Cardinal. They had, however, to abide their time.

Fearful was the vengeance the Cardinal took, not only on the nobles, but on all the people of this unhappy country. But I am anticipating.

The most terrible and remorseless instrument employed for this purpose was Peter Titelmann, Inquisitor General. Throughout the whole of Flanders, Douay, and Tournay, the most populous portions of the Netherlands, he proceeded at a rapid pace, spreading dismay far and wide, dragging suspected persons from their firesides or beds, and thrusting them into dismal dungeons: arresting, torturing, strangling, burning, with hardly the shadow of warrant, information, or process.

My heart sickens as I contemplate the dreadful scenes I was often compelled to witness, and I think of the number of those simply accused of reading the Bible who were hurried to the flames. Even the Roman Catholics, who had hitherto looked on with indifference, were now aroused, and representations were made to the Regent of the fearful proceedings of Peter Titelmann, the Inquisitor.

Still the Protestant faith was not put down, and Philip, maddened by the opposition he met with, at length issued a decree condemning to death the whole of his subjects who would not conform to the Church of Rome. The Prince of Orange, a moderate man, and one who never spoke without weighing his words, declared that, at this time, fifty thousand persons in the provinces had been put to death in obedience to the edicts.

Philip declared, that as his father had chastised his people with a scourge, he would make them feel the effect of a whip of scorpions. The edicts were enforced, therefore, with renewed vigour; and, as may be supposed, all who could escape fled out of this doomed land as soon as possible. The tide of commerce was completely changed, and whereas formerly manufactures were sent from Antwerp to England, now every week vessels came from Sandwich to Antwerp laden with silk, satin, and cloth manufactured in England.

My sagacious patron had long seen the course events were taking. I may state now that, for some years past, he had been busily employed in purchasing gunpowder, arquebuses, cannon, and all sorts of munitions of war, as well as cordage, and all naval stores required for fitting out ships. He had urged the English Government also to increase their military forces, and to prepare and fit out as many large ships as could possibly be built. He had agents in all parts of Europe, and by their means had kept himself thoroughly well acquainted with all that was going forward. The plots for the destruction of the life of the Queen of England were soon made known to him, and by his means communicated to Sir William Cecil. As long as King Philip hoped to gain the hand of Queen Elizabeth, and thereby to recover an influence in England, he pretended amity to the English. It was also Cecil's policy to remain at peace, that he might be better prepared for war, when that inevitable time should arrive.

The great object of the Pope of Rome, and of all whom he could influence, was to destroy England, because it was evident by this time that England had become, in most part, a Protestant country, and would never, while she remained free and independent, again yield to the Papal power. Queen Mary by her burnings in Smithfield, and King Philip and his father by the wholesale murders of their subjects in the Netherlands—the latter thereby driving thousands of Protestants into England—had done more to destroy the power of Romanism in that land than all the cardinals and bishops and the most talented preachers could ever repair.

My patron, in writing to the Government at home, had to be very careful in the expressions he used, lest his letters might be seen, and those he employed brought into trouble. This shipment of warlike stores was contrary to the laws of the Netherlands, consequently, when we were shipping gunpowder, we always used the words *velvet* and *silks*: *damasks* and *satins* were employed to signify very different articles. The authorities evidently suspected what was going forward, and gave orders to the custom-house officers to search all ships loading for England. However, as these custom-house officers were ill-paid by their Government, there was no great difficulty in inducing them to close their eyes during their searches, and to declare that certain casks on board the vessels, however suspicious might have been their appearance, contained the pieces of velvet mentioned in the bill of lading.

Chapter Fifteen
A Fight with Robbers

Sir Thomas Gresham had been absent for some time, and his return to Antwerp was daily expected. I was busily at work at my desk, when I heard the sound of horses' hoofs coming along the street. I looked out, and saw a party of travellers. Calling Master Clough, he and I, with others, hurried to the door. Sir Thomas led the cavalcade, with a young lady by his side. I had never, I thought, seen a more fair or graceful girl, while I admired the perfect ease with which she managed the jennet on which she rode. Who she was I scarcely dared to guess. She could scarcely be the little Aveline from whom I had parted, and yet the thought crossed me that it must be her.

Two young men followed,—one a strong, stout, broad-shouldered man, whose features were wonderfully like those of my old friend A'Dale, although somewhat concealed by beard and whisker. He formed a strong contrast to the slight, pale, sickly youth at his side. A second glance convinced me that the latter was my former playmate and companion— Richard Gresham. He seemed very sick and ill, leaning forward in his saddle, as if scarcely able to support his body. Master Clough hurried out to assist Sir Thomas to dismount, while I hastened, with one of the servants, to take the young lady's horse. The smile she gave me, as she dropped lightly from her saddle, reminded me of Aveline.

"You do not know me, Ernst Verner," she said; "am I so woefully changed since we parted?"

Her sweet voice sent a thrill through my heart. I had no longer any doubt that she was Aveline. Meantime A'Dale had thrown himself from his steed, and had helped Richard to the ground, giving him his arm to support him. Sir Thomas greeted me kindly.

"He has not borne the journey as well as we had hoped," he said, looking at Richard; "but the doctors advised change of air and scene, and we trusted that a short sea-voyage, and a visit to this busy city, might benefit him. Aveline has kindly come to assist in caring for him, and I have taken your old friend Andrew A'Dale into my service."

Poor Richard looked kindly at me as he took my hand; but he scarcely had strength, it seemed, to smile. A'Dale and I greeted each other heartily, and together we assisted our young friend up the stairs. He could not, indeed, without aid, drag himself along; but youth is buoyant, and both he and we were soon talking of what we would do when he had regained his strength. Aveline was committed to the charge of our old housekeeper—Dorothea Lipman, with whom she had some difficulty in holding conversation; Dorothea's only language being Flemish, of which Aveline knew but little.

After a night's rest, Richard had considerably recovered. Whenever he came into the public room, I could not help observing the devoted attention which Aveline paid him. She seemed to watch his every look, and attend to his slightest want. He, indeed, I thought, expected her to devote herself to him and to demand her services as a right, which she willingly rendered. At first this seemed but natural after the accounts Sir Thomas had given me; but I confess, when she appeared to have scarcely any time to attend to me or to anybody else, a feeling of jealousy stole over me. And yet why should I be jealous of that poor sickly lad? indeed, what right had I to expect that she would regard me in any other light than that of a humble secretary of her kind lady's husband? I had a sincere affection, however, for Richard, and heartily wished him to recover. Mistress Aveline had always treated me with kindness, and I was not vain enough to mistake the way in which she received any little attention I was able to pay her.

Sir Thomas Gresham was constantly receiving visitors at his house. Among them came at this time Master Thomas Cecil, the son of the great minister, accompanied by his tutor, Master Windebank. He was a young, pleasant-mannered, good-tempered youth, apparently somewhat light-hearted, and inclined to amuse himself with whatever fell in his way.

During his stay he rode out on several occasions with Mistress Aveline, and seemed highly pleased with her company. She, in return, seemed to attend to what he said, even with more pleasure than she listened to poor Richard, who was unable, while riding, to enter much into conversation in consequence of his cough and short breathing. I generally accompanied the party when they went out after our usual hours of business. It was but natural that a gay young man should pay attention to a sweet and lively girl like Aveline, and at first I did not care so much for it; but after a time, when I thought she seemed pleased with his attentions, I began heartily to wish that he would take his departure. One thing I thought I had discovered— that her heart was not given to Richard; but then I was convinced for the same reason that she did not care for me. I was very glad when Sir Thomas, at the minister's request, supplied young Cecil and his tutor with money to enable them to continue their tour which they intended making through Germany, and from thence passing on through Switzerland into Italy.

We were, shortly after this, more busily employed than ever in purchasing bow staves, as Sir Thomas urged the Government by writing frequently, and, when he went home, personally, to make every preparation for war. He had discovered the hatred which the Roman Catholic sovereigns had for England, now that Queen Elizabeth had declared herself so decidedly Protestant. At the same time, he deemed it important to supply England with the precious metals, that she might, in case of a war, have wherewith to pay her troops.

As the bullion was purchased, it was shipped, as I have already mentioned, on board vessels. At length, in consequence of the expected scarcity of shipping, Sir Thomas resolved to make a large shipment on board one particular vessel. The amount had been carefully done up inside various packages, as I believe I have before described.

"It is necessary that a trustworthy person should be on board, to see that the goods are not tampered with," observed Sir Thomas to me. "You and A'Dale will therefore go down and see them shipped, and you will afterwards continue on board and proceed with the ship to England. As soon as she is unloaded, you will return in her, and report to me all that takes place, and all the news you can hear in London. You will go to Lombard Street, and receive despatches from Master John Elliot to bring with you."

As a small portion of the goods only had been shipped when we reached the vessel, the bulk not having arrived, A'Dale and I determined to remain at the hostel instead of going on board to sleep. We were seated in the public room, and talking together in English, when, in a pause in the conversation, I heard three rough-looking persons speaking Flemish at a little distance from me. I pricked up my ears as I heard one of them remark:

"Oh! they are only two English lads; they cannot, depend on it, understand a word we say."

This made me listen more carefully, though I continued speaking with greater energy apparently than ever to A'Dale.

I still kept my ears, however, open to hear everything my neighbours said. I soon found that they were talking about our ship—the *Diamond*.

"She began to receive her goods to-day," said one; "and by to-morrow evening she will probably be able to sail with the turn of the tide. We must not let her escape us, as some of those English vessels of late have done. The question is, whether we shall attack her before she gets out of the Scheld, or wait till she reaches the broad seas."

Some of the party were for waiting at the mouth of the river, hoping thereby to make off with their prize with less risk of its being retaken; others, however, considered that they might thereby lose it, and that it would be more prudent to attack the ship while she lay at anchor.

This plan was at last, so I suppose, adopted. I looked as unconcerned as possible, as if I had not heard anything of what was said. I feared, however, that there was great danger of the *Diamond* being taken, as the pirates appeared to have a large force at their command.

I did not like to leave the room as long as the men were talking, hoping by staying to gain further information about their plans. It was evident they were thoroughly well informed of all that was going forward, and it became, therefore, very important that I should be careful as to my proceedings. I had observed near me a sunburnt, weather-beaten man, in the dress of a sea officer, who every now and then glanced up at the pirates as they spoke. Once I caught his eye, and, by the look he gave me, I felt sure that he knew I had been listening.

A'Dale and I, having finished our supper, got up, I proposing to take a turn in the fresh air before going to bed. As we had been talking of our voyage, I knew that the stranger, who must have overheard what we said, was aware that our ship was bound for London. We stood outside the door of the hostel for some minutes, before deciding which direction we should take. Just as we were moving on, I felt a hand placed on my shoulder.

"Young master," said the stranger, "excuse my interruption. I heard you remark that you were in the service of Sir Thomas Gresham, and about to sail on board the *Diamond*. I heard, too, what was said by those other men. You understand what they said, I think?"

"Not I, indeed," answered A'Dale, who now for the first time heard of the plot, for I had been unable before to tell him of it. "I do not know what you mean."

"I do, however, sir," I observed. "I would ask you whether you know anything about these men, and whether they are likely to carry out their project?"

"I feel very sure they will carry it out. The only way that I can see, is to be ready for them," answered the stranger. "I fear, however, that the crew of the *Diamond* is too small to defend her. My own vessel lies at no great distance; and if you will accept it, I will render you all the assistance in my power."

"Thank you, friend!" exclaimed A'Dale; "though I doubt not we should be able to beat back any marauders, yet a few more stout arms would be of great assistance."

But I was not quite so willing to accept the offer of the stranger. I had learnt caution. It was a quality greatly inculcated on all his inferiors by Sir Thomas Gresham. Perhaps, I thought, this very man is only a confederate, and hopes thus to obtain quiet possession of the vessel.

"Thank you, my friend," I answered, turning to the stranger. "We will communicate your offer to the captain; but we are only passengers on board; we have no command over her, and without his sanction I cannot venture to accept your offer."

"I understand," answered the stranger, promptly; "I do not take your remarks amiss. I mean you well; but you are very right not to accept such an offer without consideration. My vessel, the *Falcon*, lies rather lower down the river. Your captain will easily discover her; and if, on consideration, he wishes to receive the assistance of an honest man, who esteems his employer, and is well able to render aid, he can summon me, and I will come with a boat's crew, or two may be, and fight as I should were my own vessel attacked."

Saying these words, the stranger shook our hands warmly, and disappeared in the gloom.

A'Dale and I continued our walk. He seemed to think that I had been ungrateful in not accepting the assistance so freely offered. I explained my reasons. He saw that I was right. It was then too late to get a boat; indeed, so small was the amount of cargo as yet shipped—of which the pirates were well aware—that there was no fear of their attacking her that night. We agreed, therefore, that I should go aboard the first thing in the morning to speak to the captain, leaving A'Dale to look after the goods on shore.

I also proposed engaging a few stout fellows, well-armed, in addition to our own crew, and thus hoped to be able to repel any attack the pirates might make upon us.

The next morning, the instant the grey dawn streamed into our chamber, we sprang out of bed. We wished to leave the house unobserved, in case any of the sea-robbers or their confederates might be living there. To prevent them from discovering what we were about, should any one observe us, we took our way directly from the river; and then turning round again through some narrow streets, once more hurried towards it. We soon found a boat, and telling A'Dale to keep a bright look-out around him, I pulled down in her towards the *Diamond*.

Captain Davis, her commander, was surprised to see me thus early. I told him the reason of my coming. He was inclined, I saw, to doubt that the people whose conversation we had overheard were speaking about his vessel.

"If they had been speaking English, Master Verner, your ears might not have deceived you; but as they were talking Flemish, it is very likely, that being a foreign lingo, you may be mistaken."

"But it is not a foreign lingo to me, Captain Davis," I answered, laughing; "it is, I may say, my native tongue, and therefore I am not likely to be mistaken."

"That makes a difference, to be sure," he answered; "yet still the chances are they were speaking of something else. If they had had a plot in hand such as you suppose, they would have been more cautious."

"When the wine is in, the wit is out, captain," I remarked. "At first, I grant you, they said nothing to betray themselves; but when I tell you that some of our chief nobles act just as indiscreetly, you may more readily believe that such men as these might let out their secrets on such an occasion."

"Well, well, Master Verner, I am bound to believe you; and as night comes on we will have the men armed and on the watch. Still, I rather think it will come to nothing; but, as you observe, it is well to be prepared."

The crew were all Englishmen—twenty stout fellows; and, with well-sharpened hangers in their hands and a supply of pikes, I hoped they would have no difficulty in keeping any assailants out of the ship. I told them that there might be a chance of that sort of thing, and they all expressed their readiness to defend the ship to the last. I mentioned to the captain what I had done.

"Oh yes," he said, "my dogs will fight well; there is no fear of that. We were once attacked near the Straits of Gibraltar by a Salee rover; and although the villains outnumbered my crew as three to one, yet we beat them off, even though many of them had already gained our deck. We shall treat these fellows in the same way, depend on that, whoever they are."

A'Dale exerted himself so energetically, that before dark all the goods were on board and safely stowed away. An officer of the Customs having brought us our clearance papers, as soon as the tide served we were able to sail. Having still some daylight, and hoping thus to avoid the threatened attack, we immediately got under weigh, and dropped down the river. The night, however, becoming cloudy and dark, and the wind being contrary, we were once more obliged to bring up.

"If the pirates come to look for us, they will find us gone," observed Captain Davis, as we sat at supper round the cabin-table.

"But if they intended to attack us, depend upon it they were on the watch," observed A'Dale, "and know where we are as well as they did before."

I agreed with A'Dale that we ought to keep a strict watch, as we had intended. Captain Davis, I observed, as sailors are too apt to do, made light of the danger of which we had warned him.

"They will think twice before they attack the *Diamond*, depend on that, young masters," he answered to our remarks.

As A'Dale and I had been up since daybreak, and actively engaged all the time, both of us felt very sleepy. Yet we were far too anxious willingly to go to sleep. Without taking off our clothes, therefore, we threw ourselves down in our bedplaces in the after-cabin, hoping that we should be awakened by the slightest noise. We kept our swords by our sides, ready for instant action. The captain, however, laughed at us for our anxiety.

"Don't be alarmed, my young masters," he observed, in a somewhat taunting tone; "if we are attacked, we shall be able to give a good account of the villains, without having to call you up, so you might have taken off your clothes and gone to sleep comfortably."

He made some other remarks, much in the same strain; but as he continued speaking, his words sounded less and less distinct to my ears, and before he had concluded I was fast asleep.

It seemed to me but a minute after I had shut my eyes that I was aroused by a fearful uproar. Shouts and shrieks and cries of all sorts, the report of fire-arms and the clashing of steel. I started up, hitting my head, as I did so, against the beam above me, and sprang out of my narrow bed. I called loudly to A'Dale. He was so fast asleep that the first shout did not completely arouse him. The second, however, made him spring to his feet.

"What has happened?" he asked.

"The pirates have come, there is little doubt of that," I answered; "we must go and drive them back."

As I said this, sword in hand, I sprang up the companion-ladder, and he followed me. As we reached the deck, I saw a number of dark forms clustering in the rigging, whilst others were attempting to get over the sides. Our men were bravely endeavouring to drive them back with their hangers and pikes, a few arquebuses also being brought into use. Some were armed with cross-bows, but they had thrown them aside for the purpose of doing more service with their sharp blades. Never had I heard so fearful a din, for the object of the pirates seemed to be to overwhelm us, and frighten us out of our wits by their numbers. Two or three of our men lay wounded, dying on the deck. It seemed, indeed, that the pirates were gaining the advantage. A'Dale, who was a stout fellow and well accustomed to the use of his sword, laid about him lustily, and assisted much in keeping them at bay. It was pretty evident that the watch on deck had been taken by surprise, and that the poor fellows who lay weltering in their blood had been cut down unawares. The captain, however, to do him justice, was doing his best to make amends for his want of caution, and was fighting bravely, appearing now in one place, now in another, wherever the enemy were seen climbing up the sides. Still they were determined fellows, and there appeared too great a probability that they would take the ship. But at length we drove most of them back into their boats; several of the bravest being killed. Our men began to shout "Victory! victory!" rather too soon. In another instant the enemy were again swarming up the sides, urged on by their leaders. They were evidently a large and well-organised body, and seemed determined to conquer or lose their lives in their attempt to take the vessel. Once more they appeared above the bulwarks, several following each other in quick succession, and dropping down on our decks in spite of our utmost efforts to repel them. Once having gained a footing, they were enabled to keep a clear space, by which others entered. Our captain, seeing that a desperate effort must be made to drive them back, called on A'Dale and me and several of the men to attack them. We rushed forward, and a fiercer combat ensued than had yet taken place. I felt a sharp pang in my shoulder, and knew that I was wounded; but though the blood flowed freely, I was yet able to wield my sword. Still the number of our enemies increased, and inch by inch they drove us back, the larger portion of our crew being compelled all this time to guard the sides from the assaults of other parties who were endeavouring to climb up them. I began to fear, as I saw the state of affairs, that the *Diamond* and her rich cargo would fall into the hands of the pirates. They too seemed to consider themselves secure of victory, for with loud shouts they encouraged each other to push on, calling at the same time to their comrades, who were yet in the boats alongside, to come up and secure their victory. Already some of our men began to cry out that all was lost, and entreat for quarter. Just then a seaman, who had been on the opposite side to that attacked by the pirates, came running up to the captain to tell him that more enemies were coming.

"Better die fighting like brave men than yield," answered Captain Davis.

As he spoke, I looked on one side and saw the heads of people appearing over the bulwarks.

"To the rescue! a Gresham! a Gresham!" they shouted. I was afraid that this was only to deceive us; I recognised, however, the voice of the stranger who had offered his services. And now, before the pirates could get over to attack them, some twenty well-armed men leaped down on our decks, and springing to our side, with pikes and swords drove back our assailants. In vain the pirates attempted to resist the attack. Our friends were fresh, while our enemies had already exhausted themselves in the efforts they had been making. The pirates asked for no quarter: neither our supporters nor our crew were inclined to give it. Several were cut down and killed on the deck, others saved their lives by ignominiously jumping over the bulwarks; and so rapidly did the fortune of war change, that in a few minutes not a live pirate was to be seen on our decks. Several were hurled headlong into their boats desperately wounded, others thrown overboard.

The pirates' boats were now seen shoving off, and attempting to make their escape. As soon as this was perceived by the stranger, he called to his men, and they, returning to their boats, made chase. They were not long in overtaking them, and in the midst of the gloom we could just distinguish the boats apparently mingled together. Again we heard shouts and cries, and the sharp report of arquebuses, with the clashing of steel. Which party was gaining the victory, however, we could not tell. At length the two boats of our friends appeared coming out of the gloom, towing a third. They were soon alongside, and the stranger captain appeared on our deck with three prisoners. They were all he had been able to take. As lanterns were held to their countenances, they appeared to be ruffian fellows, from whom but little information could be obtained. They seemed also to be expecting instant death, abject terror adding to the ill favour of their looks.

Although the captain and other persons on board spoke Flemish, I, as being the best linguist, was deputed to speak to the men. I told them that now they were our prisoners we could do as we thought right, but we had no wish to kill them, even though they might deserve death. I then asked them at whose instigation they had attacked us. At length I discovered that the band was composed of persons who had been driven from their homes by the persecutions of the Spaniards; that some one among them, of superior rank to the rest, had heard, by some means or other, that the ship we sailed in had a large treasure on board, of which they hoped to possess themselves. Captain Davis consulted with us as to what we should do with our prisoners. We agreed that it might be as well to show them the cargo of the ship, and to ask them whether they thought it worth risking their lives to obtain it; and then to let them go, hoping that they would persuade their comrades not further to pursue us; for, although this first party had been driven back, we believed the assertion of the men, that there were a vast number more, who might, should the wind continue contrary, overtake us in their row-boats, and carry out their original plan.

Chapter Sixteen
Captain Rover

We had to remain at anchor for some time, as, the tide and wind being contrary, we could not proceed down the river. The information we received made it very necessary for us to be on our guard; for although we had driven back the pirates once, they would very probably again attack us with increased numbers. We proposed to the stranger captain the plan which had been suggested, and he agreed at once that it was a good one. Much to the surprise of our prisoners, who had expected to be run up at the yard-arm, or to be sent overboard with shot round their feet, we promised them their liberty — provided they would do as we directed them. They, of course, gladly consented, "We have done well," observed the stranger captain, when he saw the prisoners rowing away; "not that we can depend much upon those fellows. They may or may not persuade their companions that your vessel is not worth attacking. However, the sooner you sail away from this the better. I am also bound for England, and will bear you company. My vessel lies not far from you; and knowing what was likely to happen, I was on the watch, so that the instant I heard the sounds of strife, I was able to come to your assistance."

Captain Davis thanked the stranger warmly. "But, friend," he said, "I have not yet learned your name. I should like to know what to call you when we meet again."

"Oh! that is of little consequence," answered the stranger. "To confess the honest truth, I have had more than one name. Call me Rover. I have wandered not a little about the world, and it is a name you will not easily forget."

"But that is not your real name, surely?" observed A'Dale.

"Young master, when you have lived longer in the world, you will know that you should not ask such a question. A man, in my opinion, may have a dozen names, and slip them off and on in these troublous times as often as he lists. I beg you will remember me as Captain Rover, of the *Falcon*. We shall see more of each other ere long, probably. I hope that you will not lose sight of the *Falcon*, nor I of the *Diamond*, till we are safe in the Thames."

Saying this, Captain Rover ordered his men into their boats, and pulled away down the stream. His advice was too important to be despised. We continued to keep a bright look-out, knowing that at any moment we might be attacked. We only hoped that his departure might not have been discovered by our enemies. We soon lost sight of him, although we could hear the oars of the boat some time afterwards, as they dipped at intervals into the water, every moment growing fainter and fainter.

I had begun to feel considerable pain from my wound, though the darkness prevented my friends from observing what had happened. It was not till I went down into the cabin with Captain Davis and A'Dale that they perceived that I was hurt. The blood had stained my coat. I felt very faint from the loss of blood, and should have sunk on the deck of the cabin had not A'Dale caught me.

"My dear Ernst," he exclaimed, "you are badly hurt! why did you not let us know before?" I heard him say, though I was then unable to make a reply.

He and the captain lifted me into my berth. They then took off my clothes, and the latter examined my wound, so I was afterwards told. He had seen so many sword-cut wounds that he knew exactly what to do; and he immediately, with lint and bandage, bound up my arm, and stopped the flow of blood. In a short time I returned to consciousness, when I found A'Dale sitting by me. At first I could not recollect where I was, or what had happened. My first question, however, on coming to my senses, was whether anything more had been seen of the pirates.

"No," answered A'Dale; "but two or three boats have passed near us in the dark, and the captain is afraid that they are still on the watch for us. He proposes, therefore, directly the tide serves, to get under weigh, and to drop farther down the river. Perhaps we shall fall in with our friend Captain Rover, but if not, we must take care of ourselves, and our fellows have shown that they are both willing and able to fight."

Soon after he had said this, we heard the sound of heaving up the anchor, and other familiar noises showed us that the vessel was already moving. A'Dale told me that he had left all the men on deck, with their hangers buckled by their sides, and their pikes ready to their hands, to repel any sudden assault.

"I scarcely like to remain so long down here with you;" he added, "lest they should think I am skulking."

I begged him not to think of me, but to go on deck, if he thought fit.

"Very well," he said; "but I must come and have a look at you occasionally."

He was as good as his word. I remember his coming down once, but I was very sleepy, and soon dropped off, so that I was no longer aware of what was taking place.

The grey light of morning had found its way into the cabin when I awoke. All was then quiet; the only sounds which reached my ears being the heavy tread of the men on deck, the occasional creaking of a block, and the ripple of the water against the sides of the vessel. By this I knew that the vessel was under weigh. Feeling much better, I managed to get out of my bed, and throwing a cloak over my shoulders, crawled up on deck. We were standing down the Scheld, with all sail set, for the wind had changed. The crew were still on deck, and, with the captain and mates and A'Dale, were watching a large vessel which was following us. So intent were they in watching the stranger that they did not observe me. As soon, however, as Captain Davis's eyes rested on me, he exclaimed:

"Go down below, Master Verner, and turn into your berth again. You had no business to come on deck, and run the chance of getting the cold into your wound. I am your doctor, as well as the captain of this ship, and in both characters have a right to command you."

"I will obey you," I answered; "but pray tell me, what is that ship astern?"

"That question is one I have no means of answering," he replied; "but go down, I say, and perhaps A'Dale will tell you all about it when he is wiser than I am."

A'Dale now came to the companion-hatch, and I was very glad to have his assistance in going down again, and being helped into bed. He told me that the captain was somewhat anxious about the vessel coming up astern; that we had passed her in the early morning, and that soon afterwards she was seen getting under weigh. We, however, having somewhat the start of her, had hitherto kept ahead; but she was now fast coming up with us, and if she was an enemy we might fare ill, however bravely our men might fight.

"But does not the captain suppose she may be Captain Rover's ship?" I asked. "He told me that she was not tar off, and that he was bound for England."

"Captain Davis seemed rather to doubt that," he answered, as he went on deck.

He soon returned, however, saying that I was right; and in a short time the *Falcon* was almost abreast of us. Captain Davis had had not only my wound to dress, but those of three of his men who had been hurt. Two had been killed, and their bodies were now resting at the bottom of the Scheld.

Captain Rover hailed us through his speaking-trumpet, and expressed his sorrow at hearing that I was hurt. The two captains agreed on the course they were to steer, and promised to remain by each other, thus being the better able to beat off those who might have been inclined to attack us singly.

When the air became warmed by the sun, Captain Davis allowed me to return on deck, for I could not bear being kept below. The water was smooth and the sky bright, and our bulging sails were filled with the fresh breeze. It was pleasant to watch the tall ship as she sailed by our side, with pennants flying, and the muzzles of her guns peering through her ports, and to think of the far-distant lands she had visited. I hoped to have another opportunity of meeting Captain Rover, and of hearing an account of his adventures. Thus the voyage continued. At night our lanterns were lighted, which we carried on the poops and forecastles, so that we might not run the risk of losing sight of each other. Several times strange vessels were seen, but we held on our way without being molested.

I still continued very weak, and I knew that such a wound as I had received was not likely to be cured in a hurry. For my own sake, I was very glad, therefore, when the shores of Essex on one side, and those of Kent on the other, appeared in sight, and we glided slowly up over the bosom of old Father Thames. The same breeze carried us along which had brought us across from Flanders, and at length we cast anchor close to the Tower.

Here Master Elliot, Sir Thomas Gresham's factor, came on board, and we delivered over to him the goods we had brought. They were at once carefully transferred into boats, and carried into the Tower, where Sir William Cecil had ordered them to be stored. Here, under the superintendence of Master Elliot, the coin was taken out; neither A'Dale nor I, however, saw anything of that. Master Elliot, when he heard that I was wounded, sent a litter, and had me conveyed to Master Gresham's new house in Bishopsgate Street, which had been built during my absence from England. Lady Anne had just come up to London, and received me with especial kindness. She had many inquiries to make, not only about Sir Thomas, but about her son and Aveline. I was sorry that with a good conscience I could not give a better account of Richard. She sighed as she heard my report.

"And my sweet Aveline, how is she?" she asked.

She watched me, I thought, as I replied; and I was afraid of blushing, and betraying certain feelings which had long been agitating my bosom. I was soon sufficiently recovered to attend the dinner-table, at which Master Elliot, in his employer's absence, presided. Among the guests, much to my satisfaction, I found Captain Rover, as well as Captain Davis who had brought us over. The latter told me that, after a few slight repairs, he should be ready again to sail, and to convey A'Dale and me back to Antwerp. I learnt also from Captain Rover somewhat about the numerous countries he had visited. He had been, I found, many years from England in command of his ship, which belonged to a company of merchant adventurers, in which company Sir Thomas Gresham had a share. He had been acquainted with Sir Thomas from his youth, having always sailed in ships either belonging to him, or to those with whom he was connected.

On parting from Lady Anne, she gave me many charges with regard to her son Richard.

"And above all things," she said, "remember you bring him and Aveline ere long back to me in safety."

A'Dale joined me on board. He had been with his friends to the last moment, and had a great deal to tell me about the wonders he had seen in England, and the state of Queen Elizabeth, who had passed through the City in a magnificent coach, all of gold and silver and silk. But the grandest sight, according to A'Dale's idea, was the shooting for a great wager of archery, in Finsbury Square, Lord Robert Dudley having been the challenger.

We proceeded for some distance down the Thames aided by the tide, but afterwards were kept a week in the mouth of the Medway, waiting for a fair wind. After this, when we got to sea, we encountered a heavy gale, which drove us back again into harbour. Thus three weeks passed before we arrived at the mouth of the Scheld.

We had brought over a cargo of wool and hides, to be manufactured in the Netherlands into numerous articles.

Sir Thomas approved of all that we had done. He now for the first time heard of the *Diamond* having been attacked by pirates, and of the assistance which Captain Rover had afforded us.

"I hope that he will be here before long," he observed, "as I shall be glad to offer him my best thanks, and perchance show him my gratitude in a more substantial manner."

Having delivered my despatches to Sir Thomas, I hastened in search of Aveline and Richard. On entering the sitting-room, the noise of the opening door aroused Aveline, who was busy over her work, absorbed in thought, so it seemed to me. She started up, and, as I approached, took my hand.

"Why, Ernst!" she exclaimed, "what has happened? you look so pale and ill."

I told her of our ship having been attacked by pirates, and she listened with deep interest, so it seemed to me, to my narrative.

"And Richard," I asked, "how is he?" She pointed to a couch in a recess, shaded by a curtain, and shook her head, while a sad look came over her countenance. "He sleeps," she said. "He sleeps often now, and a long time together, and every day grows weaker; but his father does not observe it. I have not ventured to write to Lady Anne to tell her; and I fear that her grief will be greatly increased when she hears of what will, I am sure, ere long take place. I wish that he had never been brought over here, and separated from her."

I need not say what further conversation passed between Aveline and me. It was some time before Richard awoke. He seemed pleased at seeing me, but I soon observed that the account which Aveline had given of him was too correct. After the day of my arrival, I saw both him and Aveline only for a short time in the evenings, being engaged in the counting-house from an early hour in the morning till late every day. There was a large amount of work to be done, and as Sir Thomas and Master Clough never spared themselves, so they required us, their inferiors, to labour with a like assiduity.

The state of the country was also becoming every day more and more disordered. It is only surprising that this had not occurred at an earlier period. Antwerp itself suffered, as well as other places. Bands of ruffians went about the streets at night, attacking any unarmed persons they met, and sometimes breaking into houses, when they carried off whatever they could lay hands on, and had generally decamped before the arrival of the watch or guard. At length the robbers so increased in numbers, that the ordinary watch of the town could do nothing to oppose them.

The persecutions continued as fierce as ever, the Inquisitor, Titelmann, daily citing before him persons of all ranks and callings, men and women, and compelling them by force to say whatever it pleased him. Often he did so in revenge for words which they were accused of having uttered against him, although he always used the pretext of heresy. The Government of the Regent—the Duchess of Parma—was also employed in ruining the country, edicts being passed to prohibit the importation of cloth and wool from England. Shortly after this, another edict was passed, prohibiting the importation of any merchandise or goods of any sort from England; while no Flemish goods were allowed to be exported on board English ships.

I was one evening seated at my desk at work, when the porter told me a stranger wished to see me. I went down, and as the light fell on my visitor's features, I recognised Captain Rover, who had rendered us such essential service on board the *Diamond*.

I put out my hand and shook his warmly.

"I have come to have a few words with you, Master Verner," he said, "and it maybe better that they should be in private."

I led him into the room where Sir Thomas was accustomed to receive casual visitors, and where what was said could not be overheard.

"I have come on a matter of no little importance," he said.

"A great danger threatens your friend and patron, Sir Thomas Gresham. In my last passage from England, I brought over several persons of whom I had some suspicions when they came on board; yet I did not show what I thought, and they somewhat to my surprise, seemed inclined to take me into their confidence. They were Romanists, I discovered; but as such have perfect freedom to enter or leave the country, I had no wish to molest them. One of them fell sick while on board, and, as his companions neglected him, I did my best to attend to his wants. When we arrived in harbour, I kept him on board some days, and then took him on shore, and had him attended to till he recovered. He then, it appears, joined his companions; but last night he came on board my ship, and entreated me to take him back to his native land, saying that he could have nothing more to do with those with whom he had joined himself. He told me that a villain who goes by the name of Martin has laid a plot to rob this house, and either to carry off Sir Thomas Gresham or to murder him. As he is a cunning villain, it is too likely that he will carry out his plans, if care is not taken to guard against them."

I warmly thanked Captain Rover for this information, and begged that he would allow me to bring him to Sir Thomas. He thanked me, but declined seeing my patron.

"I do not require any reward of him; and if you repeat what I have told you, my object is gained," he answered. "Perchance, some day I may make myself known to him; but at present I have no desire to meet those I once knew. I have been deprived of all I cared for or loved on earth; and, if I had the power, I would begin a new existence, so as to forget the past."

"But why not see my kind patron? he will surely not be ungrateful for the important warning you have brought him; besides, he owes you a debt of gratitude for the assistance you rendered us on board the *Diamond*. I heard him say that, could he discover you, he would thankfully repay you."

"I am sure that he would, my young friend," answered Captain Rover. "He is a just and liberal man; but I require no assistance at present; when I do, I promise you I will ask for it. And now I must bid you farewell; I have myself an important undertaking on hand. I have good reason to hate the bigoted Spaniards and their fearful idolatries, and to befriend those they persecute. I have therefore agreed to assist in the escape of a number of families who dread the persecutions of the Inquisition. Already the demon Titelmann has carried off some of their relatives to imprisonment and slaughter, and they full well know that he will treat them in the same way, if he can capture them."

"I wish that I could help you!" I exclaimed. "If you can point out how I can do so, after I have performed my duty to my employer, I will join you at any place you may indicate."

"I thank you, but you cannot do that," he answered; "I have my vessel ready for sailing, and all I could do was to let the poor people know that when they came alongside I would receive them on board. All my crew are staunch, and I have no fear that they will betray any one. The instant, therefore, the poor fugitives come alongside, they will be hoisted on board and stowed away below, so that, should a Government boat follow them, by the time the officers reach the ship there will be no one to be seen. And now, Ernst Verner, farewell. We may meet, I dare hope, again. I must hasten on board to be ready to receive the fugitives."

Chapter Seventeen
A Gale

As soon as Captain Rover had left me, I hastened to Sir Thomas. He received my information very calmly, and cross-questioned me as to all Captain Rover had said. "I wished that you had stopped him," he observed; "and yet I have no reason to doubt his information. I have already received a warning to the same effect, but was in some doubts as to the truth of the account given me. None, however, now remains on my mind. I will, therefore, follow the only prudent course: I will take my treasure and my family out of the country forthwith."

My patron was prompt in all his actions. Captain Davis was in the harbour. He instantly sent A'Dale on board to the captain, telling him to get his vessel in readiness for his reception, and desired him at the same time to send a dozen stout hands, well-armed, for the protection of some goods which he proposed to ship forthwith. Litters were ordered for Aveline and Richard. He, poor fellow, was unable to sit on horseback; indeed, Sir Thomas could scarcely have been aware of his dangerous condition, or he would not have attempted to move him, especially at night, when the damp air was so likely to increase his malady. Master Clough was not unmindful of the threatened attack on the house, and secured several porters and other trusty men for its protection. A similar body was also prepared to conduct the litters and Sir Thomas down to the water-side. The men had been summoned up one by one, and did not put on their harness till they were inside the house: thus no one was aware of the preparations we were making. The tide would not serve till an hour after midnight: we therefore waited till nearly twelve o'clock before we set out.

The horses were brought round for Sir Thomas, with four stout men-at-arms, who had been engaged as his guards. A'Dale and I went on foot; he taking care of Richard, while I walked by the side of Aveline's litter. With our swords drawn, and our pistols in our belts, ready for instant use, we proceeded along the streets. Several persons passed us, but if they were robbers, they must have seen that we were too strong a party to be attacked with impunity. Thus we reached the water-side in safety. We there found, much to our surprise, a number of people, all of them with boxes and bundles on their backs, or under their arms—quite a concourse they seemed in the gloom of night. As we entered our boat, we saw that several other boats were ready, apparently for their reception. There were old men and women and children, as well as many young men. As the boats were filled, they rowed off down the river. We could judge by their exclamations that they were in great haste, and fearful of being overtaken. At length there was a cry, "The guard is coming! the guard is coming!"

THE FUGITIVES DEFENDED THEMSELVES BRAVELY.

The men faced about and drew their weapons, while the remainder of the women and children were hurried into the boats. Then their protectors slowly retreated. The soldiers rushed forward, as they saw the number of the fugitives on shore decreasing. The latter defended themselves bravely. We were, of course, shoved off forthwith, lest the soldiers might fire on us, as we saw them doing upon the helpless people in the other boats. We judged, as we pulled down the river, from the flashes of fire-arms, that none of the fugitives were longer defending themselves on shore, but that either they had thrown themselves into the water, or had escaped in the boats, unless they had been taken prisoners. From the number of people, and the boats which were rowing down the river with us, we thought there must have been one hundred or more fugitives escaping from the fearful persecution of the terrible Inquisitor, Peter Titelmann. From what Captain Rover had told me, I concluded that these people were attempting to reach his ship. I prayed earnestly that they might do so in safety. We urged our boatmen to row as fast as they could, for now numerous lights were seen on the shore, and we feared that the emissaries of the Inquisitors were getting boats ready in order to pursue the fugitives. I knew well the sort of man with whom they would have to deal, if the latter were captured.

Aveline became as much interested as I was, when I explained what was taking place.

"I wish that I could help the poor people," she exclaimed; "but I can, at all events, pray for them!"

She did not appear in any way to think of the dangerous position in which we ourselves were placed, for there was no doubt that, should we be overtaken, we should run a great risk of being cast into the prisons of the Inquisitors. Although no building exclusively used for confining those accused of heresy had been erected in the Netherlands, the ordinary prisons were so completely under the command of the Inquisitors, that they answered every purpose of those fearful edifices which existed in Spain.

Sir Thomas sat calmly in the boat supporting Richard in his arms, and endeavouring with his cloak to protect him from the night air. As I cast my eyes back toward the town we were leaving, the number of lights increased, and some appeared to be close to the water, and moving towards us. "If our pursuers have lights in their boats, it will be an advantage to us," I thought, "as we shall be the better able to avoid them." I did not, however, mention what I had observed to our crew, who were already doing their utmost to reach the ship. At length, greatly to our satisfaction, her signal lights were seen a short distance ahead, and soon her high sides appeared rising up close before us. Aveline, with her maiden and Richard, were soon lifted on board, followed by Sir Thomas. The treasure was quickly hoisted up, and, as the breeze was favourable, the ship was immediately got under weigh. Those only who knew the river well could venture down it in the dark. Objects scarcely visible to landsmen's eyes were seen by her pilot, and thus we were able to avoid any risk of striking.

We continued on till morning at length broke, when no boats were in sight; but a short distance from us appeared a large vessel, which I had little doubt was the *Falcon*, as, having watched her earnestly when I had before crossed to England, I well remembered her appearance.

It was satisfactory, I thought, to have her near us, in case we might meet an enemy, as she was, I knew, well-armed; and I was very certain that Captain Rover would do his best to support us. I had more of Aveline's society than I had enjoyed for some time, for Sir Thomas was greatly taken up with his son. Poor Richard was evidently the worse for being out on the river at night, and his father, I think, now for the first time saw his very great danger. Aveline watched the tall ship which followed us with great interest, when I told her about the poor people who, I believed, were on board, and gave her an account of the singular man who commanded the vessel.

At length we were at sea, but the wind was so light that we made but little way. The night was very dark, and during it we lost sight of the *Falcon*. After Aveline had retired to her cabin, I observed that the captain called all the crew on deck, and ordered them to take in some of the sails and to furl the rest. I inquired why he did this.

"Because I don't like the look of the weather, Master Verner," he answered. "I may be mistaken, and we may not have a breath of wind all night, and if so, our sails will do us no good; whereas, if the gale comes down upon us, it will be well they are all snugly furled."

I agreed with him; and, with the expectation of what might occur, I could not bring myself to lie down in my cabin. I consequently continued walking the deck with him. Now he stopped and looked out over the ship's side, peering, as it were, into the darkness; now, without making any remark, he continued his walk. He was at no time very communicative, being a man rather of action than of words. He was, however, brave and true-hearted, and I felt satisfied that in no safer hands could our lives be placed. We had not taken many turns when I felt a strong, damp wind in my face, which rapidly increased. In a short time the dark water was lighted up with the foam-crested seas, which rose out of its hitherto mirror-like surface. The wind howled and whistled through the rigging, the yards creaked, stray ropes lashed about, and the foam began to fly over the decks.

The vessel, like a horse to which the spur has been given, dashed onwards, plunging and leaping, as it were, over the fast rising waves. The noise I have described increased as the vessel began to plunge more and more furiously. At first, only masses of spray broke over her; but now the seas themselves dashed upwards and washed over our deck. I had gone down below to put on my sea-coat, when I heard Sir Thomas's voice inquiring what was occurring. Aveline also asked timidly if anything serious was the matter. I could only reply that a gale had commenced, which I hoped our stout ship would without difficulty ride out. Even during the short time I had been below a change for the worse had taken place. The wind howled more furiously; the water in greater volumes burst over the vessel, and she seemed to pitch and roll more desperately than before. The captain advised me to go below, urging that the sea might wash over the deck, and perchance carry me overboard; but I begged to remain on deck, saying that I could hold on to the rigging as well as the crew. Few words were spoken; only occasionally the captain issued some orders to the helmsman or to the rest of the crew, which were quickly obeyed. At length, several heavy seas struck the ship; one came roaring up, and carried away part of her bulwarks, and a breach having thus been made, those which broke on board committed yet further damage. After a time, I heard the captain order the carpenter to sound the well. He spoke a few ominous words, on his return, to the captain. The ship had sprung a leak. Orders were given to man the pumps. And now the crew began working away with might and main. However bad the leak, they might hope to keep the water under till the ship could reach a port. Thus the night passed away. I begged that I might take my part, and laboured with the rest. I was thankful indeed to see the grey dawn slowly break upon the world of waters. On every side the dark green seas were rolling and leaping up, thickly crested with masses of foam, which flew off their tops, and danced from sea to sea. No other vessel was in sight. The dark clouds hung down, as it were, covering the ocean with a thick canopy. The leak would allow of no rest to the crew. As soon as one party of men grew tired, others took their places. Several times I threw myself down on the deck to regain my strength.

I was thus lying down near the companion-hatch, when I saw a figure standing close to me. It was Aveline. She gazed about her with a look of astonishment and awe, but when her eyes fell on me, her countenance exhibited an expression of consternation. "Oh! Ernst Verner, what has happened? are you hurt?" she exclaimed.

I rose as she spoke, assuring her that I had suffered no harm, and at the same time entreating her to return to the cabin, lest one of the furious seas which ever and anon swept over the deck might carry her into the raging ocean.

"But the same fate might befall you," she said. "Oh, Ernst, how fearful!"

I showed her that I was holding on to a ring-bolt in the deck, and that the risk I ran when thus lying down was not so great as she had supposed. As I was speaking, I saw a sea rising high above the bows of the vessel. I had just time to grasp her in my arms, and to spring under shelter of the companion-hatch, before it broke on board, and rushed as others had done along our deck. Not without difficulty I saved her from injury, and, descending the ladder, placed her in the cabin, where her maiden was sitting crying bitterly with alarm. On the other side was Sir Thomas, supporting poor Richard. He himself had been too often at sea not to have been placed before in a like position, though he seemed scarcely aware how furious was the gale then blowing, nor had he been told, I found, how serious was the leak the vessel had sprung. The crew continued working energetically at the pumps; and I judged by the way the captain and mates urged them to persevere, themselves working like the rest, that the water in the hold had in no way been got under. The captain and his officers were brave men; but their countenances grew pale with anxiety, and I saw them looking constantly round the horizon in search of some vessel which might come to our assistance. At length I asked Captain Davis what he thought of our condition.

"To be frank with you, I think very bad of it, Master Verner," he said. "If the gale abates, the ship may be kept afloat; but if not, all our efforts will be unavailing; and then, unless some vessel comes to our assistance, drowning must be our lot!"

My heart sank at these words, for I had not before realised our danger. Should I go and tell those below to be prepared for death? I had not the heart to do it. At that instant my post at the pumps was left by another man. I rushed frantically at it, and worked away with might and main. As long as I was in action, I could keep off the painful thoughts which pressed on me. Was I prepared for death? Yes, I had settled that matter as every man ought to settle it; if he does not, wretched is his condition when the hour of trial arrives; but I thought of others, — my kind patron, of his gentle son, but, more than all, of Aveline, so young, so fair, thus to be summoned out of the world. Yet, surely there must be hope. I looked at the boats.

"We can be saved in them, captain," I said.

"They would not live a moment in such a sea as this," he answered.

"Then we can construct some rafts?"

He shook his head.

"The strongest man would quickly be washed off them. No, Ernst Verner, we are in God's hands. If He orders the storm and seas, they will obey Him. I know thus much about religion. We will make another effort to get at the leak, but not for a moment can we desert the pumps. Already the ship labours heavily, and a few more feet of water in her hold will carry her to the bottom."

The captain was as good as his word. A sail was got over the bows, and hauled by ropes under the ship, where the leak was supposed to be. This done, a party of men descended with bedding and clothes, and such loose stuff as could be found, in order to ram it into the leak. It seemed that these efforts were not altogether unavailing, for though the water still increased, it did so less rapidly than before. Hour after hour passed by, and I judged from the looks of the captain, and the way he spoke, that he was still very anxious.

"We can but prolong our lives," he remarked at length. "The men are now almost worn-out, and cannot, I see, continue much longer at work." Even as he spoke, several of the crew left their posts, and, throwing themselves on the deck, declared that they could do no more. Others murmured out that the ship was sinking. Some begged that spirits might be given to them.

At this juncture, as I was gazing round the horizon, my eye fell on a white spot rising above the dancing seas. At first I thought it was but a sea-gull's wing, or it might be the crest of a wave higher than those near us. I called the attention of one of the mates, who was standing near me, to it. He looked at it anxiously for some time. At length he shouted, "A sail! a sail! Cheer up, lads!"

The cry was taken up by the men. Those who had thrown themselves on the deck leaped to their feet, and once more seized the handles of the pumps. Nearer and nearer drew the ship. The wind too, I thought, was also abating.

"Cheer up, lads! cheer up!" shouted the captain ever and anon, as the men appeared to be relaxing their efforts at the pumps. "You will see your homes again, never fear, if you keep moving smartly!" Still, although the crew worked on bravely, the water continued pouring in, and rising higher and higher. It needed not now for any one to tell Sir Thomas Gresham or his companions in the cabin of the danger we were in, for already the water was rising to their feet. They now rushed with scared looks on deck; Sir Thomas supporting his son in his arms, followed by Aveline and her maiden.

Seeing the way in which the men were working at the pumps, Sir Thomas, placing Richard under shelter within the companion-hatch, seized a handle, and began himself working away like the rest.

"You should have told me of this before," he observed. "I had no right to be excused labouring with others."

His example had the effect of encouraging the crew, who even now had begun to relax somewhat in their efforts.

A signal of distress had been hoisted. It was seen by the approaching vessel. I judged from her appearance that she was the *Falcon*, and Captain Davis told me I was right. Night, however, was approaching, and the difficulty of reaching her would be greatly increased by the darkness. On she came, and by this time the sea had so much gone down, that boats could be lowered from her without difficulty. Two were seen let into the water, and, propelled by sturdy crews, they approached our ship. Sir Thomas at that time thought little of the wealth on board the *Diamond*. His desire was to save the lives of his son and those with him, but Richard seemed to engross almost all his thoughts. He scarcely regarded himself, so it seemed to me. Even though the boats were approaching, the captain urged the crew to keep to the pumps.

"Lads," he exclaimed, "it would be a base thing to let this fine ship sink beneath our feet, if any exertion of ours can keep her afloat!"

"Think not of the wealth on board, but rather run no risk of losing your own life and that of your companions, Master Davis," said Sir Thomas.

By this time the boats had come alongside.

The first who leaped out of them on to the deck of the sinking ship was Captain Rover. A glance showed him our condition, and he seemed to recognise Sir Thomas, though he did not address him by name.

"We will convey you safely on board my ship, sir," he said, "with those who cannot work; but I never let a stout ship sink under me if I can keep her afloat; and perchance a few fresh hands will help her to do that, if my friend here, Captain Davis, will accept their services."

Captain Davis's countenance brightened, and cordially thanking his brother captain, he accepted his offer.

"You shall have half a dozen of my men for those who are already knocked up," said Captain Rover.

Meantime Aveline and her maiden had been carefully lowered into one of the boats. Sir Thomas and Richard followed.

"Can I desert my charge?" I said to myself. "No; that were a disgrace while I have strength. If Captain Davis remains, so will I."

I did not forget Aveline when I came to this resolution. It was in spite of the strong wish I had to accompany her. Yet she would be in safety on board the *Falcon*, and I trusted that the *Diamond* would yet swim, and enter port at last. I therefore bade Sir Thomas farewell, telling him that I would remain by the ship and her cargo, of which I had charge.

"You do well, Ernst," he exclaimed; "and your service shall not be forgotten."

I fancied, but it might have been vanity, that Aveline looked up at me anxiously, as if she wished that I had accompanied her; but my resolve was taken, I was doing my duty, and prepared for the consequences.

Captain Rover, with our worn-out men and passengers, returned to the *Falcon*; while we, once more making sail, stood on our course towards the mouth of the Thames. The six fresh hands which had been left with us soon reduced the depth of water in the hold. Yet as night came on our anxiety returned. Though the wind had fallen, the sea was still somewhat rough, and the night was dark, and we could with difficulty keep the *Falcon* in sight. As the wind fell, a fog came on, and at last completely shut her out. Thus we were all alone on the dark ocean. Now and then the men at the pumps would cheer and pass jokes to each other, but those who had knocked off lay without speaking, resting from their toil. The only other sound was the creaking of the yards against the masts, and the splashing of the sea against the vessel's bows. I had had no rest the previous night; at length, overcome with fatigue, I descended to the cabin, and threw myself into my berth. I had scarcely time to offer up a prayer before my eyelids closed in sleep. And yet, while I asked for my own safety, more fervently did I petition for that of Aveline. The cabin, and many of the articles which she had left about in the hurried departure from the ship, brought her vividly to my mind. Yet surely I did not require any visible things to recall her. I knew full well that there were still many dangers to be encountered. Another gale might arise. Even the *Falcon* might spring a leak, or be driven on rocks or quicksands, while there were many pirates cruising about, some French and others Flemish, on the look-out for merchantmen sailing without a convoy of men-of-war.

Chapter Eighteen
The "Beggars."

I do not think I shall ever get the sound of those clanging pumps out of my ears. Daylight returned, but a thick mist hung over the sea, and concealed all objects from sight. The ocean was now calm; we wished indeed that there had been more wind, that we might with greater speed finish our voyage. At length, as the sun rose higher in the sky, his warm beams dispelled the mist, while a breeze from the south filled our sails, and once more we glided rapidly through the water. We looked round for the *Falcon*. No vessel answering her description was visible, but in the south-west were two or three sail. The *Falcon* was not likely to have been in that position. We only hoped that, should they draw near to us, they might prove friends. Now we set all the sail the vessel could carry; indeed, every one on board was anxious to take her home in safety, knowing the reward they would receive for so doing. As the day advanced, two of the strangers drew nearer. They were tall ships, their hulls being high out of the water, and their masts crowded with sail, towering above them. Our captain regarded them attentively.

"They may be friends," he observed; "but it is not impossible that they are foes, and we shall do well to keep out of their way."

The wind now favoured us, coming still more astern; and long yards were rigged out on either side of the vessel, from which sails were hung close down to the water. Active seamen went aloft and hoisted other masts with yards and sails above those already set. To the extreme yard-arm also spars were run out, from which more canvas was hung. Thus, like some winged creature, we glided rapidly over the smooth sea.

We watched the strangers. The more our captain looked at them, the more he was convinced that they were French. It was doubtful at first whether, with all our exertions, we were getting ahead of our pursuers. If taken, we should not only lose the wealth committed to our charge, but be ourselves placed in prison; and the French had a bad name for the way in which they treated their prisoners. The more anxious we appeared to be to escape, the more eager our pursuers evidently became to overtake us. They also, as they got the wind astern, set fresh sails; and it was evident that we no longer increased our distance from them, rather at times we feared the contrary. We ran on, and, had the ship been free of water, we might probably have distanced our pursuers. Still hope kept us up. At night we might have a better prospect of escaping, but night was still far-distant. On looking ahead, we observed in the horizon another sail. After looking at her for some time, we were convinced that she was standing the same way that we were; therefore, even if a friend, she would not render us any assistance.

We stood on, but every hour showed that our pursuers were gaining on us. But we also were gaining on the vessel ahead. And now, as we looked, another appeared. She, too, was a tall ship. Though we saw her, our pursuers did not; and thus, as I before said, we continued to run on, the chances of our escaping lessening every hour. At length, a flash and a puff of smoke were seen, and the sound of a gun came rolling over the water.

"Your shot will not reach us yet, my friends!" exclaimed Captain Davis; "and while you are inclined to play at long bowls, we need not fear you." Another and another followed, till the enemy ceased firing, seeing that their shot fell short. The sound, however, had the effect of calling the attention of the vessels ahead, and we now saw them coming round to the wind and standing toward us. There were two tall ships, and a third much smaller. As they approached, our pursuers seemed to think that they had followed us far enough. All their light sails were taken in, and they now also hauled to the wind. The two tall ships were evidently English men-of-war, while the third was, as I had supposed, the *Falcon*. As she passed us, Captain Rover hailed, desiring us to continue our course, saying that he would keep us company, while the men-of-war would pursue the enemy. We had now a friend near us; and although the leak gave us ample employment, we at length safely entered the Thames.

The wind continuing favourable, we ran up, and came to an anchor off the Tower.

The fugitives at once landed, and joined their countrymen who had already settled in England. The Government of the Queen had wisely and liberally made all possible arrangements for their accommodation; abodes, and places of worship where they might hold their services according to the Protestant form, being assigned to them.

I proceeded at once on board the *Falcon*, and was amply repaid for the risk I had run by the reception I met with from my kind patron. Aveline's welcome also was abundantly gratifying. I was on this occasion much struck by the way in which Captain Rover regarded the young lady.

"Yes," I heard him say to himself; "if it were not for the difference of age, I could believe that one whom I know is now in heaven had returned once more to earth. Strange! most strange!"

He did not give me an opportunity of inquiring what he meant. Indeed, it was said only as we were about to leave the ship, and to proceed to Sir Thomas Gresham's new house in Bishopsgate Street.

Lady Anne was at this time residing at Osterley. Sir Thomas therefore remained at Gresham House only one day, in order that Richard's strength might be somewhat recruited. We then proceeded to Osterley House, a beautiful residence which Sir Thomas had lately purchased, ten miles out of London. On the approach of our cavalcade, Lady Anne hurried down to welcome her husband and son, as well as Aveline, with open arms. I saw her countenance fall as her eyes rested on Richard. She, at a glance, discovered, what his father had yet scarcely done, that he was greatly altered; for he had become daily weaker since we left Antwerp. The best physicians from London were called in, but they could give no hope to the fond parents; and Sir Thomas became fully aware that he must be prepared to lose his only son. The blow was a heavy one. My patron was a strong-minded man, accustomed to deal with characters of all sorts; but his diplomatic powers, his financial talents, could here avail him nothing. He almost succumbed under the heavy sorrow. Even before he expected, Richard breathed his last. He knew, however, that the same Hand which had given him worldly prosperity had taken away his son, and he submitted without murmuring. He said little, but he suffered none the less. The pleasant house had become a house of mourning. Aveline, with all a daughter's tenderness, endeavoured to soothe the sorrow of her kind mistress; and when I next paid a visit to Osterley, I was thankful to see that both my patron and his lady had regained their usual tranquil manner. Sir Thomas had entertained the thought, common to most men who have gained rank and honours, of building up a house. The death of his son altered all his projects. He now began to speak to me of the duty of public men, who have wealth at their command, undertaking works for the general benefit of their countrymen. Numerous projects passed through his mind.

We had been one day in London, standing out in Lombard Street, where the merchants were wont to meet to transact business, and had been exposed to much damp and cold; the heavy rain frequently compelling us, with other persons, to seek shelter in the shops near where we happened to be standing, when, on our return to Gresham House, Sir Thomas exclaimed:

"Why should not a great commercial city like London possess a Bourse like that of Antwerp? It would be a great benefit to our merchants; and yet I fear that unless some private person undertakes it, we may never see such a building erected. The Government, provided they obtain the money for their wants, can scarcely be expected to care how their merchants are lodged."

I, of course, agreed with Sir Thomas, that such a building was very desirable; but that I scarcely expected that any one would be found public-spirited enough to erect it at his own expense.

"Nay," he said, "but if a man has the means, and the thought is put into his heart, it is his duty to carry it out."

To plan, with Sir Thomas, was in most cases to execute. At his dictation, I wrote out a proposal, in which he offered to build a Bourse, or Exchange, at his own expense, for the accommodation of the merchants, provided a site should be found on which the edifice might be conveniently erected. One of his principal clerks—Anthony Strynger—was directed the next day, the 4th of January, 1565, to make the proposal in due form before the Court of Aldermen. At first it was proposed to establish it in Leadenhall. But Sir Thomas wished to erect his building in the close vicinity of Lombard Street, so that the merchants might not be moved to any distance from their original place of meeting. His magnificent offer was at once accepted, and a subscription was entered into by the merchants for purchasing a piece of ground in the position he indicated. Some time, however, passed before the stone of the foundation was laid. The ceremony took place on the 7th of June, 1567; but so diligently did the workmen perform their task, that the whole was finished by the end of November in the same year. I should say that during the period I have mentioned I was sent over to Antwerp—as was also one of my patron's apprentices, John Worrall—to assist Master Clough in purchasing materials for the Bourse. The architect of the building was Flemish—Master Henryke by name. We shipped large quantities of stone, as also much of the woodwork, from the Netherlands. All the wainscoting was made at Antwerp, as was also the glass for the windows. It was adorned with numerous statues. Most of them were executed in England; but Sir Thomas desired to have one, superior to the rest, of the Queen's Majesty. This was executed in Antwerp, and received great commendation. We shipped iron also, and the slates with which the building was roofed. I now continued to reside in Flanders, where Sir Thomas only occasionally paid a visit, as business of importance demanded his presence. Master Clough, having become weary of a single life, had gone to his native country—Wales—and had there found an amiable lady to his taste, and with her he had lately returned to Antwerp, there to resume his office as Sir Thomas Gresham's chief factor. My old friend A'Dale had been residing there ever since the time I last spoke of him, and frequently I had letters from him describing events which had taken place. From these I have noted down the more important points of interest by which my friends in after years may be able to understand the state of the Low Countries at that time.

Before I commence that brief narrative, however, I must say that Aveline continued to reside with Lady Anne, and truly to act towards her the part of a loving daughter. I had for some time entertained hopes that the young lady was not altogether indifferent to me. That I myself loved her I had long since discovered. I had, however, as yet not the means of supporting her in that state to which, through the kindness of our friends, she had been accustomed. I spoke, it may be remembered, of a document which had been placed in my hands by her martyred mother. On examination it was found that it related to an estate which was rightfully the property of her father; but without his appearance to claim it, she herself could not take possession of it. Sir Thomas had expressed his readiness to endeavour to obtain it for her; but on consulting the lawyers they decided that this could not be done. Her father—Master Radford—had been outlawed in the reign of King Henry for holding heretical opinions; and unless he should appear and obtain a reversion of that outlawry, the estate would remain forfeited. By petitioning the Queen's Majesty, however, there would be no difficulty in obtaining this reversion. But Master Radford had not appeared; and great doubts were entertained whether he was still in existence.

Oftentimes I thought of expressing my wishes to Sir Thomas, and entreating him to place me in some position where my means would be sufficient for the maintenance of a wife; but yet, owing everything as I did to him, I felt that I ought to wait until he should propose to advance me, being sure that, had I patience, this he would certainly do at some time. I may mention also that Captain Davis was continually employed in the service of Sir Thomas, especially in bringing over the materials for the Bourse. Of my friend Captain Rover, however, I in vain attempted to gain tidings. He had again left England on a long voyage; his ship, the *Falcon*, being employed by a company of merchant adventurers.

I have already spoken of the fearful persecutions to which the inhabitants of the Netherlands were subjected by the officers of the Inquisition.

At length they could no longer submit to the tyranny under which they groaned. Some of the principal nobles of the land resolved to oppose the bloody edicts of King Philip. Among the chief was Philip de Marnix, Lord of Sainte Aldegonde, a Protestant nobleman and a true patriot. He having collected a number of other leading men of a similar character, they drew up a document called "The Compromise," by which all the signers bound themselves to oppose the Inquisition, and to defend each other against all the consequences of such a resistance. At the same time they professed allegiance to the King, pretending to suppose that he was unacquainted with the tyranny exercised over his subjects. Among those who first signed this document were Louis of Nassau, brother of the Prince of Orange, Henry de Brederode, the Counts of Culembourg and De Berg. De Brederode at the commencement took the leading part in this movement.

But all eyes were turned towards William of Nassau, Prince of Orange. He was nominally a minister of the Regent, and Governor of the Provinces of Holland and Zealand; but it was well-known that his heart was with his fellow-countrymen. Some of the people, however, looked towards Lamoral Count Egmont, who was considered the best soldier of his time; and it was thought he would hasten to the relief of the country. Count Horn, Admiral of the Seas, noted for his bravery, was also considered a patriot likely to come forward in the cause of liberty.

At length, the Compromise having been signed by a large number of noblemen and gentlemen, it was resolved to present the petition to the Regent, then holding her court at Brussels. Master Clough, hearing what was about to take place, sent me over there to gain information. I arrived on the 3rd of April, 1566.

On the evening of that day notice was given that a cavalcade of noblemen was entering the city, and I, with many thousands of the citizens, hurried out to meet it. There were at least two hundred noblemen on horseback, all magnificently dressed, with pistols in their holsters, and swords by their sides. Count Brederode rode at their head—a tall, stout man, with a soldier-like bearing and handsome features, his light curling locks hanging down over his shoulders. Close to him rode Count Louis of Nassau, one of the bravest and most gallant of knights. As the cavalcade advanced, slowly making its way through the streets, it was greeted from all sides with frequent demonstrations of applause. The two Counts alighted at the house of the Prince of Orange, while the rest of the company, with their numerous attendants, separated to other parts of the city. The following day the Counts Culembourg and De Berg entered the city with a hundred other cavaliers. The 5th of April was the day fixed for presenting the petition. The confederates assembled at the mansion of Count Culembourg, a short distance from the palace where the Duchess Margaret was prepared to receive them. It was a brave sight to see these three hundred young noblemen, arrayed in the most magnificent costumes, walking arm in arm through the street. There was little doubt of the risk they ran, but they had resolved to attempt the deliverance of their country from Spanish tyranny. The daughter of Charles the Fifth received them in the very hall where he had abdicated his throne, many of the nobles who appeared on that occasion being present. Among them were Orange and Egmont. Brederode, advancing, addressed the Duchess, expressing his devotion both to her and to the King, at the same time pointing out that the edicts and the Inquisition would certainly produce a general rebellion if continued. He stated, also, that there was not a man in the country, whatever his condition, who was not liable at any moment to lose his life under the edicts; and that the life and property of each individual were in the power of the first man who desired to obtain his estate, and chose to denounce him to an Inquisitor. He requested, therefore, that her Highness would despatch an envoy to the King, and that in the meantime the Inquisitors should be directed no longer to exercise their functions. Among those who stood near the Duchess was the Baron Berlaymont, who, in a voice stifled with passion, though still loud enough for the petitioners to hear, exclaimed:

"Is it possible that your Highness can entertain fears of these beggars (gueux)? See! there is not one of them who has not outgrown his estate!"

The same remark was repeated in the hearing of some of the confederates. On their meeting afterwards at a banquet prepared in the Culembourg mansion, after the wine had freely circulated, Brederode rose. He well knew the feelings which the remark I have mentioned had excited in the breasts of the confederates.

"They call us *beggars*!" he shouted, in a scornful tone. "The joke is a good one. Let us accept the name; we will contend with the abominable Inquisition till compelled to wear the beggar's sack in reality!"

He then called one of his pages, who brought him a leathern wallet, such as are worn by mendicants, and a large wooden bowl.

Hanging the wallet round his neck, he filled the bowl with wine, and lifting it with both hands, he drained it at a draught.

"Long live the beggars!" he cried, as he wiped his beard and put the bowl down.

"Long live the beggars!" resounded through the hall. The bowl went round, and each noble, pushing his golden goblet aside, and filling the bowl to the brim, drank the same toast: "*Vivent les Gueux!*"

The wine continued to flow fast. While the conviviality was at its height, the Prince of Orange, with Counts Horn and Egmont, made their appearance. Immediately they were surrounded by the now half-intoxicated beggars, who compelled each of them to drink from the bowl, amid shouts of "*Vivent le Roi et les Gueux!*"

Chapter Nineteen
Image-breaking in Antwerp

From this time forward Antwerp was in a state of constant excitement and commotion. Count Brederode took up his quarters in the city, and daily entertained a crowd of nobles at his hotel, stirring them up to oppose the Government. Count Meghem, the great enemy of the Reformers, also came into the city; and it was supposed that he was laying a plan for the introduction of a garrison, and for collecting a store of ammunition to overawe the inhabitants. The chief people of the city, therefore, resolved to send to the Prince of Orange, to request his presence, in order to try and pacify all parties. He reached Antwerp on the 13th of July. The inhabitants of the city were wild with enthusiasm at the thought of his coming. Thousands, I may say tens of thousands, from all parts of the city went forth from the gates to bid him welcome. A'Dale and I were among the number. The road along which he was to pass for miles was lined with human beings. The roofs of the houses—the ramparts—every spot whence a sight of the street could be obtained, was packed close with eager and expectant faces. A long cavalcade of citizens, with Count Brederode and a number of confederates, rode forth to escort him into the city. As soon as he appeared at the head of a small body of gentlemen, his demeanour calm and unmoved, Brederode and his companions fired a salute from their pistols. It was the signal for loud and reiterated shouts from the assembled multitude, while again and again the cry of "Long live the Beggars!" was repeated. In vain the Prince entreated them not to utter that cry.

"I have come," he said, "not to side with any party, but to endeavour to restore tranquillity to the city."

The general feeling was that he had both the power and ability to keep his word. Day after day he was engaged in endeavouring to quiet the public mind. All classes of the people were consulted. At length it was agreed that the exercise of the Reformed religion should be excluded from the city, but tolerated in the suburbs; and that an armed force of the citizens should be kept in readiness to suppress insurrection. To these arrangements the people agreed, and the Regent highly commended the Prince for what he had done: King Philip pretended also to approve of his conduct, but in reality took no steps to abolish the Inquisition or to renounce persecution. He, as was suspected, only awaited his time to destroy the Prince himself.

Shortly after this the Prince was called away to Brussels, to attend a council held by the Regent. About the same time a meeting of the confederates had been held in Duffel, the result of which was that Louis of Nassau, with twelve associates, laid before the Regent a statement of their views. They declared that they were ever ready to mount and ride against a foreign foe, but that they would never draw a sword to injure their innocent countrymen. Their proposals were received with a very bad grace by the Regent, whom they quitted, most of them feeling that the only resource left was to draw the sword in defence of their country.

No sooner had the Prince of Orange left Antwerp than the city was once more thrown into a state of commotion. I should mention that Antwerp contains numerous fine and richly adorned churches: the largest is that of Our Lady, which King Philip a short time before had converted into a cathedral.

Close to the chief entrance I had frequently seen an old woman — Barbara Trond by name — who gained her livelihood by the sale of wax tapers, little leaden ornaments of the Virgin and saints, and other Papistical trickeries. She managed also to gain many a coin by the persuasive powers of her tongue, which she wagged with considerable effect on all occasions. When she pleased, nothing could be more smooth and oily; but when angered, that tongue could utter oaths and abuse with unsurpassed vehemence. One morning A'Dale and I were strolling beside the cathedral, when a small party of idle boys and ragamuffins happened to come that way intent on mischief, if they could possibly achieve it. One of them with a grave air walked up to the old woman's table, and, taking a taper in one hand and a saint in the other, inquired the price of the articles. A loud laugh followed her reply.

"What! your whole stock in trade is not worth a tenth of the sum. Your saints if melted together would scarcely make one decent-sized bullet, and all your candles would not afford light sufficient to an honest weaver during the labours of one winter evening. Give up selling such trash, Dame Trond; try and make a livelihood in some more respectable calling!"

Such and similar remarks quickly excited the ire of old Barbara. Her replies were not such as to soothe the tempers of those who stood by her.

Gibes and shouts of laughter proceeded from every side, till the old dame, giving way to the fury of her temper, seized the stool on which she sat, and began to lay about her on every side. In an instant, the mob charged the table on which her wares were spread for exhibition, and trampled them on the ground. She retreating, and flourishing her stool, entered the cathedral, where they with shouts of laughter followed her. We should have been wise if we had kept out of the church, but instead of that we could not resist the temptation of following the old woman's pursuers, as did numbers of others who were near at the time. Her courage was worthy of a better cause, not that any one really attempted to injure her—though she, as she went up the church, seized whatever came in her way, and hurled it at the heads of her assailants. The shouts of the rabble attracted others from a distance, and thus in a short time the cathedral was full of people; some, like Barbara Trond's first assailants, inclined for mischief, but a large number merely spectators, as we were. The mob began to shout now one thing, now another. "Down with these Romish mummeries! down with the idols!" were the cries we chiefly heard. The crowd surged to and fro, but contented themselves with merely shouting, without attempting to commit any mischief. It was evident, however, that to this they would soon proceed, as several persons had already hurried off to the Town House to give information of the outbreak to the magistrates. In a short time a body of these dignitaries, in their robes of state, were seen entering the cathedral, headed by the Margrave of Antwerp—John Van Immerzeel—the two burgomasters walking on either side of him, and the senators following. He stopped in the centre of the church, and harangued the mob. By his persuasions those on the outside agreed to take their departure, hoping that their example might be followed by the rest. But the hour of evening service was approaching, and the ragamuffin crew, who certainly cared very little for masses or services of any sort, declared that they could not think of leaving the church until they had enjoyed the benefit of that about to be performed. In reply, they were told that no vespers would be held that night, and were again entreated to disperse.

"If we go, the people will follow," observed one of the burgomasters to the Margrave. "Let all the doors be closed, except the one out of which we go, and the people will swarm out like bees from their hive."

Thankful to get out of the church with whole skins, the magistrates marched forth in as dignified a manner as they could assume. The Margrave, however, remained behind, endeavouring to persuade those who were still in the church to retreat. But the rabble were not in a humour to be persuaded.

Something said by the Margrave offended them, and, in spite of his threats and exhortations, they rushed on him and sent him ignominiously flying out of the church. They instantly threw open all the other portals, and the populace, who had been retiring like an ebbing tide, now rushed back, and flowed into the building, raging and foaming like an angry sea.

A'Dale and I had remained at the further end of the church, unable, without mixing with the crowd, to make our escape. Those who had charge of the building made a vain attempt to carry off some of its more precious possessions, but they had to retreat before the threatening aspect of the crowd. Instead of the expected vespers, a hymn was raised by the multitude who filled the church. At that moment, perhaps many who joined in it hoped that it would have the effect of tranquillising the multitude. Scarcely, however, had it concluded before a band of the most ruffianly-looking of the assemblage united together, and, as if with one accord, made a rush at the figure of the Virgin—the same idol which had been carried about the city a few days previously. Before any one could interfere, it was dragged from its pedestal and hurled to the ground. It was immediately set upon, the rich robes were torn off it, and with axes and hammers, wielded by brawny arms, the figure in a few minutes was hewn into a thousand pieces, which were scattered over the floor. A wild shout of triumph succeeded. All sorts of weapons of destruction were now produced by the mob. Some had sledge-hammers in their hands, others axes, and others bludgeons; while ladders, handspikes, and ropes and blocks were brought into the church. Immediately they went to work. The images which could be most easily got at were hurled from their niches, and the pictures were torn from the walls, and the painted windows shivered to atoms. Some of the men were seen climbing up the carved work, striking with their hammers on every side; others, placing ladders against the walls or columns, ascended to dizzy heights, with ropes and blocks, and pulled down the ornaments which were otherwise out of reach. The wax candles were seized from the altars, and held by some of the party to light the others in executing their task. Everything was done in the most systematic manner. There were no less than seven chapels in the cathedral, every one of which in succession was utterly spoilt. Chests of treasure were broken open, and the gorgeous robes of the priests dragged forth, many of the mob attiring themselves in them. Casks of wine were broached and the liquor poured into the golden chalices, out of which the despoilers quaffed huge draughts to the Beggars' health. Splendid manuscripts were torn into sheds; and in a short time the interior of the richest church in the Netherlands was an utter wreck. But poor as were the despoilers, not a particle of gold or silver did any of them carry off. The ground was literally strewn with cups and ornaments of precious metals, and jewels, and embroidered garments, broken, torn, and defaced, in every possible way, mingled with the marble fragments of the images and the rich and elaborate carvings which had been cast to the ground.

Their work being complete, the band of image-breakers, each seizing a burning torch, rushed forth from the cathedral, and, as they swept through the streets, shouted with loud and hoarse voices, "Long live the Beggars!" On they went. Every crucifix, every image of the Virgin or other idol, every symbol of Romanism, was dashed to pieces. With sturdy blows they burst open the doors of the next church they reached. In they rushed with their ladders, and sledge-hammers, and other weapons, and in a short time all the images, and all the ornaments were hurled to the ground and broken in pieces. Church after church felt the effects of their fury; none escaped. With wonderful rapidity the interiors were completely gutted.

Although by this time the streets were full of people, yet but a small band—it was generally thought not more than one hundred men—performed the whole of the work. They probably had many friends and supporters; but it was strange that no one should have attempted to interfere with them.

The authorities were completely panic-struck, expecting that their own Town Hall would be the next attacked. From the churches they went to the convents, which they treated in the same way. All the altars, statues, and pictures were utterly destroyed; and, to punish the monks, they descended into the cellars, where they broached every cask they found, pouring out the wine in one great flood, though abstaining from drinking it themselves. The inmates of the nunneries fled, and in all directions they were seen in the streets, rushing here and there, shrieking and crying out as if they were pursued. Their terror, however, was imaginary, for, savage as the image-breakers might have appeared, they had but one object in view, and not a nun or monk was in the slightest degree injured. In the prison of the Barefooted Monastery they found an unhappy monk who had been shut up for twelve years for his heretical opinions, and with loud shouts of joy they liberated him from his dungeon.

When morning dawned, it was found that the interiors of no less than thirty churches inside the walls had been utterly destroyed. Not a graven image, scarcely a picture, remained in any of them.

We were out all night watching what was going forward. I, of course, have given but a very brief account of all the events which took place.

When we returned, Master Clough was not a little angry with us for having gone without his leave, although he was willing enough to receive the account we had to give him. He talked indeed of reporting us to Sir Thomas as idle varlets, who did as little as they could for their pay.

More came out of this matter, as might be expected, as I shall have shortly to describe.

Chapter Twenty
Adventure with a Witch

Master Clough punished me for what he was pleased to call my idle behaviour, during the time of the breaking of the images, by making me copy out the whole of a long letter he wrote to Sir Thomas Gresham, giving an account of the affair. He acknowledged that the mob, although he called them ruffianly rascals, had evidently been influenced by one sole motive, that was—to do away with all the symbols of Popery; that neither man nor woman had been in the slightest degree injured, nor a single article (great as was the value of many of them) appropriated by the image-breakers.

Shortly after this we were as usual seated at our desks working away, for Master Clough kept us well employed, when a courier entered the office. He brought the information that Sir Thomas Gresham had landed at Ostend two days before from England, accompanied by a lady, and that he hoped to arrive the following day at Antwerp. Preparations were instantly made for his reception. A'Dale and I were not a little interested in trying to guess who the lady could be. We cross-questioned the courier, but all we could learn from him was that the lady was not Lady Anne Gresham; indeed, he had supposed, from the way Sir Thomas treated her, that she must be his daughter. She was also, we discovered, young and fair. I had some hesitation in asking the man these questions. Her name he did not know. I strongly suspected that she must be Aveline Radford.

Madam Clough, however, at all events seemed to know all about her, and was preparing a room, though I must own that I did not venture to inquire of that lady. I have said very little about Madam Clough hitherto. She was a very good woman, but, in our estimation, not to be compared to Lady Anne. She demanded far more attention and respect as her due, and never allowed us the slightest approach to intimacy; indeed, she seemed to consider that we were in all respects her inferiors. Still she was, as I have said, a worthy woman, and knew how to do her duty. She was inclined to be charitable, as far as helping those who came to her in distress; and I have no doubt that in her own place at Plasclough, in Denbighshire, where she and her husband resided when making holiday, she acted the Lady Bountiful to perfection.

It must be confessed that, after the news we had received, I felt a strange trepidation at my heart, and made a variety of mistakes in the letters I was inditing, for which I received due verbal castigation from Master Clough. What other young lady could be coming besides Aveline? A'Dale, I rather suspect, hoped, for his own sake, that she might be some stranger; for though he admired Aveline, yet he was aware of my feelings with regard to her, and he was too true a friend to wish to interfere in the matter.

I slept very little, it must be owned, that night. I was thinking of Aveline—how she would appear; how she would treat me: whether, in the light of an old friend, or, after having seen so many great and wealthy people, be inclined to look upon me as her inferior. I kept twisting and turning the subject in every possible way, till I made myself perfectly miserable; and it was not till at last I thought that perhaps, after all, the lady who was expected might not be Aveline, that I dropped to sleep.

A bright idea occurred to me in the morning. It would be but respectful if A'Dale and I were to ride out to meet Sir Thomas Gresham as he approached Antwerp. I suggested the same to Master Clough, and, having got through all the work he required of us at an early hour, we were perfectly ready to set forth. He threw no objection in the way. We therefore ordered our horses, and as soon as we could with decency leave the office, we rode forth by the northern gate from the city. We, I must confess, had calculated, from the information gained from the courier, that Sir Thomas would not arrive for at least two or three hours after that time. We should thus have an opportunity of meeting him and his companions at some distance from the city, and enjoy the pleasure of riding back with them. We rode on for some distance, till at length we began to hope that we might soon fall in with the expected travellers. Every cloud of dust which appeared rising ahead of us gave us hopes that they were coming. As we drew nearer, and figures appeared through the cloud of dust, my heart beat quicker. A few minutes more showed us a party of travelling merchants, with their packs on led horses.

"That must be them!" exclaimed A'Dale, as another cloud rose in front of us.

We pushed on eagerly. They were a band of a dozen or more horsemen. The serviceable swords, with the hilts ready to their hands, which they wore at their sides, the pistols in their belts, and the arquebuses slung across their saddles, gave them a somewhat suspicious appearance. They eyed us narrowly, but we put on a bold and independent look. It struck me that the traders we had passed a short time before would not have been well pleased to have fallen in with them, nor would, I suspect, Sir Thomas Gresham and his companions. Thus we were doomed several times to disappointment. At length we rode on for some distance without meeting any one. The day was advancing, and we began to fear that Sir Thomas had for some reason stopped on the way.

"Well, then, all we have to do is to turn our horses and ride back again," said A'Dale.

As he spoke, however, I thought I saw another light cloud of dust. I pointed it out to him.

"We will go on for ten minutes more, and then, if Sir Thomas does not appear, we will do as you propose," I said.

As we rode on, I more than once stood up in my stirrups, eagerly looking forward, for I felt convinced that another party of travellers were approaching. I was not mistaken. The cloud of dust rose higher and higher above the horizon, and beneath it, at length, horses and riders were seen. We pushed on with more confidence. As we advanced, we could distinguish a tall cavalier on a stout horse, and a lady riding a palfrey by his side. About that there was no doubt. We felt sure it must be Sir Thomas and his expected female companion. I thought I could distinguish another female behind the first, and several other horsemen and baggage animals. All doubts were set at rest directly afterwards, as we distinguished the well-known features of our patron; but with regard to the lady we were not so certain, as her face was concealed by the veil which she wore to guard her from the dust. As we approached, however, and saluted Sir Thomas Gresham, she drew it aside, and I beheld a lovely face, though somewhat pale, which, I felt sure, from the expression, must be that of Aveline. Of this she gave me assurance, as she replied to my salutation, and a gentle blush came over her features. In truth, I had no reason to be dissatisfied with the way she received me. But I was grieved to find that she was not in the enjoyment of her usual health. Of this also, Sir Thomas informed me, by observing that she had accompanied him, by the invitation of Madam Clough, who had long wished her to pay a visit to Antwerp, in the hope that the change of air and scenery might benefit her.

"Alas! however," observed Sir Thomas, "such a change has not always proved as beneficial as we might have desired."

I knew by his remark that he was thinking of his son Richard. I was glad when Sir Thomas addressed A'Dale, who rode by his side, leaving me to drop behind him with Aveline. We had much to speak about. She assured me with a smile that there was no cause for alarm about her health, but that she had been anxious to accept Madam Clough's invitation, and that Lady Anne had kindly consented to spare her for a few months.

"I have brought over a new waiting-woman," she observed. "You remember her, though. She is the daughter of Farmer Hadden, whose hospitality you enjoyed when driven back on your voyage from Ipswich, of which you have often told me. Her father and mother are dead, and she applied to Lady Anne for employment as waiting-woman. She is very faithful and loving, and, better still, is a true Christian."

Among many private matters, interesting chiefly to ourselves, Aveline described the improvements at Osterley which Sir Thomas had lately made, as also the beautiful appearance of the Bourse, which was now nearly completed. I, of course, had much to tell her, in return, of the events which had lately occurred at Antwerp, especially of the image-breaking, and the destruction of the beautiful interiors of so many of the churches.

"They were savage hands which performed the work," she observed; "yet we should not regret the overthrow of idols, for idols they are, although in appearance full of grace and beauty. I pray that nothing worse may happen; but I fear much, that when King Philip hears of these doings, he will take vengeance on the unhappy people who perpetrated them. I cannot but grieve also that so much rich carving and beautiful decoration should have been destroyed."

I agreed with Aveline in that respect; at the same time I echoed her remark with regard to the idols which had been pulled down. So quickly passed the time, that the shades of evening stole on us unawares, and we were quite surprised when we saw the towers and stout walls of Antwerp looming through the gloom. It was almost dusk as we rode under the deep gateway, on either side of which was the entrance to the narrow passage between the two walls surrounding the city. The streets were more crowded than usual, and we passed numerous groups of men talking eagerly together. News had arrived, we found, that the example set in Antwerp had been followed in many other cities; but of that I will speak anon.

I was well pleased with the reception which Madam Clough gave Aveline. Master Clough was thankful also to see Sir Thomas, for the difficulty of obtaining money at that time was very great; and he knew that the Queen's agent would be better able personally to make the required arrangements than he could himself. One thing Sir Thomas saw—that Antwerp would no longer be the city it formerly was for commerce with England; and I may here remark, that he shortly afterwards wrote home, advising that in such brabbling times as these were, some other city should be fixed on, to which British manufactures might be sent.

We had lately had a somewhat dull time in Master Clough's house. He was out of spirits at the turn affairs were taking, not knowing what might next happen, although, England and Spain, having hitherto been on friendly terms, he was under no apprehension that the English would suffer personally. We had occasionally official banquets, but they were very dull compared to those to which we had formerly been accustomed, while no maskers or mummers were allowed to present themselves. As may be supposed, the arrival of Sir Thomas Gresham and Aveline Radford produced a very pleasant change. As Aveline had been advised to take horse exercise, she rode out, by the desire of Sir Thomas, every day; and A'Dale and I were her constant attendants, Madam Clough occasionally accompanying her, while Mistress Margery was always her companion.

One bright morning Madam Clough had been tempted to ride forth; Sir Thomas and Master Clough, having business of importance to transact, deputed A'Dale and me as usual to escort the ladies. We had two attendants, well-armed, while A'Dale and I carried pistols in our holsters. We were both of us adepts in the use of the sword. A'Dale was able to encounter any trooper, however skilful, with his favourite weapon. Madam Clough was a good horsewoman, having learned the art in Wales, where she had been accustomed to ride over her native mountains, and on the summits of the dizzy precipices. She generally took the lead, Aveline and I riding side by side. Margery often fell to the share of A'Dale, for the damsel was in no way inclined to associate with the serving-men, nor would she have been could she have understood their language; indeed, she was in all respects superior to an ordinary tire-woman. We had gone for some distance along the Mechlin road; soon after passing the village of Berchem it was proposed that we should turn off to the right, where we might enjoy a gallop over the open ground, it being there higher and drier than the surrounding country. The fresh air gave us all spirits, and we rode on rapidly, little thinking of the distance we were going. I was not sorry when Madam Clough took the lead, sitting her horse with an upright figure and stately air, apparently regardless of Aveline and me, who followed out of ear-shot. The rest of the party were still farther off. I enjoyed more than ever being alone with Aveline; and she did not, so it seemed to me, object to my society. There were many things we had to talk of, but I could not yet bring myself to speak of one subject which was at my heart. I felt myself still a dependant on the bounty of Sir Thomas Gresham. He supported me, and supplied me liberally with the wherewithal to pay for my clothes and other expenses, and to leave me an ample supply of pocket-money. But as yet he had never spoken of paying me a fixed salary; and with the possession of that alone should I feel justified in proposing to marry Aveline. She was much in the same condition, for although Lady Anne had carefully preserved the document given to me by her mother, as yet it did not appear that she would benefit thereby. Still I did not despair. I knew that Sir Thomas was generous, and that he had a true regard both for Aveline and for me; and I hoped that, if I put the matter before him, he would enable me to carry out my wishes. Several times during this ride I was on the point of speaking to Aveline, and asking her whether she could make up her mind to marry me; but as often as the words rose to my lips, I let them fall back again into my heart without utterance. There they remained, preventing me for some minutes afterwards from again speaking. On each occasion Aveline looked at me with an inquiring glance, wondering what had thus tied my tongue. Perhaps she suspected the truth, when at length, growing bolder, I approached nearer and nearer the subject, for I saw, or fancied I saw, a blush suffuse her countenance. This gave me yet further boldness, and summoning all my resolution, I was on the point of telling her the wishes of my heart, when a cry from Madam Clough made us hurry forward towards her.

She had at that instant turned the corner of a wood. She pointed to a spot a short distance from where she had reined in her horse, when we saw spread out before us a large concourse of people. They were surrounding a rough platform raised to the height of their heads. On it stood a man, who, with arms stretched out, one hand holding a book, from which he occasionally read, and the other at times lifted towards heaven, was earnestly addressing them. The words did not reach us; but so absorbed were the congregation in them, that for some time our approach was not observed. At length several horsemen, with arquebuses in their hands, galloped towards us. We without difficulty explained who we were, and the horsemen, turning round, accompanied us. The rest of our party coming up, we collected in the outer circle of the vast multitude who were listening to the preacher. He was, we found, an enthusiastic Protestant—Herman Modet by name. He was setting forth, in clear and forcible language, the great truths of Christianity, as opposed to the false teaching of Rome. He showed how the one must, when received, elevate and ennoble the human mind; while the other was calculated in every way to lower and debase it. He then, in eloquent language, called upon his countrymen to unite in overthrowing that fearful system, supported by the Pope and his cardinals, to which King Philip had completely subjected himself. "He who is a slave to such a system is unfit to rule his fellow-men!" he exclaimed. "Already he and his father have brought the most fearful miseries upon our country. What further trials is he not preparing for us? I would urge peace, forbearance, and long-suffering; and yet I cannot believe that we are called upon to submit without resistance to the horrible tyrannies to which we have been subjected for so many years."

After a time, one of the hymns of Marot, translated into Flemish, was sung with wonderful enthusiasm. I thought that Madam Clough was warmed up by it; I know Aveline and I were, and joined in it with all our hearts. Margery, although she could not understand the words, was carried away by the air, and still more so when A'Dale translated them to her.

Again the preacher continued his address. I would willingly have remained to hear more of it; but Madam Clough, who did not understand Flemish perfectly, made a sign to us to continue our ride.

We soon left the camp-meeting far behind, continuing our course in the direction we had previously been pursuing. I do not know whether the discourse we had heard made any impression on Madam Clough, for she did not allude to it; indeed, she went on in front as she had before been doing, leaving Aveline and me to follow. A'Dale, I conclude, found the conversation of Mistress Margery very much to his taste. Sometimes they laughed long and loudly together, but at other times they spoke in a more serious tone, as far as I could judge by the words I heard when we were together.

The two serving-men brought up the rear, wondering perhaps at the unusually long ride their mistress was taking. At length I thought it would be proper to advise her to return, for, looking behind me, I observed that the horizon was already dark with a bank of clouds which came rapidly rising out of the distant ocean. As, however, the sun continued shining brightly, Madam Clough was not aware of the approaching storm. As soon as I saw what was likely to occur, I pushed on, and, overtaking her, pointed out the rising clouds. She seemed somewhat astonished.

"You should have told me of this before," she observed.

I replied that I myself had not remarked the state of the sky, or I would have done so.

"Well, we shall perhaps be able to get back before it breaks," she remarked, turning her horse round.

I doubted this very much; however, there was no help for it, so putting spurs to our steeds, we galloped back, in the hopes of regaining the high road, in the neighbourhood of which we might possibly find shelter. Where we then were, we could see no house or building of any sort which would protect us from the fury of the storm. We had soon cause for anxiety, for the bank of clouds rose higher and higher every instant, and the sun became obscured, as it swept round towards the west. And now it appeared directly overhead. The wind, before soft and balmy, began to blow from the north, increasing every instant in strength, till we found a chill and furious blast in our faces. It rapidly increased in strength. The wind might be endured, but the air grew damper, and more and more chilling. I dreaded the effect on Aveline, to whom such air as was then blowing was especially dangerous. I again looked round in vain for shelter, and in a few minutes the expected storm burst, and the water rushed down from the clouds in heavy sheets. I took off my own cloak, and placed it round Aveline, though she entreated me to wear it. I replied that that would be impossible while she was exposed to so pelting a storm, and that neither the wetting nor cold would have any effect on me. Madam Clough was tolerably well guarded, so that I did not concern myself about her; and I let A'Dale look after Mistress Margery.

The wind blew more furiously; the rain descended in torrents. Notwithstanding the protection my cloak afforded Aveline, I was sure that she would be wet through in a few minutes.

As we were pushing on, I thought I saw on the side of a slight mound of earth, at a little distance, the roof of a cottage: I pointed it out to Madam Clough, and we pushed towards it. On a nearer approach, I saw that the roof rose a very little way above the ground—that it was, in fact, the covering of a sort of cave or hollow in the side of the hill, such as perhaps some shepherd or cattle-keeper might have formed to obtain protection during a similar storm to that which had overtaken us. It was somewhat larger, however, than might have been expected for that purpose; at all events, I welcomed the sight, as I was in hopes that the ladies might find shelter within. As we got up to it, we saw that there was a door to the hut, formed of rough planks. Helping the ladies from their horses, we attempted to open it, but it resisted our efforts.

"Who is there, who comes to disturb me in my retreat?" said a voice from within, in harsh, croaking accents.

It was that of a female, I thought.

"Good mother," I said, wishing to speak her fair, "there are delicate females here exposed to this raging storm—they entreat you to give them shelter."

"Let them go the way they came," answered the voice; "I shall treat others as I myself have been treated. They would not allow me to enter their gorgeous abodes; I now refuse them admittance into mine, albeit it may not be of the most splendid character."

"That were cruel, mother," I answered; "we should return good for evil; and those for whom I plead have never wronged you—of that I am certain."

"Go away, go away, I tell you!" she again cried out; "you have had my reply."

"This will never do!" I exclaimed to A'Dale, for every instant the rain was coming down heavier and heavier.

The serving-men were holding our horses. Putting our shoulders against the door, we gave a shove together, and it flew open. The hut was much larger than we had expected to find it, and would afford, I saw at a glance, not only shelter for the ladies but for all our party, and for the horses also. At the farther end sat an old crone, her white locks escaping from under her coif; and her bony arms, which were bare to the elbow, extended over a large pan, beneath which were burning coals. She glanced round at us with a look of anger.

"I pray thee, dame, be not offended," I said, approaching her, while the ladies stood at a little distance. "We have entered your abode with scant ceremony, but have no desire to treat you with disrespect; gladly will we pay, too, for the injury we may have done your door, though we could not remain outside exposed to the pelting storm when shelter was at hand. Had you admitted us without parley, the latch would have remained uninjured, and our tempers would not have been aroused."

To these remarks she made no reply, but seizing a wand, which lay by her side, began to stir the contents of the pan. As our eyes got accustomed to the gloom of the hut, numerous articles were seen about, which showed us at once the character of the inmate.

"I wish that we had braved the storm rather than have come in here," whispered Madam Clough. "Perchance, indeed, it was summoned at the beck of this old witch; and by her looks I fear she purposes to work us evil."

Nothing, could be more forbidding than the aspect of the old dame. Whether witch or not, that she wished to be thought so was very evident. I did not myself share the terror of Madam Clough, nor, I think, did Aveline; still, when I asked the old woman to allow the ladies to approach her fire, in order that they might dry their wet garments, they all drew back, evidently not wishing to be nearer than they were to the witch. She looked up, and uttered a low, croaking laugh, as she saw their terror.

"Ah! ah! ah!—your beauty and your wealth cannot guard you from the power of a wretched old woman like me!" she cried out. "Well, well, when the storm is over, you will ride away, and think no more of me; but I can follow you wherever you go, and find out your thoughts, as I know them now. You think, perhaps, that you are strangers to me—ah! ah! ah!—but I know you well—whence you come, and your future fates. You three fair dames were born in a foreign land, and so was one of you gallant gentlemen, but the other first saw the light in this hapless country. I speak true, do I not? answer me, lady!" she exclaimed, looking towards Madam Clough.

"Yes, indeed you do," said the latter; "but you might have judged by our tongues that we were not Flemings."

"Had you kept silence I should have known as well," said the old witch. "And now would you like to know the future?"

"If you can tell it to us, there may be no harm in so doing," said Madam Clough. "Can you tell me my fate?"

"Eh! that can I," answered the old woman. "Twice you have wedded, and once been a widow; again a widow you will be, and once more wedded, till the green turf on which you have been wont to trip so lightly lies heavy above your head. Think of that as you step forth over the green sward, when the air blows softly and the sun shines brightly—think what you will ere long be."

I saw that Madam Clough did not at all like these remarks, and, willing to relieve her, I asked if she could tell the fortunes of the rest of the party.

"Ay! that will I," she answered, eyeing us keenly. "There are two fair damsels here, who are ready to wed two bold youths; but danger and trouble, and battle and tempest, will intervene ere their hopes will be fulfilled. If their troubles are short, so may be their joys; but long troubles may bring longer happiness. Choose you which you will, my masters—I will read you a riddle; let me hear if you can answer it."

"We want no riddles, mother," said A'Dale; "but if you are a true sorceress, tell us plainly what is about to happen."

"A true sorceress, indeed!" exclaimed the old woman. "If I was to tell you what was about to occur, your hair would stand on end, and you would rush forth shrieking with terror amid the raging tempest. The future I see looming, and not far off. Bloodshed and destruction, fierce conflagrations, war, famines and miseries unspeakable, the graveyard overflowing, the country depopulated. All this, you Anabaptists, you preachers of the new religion, you promulgators of strange doctrines, are about to bring upon this country. Had matters been allowed to go on as they were, had the Catholic faith been undisturbed, quiet, peace, and prosperity would still have existed in the land."

"As to that, mother, you are speaking of the past, not foretelling the future!" exclaimed A'Dale. "I will not bandy words with you; and as I knew not the country during the happy times you speak of, I cannot reply to you; but it seems to me as much as saying that the man who is asleep can do no harm. Therefore, as long as the country submitted to the priests, the priests were not inclined to find fault with them."

I must observe here that Margery did not understand a word that was said; Aveline, indeed, scarcely comprehended the meaning of the old woman's remarks. She, like most persons of her class, seeing two young people together, at once pronounced them lovers. But I have an idea that her words did not fall altogether unheeded on A'Dale's ears. Whatever he might have been thinking of before, I suspected, from a glance which I saw him give Mistress Margery, that from that time he began to entertain affectionate feelings for her. The old woman had not all this time offered us seats, or shown any inclination to treat us with courtesy. It struck me, however, that the latter might probably be purchased. I therefore, taking a piece of money from my leather purse, approached her and said, "We must pay you, dame, for telling our fortunes, or we cannot hope that they will come true. Let me cross your palm with this piece of money, and we may have some expectation of finding your predictions fulfilled."

The expression of the old woman's countenance immediately changed, and, rising from her seat, she drew forth a bench and some stools, on which she begged we would rest ourselves. I saw, as she moved about, that she was far more active than her appearance betokened; and, after a little time I could not help thinking that I had seen her before. Suddenly it struck me that she was no other than Barbara Trond—the old woman who used to sell tapers and other Popish trickeries in front of the cathedral. If so, as she had frequently seen us, I had no doubt that from the first she knew who we were. I immediately guessed that, finding her old calling valueless, she had betaken herself to her present mode of life, in the hopes of preying on the superstition and credulity of her fellow-creatures. And I found that I was correct in my suspicions.

The rain meantime continued pouring down with unabated violence, and we began to fear that it would not hold up in time to allow us to return to Antwerp before nightfall. Several times I went to the door of the hut to look forth, but the heavens were still dark as at first, not a gleam of light being visible in any direction. Finding the good effect of the first piece of money, I bestowed a second of about the same value on the old woman, telling her that, as we had occupied her abode so long, I thought we were in duty bound to pay her rent. I saw that this second gift had completely secured her services; and she now seemed as anxious to please us as she had at first appeared surly and morose.

"Listen to me, young sir," she said; "for you seem to understand my language better than the rest of the party. Do not trust to appearances. You think that the Reformers have gained the upper hand. I know King Philip and his advisers too well not to be sure that they will wreak a bitter vengeance on the cities in which the churches of the faith they hold have been desecrated. He may appear indifferent for a time, for the sake of lulling the people to sleep; but, depend upon it, he only bides his time, and he will speedily spring forth like a tiger of the Far East, to crush with his mighty paws all who have ventured to oppose him."

I was afraid the old woman spoke too truly, though it required no prophet to say the same. Madam Clough seemed very little disposed to talk with her, while Aveline could only partially understand what she said. Thus the weight of the conversation fell on me; for A'Dale thought fit to endeavour to entertain Mistress Margery, who, of course, could not comprehend a single word that was spoken. I was very thankful when at last the loud pattering sound, which had continued for so long, ceased; and, looking forth, I found that it was no longer raining. Wishing old Dame Trond farewell, we led the horses out of the hut, and, quickly mounting, made the best of our way home.

Chapter Twenty One
A Battle outside Antwerp

An important event was about to occur in Antwerp. The Reformers were triumphant. They had taken possession of three churches, and in each, one of their principal preachers was to deliver an address, and offer up prayer and praise. The magistrates were greatly alarmed, believing that such a proceeding would draw down on the city the vengeance of the Regent. In their alarm, the Pensionary, Vesembeck, was sent to entreat the ministers to postpone their exercises. One of them, Taffen, a famous Walloon preacher, agreed to do so; but the others were not so easily persuaded to abandon what they believed to be the right course. Herman Modet especially was very firm. He had come into the city on purpose to preach in the cathedral, and he naturally longed for the opportunity of making known the simple Gospel of salvation, where for so many ages false teaching had alone been heard. Aveline had been very anxious to listen to a Flemish sermon from a Protestant minister; and I had promised, should Sir Thomas not object, to accompany her. On the evening before the proposed sermons were to be delivered, a stranger presented himself at the house, desiring to see Sir Thomas. He sent up his name to the room where we were seated at supper.

"Master Overton; he has come from Switzerland," said my patron. "Do I remember that name?"

"Yes, sir," I remarked; "it is the name of the priest who, abandoning the Romish faith, came over with us from Ipswich."

"Go and see, Ernst," said Sir Thomas. "If you are right, I shall be truly glad to receive him."

On going to the hall, I was glad to see my old acquaintance; and I should have known him immediately, though his countenance wore a far more happy expression than formerly, and he had altogether lost the sallow complexion of a priest of Rome. I gladly ushered him into the sitting-room, where he was cordially welcomed by Sir Thomas, and introduced to Madam Clough and the rest of the party. He had been ministering, he told us, in Switzerland for some time past to a small congregation; but at length, being anxious to revisit England, and there assist in spreading the truth among his countrymen, he had resigned his post. Aveline had so grown since he last had seen her, that he naturally did not recognise her. She now timidly approached him.

"You are my uncle," she said, taking his hand; "indeed, I know of no other relative I possess on earth."

I need scarcely describe the satisfaction with which Master Overton greeted his niece.

I had never met a man whose whole heart was more given to the desire of advancing the cause of his Saviour than was Master Overton. Scarcely even did John Foxe surpass him. I have said little of that good minister. He had now obtained, we heard, a church in Wiltshire; and frequently Master Gresham used to send him money wherewith he might help his poorer neighbours. When Master Overton heard of the proposed preaching, he seconded Aveline's wish to be allowed to go and hear it.

"I will accompany her myself," he said.

Sir Thomas no longer objected; and it was arranged that we should set out the following morning, in time to secure a place near the preacher in the cathedral. Although Margery could not understand what was said, she also begged leave to accompany her mistress. We thus formed a considerable party when we entered the cathedral. We found Herman Modet ready to ascend the pulpit, round which were piled up the various articles which had been broken off the images. Already a considerable number of people had collected within the building, and soon after we entered, vast numbers kept pouring in, till the whole edifice was crowded. Just then a body of magistrates appeared in their official garments, headed by Vesembeck, who again appealed to the preacher to abandon his intentions. Earnestly as he pleaded, warning the minister of the danger which might occur, he did so without effect. All Herman Modet would agree to was to shorten his address, and, supported by the people, he refused to agree to any other arrangement.

At length, completely discomfited, those of the magistrates who were Roman Catholics withdrew, while the remainder stopped to listen to the preacher. Ascending the pulpit, in a sonorous voice he gave forth a psalm, the words and air of which were well-known to the vast assemblage below. Hitherto a low murmur had alone been heard throughout the building. But now, many thousand voices swelled up together to the praise of Him who came on earth to die for man—the just for the unjust, that all, by trusting in Him, might have everlasting life. I have not space to give all the sermon, though I made notes of it at the time. It was eloquent, fervent, and convincing. I cannot fancy that any right-minded Romanists, inquiring for the truth, could have heard it and yet not have yielded to its arguments. I should rather say, that it is surprising that they could resist them. Yet there were, I know, many Romanists there who, though perhaps moved at the moment, went away retaining their former opinions.

Herman Modet, though he had consented to preach for a short time, carried away by his feelings, continued to pour forth his words of fire hour after hour, no one wearying even by the length of his discourse. Once again there rose a hymn of praise such as had never before been heard within those walls—not to Mary, not to any of the saints, but to the Lamb without spot or blemish, slain for the sins of the whole world, that all who believe on Him might not perish, but have everlasting life. No thoughts can be more pure and simple and holy, more full of Gospel truth than are those found in the hymns of Marot. Although we had been standing so long, we yet left the cathedral with regret. Several of our party could only comprehend a very small portion of what they had heard. Margery, indeed, did not understand a word, and yet there was that power in the speaker's manner alone which riveted her attention, while sometimes A'Dale, and sometimes I, explained to her the substance of the discourse.

Madam Clough, when we returned home, could scarcely believe that we had been so long a time at the cathedral, or that we could have been as interested as we professed with the discourse we had heard.

I must now give a short account of the numerous public events of deep interest which occurred after this.

I have said that Master Overton proposed returning to England; but when his presence in Antwerp was known, several Protestant Englishmen, as well as Reformers of other nations in the place, earnestly requested him to remain and minister to them. Sir Thomas Gresham also urging him to do so, he consented to take the charge of a Reformed Church at Antwerp till another should be found to supply his place. This was a great advantage to Aveline especially, as she thus had a relative to whom she could go for advice and instruction, which certainly her friend Madam Clough was unable to afford.

Similar scenes to those I have described in Antwerp took place in numerous towns throughout the Netherlands. In Flanders alone, four hundred churches were sacked, in Mechlin, in Tournay—a city distinguished for its ecclesiastical splendour—in Ghent, and in Valenciennes. In not one of them, however, was a single human being injured.

On the return of the Prince of Orange, he expressed his regret at what had occurred. At the same time, he did not appear disposed to treat the image-breakers with much severity. The Regent Margaret, however, on hearing of the disturbances, was seized with the greatest alarm. When the news reached Philip, he swore a deep oath that they should bitterly pay for what they had done. Owing to the representations of the Prince of Orange, in the meantime liberty of worship was granted in places where it had already been established; and it seemed at first as if the Reformers were about to obtain all they required. Bands of insurgents appeared in various places. In the city of Valenciennes the Reformers had completely gained the upper hand. But the city was declared by the Regent in a state of siege; and a body of troops under the fierce Papist Noircarmes was sent to invest it. Sad news shortly afterwards reached us, that most of the Protestant bands had been cut to pieces by Noircarmes and his troops.

The Prince of Orange was governing Antwerp, with the brave young noble, Hoogstraaten, under him, while Brederode was also in the city secretly raising troops for the defence of the liberal cause. On two occasions I attended Sir Thomas Gresham, when invited by the Prince of Orange to dine with him. The Prince received my patron with great courtesy at a magnificent banquet. From the conversation of the Prince, it was very clear that he was anxious to ascertain from Sir Thomas Gresham the disposition entertained by Queen Elizabeth and her ministers towards the revolutionary party.

"Do you think," he said, "that she will aid our noblemen and other chiefs, as she did those in France, for the sake of their religion?"

Sir Thomas, in reply, asked whether the noblemen to whom the Prince alluded had demanded any help of her Majesty. He said that he could not tell. Then said Sir Thomas, "I am myself no judge, nor can I interfere in a matter of so much importance."

Soon after this, Sir Thomas again returned to England. It was now that some of the leading Protestants in Antwerp memorialised Sir Thomas Gresham, explaining that the outbreaks which had lately occurred in the city were greatly contrary to their wishes, and entreating him that he would petition the Queen Elizabeth in their behalf, and that the ruin with which the Low Countries were threatened might be averted. They begged that she would address King Philip, in order that he might be brought to accede to their reasonable request: that they might be allowed liberty to worship God without molestation, asserting that they were perfectly ready to "render to Caesar the things which are Caesar's," should they be allowed to "render unto God the things which are God's."

I mentioned just now that Brederode was raising men in Antwerp. With him was associated the brave and gallant young nobleman, Marnix of Tholouse. He had left college in order that he might draw his sword in the cause of religious liberty.

The Prince of Orange at length thought it necessary to prohibit Brederode's enlistments. He and his followers accordingly left the city, and embarked on board several ships which they had seized. More men having joined them, Brederode took his departure for Holland, where he hoped to raise more troops. In the meantime Marnix of Tholouse, with his newly collected force, sailing up the Scheld, landed and attacked the little village called Ostrawell, about a mile from Antwerp. Here he posted himself with considerable judgment. In his rear he had the Scheld and its dikes, on his right and left the dikes and the village. In front he threw up a breastwork and sunk a trench. On this spot might truly be said to have been first hoisted the standard of liberty. A'Dale and I paid a visit to the camp. Daily numbers of men flocked to his standard, till he had collected fully 3,000 round him. If the bravery of one man could have supported a great cause, the gallant young student might have succeeded. His followers, however, had no discipline, and consequently no dependence on each other. Brederode had promised to join him shortly with a body of troops; and it was hoped that he would himself infuse his own spirit into his men, and bring them under discipline.

As the ground was perfectly level between the city and his camp, we were able from the ramparts to see all that was taking place within it.

Although the Prince of Orange would not give his open support to the patriot band, yet he did not feel himself called upon to interfere with them; indeed, he had been fortunately furnished with no troops with which he could have done so. Affairs in the city therefore went on quietly.

One morning, however, at early dawn the sound of firing from the direction of Ostrawell called a vast number of the people of Antwerp to that side of the ramparts. It soon became evident that Tholouse had been suddenly attacked, and that a fierce battle was raging. No one could tell by whom he was assailed. In a short time the roofs of the houses, the towers of the churches, and the higher parts of the walls, were covered with eager spectators. We were among them. We could hear the sound of drums and trumpets, and the sharp rattle of musketry. Then came the shouts of victory, the despairing cries of the vanquished. The glitter of the helmets and spears, the bucklers and corslets of the assailing party we could clearly see, while their standards—they were those of Spain—showed their exact position. The young Count had greatly won our admiration, on account of his youth, his gallant bearing, his talents, and his bravery. He had become a staunch Protestant, and for that cause was ready to lay down his life. A short time before, he had married a very charming young lady, who shared his enthusiastic desire to establish the liberty of their country. She was now in the city, and we could not help thinking what must be her feelings on finding that the camp had been attacked. We could see the enemy approach the breastwork in front of the camp. Alas! it was defended but for a short time: on came the assailants; now they entered the fort. Onward they pressed, some shooting rapidly, while the swords of others were kept in constant exercise.

"What say you, Ernst; shall we go forth to their support?" exclaimed A'Dale. "We shall find hundreds of brave fellows ready to accompany us; and I for one cannot stand here and see our friends butchered by their tyrants. See! see! the enemy are advancing; there is no time to lose, if we are to give them any real help!"

I was as willing as my friend on most occasions to rush into danger; but it seemed to me that already the enemy had gained the day, and that our assistance would come too late. They pressed on till we could see hundreds of the patriots driven into the Scheld. On one side was a farmhouse; round it for some time the battle raged furiously. Then the flames were seen to burst forth. Again the assailants advanced. Small bodies of the patriots who had escaped from the fight were rushing towards the town. Soon the excitement became uncontrollable. It was not surprising that the Calvinists within the city should have felt for their brothers who were thus being destroyed. For a short time, from every street and alley in the city, people were seen coming forth armed with lance, pike, and arquebus; some bearing huge two-handed swords, which had belonged to their fathers, others, battle-axes, and some carried huge sledge-hammers over their shoulders. All were determined to issue forth, in the hope of rescuing their friends ere the whole of them were destroyed. Meantime the young bride of Tholouse was seen flying from street to street, calling on the Calvinists to save their brethren on the point of destruction. Fully 10,000 men were up in arms; but the gates had been closed by order of the Prince of Orange, and they found it impossible to force their way out. The whole city was in a state of commotion. The Lutherans as well as the Calvinists had flown to arms. Some of the fiercest proposed to avenge the death of the patriots by the slaughter of the Roman Catholics. The latter also, in consequence, in their own defence, had taken up arms. A most sanguinary outbreak was, therefore, every moment expected.

Had it begun, no one could say when it would end, or the number of lives which would be sacrificed. While the dreadful scenes I have described were going on, we hurried down from the walls to the open place near the Red Gate, still hoping that there might be some time to render assistance to the defeated patriots. At this moment the Prince, without any guards or attendants, rode in among the crowd collected there. Instead of the usual signs of respect with which he was greeted, he was now received with howls of execration. A thousand hoarse voices called him the Pope's servant, the minister of antichrist, a traitor to his country. Some even proposed to cut him down on the spot. An arquebus was pointed at him, but, ere it was discharged, a hand from the crowd struck it away. Even before this the postern of the Red Gate had been forced open, and a number of the Calvinists were issuing forth.

The Prince sat calmly on his horse; then, lifting up his hand, he addressed the multitude. As he spoke, every voice was hushed. He told them that he came for their good, that the battle was over, that their friends had been cut to pieces, and that the victorious enemy were retiring; while, brave as those who heard him might be, should they go forth, they would be unable to retrieve the fortunes of the day. He pointed out to them that they were ill-armed and without discipline, and that the same force which had captured the camp at Ostrawell might with equal ease destroy them.

The remarks of the Prince seemed so just, that I persuaded A'Dale to give up his design of marching out to the relief of the remnants of the patriot force. Some hundreds, however, still insisted on going forth. Again and again the Prince and the Count Hoogstraaten, who had a short time before arrived on the spot, entreated them to abandon their design, warning them that their blood would be upon their own heads should they persevere.

Five hundred marched forth. The enemy were seen scattered about the country pursuing the fugitives. On the appearance of the city force, they were quickly again summoned together by the sound of the trumpet; and now, in a compact mass, they advanced towards the city, with drums beating and colours flying. Just before this a rapid firing was heard in the rear of the enemy. We at the time little knew what it was. Alas! the savages were shooting their prisoners, three hundred of whom they had captured, intending to ransom them. When, however, they found they had again to enter into a fresh battle, they shot the whole of the unfortunate men. Thus, in reality, this unadvised sally of the citizens was the cause of the death of a large number of their countrymen. The citizens, finding themselves outnumbered, and not relishing the firm bearing of the Spaniards, retreated rapidly into the city, the gates being shut only just in time to prevent the entrance of the Romanist force. The enemy, then advancing close to the city walls, planted the banners of the unfortunate Tholouse on the margin of the moat, sounding at the same time a trumpet of defiance. The Prince and his lieutenant exerted themselves to prevent another sally, well knowing the thoroughly trained force the citizens would have to encounter. In the opinion of the Prince the time for fighting had not yet arrived.

During the period I have been describing, the whole city continued in a state of the fiercest commotion. The Calvinists in vast numbers had taken possession of the Mere; it was here the market was held: it is a long wide place, too wide almost to be called a street, with fine buildings on either side—the streets which enter it communicating with the Exchange and many other public edifices. This place had been barricaded with paving stones, upturned waggons, and other articles which came to hand. A large body of the people had forced their way into the Arsenal, and obtained a supply of ammunition and several field-pieces; these they planted at the entrance of every street and passage. Another party stormed the city jail, and liberated the prisoners with whom they were crowded. These eagerly took up arms, and assembled in the Mere for its defence.

A'Dale and I, standing well with the Calvinists, were able to go in among them; but what we heard gave us great cause for anxiety. A large number were sincere and devoted men, excited at that moment to the highest pitch of religious enthusiasm. There were, however, no small number of ruffians, eager to commit any crime which came in their way. Some proposed pillaging the churches and the houses of the Romanists, the images only having before been destroyed.

"Let us collect all the wealth which has been so long hoarded up by these wretched drones!" cried out some; others proposed even sacking the whole of the city, and setting up a Republic of their own.

The report of these proposals spread rapidly through the city: nothing could exceed the terror and alarm of the rest of the inhabitants. It was fearful to hear the cries of the women and children, who every moment expected that the place would be given over to rapine and bloodshed.

Night was approaching: it was impossible to say what would take place during the coming darkness. Meantime the Prince summoned the Board of Ancients, the Deans of Guilds, and the Ward Masters, to consult with him at the Council Room: he had also caused eight companies of Guards, which had previously been enrolled, to be mustered on the square in front of the City Hall for its protection. It was rapidly arranged, at his suggestion, that terms should be offered to the insurgents; but who was to carry the message?

"I myself will go forth," he said; and listening to no remonstrances, he threw himself on his horse, and rode down to the Mere. He was allowed to pass by the guns, till he was once more in the centre of the fierce mob. He told them that they must appoint eight deputies to treat with him and the magistrates at the Town Hall. The deputies were soon chosen, and accompanied him back. Six articles were drawn up, providing that the keys of the city should remain in his possession; that the watch should be held by burghers and soldiers together; that the magistrates should permit the entrance of no garrison; and that the citizens should be entrusted with the care of their own charters. The deputies and the City Government at once gave their cordial assent to these articles. When the deputies returned, their constituents were not very well pleased with what had been done, declaring that they would not submit to be locked up at the mercy of any man, nor would they trust to mercenary troops for guarding their city. The Prince, hearing this, agreed that the burghers, Calvinists, Lutherans, as well as Romanists, should be employed to guard the city.

These arrangements were not made till dark. A'Dale and I returned home. I may say that not one of the household could be persuaded to go to bed. Master Clough's anxiety was very great, especially on account of his wife. A'Dale and I, therefore, willingly undertook to go forth again and learn the news. As we approached the Mere, where an army of not less than 15,000 Calvinists still remained encamped, with guns loaded, and artillery pointed, we heard cries, "Long live the Beggars!"

"Down with the Papists!" and similar shouts. We waited for some time: again and again they were repeated, till we felt convinced that they were about to march forth, and carry out the threats they had previously uttered. Thus the night passed away.

We were not the only people who kept awake. Few, I believe, slept; but there was one who, with his associates, laboured hard the whole time—that was the Prince of Orange, so we afterwards heard. He was employing every means he could devise to save the city. He had interviews with the leaders of various parties; among others, he saw the ministers and notable members of the Lutheran Churches, and induced them to persuade their congregations to take up arms for the preservation of order. He also engaged the assistance of the chiefs of the various foreign mercantile associations—the English, Italian, Portuguese, and others—and ordered us to remain under arms at our respective factories, ready to act at a moment's warning. The Romanists also were assembled, and urged to unite with all those who wished to support order. As may be supposed, they were eager enough to do so, as certainly they would be the first to fall, should an outbreak take place.

There were thus three parties in the city—the Calvinists, the Lutherans, and the Romanists. In the two latter were generally found the richest people of the community, though they were the least numerous. They, therefore, would have suffered the most, had a battle been fought in the city. Nothing could have been more horrible than such an event—desolation and destruction would have been brought into every house. Yet, strange as it may seem, all parties were willing and eager to fight. Fresh articles were drawn up, and approved by those who represented the Lutheran and Romanist parties. The Prince resolved early in the morning to present them to the Calvinists; attended by Hoogstraaten and a committee of the municipal authorities, with a guard of a hundred troopers, he once more rode towards the Mere. It had been arranged that all who were anxious to preserve order were to wear a red scarf over their armour. Thus distinguished, he and his party approached the camp. The Calvinists appeared fierce and threatening as ever; but, notwithstanding, he was once more allowed to ride into the middle of the square. It was a moment of the greatest anxiety. One of the magistrates with a loud voice read the articles by the command of the Prince. For some time it seemed doubtful whether they would be accepted. But he in a few words expressed their meaning.

"And now, my friends," he said, "let me entreat you, by the love you bear your wives and children, by the love you bear your faith, by your duty to your country and to your Maker, to agree to these terms. If you do so, repeat the words with which I will conclude my address."

There was a pause. Then he cried with a loud voice, "God save the King!"

Again there was a pause. The Calvinists were swayed by conflicting emotions, but the calmness and gentleness of the Prince overcame all other considerations.

"*Vive le Roi!*" they shouted; and the cry was taken up throughout their ranks.

"I thank Heaven that it is so!" he again cried, when silence was once more procured. "Now let me entreat you quietly to return to your homes, and show that you bear your fellow-citizens no ill-will for what has occurred."

In a short time, those in charge of the artillery restored them to the Arsenal, where all arms which had been taken were replaced. And now the citizens of all classes were seen addressing each other in friendly terms—the Calvinists, Lutherans, and even Romanists. The passions of some fifty thousand armed men were appeased. The lives of numbers were preserved, and the beautiful city of Antwerp was saved, by the wisdom and courage of William of Orange.

Chapter Twenty Two
The Duke of Alva

I was so deeply interested in the public events I have described, that I found little space in my journal for an account of my own proceedings. In truth, while at Antwerp, I was engaged the greater part of the day in my official duties, and have therefore little to tell about myself. Although order was restored in Antwerp, the city was full of mourning, especially among the lower classes, so many had lost relatives in the late fight. The person for whom I could not help feeling the most compassion was the young widow of the brave Tholouse. For some days she would not believe that he was among the slain, until one of the men who, though desperately wounded, had escaped death, was brought before her. He described how the young captain, though surrounded by foes, fought to the last, till he was struck down and cut to pieces. After the enemy had retired, we went out to the scene of the conflict. I had never witnessed so sad and horrible a sight. The ground in the camp was strewn with dead bodies. There was one pile of slain larger than the rest. Within it was found the hilt of the broken sword of the young hero, his helmet cleft in twain, and a corpse, covered with a hundred wounds, which those who knew him best declared was his. This seemed but a disastrous commencement of an attempt to establish liberty. Many abandoned all hope of their country's freedom. But bolder spirits hoped against hope; among them, even at that time, was William of Orange, or the Silent William, as he was called. He could speak, however, as I have already described. He gained the name, not so much because he was silent, as far as words were concerned, but because he kept his more important and deeper thoughts hidden in his own bosom.

It became known at this time that the Duke of Alva, the most celebrated general of his day, was marching with a Spanish army towards the Netherlands; and by the middle of August he reached Thionville, on the Luxembourg frontier.

Count Egmont and several other nobles rode forth to meet the Duke. Though at first Alva treated Egmont somewhat coldly, in a short time he appeared to be on the most friendly terms with him, and the two were seen riding side by side at the head of the forces. Of course the Duchess Margaret was very indignant at the appearance of Alva, who had come to supersede her. She at length consented to receive him without any of his attendants. But when he appeared in the courtyard with his body-guard, the archers of the Regent's household showed a disposition to prevent their entrance, and a scene of bloodshed seemed on the point of being enacted. At length he was allowed to pass, and the Duchess received him standing in the centre of her reception-room with the most chilling manner. Behind her stood the Count Egmont and other nobles. Alva, however, must have known how completely they were all in his power, and had thus less difficulty in suppressing his anger. It was said that the Prince of Orange again and again warned Counts Egmont and Horn, as well as several others, on no account to put themselves in the power of Alva. He showed his opinion of the character of that person by resigning all his offices, and retiring to his paternal estate of Dillenburg.

Alva having superseded the Regent, the country soon felt the effects of his presence. He forthwith distributed his well-trained troops through Brussels, Ghent, Antwerp, and other chief cities, and ordered the municipalities to transfer their keys to his keeping. A deep gloom settled down over the whole land. The day of vengeance with which they had long been threatened was now to overtake them. The people everywhere were oppressed with a feeling of hopeless dismay. They knew that they had no power to resist the force which had arrived to keep them down. Those who had a possibility of escaping made their way out of the ill-fated land across the frontier. Foreign merchants deserted the great marts, and the cities had the appearance of being stricken by the plague.

The Duke of Alva established a new court, for the trial of crimes committed during the recent period of troubles. It was called the Council of Troubles, but it soon acquired the terrible name of the Blood Council. It superseded all other institutions. All other courts were forbidden to give judgment on any case growing out of the late disturbances.

A reign of terror commenced, which exceeded anything that had before taken place. The Blood Council made rapid work wherever they went. In one day eighty-four of the inhabitants of Valenciennes were put to death; on another, forty-six persons in Malines. Ninety-five people collected from various towns were burned or strangled together at one place. But I sicken as I write of the horrible cruelties practised by Alva. He had come for the express purpose of destroying all the leaders of the popular movement. In spite of their high rank and the service they had rendered their King, they were condemned to death. Egmont had proved himself too faithful in carrying out the wishes of Philip, by the cruelties he exercised at Valenciennes and elsewhere, to deserve much pity.

It was at this juncture that William of Orange came forward. He published a manifesto, clearing himself of all the accusations brought against him, and declaring that he was about to make war, not against the King, but against those who had usurped his power and authority in the country. He immediately set to work to raise funds and troops. He sold all his jewels, plate, tapestry, and every other possession of value. Other nobles subscribed large sums. Count John of Nassau pledged his estates to raise funds for the cause.

The plan of the campaign was drawn out. The provinces were to be attacked simultaneously in three places. An army of Huguenots was to enter Artois on the frontier of France. A second, under Hoogstraaten, was to operate between the Rhine and the Meuse; while Louis of Nassau was to raise the standard of revolt in Freesland. A fourth force, under the Seigneur de Cocqueville, consisting of 2,500 men, also entered Artois. He was immediately attacked, and almost cut to pieces. All the Netherlanders who were taken prisoners were given up to the Spaniards, and, of course, hanged. A similar fate befel the force of Count Hoogstraaten. Louis of Nassau, however, was more successful.

His was the first victory gained by the patriot forces. It was seldom, that, ill-equipped and ill-disciplined, they were able to compete successfully with the well-trained troops of Spain. As yet, unhappily, there seemed but little prospect of the cause of liberty being triumphant. It was not man's arm which was to win the day. It was said that Alva's rage was almost uncontrollable when he heard of the defeat of his troops. In revenge, he immediately put to death eighteen prisoners of distinction, including the two Barons Batenburg, Maximilian Kock, Blois de Treslong, and others, who were executed in Brussels. Soon afterwards, the pretended trial of Egmont and Horn being concluded, those nobles were also executed in the same place. The events connected with their death are too well-known to require repetition. Though they did not die on account of their religion, for they were both staunch Romanists, yet their execution contributed greatly to forward the cause of the Protestants, as many other persons who might have remained true to Philip were induced to side with the patriots, lest they should be treated in a similar manner.

Nothing could be more deplorable than the condition of the Netherlands at this time. Every family was mourning for some of its dearest relatives. The death-bell tolled hourly in every village, while the survivors almost apathetically awaited the time when they themselves might be called to suffer in the same way.

Columns and stakes were to be seen in every street. The door-posts of private houses, even the fences in the fields, and the trees in orchards, were laden with human carcases, strangled, burnt, or beheaded. New scaffolds, gallows, and stakes were erected everywhere, ready for those devoted to destruction. All those who could escape had fled; and had it not been for the strict way in which the gates were guarded, nearly every town in the Netherlands would have been depopulated. In Antwerp, as well as in other great manufacturing and mercantile towns, once so full of industrial life, silence and despair now reigned. Poor Antwerp! it was my native city. I had known it for the greater part of my life. I had seen it once at the height of prosperity. Its commerce and industry were now well-nigh destroyed.

Chapter Twenty Three
Protestants in Antwerp

Master Overton continued in Antwerp; and as he gained a greater knowledge of the language, he became a very popular preacher among all classes. The arrival of Alva and his myrmidons had, however, put a stop to all public preaching; all meetings for prayer, whether public or private, were prohibited on pain of death. But this did not prevent people from meeting regularly, in secret, to read the Scriptures, to exhort each other, and to offer up prayer and praise together. There were many such congregations in different parts of the city. The one we attended was in a large upper room in a house not far from the Mere, where Master Overton ministered. Two flights of stairs led up to the storey on which the room was situated, besides which there was a narrow winding stair inside the wall, with a concealed door on the top, which led down to a small postern gate. The house belonged to a noble of the privileged order, and no magistrates dare enter it without authority from the Regent.

We knew one Sunday evening that a service had been arranged, and that Herman Modet was to preach. The weather was bad, the rain pouring down in torrents, the wind blowing, and the lightning occasionally flashing forth from the surcharged clouds. Still Aveline was very anxious to attend the meeting, as was Mistress Margery. Madam Clough had wished to go, but she dreaded the pelting storm. Master Overton was, of course, to be present, to assist in the services. He had hoped that the mind of Madam Clough had been somewhat awakened, and he pressed her to accompany us. Still she refused, when listening at the window, we found that the rain had ceased. This decided her, and the time having arrived, we set forth with Master Overton. Guarded from the weather as well as we could be, we sallied forth two and two, each taking a different road. Aveline and I had agreed to take the longest one. As we were at some little distance from the place of meeting, a flash of vivid lightning burst from the sky, playing along the street, as if seeking for some object to strike. Immediately afterwards our ears were almost stunned by a loud rattling peal of thunder, and once again the rain came down with even more force than before. I led Aveline under a porch, where we stood for some time watching the rain descending, and the bright flashes of lightning which came with unusual rapidity from the sky. I prayed that none of them might strike the fair girl who was beside me. She only seemed to regret being absent so long from the meeting. Once more the rain ceased, and hurrying along, we in a short time reached the side door of the building in which the meeting was being held. I having made the usual sign, the door was cautiously opened by an unseen porter. The light of a dim lamp enabled us to find our way upstairs, for no one appeared. The room was already nearly full, the larger portion of the people perhaps being Flemings who, even at the risk of their lives, had thus met together to worship according to their consciences. The preacher was at his desk, the congregation were engaged in singing in a low voice one of the hymns of which I have before spoken. It ceased; when the preacher burst forth into a fervent prayer. He prayed for all present, but especially that his country might be set free from the tyranny under which she groaned, and that all might be able to worship God in the way He desires to be worshipped, in spirit and in truth. Another hymn was sung, God's Word was read, and then the preacher began a discourse which for clearness and eloquence I have never heard surpassed. Every ear was intently listening to the words which dropped from his lips. Except the breathing of his auditors, not a sound was heard. Suddenly there was a loud cry: the report of fire-arms— the trampling of feet—the clashing of swords. A desperate struggle was going on close to us. The congregation sprang to their feet: those who had weapons drew them. At that instant the door was burst open, and the dead body of the man who kept it fell forward into the room. At the entrance was seen a body of Spanish musketeers, with weapons pointed ready to shoot down any who might oppose them. "Beloved brethren, resistance is useless—it is sinful!" exclaimed the preacher, who, being raised above the rest, had observed the strong body of men who guarded the door. "We must yield to superior power. God will know how to avenge His chosen ones."

However, in spite of the exhortations of the preacher, several of the men, who were accompanied by their wives and daughters, attempted to defend them from the rough hands of the soldiery.

"The heretics resist!—the heretics resist!" shouted the Spaniards. "Fire! fire!"

"RESISTANCE IS USELESS!"

At the fatal word the musketoons were levelled, and sent their deadly missiles whizzing through the air. The hall was filled with smoke—fearful shrieks and cries followed. The bullets had extinguished most of the lights, increasing the gloom. During the wild confusion I led Aveline to the secret door, close to which we were seated; it opened with a spring, and before the smoke cleared away sufficiently for any of the Spaniards to see us, we had passed through. Lifting her in my arms, I bore her rapidly down the narrow stair. I heard footsteps above us; they were those of friends who were endeavouring to escape by the same way. We were in total darkness, but I knew my way. The door at the bottom of the stair opened from within: I had some difficulty in withdrawing the bolts, fearing to make a noise. By this time those who were following had reached me; but I dared not speak to inquire who they were. The door was at length opened, and again lifting Aveline up, I bore her rapidly along the street. The rain had ceased, but the night was unusually dark, and favoured our escape. I dared not stop to ascertain who had escaped with us: I could only hope that they were our friends. I hurried on. Aveline entreated that I would put her down, as she felt fully able to accompany me on foot: I did so at length, and, supporting her on my arm, we took our way towards our abode. The storm had kept the citizens in their houses, so that we met no one; and even the usual guards had been keeping under shelter. Had I not been well acquainted with the city, it would have been impossible for us to find our way; as it was, I had great difficulty in doing so. More than once I feared that I had taken a wrong turning; and had I once become bewildered in that dark night, we might have wandered about till daylight without reaching the house. The porter, knowing that we were from home, was on the watch for us; he opened the instant we rapped at the door. He was a Protestant, and thoroughly trustworthy. He cast an inquiring glance at Aveline's pale face. My looks, too, probably showed that something terrible had occurred. I asked if the rest of the party had returned, and was greatly alarmed to find that they had not. A stranger, he told me, was with Master Clough.

"Shall I wait a few minutes, and see whether they will arrive, before we give the sad information to the factor?" I said to Aveline. She thought we had better go in at once, as no time was to be lost, if possible, in saving our friends from being carried off to prison. I dreaded lest some of them might have been among those killed or wounded by the cruel fire of the Spaniards. Aveline at once agreed to accompany me into the sitting-room, where Master Clough and his visitor then were. The porter assured us that he was an Englishman, and we supposed that there would be no danger in describing what had happened in his presence. I had always considered the factor a very strong-minded man; but when I told him that the meeting had been surprised by the Spanish musketeers, he was almost overcome.

"And my wife!" he exclaimed; "where is she?—why did she not accompany you?"

I explained that Madam Clough was seated at some little distance from me, and that had I waited to assist her in escaping, we should all, to a certainty, have been captured together. "Mistress Radford and I were seated close to the secret door, with which I was fortunately acquainted, or we most certainly should not have escaped," I said.

As I spoke, the stranger started and cast an inquiring glance at Aveline. Till then I had not remarked his appearance, but the movement he made induced me to examine his countenance more closely, and I then recognised the captain of the *Falcon*.

"Radford!" he exclaimed, starting up and walking towards Aveline. "Is this young lady's name Radford?"

"Yes, sir," said Aveline, lifting her eyes from the ground and looking at him. "It was the name of my father—though, alas! since my infancy I have never known him, nor even whether he is alive or dead."

"And your mother?—can you tell me of her, young lady?" he asked. "Are you her only child, or had she others?"

"I was her only child," answered Aveline, "and, alas! I lost her when very young. She died during the reign of cruel Queen Mary—put to death at Smithfield, because she loved her Bible, and held to Protestant truth."

"And your name is Aveline?" exclaimed the stranger, taking both her hands, and gazing earnestly in her face. "Then it was my beloved wife, your mother, who was thus foully murdered; and you are my own sweet child, for I was her husband! I am Captain Radford. I am your father, Aveline!"

Aveline put her hands on her father's neck as she received his kiss.

"I believe it; I am sure you are," she answered; "for even now, though I was so young when last I saw you, I remember your features, and your voice strikes on my ear like an old familiar sound."

While Captain Radford and Aveline were conversing together, Master Clough made further inquiries concerning what had occurred, and begged that I would accompany him to the place of meeting, to ascertain what had become of the prisoners. Of course, though the risk was very great, I consented immediately, and Captain Radford also desired to accompany us. "My daughter will be safe here, and I cannot let you go alone, my friend," he said. "As Englishmen, we shall not be interfered with."

The two gentlemen put on their cloaks, and taking their swords, we all three sallied out together, and made our way directly to the house I have spoken of. As we approached it, we saw torches blazing up, and found a guard of musketeers at the door. Pretending ignorance of what had happened, we inquired why the guard was posted at the house.

"Some Anabaptists or other heretics have been holding one of their assemblies in this house, and have all been seized, and are about to be carried off to prison," answered the sergeant of the guard.

"Did they yield willingly, or was any resistance made?" I asked, anxious to ascertain, if possible, who had been hurt.

"Indeed there was, and four or five met their deaths in consequence. It was through their own folly. However they have saved the executioner some trouble," answered the soldier.

Deeply grieved at these words, and anxious for the fate of our friends, I inquired if we could see the dead people.

"If it will please you, you are welcome," said the sergeant roughly; "it will be a lesson to the heretics not to hold illegal meetings again. If they wanted really to pray, there are the churches, and there is the mass for them; what more can they desire, unless they are really children of Satan?"

Taking Master Clough's arm, Captain Radford and I led him upstairs after the soldier. We entered a room near the hall. A ghastly sight met our eyes. Thrown carelessly on the floor, in a row, were eight dead bodies, just as they had been dragged out of the hall. Two were females, the rest were men. There had been many more men than women in the room, and, as might have been expected, a greater number of the former had suffered. The scene was one that might have sent a cold shudder through the hearts of people less interested than we were. Poor Master Clough could scarcely force himself to look at the dead bodies. We had to move one of the females to examine her countenance, as she had been thrown down with her face to the ground. Master Clough breathed more freely when he found that neither his wife nor Margery were among them. I was deeply thankful also to find that my friend A'Dale had escaped, dangerous as his position might be. This sad task performed, we hastened below, to inquire of the Spanish sergeant what had become of the prisoners.

"Have you any friends among them?" he asked.

"Yes, my friend, we have," answered Master Clough; "and we will recompense you if you will enable us to see them."

"You Englishmen have no lack of gold, and you will have no lack of friends wherever you go," answered the sergeant. "For the present I cannot leave my post; but I shall very likely be on guard at the prison to-morrow, and then I will assist you, if you will make it worth my while."

"But in the meantime can you tell us where our friends are to be found?" I asked.

"I will send one of my men, and he will show you," whispered the sergeant. "I am prohibited telling you, but you will understand."

He gave a peculiarly knowing look as he spoke. I doubted much whether the fellow was to be trusted; and yet we might obtain what we desired through his assistance. It was important also to find a man so willing to be bribed. By managing him properly, I saw that we might make him of use. The sergeant, telling us to wait, called one of his men, and whispered for some time in his ear.

"It is all arranged," he said, at length; "and you will remember that I consider you my debtors. I am pretty well able to look after my own interests—you will understand that."

We guessed clearly what he meant. However, as much depended upon the amount of gold Master Clough was able to expend, we knew that we should have little difficulty on that score. Should he bribe high enough, not only would the prison doors be open, but the gates of the city likewise, and not only our friends, but others in a like predicament, might be able to make their escape. Antwerp had become every day less and less fitted for our residence; and I knew that, as nearly all my patron's affairs had been wound up, we should have no difficulty in quitting the place at a very short notice. Following our guide, we passed through several streets till we arrived at one of the many new jails which had of late years been established in that unfortunate city. The soldier knocked at the gate. A warder, armed to the teeth, opened it.

"What, more prisoners?" he exclaimed.

"No," answered the soldier, and whispered a few words. "They pay well, though."

I began rather to doubt whether some trick had not been intended, and suggested to my companions that we should be cautious.

"Have two English ladies and a gentleman been brought here?" asked Master Clough.

"We recognise in this place neither ladies nor gentlemen nor nationalities. If we have here any prisoners you may desire to see, we may perchance enable you to accomplish your wish, provided always that you satisfy my just demands for any trouble you may give me."

Knowing well what the man meant, we bestowed on him a gold piece, having given a smaller one to the soldier, who immediately took his departure. We described to the warder the prisoners we desired to see.

"I will speak first to the governor of the jail," answered the man; "for myself, you will understand I can do nothing."

I saw by the leer in his eyes that he knew pretty well that he had us in his power.

"Well," I said, "we will not be ungrateful to the governor either, if he allows us to communicate with our friends."

In a short time the man returned, saying that the governor would speak with us himself, and desired us to follow him. He showed the way upstairs, through several passages, to a room, where, before a well-spread board, at which stood several flagons of wine, we found that functionary, seated in a well-stuffed high-back chair, a large napkin being placed under his chin, and fastened over his shoulders. His height was not great, but his size was prodigious; his cheeks swelling out on either side, scarcely allowed his small grey eyes to be visible. A large dish was on the table, from which he appeared to have helped himself abundantly. We stood before him with our hats in our hands.

"You want to see some prisoners?" he asked, in a somewhat inarticulate voice. "You are all honest men. Well, then, to be frank with you, I should like to see the value you set on them."

At this, without further ado, Master Clough placed several pieces of gold before the governor, who now smiled blandly.

"I see you are sensible men," he observed. "Here, Gruginback, take these people to the room where the last lot of prisoners were placed."

The governor, anxious no longer to be interrupted in his supper, which, for some reason, had been much later than usual, waved his hand, and we, taking our leave of him, followed Gruginback out of the room. With his lantern in his hand, the man led the way down numerous stairs and various passages, till we arrived at the door at the end of a vaulted corridor.

"This is one of our best rooms," he said, as he selected a key from his bunch and at length opened the door.

It was filled almost to suffocation. Some of the people within were lying down, leaning their backs against the walls. Others were sitting in various postures, to occupy as little space as possible. A few were standing up, although there was but little room for them to move. As we entered, from one of the corners where a group of females was collected, Madam Clough, uttering a cry of joy, hurried to meet her husband. She was followed by Margery and A'Dale, who had been sitting near her. He, I saw, was very pale, and from the blood on his arm and over one side of his dress, I feared that he had been wounded.

"Have you come to take us out of this horrid place?" exclaimed Madam Clough. "How brave and loving an act!"

Master Clough, of course, said that he hoped to do so ere long. After comforting our friends as well as we could, Captain Radford and I, accompanying Master Clough, set off to call on the Civil Governor of the city, to obtain from him their liberation. That functionary—Vander Vynck—a creature of Alva, received us with but little ceremony. He was about retiring to bed, after his supper, and did not appear pleased at being disturbed.

"If people attend unlawful meetings, they must take the consequences," he observed, when Master Clough made his report.

"But the meeting was held by an Englishman, and those for whom I plead are all English," answered Master Clough.

"Yes, but natives attended, as can very well be proved," exclaimed the governor. "The report has already reached me. It will go hard with them, for they have no excuse to offer. If you English come into this country, you must abide by its laws. For the security of our holy religion, such meetings are prohibited, and it matters not whether they are held by Englishmen or others. They will shortly be tried; and if, as I doubt not, they are found guilty, they will probably lose their lives. You have had my answer."

Poor Master Clough could say nothing more.

Greatly out of spirits at the ill success of our visit, we left the governor's house.

"We must unlock their prison doors with golden keys," at length said Master Clough. "I have seldom found that fail; but I fear it will go hard with the preacher. If our friend Overton cannot be liberated, these people, who have executed so many others for less offences, will shortly put him to death."

"If we cannot bribe his guards, we must carry him off by force," said Captain Radford. "I shall not lack support; and such a mode of proceeding is more to my taste than bribing these villains."

But the difficulty was to find out where Master Overton was shut up. It might have been in the same prison as the rest of our friends, though it was more probable that he had been carried to some securer jail. Finding nothing more could be done that night, we turned our steps homeward. On entering the house, we found the porter standing pale and trembling, and wringing his hands, while the other servants came hurrying into the hall in a state of the greatest trepidation and alarm.

"What is the matter—what else has happened?" asked Master Clough.

"They have carried her off! It was not our fault—they deceived us. They have borne her away!"

It was now my turn to be anxious.

"Who? who?" I asked, scarcely able to utter the words.

"It is the young lady—Mistress Radford," answered one of the servants.

"Oh! my daughter! where have they borne her to?" cried Captain Radford.

"We know not; we cannot tell," answered the servant.

"Villains! knaves!" exclaimed Master Clough, his Welsh temper rising. "How came you to allow any one to enter the house in my absence? This is an Englishman's house; you should have kept it against all comers."

"Oh! my lord, oh! master, we were deceived!" cried the porter. "The men came pretending to seek you on important business. On finding you were out, they forced their way upstairs, in spite of our opposition, with drawn swords and fire-arms in their hands. We were unprepared, and could not resist. Mistress Aveline was in her room when they rushed in. While two of them stood guard over her, the rest searched the house, pretending to look for fugitives from the meeting-house. But, as they broke open all the chests and bureaux they could find, it was clear that they were in search also of money. We are afraid that they carried away no small amount of property, for each man appeared laden with as much as he could carry, and then, placing the young lady between them, they hastened away from the house."

"Then did none of you think of following them?" exclaimed Master Clough. "For the money I care little compared to the loss of the young lady. Captain Radford, I feel for you; but even now we may discover where she has been taken to. Villains! knaves!" again exclaimed Master Clough, turning to the servants. "Why did not you follow and find out?"

"Oh! good master, they would quickly have killed us if we had attempted to do so; but immediately the strangers disappeared round the corner, Jacob Naas slipped out, and being quick of foot, followed them rapidly. Should he be unable to find them, he said he would return; but as he has now been some time absent, there is no doubt that he has tracked their footsteps, and will perchance ere long bring us tidings of the place where they have bestowed the young lady."

I cannot, even now, speak of my own feelings, nor can I well describe those of Captain Radford, on hearing this alarming account. All we could do was to wait patiently for the return of Jacob Naas. It made me almost forget the dangerous position of our other friends, for the Inquisitors were too apt to put their victims to death first, and to make inquiries respecting them afterwards; and at this time, when people were accused of heresy, a fair trial was never known to take place.

Chapter Twenty Four
A Visit to Barbara Trond

We stood in the hall, anxiously waiting the return of Jacob Naas. Several times I went out into the streets, hoping to meet him. At length I saw a figure coming rapidly out of the gloom of night towards me.

"Jacob, is it you?" I asked, as he drew near.

"Yes, Master Ernst; and I have almost lost my breath through fright and running. I am little accustomed to that."

"But have you found where they have carried her, good Jacob?" I asked eagerly.

"Yes, yes, I will tell you," was the reply; "but I am afraid even now I am followed. We will go into the house before we attempt to speak."

On entering the hall, a glass of wine restored the worthy Jacob's powers of speech.

"I hope they are not coming, though, for they would carry me off to prison too, and perhaps burn me for living in the house of a heretic!" exclaimed Jacob, who, though a Protestant at heart, had of late conformed to the Romish system.

"But say, my good friend, where they have taken Mistress Aveline!" cried Captain Radford.

"I will tell you, sir, if you will have patience," said Jacob. "I soon overtook them after they left the house, but had to keep at a cautious distance, lest I should be seen. They slackened their pace in a short time, and I was then able to keep them easily in view. I judged, from the direction they were taking, that they were making their way to the Water Gate; and my great fear then was, that they might be going out of the city altogether, and I might find it impossible to follow them. I thought of you, Master Ernst, for I knew how grieved you would be. On they went; now taking their way through the narrow streets and lanes in that direction. I had to get nearer than was prudent, for fear of missing them. Several times I was afraid that they would see me, but I suppose they did not. At length I was greatly relieved when I saw the party stop before a house a short distance from the

Water Gate. The door opened, and they all went in. I immediately hurried up to the door, on one side of which I contrived with the point of my dagger to make a mark which I am sure I shall know again. What the character of the house is I know not. Just as I was coming away, the door again opened, and I had to run to escape detection. I believe that I was followed, but I soon distanced my pursuers, and for the sake of the young lady I would gladly have run twice the risk I did."

We all, of course, thanked Jacob for the service he had rendered. He promised us that as soon as it was daylight he would gladly set out again with either of us, to try and discover the house into which Aveline had been carried. Master Clough was, however, in the meantime thinking about his wife. We were also interested in the safety of the preacher. Captain Radford longed once more to see him, as the brother of his lost wife.

The rest of the night was spent in a state of feverish anxiety, very often in silence, for after we had discussed our plans for the liberation of our friends, our minds were too much occupied to allow us to speak. Captain Radford's was the boldest plan of all. He proposed to bring the crew of his own ship and that of two or three others into the town, by scaling the walls, which he thought might be done at night; and while one party carried off Aveline from the house where she was retained in captivity, others were to attack the prison in which Madam Clough and her companions were shut up; and a third party was to liberate Master Overton, if his place of imprisonment could be discovered. As soon as morning broke, I called up Jacob, who had gone to sleep, and he, keeping to his intention, accompanied me to try and find out the house to which Aveline had been carried. We waited for some time till people were about the streets, that we might not be remarked, and then took our way hastily towards the Water Gate.

"There is the house, Master Ernst, at the end of this street," said Jacob, at length. "Let us pass by on the opposite side. I think I can distinguish the mark without looking at it too earnestly."

My heart beat quickly, for I thought that even then Aveline might be looking out of the window and observe us, though too probably she would be placed on the opposite side of the house. We went on.

"We must be close up to the door now," observed Jacob, carelessly glancing round. "Yes, there's the mark. Don't look too hard at it, Master Ernst. Yes, I have no doubt about it. And the house—yes, I see—it is one that belonged to Count Aremberg."

I looked up. The door which Jacob indicated formed the side entrance of the house. At one corner was a stout tower, and the whole of the building was of a peculiarly massive construction. It was one of those privileged abodes of the nobles into which no officer of the law could enter without a special warrant from the sovereign himself, or his representative. Count Aremberg, who had lately been killed, had left the city some time before, and the house, it was supposed, was in the hands of the Government. It was, too likely, then, they were turning it into a prison of the Inquisition, or a place of incarceration for particular prisoners. If so, the difficulty of enabling Aveline to escape would be greatly increased. However, it was something to know where she was shut up. We walked along as if we would have gone out at the Water Gate, but at that hour it was closed against us. We therefore returned, inspecting carefully the building in every direction, avoiding as much as possible making ourselves conspicuous. Having accomplished this undertaking, we returned homewards. We found Captain Radford and Master Clough preparing to set out. But it was necessary to spend some further time in consultation. The means of liberating our friends were greatly curtailed by the audacious robbery which had taken place. Master Clough, however, found that the robbers had not penetrated to one of his strong boxes, in which the largest portion of his valuables was kept.

We had still to ascertain where the preacher was imprisoned.

Should it be discovered that he had been a priest, there would be little hope of his being liberated. We must therefore in his case employ stratagem or force. I wished to set out with Master Clough, but he directed me to remain at home and look after the house.

Captain Radford meantime went off to his ship, that he might arrange his plans with his own crew and the crews of some other ships in the harbour.

I felt the inaction I was doomed to endure very much. I would far rather have been engaged in some way or other. I was pacing the room with uneven steps, after my friends had gone, when Jacob Naas presented himself.

"I have been thinking, Master Verner, that we may perhaps get some help from that old woman, Barbara Trond, whom we met out on the heath on the day of the storm some time back. I saw her only a week ago in Antwerp. Soon after the Duke Alva arrived, she returned to Antwerp; but, instead of selling wax tapers and other Popish mummery, finding her calling of sorceress and witch answer so well in the country, she now pursues it in the city. Nothing takes place with which she is not acquainted. The credulity of the Romanists is unbounded, and she finds it pay her well. Now the gold pieces you bestowed on her when we took shelter in her hut evidently won her heart, and it is my belief that if anybody can help us she can; not that I would trust to her heart or her honesty, but far rather to her avarice. If

Master Clough will give me leave to go and see her, and supply me with a dozen gold pieces, I have no doubt that, properly bestowed, they will work wonders."

I thought Jacob's plan a good one. I knew that old Barbara's public position had enabled her to become acquainted with a number of people in the city; and from her acuteness and intelligence I thought it likely she would have turned this knowledge to good account. I knew she could gain admittance into places where nobody else could find their way; and if she was determined to carry out an object, she was not the person likely to fail from any want of exertion or from over-delicacy. I wished very much to accompany him, and proposed setting out at once, without waiting for the return of Master Clough. He, however, urged that we should first see the factor, and take his advice; perhaps he might have some other means of liberating Aveline, as well as the preacher, Overton. The time appeared very long while I waited for the return of the factor. I could not help thinking that all sorts of dreadful things might happen to Aveline—that she might be taken away from Antwerp, or placed in the Inquisition and subjected to torture, to try and make her condemn her friends. The last idea was too dreadful to be entertained, and yet such things had been done day after day.

At length Master Clough returned. I inquired eagerly of the success he had had. He shook his head:

"For our friend Overton I have very little hopes," he said. "For my dear wife and her two young companions, I may possibly, by bribing high, succeed, provided they immediately leave the country, undertaking never to return; forsooth, the latter part of the arrangement would be no great punishment, as I cannot conceive any one willingly remaining in a land ruled by that despotic and boastful tyrant, Duke Alva. I was permitted to see my wife, and I was thus able to keep up her spirits. My belief is, that the authorities, who have got her in their power, keep her there, in order to see how much they can draw from me. I am now going forth to endeavour to raise the sum they require; at the same time, I have threatened to make a formal complaint to the Court of Spain of the robbery which has been committed in my house, and of the outrage to my family by the carrying off of one of its members. Of Mistress Aveline I have been unable to gain any information."

I told Master Clough of Jacob's proposal, to which he agreed, and at once placed a purse of gold in my hand, telling me to make the best use of it I could.

"Duke Alva will arrive here to-morrow, I find, for the purpose of being present at the opening of the monument he has erected to himself. As he at present, as far as I can learn, has no wish to quarrel with England, I have hopes that a personal application to him may be successful. At all events, we must leave no stone unturned to gain our object; and, once out of this country, never will I set foot in it again."

Master Clough having drawn out the papers he required for his proposed transaction, set out for the Bourse; while I, disguised as one of his serving-men, accompanied Jacob to the abode of the old fortune-teller. Flemish being my native tongue, it must be remembered I had no difficulty in passing for the character I had assumed; and I thought that, probably, the Dame Barbara would not recognise me.

We hurried on towards the part of the city where Jacob believed she resided; but to find her abode when there among the numberless mean houses which filled that part of Antwerp was not so easy. We had to ask several people, and to go from house to house before we could discover her. Some looked at us suspiciously.

"You want the Witch of Antwerp," said one, at length. "It is dangerous dealing with such as her. Maybe she has brought these miseries on our country; and the people would do well to make her remove them, or to sink her into the middle of the Scheld. However, if you desire to find her, go on to the end of the lane, and then, turning to your right, knock thrice at the first door you find. If she is disposed to admit you, the door will open in as many minutes as the times you have knocked; if not, you will hear her owl hooting from within—that is a sign that you had better make the best of your way from the house, or some evil will befall you."

We thanked our informant—a hard-working artisan of the class which mostly occupied that part of the city—and followed his direction.

On reaching the door, I directed Jacob to knock. I almost expected to hear the owl hoot, but scarcely two minutes had passed before the door slowly opened. We entered, and found ourselves in a dimly-lighted passage. The door closed behind us, without anybody being seen. We had our swords and daggers, and Jacob carried a pistol in his belt, so that, should we be suddenly attacked, we might defend ourselves. We advanced quickly along the passage, till at the farther end we came to another door. Jacob knocked three times with the hilt of his dagger, when the door by unseen agency opened slowly, as the other had done, and we saw a curtain hanging in front of us. On drawing it aside, we found ourselves in a vaulted chamber of considerable size; several lamps hanging from the roof gave sufficient light to show the various objects within. The trade carried on by the old witch must have paid well, as the various articles the chamber contained could not have been procured unless at a considerable expense. There were stuffed animals and creatures of various sorts: a huge crocodile, from the Nile; a vulture, with expanded wings, and talons tearing its prey, at which its bloodshot eyes looked down with an expression of life-like savageness. On one side there was a human skeleton of gigantic proportions, with a club in its hand, in the attitude of striking. Toads and lizards abounded. There were mummy cases, with their lids off, exposing the dried remnants of mortality within. In huge bottles were children, some with two heads, or three arms, and other deformities, hideous and disgusting to look at. There were also all sorts of incomprehensible instruments, but whether constructed for any purpose, or merely for the sake of deception, I could not ascertain. At the farther end of the chamber sat the old witch, habited much as we had seen her in her abode on the heath, with a few fantastic additions, which increased her weird appearance. Beyond her was an open space, and on the ground was seen a fiery line forming a circle. A mist seemed to fill the end of the vault, or else it was a veil so cunningly devised as to represent a mist. Before her, on a tripod, stood her magic cauldron, out of which deep red flames rose up, casting a lurid glare around.

I saw that Jacob looked very pale. He was not prepared for such a scene. He perhaps thought that I, too, had lost my colour; or possibly the nature of the light in the room added to the pallor of our countenances.

The witch took no notice of our approach, but continued her apparent incantations. We advanced slowly between a row of hideous monsters, who grinned down upon us from the pedestals on which they sat or stood. They reminded me somewhat of the deities of an Indian temple, from which possibly they may have been carried away by some Spanish or Portuguese adventurers.

As we drew close to the witch, she waved her wand, and in a low, croaking voice ordered us to stop.

"What seek you with me?" she asked, in the same harsh tone.

"Your assistance, good mother," answered Jacob.

"Good mother, quotha? People don't often call me good. As to whether or not you will or will not obtain my assistance, time will show. We have not met for the first time. I don't forget you, young sir, with a liberal hand. Tell me, however, what you require, and I doubt not that I shall have the power to obtain it for you."

"The task is not an easy one that we desire you to perform, dame," I answered. "I am ready to purchase your services on your own terms; and perhaps, as the affair is altogether connected with this world, we can dispense with your incantations on the occasion, and proceed at once to business."

The old woman uttered a harsh, cackling laugh: "I know not that," she said; "but where work can be done by human means, I have no desire to summon the spirits of the dead to my assistance. See yonder relic of mortality. At my will I can clothe him with flesh and skin and garments, and send him forth to accomplish my behests; but I tell you I often have to pay dear to maintain my power, and therefore would I rather trust to such means as my native wit affords me."

She pointed as she spoke to the skeleton of the giant. I had no wish to dispute the matter with her, however much I might have doubted the power she possessed, though I had great confidence in her wit and knowledge of what was going on in the city. I at once, therefore, explained what had happened—how Master Clough's house had been attacked, and Aveline carried off. I did not at first tell her that we were aware of the place in which she was imprisoned, that I might judge whether she knew anything of the matter. But she must have suspected that we knew more than I told her, for she declared that she could do nothing unless she knew the place in which Aveline was shut up. I accordingly told her that we had discovered the house, and were eager to undertake any plan she might suggest for rescuing her.

"Well, sit down there on those stools," she said, pointing to some which stood on the opposite side of the chamber, "Rest there, and meditate; I must have time to consider the matter. Perchance I may have to consult my familiar, and, if so, you must promise to remain quiet, and not to be alarmed at my proceedings. Is there any other matter about which you desire to consult me?"

I told her of Master Overton's capture, and of our dread lest he might—as so many other Protestants had been—be led to the stake, in spite of his being an Englishman.

"He deserves to die for his folly!" she muttered. "Why not let people remain in their ignorance? If they are once enlightened, they will allow the priests and witches and wizards, and such-like persons, who live on the credulity of their fellow-creatures, to starve and sink into pauper's graves. However, if you pay me well—although I have no love for the man, or such as he—I will honestly win my wages, by doing all I can to obtain his liberation."

"A sensible answer, dame," I replied, being more convinced than ever that the old woman worked rather by art and cunning than by any power she possessed over the spirits of the air or earth.

"Well, young sir, let me hear what means you have at your disposal for liberating the young lady. Can it best be accomplished by force or fraud?"

"That is the very question on which I would consult you," I answered, not wishing to inform her of the plan I proposed, lest she should prove treacherous—for even then I did not altogether confide in her.

"Perchance it might be well to unite the two," she said. "If I can manage to get the young lady to the street-door, think you that you could protect her till you have her safely out of the city? for I warn you that it would not be safe to conduct her back to Master Clough's house."

I did not answer immediately, though the plan she proposed was similar to what I had from the first thought of.

"I will try and find a few trusty friends who will help me in the matter," I answered, "if you can manage to place the young lady in our hands. It must be done, however, without delay."

"You are right, young sir," she answered; "I have thought over the matter. To-morrow our great Duke is to unveil before the eyes of his admiring worshippers the mighty statue he has erected to his own honour. Men's thoughts and tongues will wag different ways, I suspect, at the spectacle; but all will be eager to show themselves present—magistrates and people, soldiers and civilians. The streets will be empty, and many a strong post left unguarded. It is a pity the Prince of Orange has not a few thousand men ready to rush in on one side of the city while the Spanish hero is singing his own praises on the other. However, it will be some time before the Prince can recover his losses; though I tell you, as long as any life remains in the land, he is the man who must take the lead. Now, then, listen to my plan. You have marked the house well, you say. Two hours after noon to-morrow, when the lieges of this city are kneeling before the statue of their tyrant, do you come to the door and knock thrice. I will be within; and if the young lady has not in the meantime been removed, I will find the means of bringing her down and delivering her into your hands. The rest must depend upon your courage and resolution. The risk is great, and so must be my reward."

Knowing well what she meant, I placed a portion of the gold I had received in her hand, and promised her a yet further sum as soon as, through her means, Aveline was rescued.

"And now, dame," I said, recollecting the preacher and his too probable fate, should he not be set at liberty, "what help can you render the other prisoner I spoke of? will gold not find its way to his jailers' hearts?"

"That task would be a more difficult one even than the other," she answered; "yet, could I find out where he is shut up, I might perchance accomplish it."

"Cannot your art help you?" I asked.

She turned a quick glance round at me.

"It is a matter in which I am not disposed to exercise it," she answered. "Now go your ways, and make your arrangements for rescuing the young lady. Come here again to-night at ten o'clock, and perhaps by that time I may be able to give you further information."

Having said this, the old woman, as if suddenly recollecting that she had been too matter-of-fact in the way of dealing with us, went to her cauldron, and poking up the fire, began to mutter various cabalistic words, at the same time stirring its contents with her wand.

Taking this as a sign that she wished our visit to terminate, without further waste of words we returned by the way we had come, the doors opening as before, without our touching the latch, while the last one shut with a loud slam behind us, and we heard bars and bolts immediately drawn across it, showing us that some person had been concealed close to the door. Soon after we reached the house Captain Radford arrived.

Chapter Twenty Five
The Escape from Prison

I need not describe the inquiries made by Captain Radford. I briefly explained the plan I proposed for recovering Aveline; he approved of what I had done.

"I can bring a force of twenty seamen, who will fight to the death," he observed; "but I have hopes that we may so manage it as to encounter no opposition. The sea-wall can easily be scaled, and I propose, therefore, to have ladders in readiness, so that, climbing over them, we may avoid the gates. As the Spanish troops will be in the citadel in attendance on Duke Alva, we may manage even in daylight to do so without being observed. The boats will be in readiness to receive us, and we may speedily get aboard my ship."

I do not here mention all the details of our plan. Having arranged it thoroughly, I then told him I had hopes that some means might be found of rescuing Master Overton. For that also he was prepared. His idea was, that if the prison could be found, to force the gates while the troops were away in the citadel. He believed that many of the citizens would unite in the attempt, in the expectation of rescuing their own friends. Indeed, so great was the hatred felt by the great mass of the population towards the Spaniards, that the instant they were removed, without considering the consequences, the people were ready to rise, for the sake of doing any mischief which might present itself.

We found that Master Clough had returned, and once more gone out. We now waited anxiously for his return, as we could do nothing till the evening, when Captain Radford proposed once more going among his brother captains, in order that he might obtain further assistance. We waited and waited. Still he did not appear, and our anxiety increased. At length, as it was growing dusk, and Jacob and I were about to prepare for our expedition, a knock was heard at the door.

"That's the master's!" exclaimed Jacob, hurrying down.

We followed him, when the door opened, and Master Clough appeared with his wife leaning on his arm, followed by A'Dale and Margery. Both were agitated and trembling, and could with difficulty find words to explain what had happened. Till the very moment of their liberation they had believed that they were to share the fate of many of their fellow-prisoners, who, it was reported, were to be carried forth and executed outside the walls on the following day, in honour of the Duke Alva's appearance in the city. How far the report was correct we could not tell, but it had served very naturally to agitate them greatly. They had no time, however, for giving way to their feelings; for the condition of their liberation, Master Clough informed us, was, that they were to leave the city that very evening. If found within the walls by daybreak, they would run the risk of being again incarcerated, and sharing the doom of the numberless Netherlanders put to death by the Blood Council. A'Dale was anxious to hear what I had done; and, in spite of the danger he would have to go through, he insisted on aiding me in the undertaking. But our first care was to see Madam Clough and Margery placed on board Captain Radford's ship. Some time was occupied first in collecting all their jewels and other valuables, loaded with which they bade a hurried adieu to the house they had so long inhabited, and to their domestics. With as many men as could be spared from the house, well-armed, we then set forth, lighted by torches, to the Water Gate, where Captain Radford had his boat waiting. He had a pass ready, so that the rest of the party had no difficulty in getting through the gates. Jacob and I, having seen them thus far safely on their way, turned back, in order to pay our promised visit to the old witch. As we walked down to the gate, A'Dale told me that he had resolved to return on shore again at all risks, if there was any work to be done. I briefly told him the plans for rescuing Aveline. "That will just suit my taste," he answered. "I would rather, if a blow is to be struck, be ready to join in the fray."

As soon as Jacob and I had seen my friends through the gates, we returned into the city, and made the best of our way towards the abode of Barbara Trond. The door opened as before, and we entered the vaulted chamber. She was seated, as she had been at the first visit, before her cauldron, as if busily employed in her incantations. There was, however, the smell of a rich stew, and I saw a vessel steaming away on one side of me from which it appeared to proceed. I had little doubt, therefore, that the old woman was not unmindful of her creature comforts. It was most likely that she had only put on her cauldron as our knock was heard at the door. But she would probably be more useful to us by the information she managed to pick up in the world than by her sorceries.

"I judge that you are my visitors," she said; and putting aside her magic wand, she turned round, as if to discuss matters in a matter-of-fact way.

"Now, my young sir, do you think you possess sufficient courage and nerve to enter one of the prisons of the Blood Council? If you do, I may promise you the freedom of your friend. But recollect the risk you run is a very fearful one. If you are captured, your life will pay the penalty."

I replied that I would run every risk for the sake of saving the life of my friend, and asked what plan she proposed.

"I have, you understand, assistants in every direction," she said. "I have made it to be understood that the minister, Overton, would, if duly instructed, be disposed to return to the old faith. I have therefore suggested that a certain learned friar should be allowed to visit him, who will bring forward such irresistible arguments that he will be unable to withstand them. I have bribed the guards to shut their eyes, should they observe anything suspicious, especially if two friars are seen to go out instead of the one who might have entered. Now see!"

As the old woman spoke, she rose and took from a chest on one side of the room two bundles.

"Here are two friars' dresses, with all things requisite," she observed. "Do you dress in one of them, and conceal the other round your body beneath your gown. I have a pass ready to admit you into the prison; when there, I must leave the rest to your discretion and judgment. To-morrow before noon will be the best time to visit the prison, when the attention of the people will be drawn off towards the ceremony I was describing to you. This will give you time to see your friend in safety, and to assist in the rescue of the young lady."

My spirits rose on hearing the plan of the old woman; and I should then and there have given her the whole of the money with which I hoped to bribe her, had I not thought it possible she might take the bribe and neglect to perform her part of the contract. Having a great deal to do, I took leave of her as soon as these arrangements were made, and hastened back to Master Clough's house.

Here I was engaged till daylight in seeing his property packed, which was to be shipped in the morning, and in making arrangements with the clerks and servants who were still to remain. At length, overcome, I lay down for an hour on my bed, charging Jacob to call me in ample time to prepare for my hazardous undertaking. When I arose again I need scarcely say that I prayed earnestly for protection, that all those in whom I was interested might escape from the dangers which surrounded us. I had still much to do, so there was but little time for thought. My chief consolation was, that should I fail and be captured—when I knew that my death would be certain—I should leave Aveline under the guardianship of her father. She would mourn for me, but would, I trusted, in time, find a balm for her sorrow.

Antwerp was full of prisons, many of the residences of the murdered burghers and nobles having been converted for that purpose. Dame Trond had, however, indicated clearly the one in which Overton was confined. As the hour approached, accompanied by Jacob Naas, I took my way to a spot near the city walls, where a deep archway existed. The neighbourhood was little frequented, and we there hoped that I might be able unperceived to put on the friar's dress. The change could very quickly be made, so that there was not much risk of being interrupted, while Jacob kept watch outside, to give due notice of the approach of any intruder. I sallied forth, still in my servant's dress, with the faithful Jacob. I did not for a moment conceal from myself the danger of the undertaking. We hastened along, with two small valises containing the dresses on our shoulders, like a couple of serving-men carrying their master's property, looking as unconcerned as possible when we met any passers-by. I encountered several persons who knew me, and looked at me very hard; but the change of dress had so altered me, that they evidently thought they must be mistaken.

We hurried on through the streets till we approached the spot I have described; then, stopping, we looked round, to ascertain whether any one was observing us. Finding that the coast was clear, we again hastened on, and, as we believed, gained the arch without being discovered. Unpacking our valises, I immediately commenced rolling Overton's disguise round my body, and fastened it securely. I then hurriedly put on the dress arranged for myself, with a belt of rope round my waist, and a large rosary of wood attached to it. As soon as I was dressed I called Jacob.

"You are the monk to perfection, Master Ernst," he said. "Surely no one would hesitate to admit you, wherever you may desire to go; and if you can persuade the minister to dress up in the same way, you will have no difficulty in getting through the gates of the prison."

These remarks encouraged me greatly, and, with more confidence than I had expected to feel, I made my way by a circuitous route toward the prison I have mentioned, while Jacob, putting one valise into the other, returned homewards.

As I passed along, many of the people I met bowed and saluted me, as they are accustomed to treat their priests. I in return muttered a few words such as are used by the friars on similar occasions. I was afraid of walking fast, as my inclination prompted, lest I should betray myself. The streets were already crowded with people in their holiday attire, prepared to assemble at the festival, though their looks did not wear a joyful aspect. Fear and doubt rather were visible on every countenance. The name alone of the Duke and his murderous musketeers kept them in awe. They had no leader in whom they could confide, even should they have ventured to resist the tyrannical treatment to which they were subjected. They knew themselves to be slaves; but at the same time they were slaves panting to be free, and only waiting an opportunity for striking a blow for liberty. I could distinguish, as I walked along, the Protestants from the Romanists, by their looks, and the way in which they regarded me. The Protestants cast a glance of defiance as they passed, and made no sign of respect. The Romanists, on the contrary, wore generally a look of stolid indifference, or made an abject bow.

Arrived at the prison door, I mustered up all my courage. I required it to withstand the scrutiny of the jailer when I presented my pass.

"You are the monk who has undertaken the conversion of the heretic minister?" he observed. "It is well, though I should think half a dozen will be required before he is brought to the truth. They are fearfully tough subjects to convince. I have had five or six under my hands, and one and all preferred going to the stake to recanting."

"Perhaps two of us may work the desired change," I answered; "my brother, Father Peter, and I hope to get the captive free from his thraldom; and if we don't succeed to-day, we must try again."

"When is Father Peter coming, then?" said the jailer.

"What! has he not already arrived?" I inquired; "surely, I hoped that he had been with the prisoner some time already."

"If so, he must have come before I was on guard," answered the jailer.

"Very likely," I replied; "he is always zealous, and would rather be before than after his time. And was he not here yesterday?"

"Not that I am aware of," answered the jailer.

"I see how it is!" I exclaimed; "they wish to throw all the work upon me. However, I must waste no longer time. Let a warder show me to the prisoner, for unless he is brought to the truth very soon, it seems probable that he will be sent to the stake."

The jailer on this called one of the warders, and directed him to lead me to the English minister's cell, and on no account to interrupt us. By the glance the warder gave me, I hoped that he had already been bribed by old Dame Trond, and that he would not interfere with our proceedings. I therefore followed him with a light step, passing through numerous passages to the room in which the prisoner was confined. The house had been hurriedly fitted up as a prison, the lofty rooms being divided into two storeys, and each room being again subdivided by passages into cages, rather than cells, so that the prisoners could be confined separately from each other. Many of them had very little light, and still less air; and, as far as I could judge, every cell almost had an occupant. It was fearful to contemplate what would be the probable fate of all those human beings, for it was well-known that of those imprisoned but a very small number escaped death.

"I conclude that Father Peter is already with the prisoner," I observed, as I walked along.

The man glanced quickly round at me.

I showed him a gold piece in my hand. He immediately put out his to receive it, nodding at the same time.

"There," he said at length, as we reached the door of the cell; "I need not look in, for I should not like to interrupt Father Peter, should he be at his devotions with the poor heretic. Go in, and may you have success in your undertaking."

I observed that when he shut the door he did not again lock it or push to the bolts. The minister was seated with his back to the door when I entered. When at length he discovered that there was somebody in the cell, he rose from his seat, and, turning round, confronted me.

"I regret, sir, that you should have come," he said, in a courteous voice. "You perhaps wish to make known to me the articles of your faith; but let me say in return that I know them thoroughly, and have no wish to embrace those which differ, I conceive, from the teaching of the Gospel."

"I see you do not know me, Master Overton," I said, in a low voice. "Do not utter any exclamation of surprise; I have come in the hopes of liberating you!"

"Who—who is it?" he exclaimed, in an undertone. "Ernst Verner? No, indeed, I should not have known you. But how do you expect to set me free?"

"You must assume the same disguise I wear," I answered; "I have it prepared for you. They have allowed you, I see, a pallet-bed. You must leave your clothes upon it, stuffed out as we can best arrange them; so that, should the warder look in, he may suppose you to be asleep. Quickly put on these monkish habiliments. I have already spoken to them of having a companion; and I hope, before they expect any deception, we may have got outside the prison gates."

Master Overton quickly understood what was necessary to be done, and, dressing himself in the friar's robes I had brought under mine, soon appeared quite as respectable-looking a friar as I did.

"We must frame an excuse for leaving the prison so soon," I observed. "I must assert that the prisoner is too obdurate to be moved at present; and that, unless he is subjected to a little more discipline, I fear that we cannot hope to be successful."

I now spoke loud enough, should the warder be passing, to let him suppose that I was arguing with the prisoner. After some time my voice rose higher and higher. At length I whispered to him, "It is time that we should set forth." He was more agitated than I should have expected.

"I cannot go in my own strength," he said. "Let us kneel down and pray."

We did so, and rose greatly refreshed.

"Now," he said, "I am prepared."

I had a staff such as friars were accustomed to use, and requested him to take it. Pressing against the door, I gladly found it opened. I had marked the way we came, and was thus able to go forth without hesitation, till we reached the door where the jailer was stationed.

"Father Peter and I have had hard work," I said, as I saw him, "and I am afraid we have made but little way. However, we must not despair, and hope to come again to-morrow."

The jailer looked from me to the pretended Father Peter. It was a critical moment.

"We must not delay," I observed, "for we have several more heretics to visit. Come along, Father Peter, come along!"

The jailer, deceived by my coolness, and either believing or pretending to believe that my companion had been admitted by his fellow, drew forth the key of the door, and, pulling back the bolts, to my infinite satisfaction opened it. I almost shoved the seeming Father Peter out of the door in my eagerness to get him free, and, bestowing a blessing on the jailer, I followed him into the street. But I did not consider that we were clear of danger. In the first place, our flight might soon be discovered by one of the warders who had not been bribed by Dame Trond; and, should we be pursued, we were too likely to be recognised. I now wished that we had made some arrangement for changing our dresses, but it was too late to do that. Unwilling to return to Master Clough's house, we agreed that our best plan was to make our way direct towards the Water Gate, in which neighbourhood we hoped to fall in with Captain Radford and his party. There were one or two spots in that neighbourhood where I knew we might possibly have time to take off our friars' dresses. Master Overton had been so long accustomed to wear a similar costume, that he was perfectly at home in his; and, though it was much against his will, he followed my example in making the usual signs to the passers-by who saluted him.

By this time people were proceeding in greater numbers towards the citadel, literally leaving a considerable portion of the town depopulated. At length we reached the part of the wall near the Water Gate which Captain Radford had pointed out as most easy to scale. It was about an equal distance from the towers, from which, although sentries were generally placed in them, we hoped that, on this occasion, they might be withdrawn. The wall, I think I said, was very thick, there being a passage within it, running completely round the city, with here and there openings in the inside, to afford light and air. At the top also was a walk communicating with the various towers. There was but little difficulty in scaling the wall from the inside to the upper wall, as from the numerous buttresses and turrets, concealment might easily be obtained. The risk was in descending on the outer side, where it was far more open to view. The streets in this part of the city were especially narrow, with numerous dark passages and archways. The inhabitants, too, were nearly all Romanists, and they appeared mostly to have gone out to welcome the Duke; so we had not much difficulty in finding a secluded spot, where we could get rid of our friars' costume. Master Overton had been dressed in his gown when taken. Under this he had the dress of a civilian, which he usually wore. The gown he had left in the prison when he put on the friar's dress. We both of us therefore were sufficiently clothed, after getting rid of our friars' robes, to appear in the streets. Scarce a minute was occupied in throwing them off. Shoving them up into a dark corner, we again hurried out, in the hopes of falling in with Captain Radford. It still wanted several minutes to the time when I expected to meet them. We had taken our station near the wall at a convenient spot whence we could watch it. Great was our delight when we saw a rope ladder let over the wall, and, one by one, a number of armed men descending by it. Among them I recognised Captain Radford and A'Dale. We hurried forward to meet them. The former Master Overton warmly embraced.

"Brother of my sainted wife," said the captain; "I little expected thus to meet you! We parted in anger: we meet as real brothers."

There was no time for the exchange of further words, but the men forming in close order, we marched steadily along the narrow streets. At another time this would have been impossible; but there was, at present, little risk of any one interfering with our proceedings. At length we reached the door which Jacob Naas had marked, and, with an agitated heart, at once stepped forward and gave the number of raps agreed on with old Dame Trond. It was an anxious moment. I counted the seconds as they passed by, dreading lest, after all, she might have played us false, or have been unable to accomplish her purpose. Crowbars had been brought by our party, and it was agreed that, should the door not be opened, we should force our way in. I waited anxiously, drawing my breath with an unusual quickness. I listened: I fancied I heard a bolt withdrawn. Slowly the door opened. I sprang forward, and caught sight of a figure in the doorway. Could it be Aveline?

"Hush!" said a voice from within; "I will trust to you for my reward."

In another instant Aveline herself fell almost fainting into my arms. She quickly recovered herself.

"Where is my father?" she asked. "Is he safe?"

Captain Radford stepped forward, and, supporting Aveline, we all hurried towards the walls. There was no time to hear who had carried Aveline off, or by what means she had been set free. I only knew that it was by the promised instrumentality of the old woman, and felt that she, at all events, deserved the reward I had agreed to pay. Few words were exchanged among us till we got safely back to the wall. This had now to be scaled. As yet, as far as we could ascertain, we had been undiscovered. Two of the seamen volunteered to mount the wall first, to see that our road was clear, and to guard the top till the rest had gained it. The first having mounted and made the signal that no one was near, the rest of the men followed. Captain Radford then, taking Aveline in his arms, mounted the ladder, Master Overton and I holding it below. As he reached the top, she was safely lifted up. The rest of the party quickly followed, when the ladder was once more drawn up, and let down again on the other side. We had now to descend. While I stood on the top, I could not help looking anxiously round, lest we might be observed from any of the neighbouring towers.

The place at which Captain Radford and his men had landed was upwards of a mile from the part of the wall we had scaled. He had directed those in charge of the boats to row some little way down the river, and not to return till he should make a signal for them to do so. On our way Aveline gave me a brief account of what had happened to her, more of which I heard afterwards. She was on her knees, praying that those dear to her might be protected from the dangers which threatened them, when she was startled by hearing the footsteps of several persons approaching the room. Before she had time to secure the door, they burst it open, and one of them, throwing a cloak over her, bore her downstairs. In vain she struggled—in vain she cried out. Overawing the servants, they hurried her into the streets, and carried her rapidly along till they reached the door of a large house which stood open. They entered, and she was conveyed upstairs into a handsome room, when she was placed on a sofa and left alone. Her sole attendant was a young girl who seemed to be dumb, and, at all events, from her she could not obtain the slightest information of any description.

From the behaviour and language of the persons who had committed the outrage, she was of opinion that they were far above the lower classes. They had treated her with perfect respect; and it seemed that their chief object in carrying her off was to obtain a ransom, under the belief that she was the daughter of Master Clough or of Sir Thomas Gresham. She added that, on the previous day, an old woman had come to the house, and had had some conversation with its inmates. She had visited her also, and told her to keep up her spirits, and to be prepared to return to her friends within a few hours. True to her word, she had appeared that morning, and, no one interfering, had, at the time she had promised, led her downstairs.

"She, however, made me undertake that you would carry the promised reward to her house this afternoon, as soon as you had seen me in safety on board."

I, of course, told Aveline that I felt myself bound at all risks to fulfil my promise to the old woman, and that I should do well to hasten back at once and pay her the money; I should be able to do so and to overtake them by the time they reached the boats. A'Dale insisted on accompanying me.

"I wish that some other means could be found for sending the old woman her reward," said Captain Radford; "for I fear the risk to you will be very great, should the part you have taken in liberating my dear brother-in-law and daughter be discovered."

I answered that I considered that, duty should be first thought of, and that a promise, to whomsoever made, was a promise still, and that therefore, at all risks, I would willingly undertake the task.

Aveline was, I saw, very anxious on the subject; and I did my best to console her by pointing out that I had passed through so many dangers, that I had every reason to hope that I might be preserved as before.

With the purse of gold, promised to Dame Trond, under my cloak, I once more, with A'Dale, entered the ill-fated city of Antwerp.

Chapter Twenty Six
A Brave Defence

As we approached the northern gate, by which we purposed entering Antwerp, we met some straggling parties of persons who had come out of the city, slowly proceeding towards the river. They none of them carried anything, neither baskets nor bundles, nor visible property of any description. Yet there was something in their looks which made me fancy that they were anxious to escape from the place.

We hastened on to Dame Trond's house. As we passed through the streets, loud salvos of artillery and the rattling sound of musketry reached our ears, fired in honour of the ruler of the Netherlands or his statue; as A'Dale remarked, it was hard to say which. On reaching the witch's abode, I knocked as before at the door. We were speedily admitted. People who come with gold in their purses are seldom denied. The old dame was highly pleased, and promised us every possible good luck to the end of our days.

"You are fortunate, young sir," she said, "in being able to make your escape from this city; for, from all I have seen and heard, by the study of my art I perceive that ere long even worse days than the miserable ones at present are coming upon it."

"It needs no witch to tell us that, mother," observed A'Dale. "When Duke Alva finds that he can so easily fill his coffers by murdering his loving subjects, he is not likely to end his system, until he has no more subjects worth murdering."

The old woman gave a keen, quick glance up at A'Dale.

"Those are dangerous words to speak, young master," she observed. "It is well that my walls have no ears; but if a Netherlander were to utter them, I would not answer for the consequences."

I could not understand Dame Trond's character. That she was an impostor I had no doubt. She certainly was not an adherent of the Church of Rome, and still more certainly she had no knowledge of Christianity. I am afraid she was like others, who found it profitable to impose on their fellow-creatures in spite of all consequences. Yet she was apparently kind-hearted, and possessed some of the milk of human nature, though it might turn rather acid at times. When we bade her farewell, she hobbled after us to the door, again thanking us for our liberality, and praying that we might be protected from all dangers.

Having thus far satisfactorily performed our mission, we turned once more to the North Gate of the city. We were again surprised by the number of persons we saw emerging from the gate; as we passed through it, we observed the guard as usual standing at their posts, and not seeming in any way disposed to interrupt them. I remarked, however, among them two or three men I knew, and whom I had always felt sure were strong Protestants. They saluted us as we passed. One of them, stepping forward, whispered to me, "Hasten on without delay!"

I thanked the man, and we took the hint, walking rapidly forward to the place Captain Radford had appointed. I now became very anxious for him and Aveline and Master Overton, fearing lest by waiting for us they might become involved in the dangers to which the fugitives would too likely be exposed. Shortly afterwards, as we looked back, we saw the people behind us increasing their speed, and in a short time the very guard we had left at the gate overtook us. Seeing the man who had spoken to me, I asked him what had occurred.

"Taking advantage of the absence of the soldiers in the citadel, we surprised the Spanish guard at the gate," he answered, "and occupying their post, allowed our friends to go through. We have left the Spaniards bound in the guardroom. We have closed the gates behind us, and are now hastening to get on board ship before our flight is discovered A good reason then have we for making haste."

We observed that not only the men who had formed the guard at the gate were armed, but so also were a large number of the persons who accompanied them. I remembered well the escape of fugitives I had many years before witnessed, when the Romanists, without remorse, attacked them. We were still some distance from the point of embarkation towards which the fugitives were making their way, when a shout from those still behind us reached our ears:

"The Spaniards are coming! Fly, friends, fly! the Spaniards are coming!"

We looked over our shoulders, and saw a body of horsemen sweeping along the road which led from one of the further gates of the city. They were galloping furiously, and by the glitter of their leader's sword, which was pointed towards us, we were left in no doubt as to their intentions.

"Countrymen, we must stand and fight, and hold the ground till the women and children have embarked! Who will rally round me?" cried one of the fugitives.

The speaker was a sturdy artisan—a master blacksmith of the city, well-known for the valiant way in which he had, on more than one occasion, wielded his double-handled sword. Others repeated his call, and some fifty brave fellows collected together, forming a strong body across the road. Happily, in consequence of the number of canals and ditches, the horsemen were compelled to keep in the causeway, and were thus unable to cut off the fugitives by making a circuit in any other direction. We could not help answering to the brave blacksmith's call, by joining those who rallied round him. The order was now given slowly to retreat, that we might afford ourselves a better chance of escaping after the women and children had embarked. The Spanish horse were drawing nearer and nearer. They were well-trained ruffians, whose swords had often been dyed in the blood of the unhappy Netherlanders, and no sensation of pity was likely to prevent them from slaughtering all they could now overtake. As they came within a hundred yards of us, their commander ordered them to charge.

"Slay! slay! cut down all your swords can reach!" we heard him shouting out.

We had a few pike-men with us, who, springing to the front, knelt down to receive the horses. Those with pistols formed the second rank, while those with arquebuses and musketoons drew up behind them. We thus presented a formidable front, while a deep ditch on either side prevented our being taken in flank. The Spaniards, nothing daunted, however, galloped forward. We received them firmly. Several saddles were emptied of their riders, and five or six of the leading horses slain or badly wounded. The bodies of the animals encumbering the road, prevented the advance of those in the rear, thus giving time to us to reload our fire-arms, while the Spanish commander, seeing that he could not break through our line, gave the order to his men to wheel about and retire. Several others were shot as they fled, but their fleet horses soon carried them out of reach of our fire-arms. On seeing this, our brave leader gave the order to his followers to retreat towards the boats. But before we had made good fifty yards, the Spaniards had once more wheeled about, and came galloping at a furious pace towards us. Again we threw ourselves into the same position as before. Thundering over the ground came the Spanish horsemen, with the determination of crushing us. The artisans of Antwerp, however, well-trained to arms, were not men to be cut down without fighting hard, when given the opportunity of resisting in a body. Still the Spaniards charged courageously, and several of the front rank were cut down, while others were killed or wounded by the discharge of their musketoons. The places of those who were killed were instantly supplied by others from the rear, and once more the cavalry had to retreat. At that instant a man came running up from the bank of the river, which was elevated considerably above the ground on which we stood, with the alarming intelligence that a body of musketeers was seen in the distance advancing towards us. Those dreaded musketeers! even the bravest well knew that we could not hope to withstand them! The possibility that Aveline might be among those we saw on the banks gave courage to my arm, and made me resolve to fight to the last, in order to stop the progress of the hated Spaniards. Once among that crowd of helpless women and children and old men, I knew too well the fearful havoc they would commit. The atrocities which they had been guilty of at Valenciennes and many other places were still too fresh in our memory not to be thought of. Once more, therefore, we retreated, facing the foe, who again galloped towards us.

On looking round as we approached the river's bank, my worst apprehensions were realised, for there I recognised Captain Radford, though his back was turned towards me as he waved to a boat coming up the river to hasten onward. Our retreat had now become almost a flight, for our pike-men, not daring to kneel to receive the horsemen, were unable as before to drive them back. Headed by the blacksmith, however, the bravest of the party stood their ground, giving blow for blow as the horsemen rode among them. The latter must have been aware that the musketeers were advancing to their support, and this for very shame made them eager to finish the fight with the half-armed citizens with whom they were contending. The horsemen were approaching the spot where Captain Radford and his companions stood. Neither he nor Aveline, engaged in watching the progress of the boat, were aware of the near approach of danger. Though I shouted to them, amid the din of battle they did not hear my voice. Calling on A'Dale, therefore, I could no longer withstand the temptation of springing forward at all events to be by the side of Aveline, should the horsemen reach her, although our doing so might appear as if we were taking to flight. The moment was a fearful one. It seemed scarcely possible that any human power could save us. Although several of the troopers had been killed, still they were a strong body, and, rendered furious by their previous defeats, fought desperately, slashing on every side, and cutting down all their swords could meet. At a quick march the formidable musketeers were advancing towards us. The boats, by which alone we could escape, were not to be seen from where I stood. I could only hope, therefore, that they might be approaching. Still the brave blacksmith, surrounded by several of his workmen, stood his ground, not only defending himself with his formidable double-handled sword, but cutting down many of his opponents. This enabled A'Dale and me to rush up the bank. I called out Aveline's name. She sprang towards me.

"I'll fight for you to the last," I said, pointing to the Spaniards.

Then, for the first time, I saw that the *Falcon's* boats were only a short distance from the bank. A'Dale joined me, armed with an arquebus which he had taken from one of the Spaniards who had been shot. He had also provided himself with the man's ammunition-pouch and belt.

"I'll stand by you, Verner," he said, "to keep the Spaniards at bay, while you retreat with Mistress Aveline."

I thankfully followed his suggestion, and, lifting Aveline from the ground, bore her down the bank towards the first boat which approached the shore. Scarcely had the stern touched the ground before a number of the unhappy fugitives rushed towards it, and attempted to force their way on board. It seemed cruel to prevent them, and yet there was not room for all. Keeping Aveline out of the water, I waded in and deposited her safely in the stern of the boat; then shouting to Captain Radford, I entreated him also to come on board. The *Falcons* crew had meantime driven back their assailants, and taking the opportunity, before the Spaniards again rode at them, they hurried down the bank and gained the boats, already half full of fugitives. It was a sore trial to Captain Radford when he had to insist on many of the unfortunate people again landing; but there was no help for it. The boats would have sunk had he allowed all to remain. As it was, they were already too deeply laden for safety. The sailors had literally to lift out those who had last got in, and to place them on the shore, ere we shoved off into deep water. It was heartrending to see the whole shore lined with fugitives: some rushing into boats which had already come up, some waving frantically to other boats which were approaching. Here, Spanish troopers charging the unhappy people with lances, or sabring them as they attempted to fly into the water. Here and there were knots of brave men struggling with their foes. Several of the unfortunate citizens were swimming off, either to overtake the retiring boats or to get on board those they saw approaching. Now and then a shriek was heard ere the unhappy fugitive sunk below the surface.

We rowed away as fast as the crowded state of our boats would allow. I could not withdraw my eye from the shore. Simultaneously a cry arose from the hapless fugitives who had not yet reached the boats, and at that instant the heads of the musketeers, with their glittering arms, appeared above the bank, forming a deadly line—and instantly their weapons were levelled at the ill-fated people. There was a general rush into the river. Even those who could not swim trusted rather to the waters of the Scheld than to the mercy of their fellow-creatures. In spite of the hot fire opened upon them, the brave boatmen rowed here and there, receiving all they could, though often a man, woman, or child was taken on board immediately afterwards to be slain by the murderous bullets of the Spaniards. Even at the distance we had already gained, several bullets reached us. Two or three of the *Falcon's* men, and some of those we had rescued, were struck. Now we saw the Spaniards hurrying along the banks, evidently hoping to get possession of some boats in which to pursue us.

THE PURSUIT OF THE FUGITIVES.

"Were we not overloaded, they would find us rough customers to deal with on our own element," observed Captain Radford. "As it is, if they come near us, we will give them a warmer reception than they expect." In vain the Spaniards shouted to the people on board some of the boats, which had as yet got to no great distance, to return. They, happily, would not trust themselves to their tender mercies. We meantime continued to row away towards the *Falcon*. The mate, who had been left on board, seeing us coming, had already loosened sails, ready to get under weigh directly we should reach her. There was no time to be lost, for several Spanish horsemen, each taking a foot soldier behind him, had galloped along the banks till they reached some boats which had been moored there. Unfortunately, as it appeared, the crews of several were in the neighbourhood, and at the sword's point were forced to man them. This I heard afterwards. With the musketeers on board, they rowed rapidly down the Scheld in pursuit of the fugitives. Although the latter had a considerable start, some of the boats were heavy, and the crews of others were severely wounded, so that they could make but slow progress. Our hearts burned with sorrow and indignation as we saw one after another taken, and the unfortunate people in them mercilessly butchered. The delay, however, enabled us to keep ahead of them, as it allowed also other boats to escape.

Close to the *Falcon* lay two vessels which had been prepared for the reception of the fugitives. Their crews, with arms in their hands, received on board all who could reach them; and, waiting till the last boat-load of the survivors had got alongside, they cut their cables and made sail just at the time that we did.

There was, happily, a strong and favourable breeze. The Spaniards continued pursuing us, firing their muskets as long as we remained within their reach. No one was hit on board our vessel, although the others more or less suffered. We returned their fire, every now and then sending a shot from our great guns, in the hopes of sinking their boats. This we did not succeed in doing, but I suspect we somewhat damped their ardour, and at length they ceased rowing, and, firing a parting volley at us, turned their boats' heads up the river.

We had yet many dangers to encounter. There were forts on either side of the river, and should intelligence of what had occurred reach them, they would undoubtedly attempt with their guns to stop our progress. But night was now approaching, and we might possibly pass them in the dark. At all events the risk must be run. We communicated with the other vessels, Captain Radford promising to lead, and urging them to follow closely in his wake.

"There would be no use firing in return," he observed; "our shot would only knock off a few pieces of their stone walls, and would in no way assist us to escape."

The wind was fair, and there was enough of it to fill our sails, so that we glided steadily down the stream. We felt a considerable amount of anxiety as we approached the first fort; but, hoisting our colours, we stood on, as if we had no reason to dread their power. All the women and children on board had been sent below, as were most of the men, lest their numbers should excite suspicion. The crew only were allowed to appear, and they were placed at their proper posts, or directed to walk unconcernedly up and down the deck while we remained in sight of the fort. We observed the gunners at their stations in the castle, and every instant we expected to see a cloud of smoke with its attendant flash, followed by a round shot, issue from the muzzles of the guns. Slowly we glided by, dipping our flag, in mark of respect, as we passed that of Spain waving on the fort. All on board breathed more freely as we found ourselves getting past, though we still looked with anxiety to see how our consorts would be treated. They likewise sailed by with impunity.

The first great danger had now been escaped. There was still another fort to pass on the same bank of the Scheld as Antwerp. We stood on, however, under all sail, hoping that news of our flight might not have reached it. Gradually we drew near. Just then we saw through the thickening gloom of evening a horseman galloping at full speed along the causeway which led to the fort. We guessed too well his errand, but we had no means of avoiding the danger. Keeping our colours flying, therefore, as before, we stood on. Happily, at that moment the breeze increased, and we ran on more rapidly. The tide, too, was in our favour. Still the fort had numerous guns, and the deep water was very close to their muzzles.

The horseman was yet at some distance. We watched him anxiously, hoping that horse and rider might come to the ground, or that some other accident might happen before he could deliver his message. Providence favoured us more than we could have dared to hope, for one of the seamen, noted for his sharp sight, and whose eye had been kept on the horseman, exclaimed:

"He has rolled over the bank!"

The crew could scarcely refrain from giving a shout of satisfaction. A dark object, supposed to be the horseman, was seen directly afterwards climbing up the bank and making his way towards the fort, though the thickening gloom prevented our distinguishing who he really was. On we went. We could see lights, which made us fear that the gunners were preparing their slow-matches, but it was now too dark to distinguish any objects beyond the outline of the fort. The navigation of the river was so well-known to Captain Radford, that without hesitation he stood boldly on.

We calculated that the horseman would not be long in reaching his destination, and every instant we were expecting to have a shot sent between our masts or into our hull. Already we were under the guns, a discharge from which, well directed, would quickly have sunk us. I held my breath in my anxiety, looking intently towards the embrasures, out of which I knew the guns were protruding. How anxiously we marked the line of bristling cannon as we passed along in front of it! At length, we had but a few more guns to pass. Suddenly there was a loud shouting in the fort. Lights were seen moving rapidly along. In an instant afterwards we could distinguish the small sparks of the slow-matches in the hands of the gunners.

"Fire! fire quickly!"

The words were heard distinctly as they were uttered by the commandant of the fort.

Chapter Twenty Seven
Captured by Spaniards

We expected the next instant to be sent to the bottom of the Scheld, when a sudden blast filled our sails, almost tearing them from the bolt-ropes, and sending us gliding rapidly through the water. The guns aimed at our vessel sent their shot astern of us, two or three only passing through our mizzen, but doing no further damage. The next vessel could not have escaped so well, but we saw her still standing close to us through the gloom. The other was following, and we feared she must have received greater harm than either of us. But by the flashes of the guns, we saw her sails close astern of her consort. We flew on over the tide, but it required all Captain Radford's skill to steer his vessel through the intricate navigation of the river. The shores were so low that they could with difficulty be discerned, and there were numerous banks on either side of us. To run against one of them, at the rate we were going, might have proved the destruction of the ship. Still there was no help for it. The Spaniards had vessels, we knew, up the river, which would be soon sent in pursuit, and, should they find us aground, we could not hope by any possibility to escape. They were, however, not likely to venture down in the dark; and therein lay our chief prospect of safety. The wind, which had so favoured us when passing the fort, again fell, and, with loosened sails, we proceeded slowly and more securely down the stream. Daylight found us a considerable distance on our way; but just as we were about to get clear of the mouth of the river, the tide setting in, the wind fell, so that we were compelled to anchor.

A'Dale and I took the opportunity of visiting the other vessels, to ascertain the fate of the relatives of some of the unfortunate people who had escaped on board our ship. Sad indeed were the scenes we witnessed. Several of the poor people were severely wounded, and many more were mourning for relatives whom they had lost. We had, however, the happiness to restore a wife to her husband, and, in another case, a daughter to her mother, though the men of the family had lost their lives. I was glad to find that our sturdy friend the blacksmith—I forget his name—had escaped. As our vessel was somewhat overcrowded, and the others had prepared for many more refugees than had escaped, we conveyed some of our passengers to them, while they bestowed some provisions on us, of which we were in great need.

All arrangements being made, and the wind coming fair again, we continued our course towards the Thames, thankful that we had escaped thus far. But we knew very well that we were not yet safe. Several of the Duke of Alva's ships or other Spanish craft were sailing about in all directions in search of prey, and, we heard, were not at all particular what vessels they captured; certainly they would not scruple to capture us. In spite of this we kept up our spirits, thankful for having already escaped so many dangers.

I should have been blind indeed had I not seen by this time what Aveline's feelings were towards me. I was sitting by her side on deck, our eyes wandering over the blue ocean, which now sparkled in the bright sunlight. The air was soft and balmy, and the sky undimmed by a cloud.

"Aveline," I said, "you have now a father whose permission I should wish to ask, and if he grants it, will you consent to be my wife?"

"Yes, I will," she answered. "I am sure I could never consent to be the wife of anybody else."

I pressed her hand. I had felt almost sure that she had understood my feelings, and yet, without pointedly asking her, I had no right to be quite sure.

"I have no fears," she said, "about my father giving me leave to marry you. I am sure he regards you already as a son. I only wish that I had a dower to bring you."

"You have one," I answered, just then recollecting the document in Lady Anne's hands. I told her of it, and added:

"And, now your father has appeared, I have little doubt it will enable him to obtain possession of the estate of which it speaks. And yet I almost wish that you had it not, as I would rather feel that I were labouring for your support; and I am sure that my patron will place me in a position by which I may obtain sufficient means for that object."

We agreed that I should speak forthwith to Captain Radford on the subject. I did so. He smiled when I asked his permission to marry Aveline.

"You have very fairly won her, young sir," he said; "and in truth I feel that I have no right to withhold her from you, or rather that you have a greater right to her than I have. I saw from the first how matters stood; and I need scarcely tell you that I feel great satisfaction in the knowledge that she has obtained one I believe well able and willing to protect and support her through life."

No lover could have desired a more satisfactory answer, and indeed I hoped that in our case the course of true love was about to run smoothly. To be sure, we had gone through many dangers, and I knew very well that we were not free from them yet altogether.

When, afterwards, Aveline had retired to her cabin, and I told A'Dale what had occurred: "It is time, then," said he, "to confess that I have been talking on the same subject to Margery. My good father and mother would, I fancy, not object to my marrying her; and, as she has no parents whose leave she need ask, I had an idea there would be no difficulty; but, somehow or other, there is. She says that she cannot make up her mind—that she had not thought of marrying—that she cannot leave Mistress Aveline or Lady Anne—in truth, she, against all my expectations, will not do as I ask her. My only hope is that the jade may change her mind when we land on the shores of Old England."

"We are not in sight of them yet, A'Dale," I answered. "I thank you for your congratulations, but remember the old proverb, 'There's many a slip between the cup and the lip.' We must not be too sanguine."

I said this in joke, not thinking at the time, so buoyed up was I with hope, that there was any risk of the saying coming true. That evening, the wind, which had been light all day, shifted, and blew directly in our teeth, driving us back again towards the coast of Flanders. All night long we lay closely hugging the wind, in the hopes of again working our way off shore. When morning broke, a man went to the mast-head, to look out and ascertain whether the coast was in sight. He had not been long there when he shouted out:

"Several sail of ships to the southward, standing towards us."

The announcement was alarming. They could scarcely be friends, and if they were Spaniards or Flemings in the service of Alva, we were likely to be sufferers. We announced the fact to our consorts, who had, indeed, discovered the same themselves. The wind having somewhat fallen, the captains of the other ships came on board; and it was agreed, in order that we might have a better chance of escaping, that we should steer in different directions. Thus the enemy would probably, not wishing themselves to separate, steer after only one of us. With earnest prayers that we might all providentially escape, our friends returned to their vessels; we continuing to steer as before to the west, while they stood away on the opposite tack. The plan seemed to be giving our friends a chance of escaping, though we judged, from the way the strange ships were sailing, that they were standing towards us. As, however, the *Falcon* was a fast ship, we still hoped to distance them.

Our hopes soon appeared likely to be vain. As the sun rose we saw the strangers had gained upon us—the wind apparently favouring them more than it did us. It had again begun to fall, and in a short time we were becalmed, while they still stood on with their sails full. From some reason, for which we could not account, several of them stood back again towards the land, three only continuing the pursuit of us. But they were fast vessels, and though we soon again got the wind, they continued gaining on us. At length the breeze once more became favourable, and with our sails spread, we stood away across the Channel, hotly pursued by the strangers. Although they gained upon us, yet it was evident that the chase would be a long one; and we hoped in the meantime that something would happen in our favour. It was satisfactory also to believe that our consorts, with the unhappy fugitives on board, had escaped; for it was very certain that, had they been captured, the lives of all would have been sacrificed. We trembled for the fate of the poor people with us, for so barbarous were the orders issued by Alva, that the commanders of any of his ships finding refugees on board, might, without ceremony, either hang them to the yard-arms, or cast them into the sea with weights round their feet, or shoot them as they floated when thrown into the water.

Whether our captors, should we be overtaken, would venture to treat the English on board the *Falcon* in the same manner was doubtful; at the same time, it was too probable that they would do so first and apologise afterwards.

As to offering any resistance, that would certainly be useless. Master Clough especially entreated that they would not. He, however, was far from contented with the prospect of what was too likely to occur, as even, should his life be spared, they would not scruple to take possession of all his property, of which he had contrived to get a considerable amount safe on board the *Falcon*.

Hour after hour we watched the strangers, calculating how much they had gained upon us during the time. Every particle of canvas we could set was spread, but all we could do would not drive her at a greater speed through the water. If we could keep ahead during the whole of the day, we might still, as we had before done, escape during the darkness. But this was not probable. Long before that we should be within range of the enemy's guns. It was a time of great trial to all of us, to the unhappy refugees especially; yet we could do nothing but hope. Captain Radford not only maintained his own serenity, but did his best to keep up the courage of all on board.

Although we had little appetite, our meals were taken as usual. We had gone below for that purpose, and were seated in the cabin, when the sound of a gun was heard, and a sharp cry reached our ears from the deck. A'Dale hurried up to inquire what was the matter.

"The enemy have fired, and one of our poor fellows has been hit," he answered, coming back. "To escape is no longer possible. The captain has, therefore, ordered the sails to be lowered, but advises that all the passengers should remain below, lest when the enemy first come on board they may be inclined to treat them roughly."

Although Captain Radford had shown that he had submitted, the enemy continued firing as they approached, and not till they had got close to us, and had hove to, did they cease attempting to injure us. Several more of our people were hit, and two poor fellows killed outright. We had no barber or surgeon on board, and it was sad to see the poor fellows who were injured suffering without the means of helping them. Some of the women did their best, however, having attended to their friends wounded on different occasions by the Spaniards. A'Dale and I could not resist going up on deck to ascertain how matters were proceeding. Three boats from the leading ship of the enemy were approaching us. The crews sprang on board, their officers demanding in fierce tones why we had attempted to escape.

Captain Radford answered that his object was to make as quick a voyage as he could to England, having British subjects on board, who desired to reach their native land without delay.

"Let me see them immediately," answered the officer; and Master Clough and the rest of his attendants were summoned on deck.

"They are returning to England, having received orders to quit the Netherlands," observed Captain Radford, as he introduced them.

"But you have many more passengers: who are they?" inquired the officer.

"They are poor people desiring to settle in England," said Captain Radford. "They came on board my ship, requesting a passage, and I saw no reason to refuse them."

"In other words, they are rebels, escaping from the laws and justice of their country!" exclaimed the officer. "I understand it all. It is fortunate for you that you are an Englishman, and that our countries are at peace, or you would very speedily be dangling at your yard-arm. As it is, you will accompany us back to the nearest port in Flanders we can make, where all your Flemish passengers must be landed, and such property as belongs to them; and your ship will be confiscated, and you yourself will have to undergo your trial for breaking the laws. If you escape with your life, you will be fortunate; but I doubt it. Duke Alva is determined to put a stop to the flight of King Philip's subjects from his paternal sway."

We were very certain, from the way the officer spoke, that these threats would be carried out. Worse, however, was to come. While he walked aft, to speak to the next ship which was coming up, his men, I felt very sure, with his full knowledge, dispersed themselves about the decks, disarming our crew, and taking all articles which seemed to please them. Drawing pistols from their belts, they placed them at the heads of our people, and threatened to blow their brains out unless they gave up all the money they possessed. Dreading what would next occur, A'Dale and I hastened to the cabin, that we might protect the ladies from insult. Our enemies having taken all the coin they could find on their prisoners, now approached the cabin door, which we had bolted on the inside. Thundering at it, they demanded admission. I replied from within that it was the cabin devoted to the ladies, and that no intruders could be admitted.

"Withdraw the bolts!" cried a voice from without, "or we will burst open the door."

"Do so at your peril!" I answered. "The first person who makes his appearance will meet his death."

WITH A LOUD CRASH THE DOOR WAS BURST OPEN.

304

Scarcely had I ceased speaking before some thundering blows were inflicted on the door by handspikes. Fortunately the door was a strong one, and resisted the efforts of those who were trying to break it open.

"Bring a crowbar, or a stout spar," I heard some one cry out; "we shall then soon be able to force open the door!"

"I have told you, you will do so at your peril!" I shouted again.

The men outside laughed hoarsely at this threat. I felt indeed how little we could do to oppose them. Our anxiety was yet further increased by the shrieks and cries which came from other parts of the ship. It was evident that the savages were ill-treating their unfortunate prisoners. We could scarcely hope to meet with a better fate. At length the laughter and the shouting outside the cabin door increased. A'Dale and I stood with our drawn swords ready to attack any who might approach. Some thundering blows on the door followed. It creaked and groaned on its hinges, the panels gave way, and with a loud crash it was burst open. Two seamen with savage looks were the first to attempt to enter. Feeling sure that we should receive no mercy, whatever we did, we at once ran them through with our swords, and they fell at the entrance of the cabin. The others, seeing their fate, drew back for an instant. We followed up our advantage.

"If any others wish to share the fate of these ruffians, let them come on!" we cried out boldly.

Our assailants soon recovered from their surprise, and several shots were fired into the cabin, filling it with smoke, under cover of which they attempted again to force their way. The next two were treated as had been the first. The shrieks and cries of Madam Clough and the poor women within nearly unnerved us. However, we had resolved, if we could not save them, to sell our lives dearly. We therefore stood at our posts, prepared for the worst. Again our enemies pushed forward, led by their boatswain, with a huge battle-axe in his hand. Fortunately he was not able to wield it with due effect in the confined space of the cabin entrance. A'Dale's sword, as he attempted to keep the ruffian at bay, was struck down, and the man, again lifting his axe, was about to bring it down with terrific force on A'Dale's head, when, springing forward, I plunged my sword into his bosom. The fall of their leader seemed to enrage the rest of the men, and with terrific execrations they again made an attempt to force their way into the cabin.

Chapter Twenty Eight
The Beggars of the Sea

At the moment I have described, when we felt that all hope of escape had gone—for we could scarcely expect ourselves to resist the numbers who were rushing down with cries of vengeance to force their way in—a voice of authority was heard, ordering them to desist. At first they seemed in no way inclined to obey. One who appeared by his rich costume to be an officer of authority made his appearance. He spoke with a Spanish accent:

"Hold! men, hold! what are you about to do? We come not to war against helpless women. On deck, all of you; or expect the punishment of mutineers!"

He spoke with a tone of authority not to be disobeyed. Our enraged assailants quickly retired, without attempting any further violence. The officer started back with surprise when he found the dead bodies at the entrance of the cabin.

"You have defended yourselves well, gentlemen," he said, addressing A'Dale and me, as we still stood with our swords in our hands, and at our posts. "These men met their deserts. I do not therefore blame you; on the contrary, I may compliment you on your gallantry. Here!" he exclaimed, "some of you come down and convey these dead bodies away, and throw them overboard. If a few more of you had been treated in the same way, the loss would not have been great."

The bodies having been dragged away by some of our late assailants, who obeyed the order, the officer entered the cabin. He bowed with all the grace of a Spaniard to the ladies, and expressed his regret that they had been caused so much anxiety and terror. We found that he was Don Alfonzo de la Fuente, the commander of the squadron, and though obeying his master, Philip, in carrying out his laws, yet he did so with a feeling of commiseration for the unfortunate victims of his cruelty.

"I will send for an officer I can trust," he said, "who will remain on board your ship, and protect you from the lawless violence of the prize crew. All I can I will do to make amends for your disappointment. If you will permit me, I will write an order, and send to my ship, and will not leave you till the officer arrives; for I regret to say there are not many in whom I can confide, who will treat you as I should desire."

We supplied Don Alfonzo with writing materials, and he summoning some of the men, a boat was despatched to his ship, which it appeared was the last of the squadron. On going on deck with him, I found that the wind had again greatly fallen, and Captain Radford told me that he believed it would soon be a perfect calm. In a short time the officer who had been sent for arrived, and Don Alfonzo took his departure, giving him directions how he was to behave.

The officer, who, though young, had an expression of firmness and courage in his countenance, which was at the same time very pleasing, introduced himself as Don Rodrigo Ruiz. He spoke Flemish but slightly, but I was able to understand his Spanish sufficiently to carry on a conversation with him, and to interpret to the rest. I soon judged from his expressions, although he spoke with caution, that he was not unfavourable to the Protestants. I could not help suggesting to him that he should endeavour to come over to England, where he might not only declare his principles, but worship in public according to his conscience. At length, urged by Don Rodrigo, I retired to the cabin, where, rolling myself in my cloak, I lay down to sleep. He observed that he must remain on deck to keep watch over his men.

I was awoke by the sound of voices on deck, apparently shouting to one of the other ships. Hurrying up, I saw the crews busily engaged in setting sail, though as yet there was but little wind to fill them. Bowing to Don Rodrigo, who was on deck issuing his orders, he pointed towards the east, where I saw, scarcely three miles off, the sails of numerous vessels, the sun rising behind them, throwing them into the shade, and making them stand out in bold relief against the sky.

"What are they?" I asked, turning to the young officer.

"That remains to be discovered," he answered; "but our Admiral evidently believes that they are not friends, and has ordered us to set all sail, and to do our utmost to escape."

"But who do you think they are?" I again asked.

"The much-dreaded Gueux—the Beggars of the Sea," he answered. "They are known to have a large squadron afloat, under the command of that fierce captain, De la Marck—the descendant of the Wild Boar of

Ardennes. If they come up with us, the tables will indeed be turned; and it will go hard, I suspect, with our men. The hatred between the two races is so great, that I fear little mercy will be shown to any of us."

"I am glad, then, that you are on board this ship," I replied; "for, after the courtesy you have shown us, I trust that you will escape injury."

"I have no great confidence on that score," he answered. "Though you, I am sure, will do your best to save my life, the Beggars of the Sea are not likely in the heat of battle to listen to your wishes."

"But surely your Admiral will not attempt to fight with such a superior force as there appears to be approaching us?"

"It will matter little whether we fight or not," answered the officer. "To the Spaniards, at all events, among our crews, no mercy will be shown, though the lives of the native Flemings may be spared, if they agree to join the Gueux; and probably very few will refuse to do so."

The Beggars of the Sea—for such there was no doubt were the strangers—came on with a fresh breeze, rapidly approaching the Spanish squadron. In vain every sail which the Spanish ships could carry was set to woo the breeze. Their enemies came up rapidly with them. Seeing this, the Admiral ordered Don Rodrigo to alter his course, and to do his utmost to escape, directing him to return to the first Flemish port he could reach.

"There may be some who will dispute that matter with him," whispered Captain Radford to me. "Does the Don fancy we should submit to be carried off prisoners when we more than equal in number our captors?"

"Certainly," I said; "but I trust, whatever is done, the young Spanish officer may not be injured. Pray let us do our best to save his life."

We now once more stood out from among the Spanish squadron. The *Falcon* being a fast vessel, and having all the sail she could set now put on her, gradually distanced them. In the meantime, however, the Beggars of the Sea came up at a rapid rate, and soon got the Spaniards within reach of their guns. We watched them with great interest. Our fate might possibly depend upon the result of the action. The Beggars far outnumbered the Spaniards both in ships and men, although the latter had larger vessels and carried more guns. As the Gueux came up, they opened their fire hotly on the Spaniards, who, to do them justice, showed every inclination to defend their ships. Three of the largest of the Beggars' ships attacked the Admiral, the others tackled his consorts, the two squadrons running on together. The Admiral's was the leading ship. One of the Gueux was stationed on her broadside, another rather more on her bows, and a third hung on her quarter. The breeze blew away the smoke every now and then, so as to allow us a clear view of the fight. Never had I seen shots exchanged with so much rapidity. Both our crew and our captors were looking on with intense anxiety at what was going forward. At length our men uttered a loud shout as the foremast of the Spanish Admiral went by the board. Still the other masts stood, but the Gueux seemed to be redoubling their efforts, and kept pouring broadside upon broadside into the ship. Hearing what was going forward, all our passengers assembled on deck, the Spaniards in no way attempting to prevent them. We had by this time got out of the line of shot, keeping somewhat ahead of the combatants. At length another shout burst from the throats of our men as the mainmast of the Spanish Admiral was seen to sway first on one side and then on the other, and at length, with its streamers and flags flying, to fall forward over the wreck of the other mast. The other ships seemed to be suffering in the same way; first one mast and then another went. And now the Gueux were seen to be crowding round the ships, the masts and spars of which were one by one shot away.

I observed, meantime, Captain Radford going about the decks, and speaking to the crew. Don Rodrigo did not see him. I guessed Captain Radford's intentions; but he, having observed the terms I was on with the young officer, evidently did not wish to ask me to act a treacherous part towards him. The Beggars' ships which had come up after the others were engaged, their services not being required, were now seen standing after us. But it was a question, being evidently slower ships, whether they would overtake us; indeed, I judged that they would not, when we both had an equal amount of wind. I could fancy, more than actually see, the scenes which were taking place on board the captured ships. They and the Gueux appeared locked together in a deadly embrace. The crews of the latter were evidently swarming on board, and, after so hot a fight, there was no hope that blood would be spared. Still, from the flashes of pistols and arquebuses, it was evident that the fight continued, and that a desperate resistance was being made. Suddenly flames burst forth in the midst of the combatants. The Gueux vainly endeavoured to extricate themselves from their almost conquered antagonist. In another instant there was a loud explosion. The remaining mast of the Admiral's ship was seen to shoot up into the air, while her deck and broken spars and everything on it rose up many feet. There was a roar like thunder, and flames and smoke ascended with terrific fury, high above which were seen burning fragments of the wreck spreading far and wide, which again came down upon the decks of the conquerors, and fell hissing all around into the ocean. The next moment the Spanish ship had disappeared; but flames were bursting out from those of the Beggars which had been in contact with her. They, however, were at length extinguished. I heard a sigh escape the bosom of the young officer, near whom I was standing.

"He was my friend and guardian," he said. "Alas! he deserved a better fate!"

At that instant there was a cry from the Spaniards, and though I turned round instantly, I saw that every one of them had been tackled by one of the English seamen, aided by the Flemish passengers. Several had been cut down, but others had been captured without bloodshed.

"I must ask you for your sword, sir," said Captain Radford, holding a pistol to the young officer, who turned round, but had not time to draw his weapon. "You are our prisoner, and resistance will be useless!"

The capture of the Spaniards had not been accomplished a minute too soon, for the Beggars' ships were almost within gunshot, and would have opened their fire upon us. Instantly the Spanish ensign was hauled down, and that of England hoisted. The officer, seeing that he could do nothing, at once, with a bow, handed his sword to Captain Radford.

"Pray keep it, and promise that you will not use it against us," said the captain, handing it him back.

Our sails were on this furled, and a boat, by Captain Radford's orders, was lowered.

"To prevent mistakes, I must go on board the Beggars' ships, or they may perchance open their fire without inquiring who we are. They are not very scrupulous in that matter."

This precaution of Captain Radford I believe saved us. He quickly reached the headmost of the two vessels, and explained how matters stood to the officer in command—the gallant Treslong.

I need not describe the joy of the poor Flemings at this happy turn of affairs. Instead of prisoners, they were now at liberty, and warmly congratulated by their countrymen who came on board. It would have fared but ill with Don Rodrigo and his men had they not already been made prisoners, and had we not interfered in their favour. When the officer from the Beggars' squadron came on board, we at once explained how he had behaved towards us, and begged that he might be treated with courtesy and consideration, of which he was certainly well worthy. Finding that the heart of the Beggar officer was still unmoved, I whispered to him that I felt sure he was himself a Protestant, and served the King Philip very much against his will. This seemed to have very great weight with the officer, and he only advised that he should remain with our party, promising that he should receive neither insult nor injury.

A'Dale and I were anxious to visit our late captors, as well as some of the Beggars' squadron. The two captured vessels lay together, almost wrecks, and it was evident, from the way the pumps were going, that they could with difficulty be kept afloat. We went up the side of one of them. I had witnessed several sad scenes, but my heart sickened when I beheld the perfect shambles the deck had in a short time become. It seemed as if the whole of her crew must have been shot down by the guns of the Beggars!

"These scenes," I exclaimed, "will sicken me for war for the rest of my days!"

"I cannot say that it has that effect on me," said A'Dale. "It is very horrible, but people fight to kill, and know that they run the risk of being killed. Now I am rather weary of the merchant's desk, and if some of these gallant captains will receive me as an officer on board their ships, I propose joining them."

"You an officer, A'Dale?" I said; "you know but little of nautical affairs."

"But I can soon learn," he answered. "Very few of them knew much about the sea a few months ago. Besides, I have a fancy for a rover's life on the ocean."

"But what is to become of Mistress Margery?" I asked, in a low voice.

"Ah! there's the rub," he answered. "I will tell you about it by-and-by. It is not that I do not love her, or that she does not return my affection. Do not suppose that; but this is not the place to talk about it."

We had returned to our boat when he said this, and were pulling towards one of the Beggars' ships which lay between us and the *Falcon*. On stepping on board, the commander received us very courteously. I found that he was a well-known noble, William de Blois, of Treslong. Fearing, notwithstanding the promise of the first officer who had visited us, that Don Rodrigo's life would be endangered, we begged Captain Treslong to interfere in his favour, explaining who he was, and the generous way he had behaved towards us. He promised faithfully to do so; and our minds were thus greatly relieved with regard to Don Rodrigo. I proposed returning to the *Falcon*; but, to my surprise and regret, A'Dale there and then tendered his services to Captain Treslong, who accepted his offer.

"You must not expect any high rank given to you at first," he said; "but you will fight your way up to that in time, I doubt not, from the account you give of yourself; and I fully believe you will be a credit to the cause. You had better go back to your ship and see your friends, and come on board before we part company. We shall probably see you safe in sight of the English coast. By the bye, your captain must not expect to escape without paying salvage. Our men are disappointed at having lost the Spaniard's large ship; and they will be in no good humour unless they collect a little prize money."

With this not very satisfactory message, we pulled back towards the *Falcon*. I asked A'Dale again on our way how he could bring himself to give up little Margery.

THE BEGGARS OF THE SEA OFF DOVER.

"I do not give her up," he answered; "but I hope to collect a good sum with which to set up house, far more rapidly than I have any chance of doing with Sir Thomas Gresham. He has treated me very kindly, and made good use of me; but I have no great hopes that he will place me in a position where I can obtain a sufficient income to support a wife, for a long time to come, at all events."

I felt really sorry for Mistress Margery that A'Dale had come to this resolution. I did my best, however, to persuade him to alter his mind; but the more I urged, the stronger appeared his determination of joining the Gueux. At length, by the great exertions of the rovers' crews, the two Spanish ships were got into a condition for again making sail, and then, with the whole of the fleet, we steered a course for England.

Once more the shores of Old England appeared in sight, and, rounding the Goodwin Sands, we came to an anchor in the Downs. Glad as we English were to see our native land, the joy of the unhappy refugees seemed far to surpass ours. As they gazed on the land of freedom, they fell down on their knees on deck, and together joined in a hymn of praise and thanksgiving. Eagerly they packed up the few articles which they had been able to bring away. Master Clough having paid a handsome sum out of the property he had brought off to the Beggars, the rest was landed, and under an escort of soldiers, whom he engaged for that purpose, he prepared to send it off to London.

I will not describe the parting of Mistress Margery and A'Dale. He commended her to Aveline's care—who promised to look after her rather as a sister than a dependant, and, shaking me warmly by the hand, returned on board Captain Treslong's ship. We assisted, with the *Falcons* boats, in landing the emigrants. They were received, on setting foot on the English shore, with the greatest kindness by the inhabitants of Dover and other places. Their destitute condition becoming known, subscriptions were raised for their support, houses found, and a place of worship allowed them.

Master Clough kindly invited Don Rodrigo to accompany him to London—an offer which our Spanish friend was glad to accept; while his men, many of whom were Flemings, volunteered on board the Beggars' fleet.

Two or three Spaniards were put on shore to find their way back to their country by the first vessel under the Spanish flag which might visit Dover. We then all set forward for London, with the escort in charge of Master Clough's chests of gold.

Chapter Twenty Nine
Romish Plots

On reaching Gresham House we were received by Sir Thomas and Lady Anne with their usual kindness. Aveline was especially welcomed. Master Clough and his lady were also gladly received. They did not remain long, being anxious to set forth for Wales, in order to visit their relatives, and to see the new house they had a short time before caused to be erected. Sir Thomas was somewhat vexed on finding that A'Dale had quitted his service and joined the Beggars of the Sea.

"Not that I object to their cause," he observed; "that is a right noble one, though they carry it on in a rough and somewhat barbarous manner. But I consider that mercantile pursuits are among the most honourable in which a young man can engage, and A'Dale, had he persevered, had every prospect of success."

I saw poor Margery, who was present, look very sad and uncomfortable when these remarks were made, so much so that Lady Anne observed her.

"What have you to say to this matter, Mistress Margery?" she asked. "Are you the cause in any way of the young man's joining the Sea Rovers?"

Poor Margery burst into tears.

"I had far rather he had returned home than have done so," she answered; "but he told me that he could not expect to make a fortune sufficient to marry me, and to live as we ought to do, for a long time, if he followed commerce; but that he hoped by some lucky stroke to gain enough in a short time to come home and settle comfortably."

"He is more likely to gain a broken head, the silly lad," observed Sir Thomas; "but we must not have you weeping. Mistress Margery, about the matter. I will send to him and induce him to return. I had purposed considerably increasing his pay, or obtaining some post for him in which he would enjoy a good income."

Margery, drying her tears, thanked Sir Thomas for his kind intentions, and was not in any way chary of her abuse of poor A'Dale for his conduct.

"You say he is on board the Captain de Treslong's ship, do you, Ernst?" he asked, turning to me. "You shall forthwith write a letter to him, which I will sign, and despatch it without delay. Perchance it may reach him before the ship leaves the English coast; if not, it may be some time before it overtakes these roving gentry."

I had purposed waiting the arrival of Captain Radford before I told Sir Thomas and Lady Anne of my engagement to Aveline. Seeing my patron, however, in so kind a mood, and believing that he would not be less inclined to obtain a post for me than he was to find one for A'Dale, I mustered up courage to confess to him that the chief object of my heart was to marry Aveline.

"Eh! is it so?" said Sir Thomas, turning to her.

A blush rose to her cheeks as she confessed that she had resolved to marry no one else, having also, she added, her father's permission; and she then narrated the way in which she had discovered her father at Master Clough's house. Sir Thomas was not a little surprised to find that he was the Captain Rover whom he had for so long known, who was employed in the service of the merchant adventurers. Still more surprised was he when I introduced the minister, Overton, and told him how we had again met each other.

"He will, then, be glad to meet a friend who is in the house—that most excellent divine, Master John Foxe," he observed. "He lately came up to London from his living in Wiltshire, which he has for some time held. Happy is the parish which enjoys his ministrations; for not only does he preach the word of truth from the pulpit, but he carries the Gospel from door to door, and ministers both to the temporal and spiritual wants of his people. He is indeed a true shepherd of sheep, and spends his life in imitation of the blessed example set by our Lord and Master."

While he was speaking, Master John Foxe entered the room. He looked considerably older and somewhat thinner than when I last had seen him, but the same pleasing smile lighted up his countenance. He welcomed Master Overton and me warmly, knowing us both immediately.

"And now, my friend," he said, turning to Master Overton, "you will continue in this country, I trust, to preach the Word, as I hear you have been doing in Antwerp; and that you may have the means of so doing, I will forthwith endeavour to obtain a cure for you."

Master Overton warmly thanked the minister, saying that it was his wish to devote himself as heretofore to the work of the Lord. That first evening we spent at Gresham House, after our arrival, was one not easily to be forgotten. We all had so many adventures to relate. John Foxe narrated the circumstances which occurred while he resided in Switzerland; Master Overton described his wanderings, and his numberless escapes. Master Clough had to give an account of many events, especially of those which had taken place in the Netherlands since he last wrote.

Two days after Master Clough and his lady had taken their departure, Captain Radford arrived. Aveline had promised that, should he not object to it, she would be mine as soon as arrangements could be made for our marriage. I had not forgotten the packet in the possession of Lady Anne, though of the contents I had no distinct recollection. We now applied for it. Great was Captain Radford's satisfaction when it was delivered to him. After examining it, he rose up and kissed his daughter.

"There can be little doubt," he said, "that you will become possessed ere long, through means of these papers, of considerable property. I am not sorry for it, being assured that you will have one well able to manage it, and to be your true protector as long as you two remain in this life."

"The course of true love does continue to run smooth," I whispered to Aveline.

"I pray it may; but we are not married yet," she answered.

I do not deem that the matters concerning the estate in question will prove interesting to my readers. I will, therefore, merely state that, being placed before the law authorities, it was finally decided that she was its rightful possessor. It consisted of upwards of five hundred acres; and, greatly to my satisfaction, I found that it was situated in the same parish in which Master Foxe ministered. Still our marriage was not to take place just yet. Lady Anne insisted that she could not, after so long a separation, be again parted from her young attendant; besides which, Sir Thomas had received notice that a certain lady of rank was to be committed to his charge—of whom more anon. It was necessary that Lady Anne should have a younger and more active lady than herself to assist in taking charge of the said personage.

Shortly after this, Sir Thomas received notice that a foreigner of rank and consideration had arrived at Dover, and also a request from Cecil—the Queen's minister—that he would receive him into his house. The stranger was the Cardinal Chastillon, as he was still called, the brother of the famous French Admiral, Gaspard de Coligny. He had been educated for the Church, in which he was placed in his childhood; and, from the powerful influence of his family, he had been appointed to the Deanery of Marseilles, as also to the dignity of Cardinal. When only thirteen years of age, he was promoted to the Bishopric of Beauveax; and by the time he was twenty-two, he had been made Archbishop of Toulouse. It might have been supposed that so great a number of honours, bestowed on so young a man, would have bound him to the Church from which they had proceeded; but, instead of that, the abominable system which could produce such a result struck him forcibly. Having thus seen some of the abuses of Romanism, he did not fail to discover many more; and, at the age of twenty-eight, he had openly embraced Protestant opinions, and threw in all his support to the cause of the Lutherans.

The house in Bishopsgate Street having been got ready for his reception, I, with Sir Thomas Gresham, rode down to Tower Wharf, where the Cardinal arrived at three o'clock in the afternoon. Here other persons of distinction joined us, to do honour to the illustrious stranger, and, together, we all accompanied him to Gresham House. He was a remarkably handsome, courteous man, excessively insinuating in his manners, at the same time with a firm and determined look. He was said to be a refined courtier and a consummate politician. Probably the Romanists had no more watchful enemy. His eagle eye was everywhere, and his great aim was to counteract all their plots and machinations, at this time especially so rife in England for the destruction of Queen Elizabeth and all who desired to support Protestant truth. Though people still called him a Cardinal, he wore the dress of an ordinary gentleman, with a short cloak over his shoulders and a rapier by his side. Soon after he arrived, the French Ambassador came to pay his respects, whom Sir Thomas invited to stop to supper. It was very evident that there was no great friendship between the two, and that the Ambassador's object was rather to act as a spy on Chastillon—of which fact the latter was well aware. In the train of the Cardinal, among other noblemen, came the Bishop of Aries, who, I concluded, had embraced Protestant principles.

The Cardinal remained at Gresham House for a week, during which time banquets were given to him, and every respect shown. Sir Thomas had the pleasure of exhibiting to him his new Bourse. We then rode on to Saint Paul's Church, and came back to dinner—having first, I should have said, attended the Protestant service in the French Church. Meantime the Queen had directed Zion House to be prepared for the Cardinal's residence. Here, at the end of that time, he went with his attendants. The Queen was greatly pleased with him, it is said, and bestowed on him much favour. Her minister,

Cecil, too, held him in high estimation; indeed, the Cardinal afforded him the greatest assistance with regard to the unravelling of Popish plots.

I had by this time many friends in London. Among the principal, and certainly the oldest, was Sir John Leigh, who resided in a handsome house in the Strand. I frequently paid him a visit, and was now sorry to see that his health was breaking, and that he was becoming gradually weaker and weaker. Still he was as vivacious and full of anecdote as ever, while he took a keen interest in public affairs.

"Ernst," he said one day, soon after I came in, "see to the door, that no one is near. I have a matter of great importance which I know I can entrust to you. You always supposed that I was a Romanist; and so I was, as far as I could be said to have any religion; but the things I have witnessed in England, and which are now going forward in the Netherlands, in France, and in Spain, and which are, I have undoubted proof, encouraged in every possible way by the head of the Romish Church, have made me inquire into the claims and authority of that Church. I find that the Pope has no ground whatever on which to support his claim to be head of the Christian Church, and that the religion he promulgates is rather a system organised by Satan for leading souls to destruction than one for teaching them the way to attain to happiness in another life. I say this, that you may understand why I have taken the part I have done in an important matter. You are well aware that the Romanists consider any means lawful to attain their ends. They are resolved to re-establish their faith in England; and I, as a patriot, consider that no greater curse could happen to the country. Every effort has been made to induce the Queen to accept a Popish husband. They think possibly that, if they could get rid of Cecil, they might succeed in inducing the Queen to marry as they have proposed; but if not, I know to a certainty that they will not scruple to use violence, even to the taking away of her life. I have thoroughly fathomed the plot to ruin Sir William Cecil, aided by the information I have received from Cardinal Chastillon, who is himself well acquainted with it. I wish you to communicate faithfully to Sir Thomas Gresham the matters of which I shall speak to you, and he will then take such steps as he judges best for informing Sir William. There is now residing in London a Florentine gentleman, Roberto Ridolfi, who pretends to be a merchant. He by some means became acquainted with Lords Arundel and Lumley, to whom he offered the loan of a sum of money. Now this Ridolfi is an agent of the Pope, and receives express instructions from Rome on all occasions how to act. When meeting the two lords I have mentioned on the business of the loan, he managed to win them over to support the plot he had arranged. They agreed readily, and undertook to gain over the Duke of Norfolk. Many other nobles averse to the Protestant faith have joined them; among the most influential of whom are the Earls of Northumberland, Derby, Shrewsbury, Pembroke, and Leicester. They hope to accomplish their object, as I have said, without bloodshed or confusion. Sir William has, I doubt not, been greatly surprised at the way in which they have absented themselves from the Queen's Council. 'To be forewarned is to be forearmed.' A man of Cecil's judgment and discretion, when once he has a right clue to their conduct, will know how to act; but let both him and the Queen beware of foes of every description, and especially—I scarcely like to speak it aloud, Ernst—of poison. There are those who are fully capable of using it, if they think their ends can be accomplished by no other means. Not only does a good understanding subsist between them and the Pope, but they have secured the Duke of Alva. They have also opened a negotiation with the Kings of France and Spain. They have traitorously suggested that the former should issue an edict forbidding all commerce with England; and, more than that they have urged the Pope to send his troops which have lately come out of Italy to the coast of Normandy and Picardy, in order to give the English Roman Catholics courage to proceed; so that, should matters come to extremities, they would have the support of a Papal army of mercenaries. That fact, my young friend, as much as any other circumstance, has made me, as a patriotic Englishman, feel not only a repugnance for their scheme, but a hatred and disdain of principles which can so blind their eyes, and induce them thus to act. Should the plot be successful, one of the first things which Alva would do would be to make a descent on the English coast; thus, as he would hope, preventing the English from aiding the Prince of Orange.

"Ernst Verner, our beloved country is at the present moment in a very dangerous position. On one side we have, as I have shown you, France and Spain, urged by the Pope, wanting nothing but ability to attack us. By Alva's designs our commerce in the Low Countries has been crippled. In Scotland there is a strong Roman Catholic party, who are doing their utmost to subvert the throne of Elizabeth, and to substitute Mary Stuart in her place. The disaffected, whether in religion or politics, make that unhappy lady their rallying-point. Ireland is in a state of rebellion; and, as if this were not enough, there are those traitors of whom I have spoken to you, and many more at home, seeking again to introduce the despotism of Rome, and to keep the nation in that state of ignorance and superstition which the Papal power finds to best answer its purpose."

These remarks, as may be supposed, made a deep impression on me; and, after some further conversation with my old friend, I bade him farewell, promising faithfully to convey the warning given, through Sir Thomas, to the Secretary. I felt eager to be of service in the cause, and saw the importance of every man of intelligence and influence rallying round the statesman who alone appeared capable of counteracting the numerous evil influences associated for the destruction of the State. Though only half an Englishman, as a true Protestant all my sympathies were now enlisted on behalf of my adopted country.

Chapter Thirty
Dame Trond's Treachery

On leaving Sir John Leigh, I hastened back to Gresham House, where I found Sir Thomas. He listened attentively to my account. "The traitors! the unhappy bigots!" he exclaimed more than once as I proceeded with it. "Order my horse and four attendants; I will set forth immediately and visit the Secretary, and inform him of this matter. Every hour may be of consequence."

On his return, Sir Thomas told me that Sir William Cecil had received the information with great calmness, fully believing, however, the whole account.

"He will not forget you, Ernst, depend on that," he said, "should you prefer any other calling to that in which you are engaged."

It was evident that the object of the other ministers in absenting themselves from the Queen's Council was, should anything go wrong, to throw all the blame on Sir William Cecil. The wise way, however, in which the Queen acted, by affording him her utmost support, showed that she was well aware of their purpose, and that she was resolved to take the responsibility on her own shoulders. Thus it was by the wisdom and firmness of these two illustrious persons that that fearful storm was weathered, and England saved from Papal tyranny.

Soon after this, news reached us of the illness of Master Richard Clough, and in another week came the sad intelligence of his death. He had ever been a faithful servant of Sir Thomas Gresham, and one of those, who had enabled him to build up his fortunes.

His last will and testament was sent over from Hamburg. It was to the effect, that having made all his money in the service of Sir Thomas Gresham, he freely gave to his said master all his moveable goods, his lands only excepted, that Sir Thomas might do his pleasure therewith, adding that he would leave it to him whether he would suffer his wife, children, and friends to enjoy them or any parcel thereof, according to his previous will and testament. The paper concluded with the following words:

"Oh! my master, do unto my poor wife and children as you would I should do unto yours, if you were in the same place, for they have no one to trust to but to you; and therefore I bid you and my lady farewell, till it please God to bid us a meeting.

"Your old servant—

"Richard Clough."

I suspect that this letter was written in order that our friend Richard Clough might show his confidence in his old master. It was not misplaced, as Sir Thomas renounced the power given to him, when the earlier will was proved. I should say that Sir Richard Clough, to show his love of his native town, Denbigh, sought to bestow on its future inhabitants the blessing of education, by leaving 100 pounds towards the founding of a free school—a very considerable sum, let it be understood.

I was now very anxious no longer to delay my marriage with Aveline, especially as Captain Radford was in England, and purposed shortly making another voyage to some distant part of the world. The spirit of adventure had increased on him, and he could with difficulty remain quietly in England without employment. I expressed my wishes to Sir Thomas.

"I am sorry to hear this," he said, "because I was about to propose to you to go to Antwerp on important business. There is no one I would so willingly employ in it as yourself; and you will be conferring a favour on me if you will postpone your marriage to Mistress Aveline for another month or so. We will do our best to entertain Captain Radford in the meantime, and on your return I will invite that excellent minister, Master John Foxe, to leave his books and his parish for a time, and come up and perform the ceremony. Her uncle Overton must also be drawn forth from his quiet parish for a few days to assist in the ceremony."

I, of course, could not decline so flattering an offer as that now made to me by my patron, though my dear Aveline, I must own, pouted her lips and looked about to cry when I told her of it.

"If I had you here, I should not so much mind," she said; "but to let you go forth into that land where the cruel Duke practises his barbarities, and may perchance seize you and cast you into prison, I cannot bear to think of it!" and again she burst into tears.

I tried to console her, believing that her fears were vain, and that, under the protection of Sir Thomas Gresham and the English Government, no harm could possibly happen to me.

I travelled down on horseback to Harwich, and from thence crossed in a frigate, sailing for Ostend. From that city I travelled post, as Sir Thomas himself had often done, at a rapid rate to Antwerp. Here I took up my abode in the house of my patron's old servant, Jacob Naas, who had been left in comfortable circumstances by the liberality of his master. He had held to his former principles of conforming outwardly to the Romish faith. I talked with him for some time before he knew who I was. He then received me most cordially, and gave me the best entertainment his house could afford. He shook his head when I asked how things went on at Antwerp. "Oh! Master Verner," he said, "they are bad times. Our artisans have fled, the commerce of the place is ruined, grass is growing in many of our streets, springing up from the blood of the citizens shed on them. And then look at that frowning fortress. While that remains, how can we ever hope to regain our lost liberties? It is refreshing to be able to speak to you of these matters, but I dare not utter them aloud."

I asked after many of my old acquaintances. Again he shook his head with a sorrowful look. Some were dead—broken-hearted; many had been executed; others had fled, and the rest were living in poverty. A few only were flourishing, and they were among those who had abandoned the Protestant faith.

"Then I suppose that that is a proof that they have acted wisely and rightly," I observed.

"No, no, Master Verner, you do not think that," he answered: "I know enough of the truth to know that it is not always those who flourish in this world who are most favoured by God. Look at me, Master Verner, I am not happy; and when I pass them, and observe their countenances, there is little contentment and cheerfulness to be seen in them."

"And Dame Trond," I asked, "is she still alive?"

"Ah, that she is," he answered, "and drives a more flourishing trade than ever. People of all ranks go and consult her, and believe that she can work all sorts of miracles, and has numberless familiar spirits at her command."

"She is a strange woman," I observed; "but I ought to feel grateful to her for the assistance she afforded us in helping our friends to escape."

"Ah! but still I am afraid she is a *very* wicked old woman," said Jacob. "I cannot tell you how many bad things I believe she has done; and she will do many more, I suspect. I, for one, would not trust her."

"I have no wish to do so," I said, "and, indeed, doubt how far I should be right in obtaining her services, now that we know more of her character."

Finding that there was a considerable amount of ill-feeling towards the English among the Spaniards and the Flemings who adhered to Alva, I went very little abroad while at Antwerp, except when I was compelled to call on the merchants and others with whom I had business. I found, however, that it was absolutely necessary for me to proceed to Brussels. I was there going into the lion's den; but yet, as the English Government had an envoy at the Duke's court, I considered that I had no cause for fear. I accordingly went with Jacob Naas, who earnestly begged that he might accompany me.

At this time the Duke of Alva was endeavouring to force upon the provinces a tax which was known as the Tenth Penny. Expostulations had been sent to King Philip; but, though the tax was not formally confirmed, the King did not distinctly disavow his intention of inflicting it. The citizens in every town throughout the country were therefore in open revolt against the tax; and, in order that it should not be levied on every sale of goods, they took the only remedy in their power, and a very effectual one that was—namely, not to sell any goods at all. Thus, not only was the wholesale commerce of the provinces suspended, but even the minute and indispensable traffic of every-day life was at a standstill.

Every shop was shut. The brewers refused to brew, the bakers to bake, the tapsters to tap. Thus multitudes were thrown out of employment, and every city swarmed with beggars. The soldiers were furious for their pay, which Alva was unable to furnish. The citizens, maddened by outrage, became more and more obstinate in their resistance; while the Duke seemed to regard the ruin he had caused with a malignant spirit scarcely human. In truth, the aspect of Brussels at this time was that of a city stricken by a plague. Articles of absolute necessity could not be obtained. It was impossible even to buy bread, meat, or beer.

My stay in Brussels was short, and I was thankful to leave the city, albeit Antwerp was scarcely in a better condition. I purposed remaining only two days at that place, intending to return home by the way I had come.

The day after my return, just as I got to my lodgings, having transacted some business with one of the few remaining correspondents in the city, Jacob came to me with a look of alarm.

"I was passing through the Mere, close to the hall where the Blood Council hold their sittings, when who should I see hobbling away but old Dame Trond! She cast a suspicious glance at me, which I could not help feeling meant mischief. I have a relative who is employed as a porter in the hall. He has no love for his post, but he cannot help himself, so he says. I bethought myself that I would go and see him, and try to learn why Dame Trond had paid this visit to the Council. 'It is curious that you have come in,' he whispered; 'for I was wishing to come to you. You have a guest in your house who has come here as an Englishman, but is, as you should know, a Netherlander born, and a heretic. You are aware of the penalty of harbouring such; and, as he is supposed to be wealthy, the person informing against him will obtain a rich reward, being entitled to a large share of his property. The old witch Barbara Trond has found this out, I doubt not, by consulting her familiar, and she just now came here to lay information against him before the Blood Council. Now, Jacob, if you are a wise man, you will do as I intended to advise you. Go at once before the Blood Council, and say that you have just discovered that your guest is a heretic whom you received ignorantly, and thus obtain the reward yourself.' I did not dare to tell my relative what I felt when he said this; but, thanking him for his advice, I concealed my feelings, and hurried back, Master Verner, to tell you, and to urge you to make your escape without a moment's delay from the city. The Government are too much in want of funds to allow you to escape, if they can by any possibility lay their hands upon the property of which you have charge; and especially, if it is believed that it belongs to Sir Thomas Gresham, they will be the more ready to appropriate it, in revenge for the advice he is known to have given the English Government sometime back with regard to the treasure seized in the Spanish ships."

I saw at once that prompt action was necessary.

Instantly, therefore, with the aid of Jacob, putting on the guise of a courier, I hastened out to the stables, at which I engaged horses for my journey. Mounting, and followed by my English servant, I rode rapidly forth from the gates of the city.

I had got to some distance, when, turning my head, I saw a horseman galloping after me. I could not help fearing that he was some officer sent by the Blood Council for my arrest; and I doubted whether I should endeavour to defend myself and refuse to return, or to yield myself a prisoner. As he drew nearer, however, I saw that he was my faithful friend Jacob.

"Ah! Master Verner," he said; "I could not resist the temptation of following you, and endeavouring to assist in your escape. It would be sad to think what would happen if you were taken. I should never forgive myself, if I had not done all I could to preserve you."

Thanking Jacob for his kindness and generosity, I yet thought it my duty to expostulate with him, and show him the danger he was running in accompanying me.

"To be honest with you, Master Ernst," he said, "I think it will not be greater than it would be if I were to remain; for when it becomes known that

I warned you and assisted in your escape, I am very well assured that the Blood Council would condemn me to death."

On this, of course I no longer urged Jacob to return, though well assured that his regard for me was his principal motive. As we increased our distance from Antwerp, I began to hope that we should escape from the country without further danger. Instead of riding to Ostend, however, we took a different direction, towards Zealand. We had passed through Breda beyond which we proceeded a couple of stages, where, the night overtaking us, on the second day of our journey, we were compelled to stop and rest. Wearied by my ride, and the anxiety I had gone through, I slept soundly. How long my slumbers had lasted I know not, when I felt a rough hand on my shoulder. I started up, wondering what was about to happen.

Chapter Thirty One
In Prison at Brill

As I have before mentioned, I was aroused out of my sleep by a heavy hand on my shoulder. "Your name is Ernst Verner," said a voice. "You were born in the Netherlands, and your father was a Netherlander?"

Scarcely having yet gained my senses after being awoke out of my heavy slumbers, I answered immediately: "Of course. You are perfectly right in what you say, whoever you are." Directly afterwards I regretted having thus spoken, but it was too late.

"He acknowledges who he is!" cried the same voice; and by the light of a lantern which another man held up before my face, I saw that several armed persons were in the room. "Get up and dress yourself immediately; you will accompany us!" said the man who had first spoken.

I now too clearly guessed what had happened: I was in the hands of Alva's officers, and had no means of escape. Jacob had been taken in a like manner, as was also my servant John, who, however, being an Englishman, was in less danger than we were.

Immediately we were dressed we were ordered downstairs, where we found our horses, and, being compelled to mount, we set forth immediately, two men going before with torches to light us on our way. We proceeded for some hours in the dark, our guards refusing to give us any information. We stopped for a short time only for meals, and, after crossing several ferries, we found ourselves entering a fortified town. Neither Jacob nor I knew the place; but I guessed from its position that it was Brill, on the river Meuse. Why we were carried there I could not tell, except, perchance, that it was considered necessary, in order to keep the inhabitants in recollection of what they would suffer should they show any signs of rebellion, that we were there doomed to be sacrificed. It was not a pleasant thought, yet it seemed too probable. It might have been considered a more suitable place than Rotterdam for our imprisonment. Be that as it might, we were conducted to the jail, and there cast together into a loathsome dungeon, cold and damp, into which but a single ray of light penetrated. That ray came through a small grated aperture on one side of the arched roof. Although I had had some experience of a prison in England, I scarcely thought it possible that human beings could be confined in a dungeon so horrible as the one in which we found ourselves. My two companions seemed inclined to give way to despair.

Honest Jacob, however, thought more of me than of himself.

"And you told me, Master Verner, that you were about to be married to that sweet young lady, Mistress Aveline; and oh! if they hang you, she will surely break her heart! My good dame is laid in her grave, that's one comfort. There is nobody to mourn for me and poor English John here. They will scarcely kill him—though I do not know; for it seems to me that the Spaniards and those who serve them have a delight in destroying their fellow-creatures. They will probably kill us first, and then bring us to trial."

I felt that it was my duty to try and keep up the courage of my companions. Fortunately, John could not understand the remarks made by Jacob. I told him to be of good cheer, and that I hoped we might still by some means make our escape with our lives. My valise, containing a large amount of valuables, had been taken by our captors; but I still retained a considerable portion of jewels about me, besides several rolls of gold which I had concealed in my dress. This had escaped observation, our captors being delighted with the rich booty they had found in the valise, which they probably supposed was all I possessed. I hoped by bribing our jailer to induce him to help us to escape, or, at all events, to send off a letter, which might be transmitted to Sir Thomas Gresham. I told John also, what I knew would be some consolation to him, that we might possibly be able to procure a larger amount of provisions than the prison fare, which was likely to be scanty enough. Before, however, I in any way committed myself by showing that I had any money in my possession, I determined to try the temper of the jailer.

We were allowed to remain alone for several hours. At length the door opened, and a ruffianly-looking fellow appeared carrying a jug of water and a loaf of coarse bread—for coarse it seemed, even by the light of the dim lantern which he bore in his hand.

"This is but poor fare for prisoners uncondemned," I observed. "Could you not, friend, obtain us something better?"

"Good enough for men who have only a few days to live," he answered, in a gruff voice.

"They will not venture to execute Englishmen, or those under English protection," I answered, in as bold a voice as I could muster; "so you will not frighten us out of our appetites, friend."

"Caged birds don't often crow as loudly as you do," observed the jailer. "However, it is as well to enjoy your life while you have it; so I will not try further to put you out of humour."

Hoping that I had by degrees softened the jailer's feelings I took from my pocket a single piece of gold, which I placed in his hand. As he looked at it, his countenance brightened.

"Ah! now we understand each other," he observed. "And what is it you want me to do for this?"

"To bring us better food," I answered; "and let me know what is going forward without the walls. The man who would help us to escape would find it to his advantage; for, although the British Government would desire to protect us, Duke Alva is occasionally apt to execute his prisoners first and then to apologise afterwards, when he has found out that they were guiltless."

"We must not speak against the authorities from whom we take our bread," answered the jailer; but he still lingered, willing apparently to hear what more I had to say. I, however, thought that I had said enough to show him what were our wishes and intentions. At last he took his departure, looking far more pleasantly at us than he had done when he entered. We were left, therefore, alone to discuss our rough fare. As we had been kept without food for some time, we were glad to eat it, coarse as it was.

We had no other visitor after this till the next morning. We employed the time in examining our cell, to ascertain if there was any possible means of getting out. Jacob said that he had heard of men burrowing under the walls, others had got out the iron bars in the windows, or worked their way through a hole which they managed to form in the roof. But there appeared very little chance of our getting out that way. Our only hopes lay in the assistance the jailer might afford us. I cannot say that we slept very pleasantly, for our beds were composed of heaps of half-rotten straw; and though we could not find any way of getting out of our dungeon, rats and other vermin found their way in, and continued running about the floor, and frequently jumping over us during the dark hours of the night.

The next morning the jailer again made his appearance, with a basket, in addition to the usual prison fare, containing some white bread and pastry, and several other articles of food. Without hesitation I paid the price demanded for it, and then asked him if he had any news.

"Not much," he said. "Three men going to be hung, two to be burned; the latter for attempting to assist a heretic prisoner to escape, the other, who had been a priest, for preaching heretical doctrines." He looked at me very hard as he spoke.

"That may be," I answered. "It is the fortune of war; we must all run risks if we are to achieve any important object."

"Ay, ay, I see you know the world, young sir," he answered.

I again plied him with questions about the prospect of escaping, but he only shook his head, repeating: "You would not ask me if you had seen the poor fellow burned yesterday."

His argument was a powerful one. Though I did not like the thoughts of bringing the man into such fearful danger, I still could not resist the temptation of trying to induce him to help us in getting free. "If we escape, you will escape with us," I observed; "so that the risk will not be greater to you than to us."

Still the man shook his head, answering: "I have no fancy for burning!"

Once more we were left alone. The hours appeared very long. Though I had my two companions to talk to, they were so unhappy that they were little able to speak on any pleasant subject. At length the silence which had hitherto reigned in our prison was broken by loud shouts and cries, which proceeded from the streets beyond us. That something extraordinary was taking place we had little doubt, yet what it was we of course could not divine. At length at the usual hour the jailer made his appearance with our provisions, which were, as he had promised, far better than the usual prison fare. The man's countenance also showed us that something had happened. I eagerly put the question to him.

"I don't know what to say; I don't know what to say," he answered; "but I am not quite certain whether you will be outside this dungeon and I in before the day is over."

"It is honest in you to say that, my friend," I answered; "but how can that be?"

"Why, to confess the truth," answered the man, "this morning at daybreak a strange fleet was seen coming up the river Meuse. No one could tell whence it came. Some thought it was a fleet of merchant vessels for Rotterdam: but the question was soon set at rest by my friend Peter Kopplestock, the ferryman, who, going on board one of the ships, found them to be no others than those fearful desperadoes and pirates—the Water Beggars. They sent him back to tell the magistrates that two hours would be allowed them to decide whether or not they would surrender the town, and accept the authority of De la Marck as Admiral of the Prince of Orange. That if they will do so, their lives will be spared; but if not, every man who attempts to resist will be put to the sword. Our Burgomaster is a mighty brave fellow, and so are our chief burghers, but they know very well what a desperate fellow the Admiral De la Marck is; and he has got some five or six thousand men, so Peter says, on board the fleet; and what can our citizens do to resist them? He says that he comes simply to free the land from the Tenth Penny, and to overthrow the tyranny of Duke Alva and his Spaniards. The magistrates, it seems to me, do not much like to face Admiral De la Marck, and so they have been busily employed in packing up ever since, and making their way out of the town."

While the jailer was still speaking, the sound of musketry was heard, and shouts and cries proceeding from our side of the town. "I must go and see what it is all about!" exclaimed the jailer, rushing out. We thought he had left the door open behind him, but, greatly to our disappointment, we found that, even though frightened, by instinct rather than intention he had bolted it.

The noise increased, and we felt almost certain, by the shouts and cries we heard, that the patriots had forced an entrance into the town. We thought, indeed it was no delusion, that we heard a voice proclaiming liberty to the Netherlands, and the cry of "Long live the Prince of Orange! long live our noble Stadtholder!" Again loud noises reached our ears, and thundering blows echoed through the building. There could be little doubt that the jail was being forced. Then came crashing sounds, as if doors were burst open. We endeavoured to force open our own door, for we knew not what might happen. Directly afterwards, a stifling smell of smoke found its way through the crevices of the door.

"We shall be baked alive!" exclaimed Jacob Naas. "We must force the door, even should we break our shoulders in the attempt! Here, you English John, dash at it with your head, if that is the hardest part of you." We all shoved at the door together, but in vain. It resisted all our attempts. The smoke grew thicker and thicker. We could with difficulty breathe. Again and again we dashed at the door frantically. We were giving way to despair, when voices were heard. It seemed as if a body of men were rushing along the gallery, breaking open the doors of the cells.

We thought they were going to pass us by. We shouted—we shrieked—

"Here! here! my brave Beggars, my daring rovers, here are men shut up in this corner! Bring crowbars, or we and they shall be burnt together!"

The words, though spoken in Flemish, were uttered, I was certain, by an Englishman, and I thought I knew the voice. At that instant the door, which had so long resisted our efforts, gave way, and we rushed out, being seized instantly by the men who had come to our rescue; though, in the thick wreaths of smoke which curled round us, it was impossible to recognise their countenances. Confused, and almost stifled by the smoke, we did not see where we were going till we found ourselves in the open street, where the fresh air quickly revived us.

In the centre of the square, near the prison, stood on an elevated spot, a fierce-looking warrior, with a black casque, and a lofty plume on his head, a huge red beard projecting from his chin and covering his breast, his shaggy locks hanging down over his shoulders, and his moustache almost hiding his mouth. He rested on a huge richly-gilt double-edged sword. His very look was calculated to inspire terror. I asked some of the men round us who he was.

"That is our Admiral, De la Marck," was the answer.

His appearance was just then more terrible than the words he was uttering. Indeed, he was assuring the people that no harm would be done them if they would yield willing obedience to the commands he might issue in the name of their Prince. A grim look of pleasure lighted up his countenance when at that instant the governor of the city was brought before him, having been taken just as he was endeavouring to make his escape. While I was looking about me, my eye fell on the officer who had led the party to our rescue from the burning prison. He turned round at the same moment; I was not quite certain, yet I thought I could not be mistaken when, in the well-bearded, huge-whiskered, long-haired seaman I saw before me, I recognised my old friend A'Dale.

"A'Dale!" I shouted.

He sprang towards me, and almost wrung my hands off as he shook them in his joy at seeing me. "And you are the fellow we got out of the prison?" he exclaimed. "I little knew who I was saving: however, all is well that ends well. You shall tell me all about yourself by-and-by, for we have something to do to keep these citizens in order. The honest truth is, we have taken the place with scarcely three hundred men—they thinking that they were attacked by five thousand or so. However, when they find we wish to treat them well, we shall have plenty on our side, for few of them have love for Alva and his Tenth Penny."

Before sunset the whole city was brought into obedience to De la Marck. The gates were again closed, and guards set, to prevent any enemies entering; and A'Dale and I took possession of a remarkably comfortable residence, stored with all sorts of good things. The next day De la Marck employed himself in appointing fresh magistrates, and establishing a regular government in the name of the Prince.

It is very remarkable that, while the Duke of Alva was negotiating with Queen Elizabeth, and inducing her to compel the Sea Beggars to quit the shores of England, hoping certainly in the end to deceive her, the result of his devices should have been their establishment on the mainland, and the commencement of that power which was ultimately to produce his own overthrow and the success of that very cause which it was his great aim to destroy.

Chapter Thirty Two
Conclusion

I was very eager to return to England, and happily found a merchant vessel at the mouth of the Meuse on the point of sailing. I did my best to persuade A'Dale to accompany me. He confessed that the life he led on board the rover fleet was not altogether to his taste. They had on several occasions been very nearly starved, as they were when they arrived before Brill. He had, however, collected a considerable amount of booty, and, being a prudent man, he had not gambled it away, as some of his companions had done. He could now also, without dishonour, retire. We both of us visited Captain Treslong, and I explained that I was in the service of Sir Thomas Gresham, whom he well knew, and that probably A'Dale would be again employed if he returned to him. I truly rejoiced when the captain gave him leave to retire and go with me and my two attendants on board the vessel I spoke of.

We had a quick passage; and my dear Aveline received me as she ever had done, with true affection. We were married immediately afterwards, for I was determined to allow no considerations any longer to put off that event.

Margery blushed somewhat when she saw A'Dale, and though she thought that he ought to be punished for his continued absence, yet she speedily relented, and their marriage took place on the same day as mine. I will not describe it. We were honoured by the presence of Sir Thomas Gresham and Lady Anne, and a large number of persons of consideration.

My bride and I took up our residence in Lombard Street, where we had very pleasant apartments not far from A'Dale, who went into the service of his old master.

My noble patron, after the experience of a long life, had arrived at the simple conclusion that the cultivation of the understanding, and the education of the heart, gave birth to the purest pleasures, as well as the noblest aspirations, and that the best gifts which the State has in its power to bestow on its youthful members are sound learning and religious principles. He had long contemplated the establishment of a college for the accomplishment of this object. Indeed, while building Gresham House I feel very sure he had this in view. The building itself has a collegiate air. Within there is a great reading hall, while the distribution of its apartments are susceptible of every purpose of a college. He now openly expressed his intention, though I am sorry to say the University of Cambridge endeavoured to divert him from his purpose, being jealous that London should have a college, the authorities wishing that he should rather endow another hall in their University. By his will, which he now drew up, he ordained that Lady Anne Gresham should enjoy his mansion house, as well as the rent arising from the Royal Exchange, during her life, in case she survived him; but after her death both these properties were to be vested in the hands of the Corporation of London and the Mercers' Company. These public bodies were jointly to nominate seven professors, who should lecture successively, one on every day of the week, on the seven sciences of Divinity, Astronomy, Music, Geometry, Law, Medicine, and Rhetoric. The salaries of the lecturers were defrayed by the profits arising from the Royal Exchange, and were very liberal. The wisdom of my patron is shown by the sciences he directed should be taught. He considered Divinity to be the most important, and after that, holding as I know he did in great contempt the foolish art of astrology, he desired that the noble and soul-elevating science of astronomy should be chiefly cultivated. On music, too, he set high value, while geometry he considered did not only help forward astronomy, but is a fine exercise of the mental faculties. The great Copernicus has written on astronomy, but his work is little known in England; indeed, the science is but slightly cultivated or respected.

Sir Thomas also, some time before this, constructed eight almshouses, immediately behind his mansion, in the parish of Saint Peter the Poor, and in his will he provided liberally for the inmates. This, however, was only one of many charities which he established.

My wife and I frequently paid visits to our kind friends at their new mansion of Osterley; and while we were there in May, 1576, they had the honour of receiving a visit from the Queen's Majesty. I have not space to describe the magnificent arrangements which were made for the reception of her Majesty, or the numerous entertainments prepared to render her stay agreeable. I may mention, however, that a play was represented, written by my patron's old friend, Thomas Churchyard, as also a pageant, "The Devises of War." Her Majesty was greatly pleased with all she saw, but she found fault with the courtyard as too great, affirming that it would appear more handsome if divided with a wall in the middle. Scarcely had the words been spoken than Sir Thomas slipped away and sent off for workmen to London, who, in the night time, so speedily and silently laboured, that the next morning discovered the court double which the night had left single. It is questionable whether the Queen next day was more contented with the conformity to her fancy, or more pleased with the surprise and sudden alteration when the courtiers disported themselves with their expressions, avowing that it was no wonder he who could build a *change*, could *change* a building. I have, I am afraid, given but a very imperfect idea of the character of my kind and noble patron. I had met him in the afternoon at the Exchange on the 21st of November, 1579, being Saturday. Parting from him, I returned to Lombard Street. While sitting with my wife and children about seven o'clock in the evening, a serving-lad came running to say that Sir Thomas had suddenly fallen down in the kitchen soon after he came home, and was then speechless. I hastened off. When I arrived, I found my kind friend laid on a bed. A glance at his countenance told me too truly what had happened. I felt his pulse: it had ceased to beat. Thus, at the age of sixty, after having served the State for nearly thirty years with unsullied honour and integrity, Sir Thomas Gresham was taken to his rest. Surely the annals of the City of London can boast of no more illustrious name. He greatly raised the credit of the Crown in foreign parts by the skill with which he contrived to manage the exchange with foreign countries. He laid the foundation of England's commercial greatness. He elevated the character of the English merchant, and dignified the pursuits of trade by showing that they are far from being incompatible with the taste for learning; while a large portion of the fortune he had acquired in the service of the State he restored to it by numberless acts of public munificence and private charity. The funeral was more splendid that that of any nobleman I have ever seen. Could he have known what was going forward, I think he would have been more pleased by seeing the tears shed by several of the two hundred poor men and women, clothed in black gowns, who, according to the directions given in his will, followed the body to the grave.

England has had trying times since then. The Pope, not content with the massacre of Saint Bartholomew in France, when tens of thousands of Protestants were murdered by night, seemed resolved to take the life of our Protestant Queen. A large body of Jesuits were introduced, under various disguises, into England, hoping to re-convert its Protestant inhabitants to the Romish faith. Their great object, however, was to destroy the Queen. Of these plots, Sir John Leigh, as I have before mentioned, gave me warning.

At length King Philip, finding that he could not succeed by treachery, resolved to invade England with a mighty army in a vast fleet, which he called his Invincible Armada. We were for a long time in expectation of its coming, and all classes of her Majesty's subjects united for the defence of her kingdom. Even the Roman Catholics, who had no desire to have the

Pope place his foot on their necks, as he had done on the people of the Netherlands, willingly came forward for the protection of the Queen. Philip boasted that in a few months he would bring back all England to the Catholic faith, and several of his ships had large quantities of books on board abusing the Queen, and full of the foulest falsehoods. Besides this there was a large force of priests and friars, and all sorts of instruments of torture—racks and thumb-screws, and every device for inflicting agony on the bodies of people, in order to induce them to conform to what the Spaniards called the true faith. The mighty fleet of Spain sailed up the Channel, Philip's generals and officers boasting of the great victory they were about to achieve. Elizabeth and her people had done their best for the defence of the country and their liberty; but the Queen trusted not alone to an arm of flesh. She offered up a prayer to God for the protection of her realm, and sent it to her General at Plymouth, that he might in the same terms pray for victory:—

"Most Omnipotent and Guider of all our world's mass, that only searchest and fathomest the bottom of all hearts' conceits, and in them seest the true original of all actions intended, how no malice, revenge, nor quittance of injury, nor desire of bloodshed, nor greediness of lucre, hath bred the resolution of our now set-out army, but a heedful care and wary watch that no neglect of foes nor over-surety of harm might breed either danger to us or glory to them. Thou that didst inspire the mind, we humbly beseech with bended knees prosper the work, and with the best fore-winds guide the journey, speed the victory, and make the return the advancement of Thy glory, the triumph of Thy fame, the surety of the realm, with the least loss of English blood. To these devout petitions, Lord, give Thou Thy blessed grant! Amen."

The very day on which that prayer was being offered up, it was said that Don Bernadins de Mendoza, the Spanish Ambassador, rushed into the Church of Notre Dame in Paris, flourishing his rapier, and exclaiming in a loud voice, "Victoria!" by which it was supposed that the English were vanquished.

Up Channel the mighty Armada steered in the shape of a half-moon, with the wind from the south-west, on the 21st of July of that year. While Lord Howard began the battle by attacking in his own ship, called the *Ark Royal*, one of the large ships of the Armada, Drake, Hawkins, and Frobisher soon joined him, for two days pursuing and attacking the enemy with the greatest fury, joined by Sir Walter Raleigh and other brave commanders. For one day, the 24th, there was a rest; but on the following, Hawkins, in the *Victory*, attacked a great galleon, which yielded herself up; but now came on another desperate battle, till at length the Spaniards anchored before Calais. Here, after a week of furious fighting, they expected to find rest, but that was not given to them. Again the English attacked with fire-ships, by which many more of the Spaniards were destroyed. Then they cut their cables and ran up Channel, many, however, going ashore on the Flemish coast, Drake, Fenner, Hawkins, and other captains pursuing them. Other fierce battles were fought and numberless single combats, when the English never failed to come away victorious. Some escaped round the north of Scotland, pursued to the last by the English fleet; many foundered; others were cast on shore by a mighty storm which arose. A small and shattered remnant only of the mighty Armada returned to Spain, eighty-one ships of the expedition having been lost, and upwards of 13,500 soldiers.

On the 24th of November the Queen went to Saint Paul's, to return thanks for the victory graciously given. The streets were hung with blue cloth, and the City Companies ranged themselves on either side in appropriate order. The great captains who had fought so bravely, surrounded the Queen. The trophies they had won were carried in procession. A solemn thanksgiving was offered up, and the glory ascribed to God only: while, in every other church in the land, public thanks were given to God for the favour thus mercifully bestowed upon England.

Although Philip had been thus signally defeated, he still persisted in his belief that he should finally conquer England, and destroy the Protestant institutions which had been established there. May God bring to nought his attempts, and the efforts of all the enemies of the holy and blessed Gospel! This is the earnest prayer of ERNST VERNER.